"MICHAEL. WHAT ARE YOU DOING HERE?"

Catherine's hand crept to her throat and she could feel her pulse there, hard and fast, as if she had been running.

"The same as you, I gather. I am applying for a post at this august bastion of British medicine." He stared at her, his eyes as hard as agates.

"You are no longer at Scutari? You have left?" She continued to state the obvious; she couldn't help it. She could not believe the truth of what she saw.

"So it would seem."

Michael was always impatient with stupidity, and she felt remarkably stupid at this moment. Her brain refused to move beyond the astonishing fact that Dr. Michael Soames, instead of being a continent away in Turkey, in the cold and stench and blood of an Army hospital, stood before her in London.

Michael had shared the best and worst experiences of her life, had understood her as no one else ever had. Not even Lucinda or Rose, her closest friends among Miss Nightingale's staff, had perceived the fire within her that drove her to battle disease and death wherever she could.

But Michael had. Then he had kissed her and changed her life . . .

Dear Romance Reader,

In July, we launched the Ballad line with four new series, and each month we'll present both new and continuing stories set everywhere from medieval England to the American West—the kind of passionate, romantic stories you love best, written by the most gifted authors. At the back of each book, we'll tell you when you can find subsequent books in the series that have captured your heart.

Martha Schroeder's atmospheric *Angels of Mercy* debuts this month, chronicling the dreams and desires of three women stubborn enough to join Florence Nightingale on the battlefields of the Crimean War. In **More Than a Dream,** a young woman of privilege wants nothing more than a life as a healer—until a brooding physician tempts her wish for love. Next, Corinne Everett begins the *Daughters of Liberty* series, in which three young women chart their own passionate courses in the wake of the War for Independence. An ardent Patriot meets her match in a dangerously attractive man who may be Loyalist—and who threatens to steal her heart—in **Loving Lily.**

Next, rising star Tammy Hilz continues her breathtaking *Jewels of the Sea* trilogy with **Once a Rebel.** When a woman who despises the nobility's arrogance encounters a handsome aristocrat, she never imagines the adventure that awaits them on the high sea—or the thrilling fulfillment she finds in his arms. Finally, the second book in Kate Donovan's *Happily Ever After Co.* series presents a Boston society beauty and a widowed sea captain marooned on a tropical island—and the once-in-a-lifetime love that results when they're **Carried Away.**

Kate Duffy
Editorial Director

Angels of Mercy

MORE THAN A DREAM

Martha Schroeder

ZEBRA BOOKS
KENSINGTON PUBLISHING CORP.
http://www.zebrabooks.com

ZEBRA BOOKS are published by

Kensington Publishing Corp.
850 Third Avenue
New York, NY 10022

All Kensington titles, imprints and distributed lines are available at special quantity discounts for bulk purchases for sales
promotion, premiums, fund raising, educational or institutional
use.

Special book excerpts or customized printings can also be created to fit specific needs. For details, write or phone the office of
the Kensington Special Sales Manager: Kensington Publishing
Corp., 850 Third Avenue, New York, NY, 10022. Attn. Special
Sales Department. Phone: 1-800-221-2647.

First Printing: February, 2001
10 9 8 7 6 5 4 3 2 1

Printed in the United States of America

*This book is for my niece
Katherine Anderson O'Hara,
with love and admiration.
When I needed a heroine who was
blond, brainy, beautiful,
incredibly competent,
and an intrepid traveler to Turkey,
she just naturally had to be
named after you.*

Chapter One

A ghost had arrived at the mansion in Grosvenor Square.

Catherine Stanhope descended from the hackney carriage and climbed the steps to her father's house. Clad in gray from head to foot, she felt as insubstantial as fog, and as far removed from humankind as a figure conjured from smoke.

The heavy oak door swung open. Had she knocked? She could not remember moving.

"Miss Catherine!" An old man was smiling at her, his eyes wet with tears. "Oh, Miss Catherine. You are here a day early. What a surprise we had when your telegram arrived!"

He ushered her into the vast entrance hall, with its floor of huge black and white marble squares and the grand staircase that led . . . where? She couldn't remember.

"We read all about you and Miss Nightingale every day in the *Times*. Why, you're a heroine, miss. You and Miss Nightingale and the other nurses."

She managed a smile. "Thank you, Holden." The name came to her automatically. He was her father's butler. She could remember, it seemed, when she had to.

She was home.

"Wait till I tell Sir Everett, miss. He's been that worried about you." The old family retainer beamed at her and Catherine managed another smile back.

If only she weren't so cold.

If only she had been able to sleep.

All during the long journey from Scutari to Malta and from Malta here, she had lain awake night after night, thinking of the days before she left England and the day she had arrived at the Army Barracks Hospital at Scutari, Turkey.

The last and the first.

She remembered those last days before she left and her father's attempts to order her life to his liking . . .

She had come into the house that afternoon feeling exalted, as if she could fly.

"Sir Everett wishes to see you, Miss Catherine."

Her thoughts still taken up with her interview with her heroine, she had heard the butler's words only as a faint buzzing in her ear.

"Miss Catherine." This time the words penetrated. "Your father wishes to see you. The moment you returned, he said."

Holden sounded worried. Catherine looked at him and could feel some of her triumph seep away. Father. She still had to convince Father.

"Is something wrong?" She and Holden looked at each other in perfect understanding. Sir Everett Stanhope was the sun around which everything in the Stanhope household revolved. If he was angry, everyone walked carefully.

"No, I don't think so," Holden responded. "But he was very

emphatic about speaking with you. And," he added, *"a letter arrived by the early post."*

"Oh, dear," said Catherine, a little more of her elation evaporating. She smiled at Holden, a conspiratorial smile that thanked him for warning her. Then she proceeded to her father's study.

Before she knocked, she took a deep breath and told herself not to give way before her father. This time she was going to do whatever was necessary to convince him her chosen path through life was the right one for her.

This morning she had met again with the woman who had made it seem possible her dream could come true. She had left the Harley Street nursing home with her heart soaring.

Now she had returned to face the reality of her father's total incomprehension and solid disapproval. Already she could feel some of her buoyant purpose ebb.

Nonsense, she could do it. She nodded once to herself and opened the door without knocking.

"You wanted to see me, Father?" Her voice was confident, she thought.

"Yes, yes, my dear, come in." The baronet beamed at his only child and all but rubbed his hands in obvious excitement. *"I have some news for you."*

"And I for you, Father," Catherine said, smiling back, her heart apprehensive. Whatever her father had planned for her, it wasn't backbreaking work in the Crimea with Florence Nightingale.

"Sit down, Catherine." The baronet was bursting with news. *"I have great news."* He took a deep breath. *"I have arranged a marriage for you."* He must have seen the shock and denial in her face, for he hastened to add, *"Now, now, wait a minute and you will see how well it will suit. It is Julian, my dear. Your old friend, Julian Livingston! What do you think of that?"*

"No!" Catherine was on her feet, her fists clenched. *"I have told you, Father. I will not marry. I am a nurse. I have talked to*

Miss Nightingale this very day. She is willing to take me with her to Turkey. To nurse the soldiers!"

Her father's face took on the mulish look she had grown used to seeing whenever the word "nurse" was mentioned in his hearing.

"Now, Catherine, we have talked of this. You cannot be a nurse. Only poor creatures with nothing else they can possibly do except—" He broke off, his face turning red. He had almost mentioned women in the oldest profession in front of his daughter. Seeing the determination in her eyes, he grew angry. "I forbid it! You are to marry Julian. We have planned a party to announce it before he leaves with his regiment. It is all arranged, Catherine."

So her father had laid his plans in those days, but she had been just as adamant. Now she laid her threadbare gray cloak on the back of a chair. Holden had forgotten to take it from her.

A faint smile touched her lips. A stickler for such things, he would be horrified. So many people here seemed to care a great deal about the most inconsequential things.

She had read the *Times* on the packet from Calais and the train to London. It had been full of news of debates in Parliament, parties, and the queen, an endless, meaningless round by people who had faced no greater challenge than deciding what to wear in the morning. It all seemed unreal, like a children's game.

"Catherine, my dear!" Her father hurried into the room and hastened to embrace her. He kissed her cheek and then held her a little away from him and looked at her, concern in his eyes. "You seem tired, Catherine. So illness sent you home before the fighting ends. I thought it must be so, though Miss Nightingale's telegram gave no reason, just that you were coming. But I knew nothing less than dire illness would make my Catherine quit the field, and so I told everyone at the club."

He beamed at her and chafed her hands between his. "You are cold, my dear. Let me ring for tea—though that is your job again now that you are home, isn't it?" He led her over to the maroon leather armchair that faced the fireplace. "It is delightful to have you in your place again. Sit here, my dear, and rest for a while."

Her place? How absurd. And yet what did it matter? What did anything matter?

"Yes, Father." They were the first words she had spoken since he had entered the room. She leaned her head back against the smooth, worn leather of the chair and closed her eyes.

If only she could sleep. She couldn't remember the last time she had slept except in snatches, disturbed by dreams of things she did not wish to remember and people she could not forget.

Michael.

She was not going to think of Michael.

Her father was talking. Something about a party.

There had been a party before she had left for Turkey, one her father had insisted on holding despite her refusal to agree to a betrothal. She and her father had been at a standstill, he insisting she become a proper young lady and she determined to be a nurse. The party had been a huge affair, with champagne and dancing and what had seemed a million candles. Catherine had not been able to stop her father. He was a juggernaut, rolling over obstacles.

As always, Julian was the life and soul of the fun. He had danced with Catherine, swinging her through a waltz.

"What can I do to make you laugh, Cat?" he had said, grinning down at her. "Or at least smile? People will think you don't

like me. Bad for my reputation. Women always swoon over the cavalry."

"Tell my father you don't want to marry me," she replied.

"Oh, that." He shrugged off the looming threat to her happiness. "Glad you asked. I've already solved that!" With those words, he laughed and danced her out into the hall and down the corridor to her father's study and then, still dancing, swung her into the room and closed the door behind them.

"Suppose we become engaged," he said.

Catherine had gazed at her oldest friend with the combination of exasperation and affection he had always inspired.

"Haven't you listened to anything I have said for the past week?" She tried to keep the fury and panic out of her voice. "I have been trying to explain. Miss Nightingale is leaving for the Crimea in a week and Father refuses—won't even listen to why I must go with her." Catherine, usually so cool and serene, was wringing her hands in frustration.

"Allow me to finish, please," said Julian, unperturbed by her emotion. "Suppose we become engaged and I tell your father I think you should be allowed to go the Crimea with Miss Nightingale. After all, I will be there, too, and well able to protect you." He grinned at her. "Then when we get back, we can say we won't suit and cancel the engagement."

Catherine gazed at him, exasperation coupled with hope in her eyes. "That is so typical of you, Jules, to let tomorrow take care of itself. It will cause a dreadful scandal if we don't marry after a formal betrothal."

"We will worry about that when the time comes. Meanwhile, we will both have gotten our heart's desire—action." He looked down at her. "Besides, you're not bad looking by half, Cat, particularly when you wear a pretty dress and aren't frowning. The way you are now. I might decide to marry you after all."

Cat was unimpressed. "I would think again if I were you. I should end up killing you within the first fortnight."

"It was just a thought." Jules grinned at her. "Notwithstanding your disrespectful attitude toward the leading light of Cardigan's Light Brigade, I am willing to become your fiancé pro tem. What about it?"

Catherine laughed and agreed. She had laughed, that other Catherine who had lived in this house a thousand years ago.

Before Scutari.

Now she listened as, once again, her father proposed a party.

"Of course, it will have to be small," the baronet was saying. "No more than a gathering of our closest friends. Not above fifty, I shouldn't think. Not like the one before. Julian is still missing, and the earl is much too distressed to celebrate anything, even your safe return."

"Julian is not missing," Catherine said, her eyes still closed. "He is in hospital at Scutari."

"My God, Catherine, why did you not say so at once! This is splendid news! I must tell the earl—"

"They know, Father. His wound is very serious. They may not want anyone to know until he is out of danger."

"Will he die? Did you see him?" Worry laced the baronet's voice. He had known Julian all his life and regarded the charming daredevil almost as the son he'd never had.

But Catherine could not tell her father about the Julian she had left in the Barracks Hospital at Scutari—the sad, bitter man with the same distant, chilly look in his eyes that she saw when she looked in the mirror. Julian, who might very well lose his leg or his life.

Julian, whom she would have to marry.

* * *

After drinking a cup of tea with her father, Catherine excused herself and went to her room. Conversation was beyond her, and the effort to respond exhausted her. If she had the energy, she would be amused at her father's attitude. She was no longer an embarrassment. No, now she was a heroine, thanks to the almost daily dispatches from John Russell to the London *Times*, extolling the work of Miss Nightingale and her nurses.

Neither view bore any resemblance to who she was.

It was tiring to try to relate to someone who loved her but didn't understand her. It had always been difficult, but now, tired and sick at heart, she found it impossible.

Her love of nursing, her dedication, had set her apart from her contemporaries from an early age. She had laughed and played and later danced and flirted like any other privileged young lady, but she had never thought of that world as the one she would ultimately live in. She knew herself better. A profound need to be of service to others, to succor them and bring them back to health when they were ill—for some reason she could never explain, that was the paramount fact of her life. She had told very few people of this desire after her father and her best friend failed to comprehend what she felt.

The baronet had thought it a whim, a childish fancy she would soon outgrow. Julian had simply ignored it. Both thought she would get over it once she went to London and had a whole new wardrobe of pretty dresses and a whole new group of fellows to slay with her big blue eyes.

Only a few women—Lucinda and Rose, her fellow nurses at Scutari—had understood. A few women and one man.

Michael.

She would not think of Michael.

Oh, God! This place was not real. Reality was in Turkey, in the dark, forbidding hospital that loomed atop the cliff rising from the sea at Scutari. Reality was the screened-off operating area in the ward where surgeons fought against death, armed only with skill and a scalpel. Reality was dirt and blood and relentless cold.

The room that had been hers since childhood was now that of a stranger. The soft bed, the fire that crackled on the hearth and spread warmth throughout the room, the clean sheets, the comforter all seemed to belong to another life. Had she ever really taken being warm and clean for granted? Had her rest ever been undisturbed by dreams of blood and the screams of the wounded?

She lay down without bothering to take off her dress and pulled the satin-covered down comforter over herself. Closing her eyes, she willed her mind to quiet and rest. She would not think.

She would not dream.

She would not.

Chapter Two

The clothes she had left behind seemed garish and fussy now. She was used to wearing simple gray and black dresses relieved only by white caps and collars. The blue silk she allowed her new lady's maid to choose for dinner that night startled her eyes and felt insubstantial on her body.

But she had enjoyed the bath in the copper tub in front of the fire. When she had first left England, she had yearned for a bath more than anything, and she found with surprise she could enjoy it. That was something, some connection to the Catherine who used to live here. She would cling to that. Perhaps in time she could use that small pleasure as a lifeline and scramble back to some semblance of a life.

A life without purpose if she was no longer a nurse.

A life without meaning if Michael continued to hate her.

What difference do his feelings make? she asked herself, clenching her fists in fury and pain. She would never see him again. He was Scots and he hated London.

If he lived next door to you for the next forty years, she told herself, *you would never see him. He would make sure of that.*

"How do you usually wear your hair, miss?" the little maid wanted to know, her face anxious as she looked at Catherine in the looking glass.

Catherine smiled, the first genuine smile she had felt in weeks. "Well, Betsy, recently I braided it as fast as I could and bundled the braids under a very ugly white cap."

"Miss!" Betsy was shocked. "You never did!"

Was that old hospital life still so surprising? Would no one who had not known her there believe she had lived it, loved it above everything? Catherine felt her amusement drain away. "Do whatever is easiest for you," she said, losing interest.

Catherine closed her eyes as the girl's eager fingers began to work. She remembered learning to braid her hair in the dark on board the leaky little ship that had taken them to Scutari. How she and Lucinda had laughed at the lopsided mess they had made of it.

Dear Lucinda. She would be home sometime. Home to London. A friend who would understand. Aboard ship, she and Lucinda had been the only nurses not to succumb to seasickness. They had taken turns nursing the others, some of whom had already been complaining and regretting their decision.

"We're going to have trouble with some of our friends," Lucinda had said, rolling her eyes and giving Catherine a wry grin. A small woman with gleaming black hair and dark blue eyes, Lucinda had a wicked sense of humor that managed to make light of their uncomfortable situation. Catherine had quickly learned to consider her a friend as well as a valued colleague.

She had also met Michael on board the ship—Dr. Michael Soames. Her heart gave a sudden, sharp pang at

the very thought of his name. He had no use for female
nurses and had told her so in no uncertain terms. They
had encountered each other on deck and had spoken for
the first time. He had told her to get below with the other
nurses, that the crew had work to do.

She could see it as clear as a scene upon a brightly lit
stage if she kept her eyes tightly closed.

*She had rounded on him in fury. "I am not playing! I am a
nurse. I'll have you know I trained with the Sisters of Charity in
Paris."*

*If she had impressed him with the fact she had studied and
worked at the foremost nursing facility in Europe, the Salpêtrière
in Paris, he did not show it, though one auburn eyebrow arched
for a moment. In silence, he turned and headed toward the crew's
quarters, where more than a dozen sailors lay catching what rest
they could in their hammocks, victims of bad food and worse
weather.*

*"If you need me, Doctor, I will be with the nurses," she called
after him, bracing herself against the bulkhead as a particularly
vicious wave struck the ship broadside.*

*She had expected him to ignore her offer. Instead, he turned on
her, ice in his voice but hot anger in his eyes. "I don't need your
services, no matter where you were trained. The Army doesn't need
you, either. You had better book your return passage as soon as
you arrive in Turkey. You won't stay. None of you will, particularly
you ladies, once you see what really goes on in an Army hospital."*

*Catherine looked at him gravely. "I would have expected a more
open mind from a medical man, Dr. Soames."*

*Surprisingly, he gave a snort of incredulous amusement. "Then
I fear your expectations are doomed to disappointment," he said.
"Medical men know better than most that war and medicine are
not fit occupations for a lady."*

There was a muffled cry from the crew's quarters and he turned quickly and entered, leaving Catherine looking after him. She had been disappointed, but she'd shrugged and entered the nurses' cabin, only to be knocked almost to her knees by another enormous wave.

"Watch out and keep hold of the hammocks' ropes," Lucinda said, helping Catherine regain her feet. "What has you frowning?"

"Dr. Soames," Catherine responded. She and Lucinda had talked about the dour Scotsman before. Catherine had voiced her disappointment in him. "He's such a good doctor," she had said in puzzlement, speaking in a low tone as she gently bathed the face of one of her fellow nurses. "I don't understand how he can be so rude and stupid about nurses."

He had treated several of the nurses who were the sickest, and though he had refused her offer of help then just as he had today, she had been impressed at the quick, gentle way he had looked them over, listened to their symptoms, and given each one a weak dose of morphine and water.

Lucinda had shrugged and lightly commented that most men were fools when it came to judging women. "They only want curls and simpers and 'oh my you're wonderful' from us," she had said.

But Catherine had protested. "Doctors are different. Medicine is a calling, and doctors have to see people more deeply than ordinary men."

Lucinda had laughed. "All men are alike, Catherine. You'll see."

Catherine had frowned, sure Lucinda was wrong.

"Is everything all right, miss? Did I pull your hair?" The girl who was doing her hair—what was her name?— sounded anxious.

Catherine's automatic kindness to those who served her

made her smile and say, "No, I was thinking of something else. You have a very deft touch."

The girl—Betsy, that was her name—beamed. "It is a pleasure to work with such hair, miss. So soft and shining. You look beautiful no matter how you wear it."

"Thank you, Betsy." Catherine looked at her reflection without interest. The blond woman with the troubled blue eyes who looked back at her seemed unfamiliar in her rich gown and careful coiffure.

As she descended the stairs, she thought of Lucinda's cynical appraisal of the male sex. And she thought of Michael, who had refused to listen, had believed the worst. Michael, the surgeon, the healer who had come to appreciate her talents but believed the worst about her character.

It seems Lucinda was right after all, she thought as her father's eyes lit up at the sight of his now fashionably dressed daughter.

"I am so happy to have you back, my dear. You look lovely as ever." Her father beamed at her. Catherine remembered that the baronet was always happy with her when she looked fashionable and pretty.

"Thank you, Father. I am glad you are pleased." She felt ill at ease and faintly ridiculous. She had forgotten how to walk in the fashionable crinoline. Movement was difficult, and every change of position had to be planned lest her skirts fly up and betray her.

"We have a number of invitations for this evening," Sir Ernest said. "There are musicales and after-dinner soirees. Or perhaps we could go to the opera. What do you think? You have been denied the pleasures of civilization for too long. Now that you are home, I expect you will want to sample them all."

"No, I grew used to going to bed very early in Scutari. We worked so hard that any chance we had we would snatch a little sleep." She smiled reminiscently. "I remember once—"

"Catherine, please." There was a pained expression on her father's face. "You are home now. There is no need to think of that place ever again. It was terrible, I know. You saw things no gently reared woman should ever have to endure." His voice shook a little as he thought of what his daughter had been through. "But now I have you safe and you will never have to think of any of it again."

"But, Father, some of those experiences were terrible, yes, but others—" Catherine paused, trying to think how to explain to her father. "Other things were wonderful. I was helpful, Father. I was needed. I actually saved lives. Those weeks in Turkey with Miss Nightingale were the greatest experience of my life."

Her father sighed. "I know men often feel that way about war, my dear, and I suppose I can understand how you might feel somewhat the same way." To Catherine's surprise, he rose and came around the long table to her end and raised her to her feet. "But, Catherine, you must know that women should not share those feelings. They are masculine and entirely inappropriate for you. Please do not speak of it again. People are well aware of the kinds of dreadful things you went through—the newspapers have seen to that—but you must not speak of it to anyone. You will seem coarse and unfeminine if you even allude to it. It makes you seem different from other girls. It must be kept secret."

Catherine said nothing, but excused herself soon afterward and returned to her room. So nothing had changed. Her father still did not understand, still was ashamed of his strange, difficult daughter.

Did all men feel that way? she wondered in despair. Did

they all want women who were china dolls? Lucinda had often said much the same thing.

No, she thought sadly. Michael would have understood, would have shared her feelings.

But Michael hated her now and had ordered her out of his life.

There had been a time when they had been friends, shared their thoughts, had talked long and deeply.

It had happened on their way to the camp at Balaklava. She and Michael had traveled up the Bosporus and across the Black Sea together. The only passengers aboard the transport ship that had lurched and wallowed its way to the Crimea, they had been thrown into each other's company for most of the voyage.

It led to a strange friendship between them. At night, after they had shared a meal with the captain, they would go on deck and stand looking out to sea, talking. Perhaps it was the dark or the isolation, but Catherine found herself drawing closer to the taciturn, fascinating doctor than she could have believed.

He shared her passion for healing. That was the great thing about Michael, she often thought. Not only did he have that passion himself, he seemed to understand her answering need to heal completely understandable. Once he had worked with her, it seemed he understood and equated her needs with his—a surprising and intoxicating discovery. He was the only man she had ever met who felt that way. They had shared their ideas and dreams diffidently at first but then, toward the end of the voyage, with increasing candor.

Their last night at sea she had attempted to tell him why his friendship was so different and so important to her.

* * *

"You do not find me odd. You do not think I should be embroidering or paying calls," she told him, half in fun.

He laughed, and that laugh all but sealed her fate, for it made him more than attractive. It made him devastating. He looked young for that moment and carefree, the way he might have looked if he had not had to work his way through the Edinburgh College of Medicine—if he'd had the advantages a man in her station of life would have taken for granted.

"Embroidering? Why would you do that if you did not enjoy it?" he had wanted to know, sounding surprised.

"Because it is expected of women," she had explained.

"But you are rich and beautiful and intelligent," he had responded, "and your father loves you. Why should you have to embroider or—what was the other task?—pay calls if you do not enjoy them? I know some women enjoy them, but if you do not, why bother with them?"

She had felt a flash of pure feminine pleasure that he thought her beautiful, but she had stuck to the point of the discussion. "I am not rich. My father is rich. Like all other women, I am subject to a man's governance unless I can pay my own way in the world."

"Well," he said matter-of-factly, "now you can. You are a nurse, and a damned fine one. You should be able to find a job when you return to England. If you can bring yourself to do that," he added, glinting a quizzical glance at her, almost as if he dared her to take her life in her own hands.

By the cool, clear light of the stars, Catherine thought she saw challenge in his eyes. He was asking if she had the courage of her convictions. Would she choose to forego all the ease and comfort of the life she knew and instead embrace a life of service and simplicity?

"I don't know if I am strong enough to do that," she admitted *slowly, feeling her way.* "I have disappointed my father in so many ways by insisting on my need to nurse. It has taken me years to convince him I was serious. Why, before he would let me come with Miss Nightingale, I had to——"

Seduced by the night, Catherine had almost revealed her sham engagement to Julian, but she couldn't bring herself to tell Michael of her deception. Honest to a fault himself, he would never understand her need to placate her father's desire for her to be a normal, docile daughter. Michael never placated anyone, she was sure.

"You had to what?" he asked.

"Oh, promise all sorts of things. That I would keep warm and write him once a week and always stay near Miss Nightingale." Catherine knew she sounded unconvincingly casual, but Michael said nothing further.

"So you are hemmed in by convention and a father's devotion," he said, irony tinging his voice. "I know many girls who would jump at the chance to suffer with you."

"I know, I know." She felt a spurt of anger at his dismissal of her feelings. "I am not complaining. I am explaining what restrictions I am subject to. You may find my circumstances enviable, but I find your freedom equally desirable."

He frowned. Starlight lit his dark mahogany hair into fire but cast his face in shadow. "What you call freedom I think of as servitude. I am a slave to the one thing I vowed never to worship— money. I detest having to constantly think of it, work for it, be driven by it."

His smile looked bitter in the dim light of the stars, and a passionate anger made his voice a rasp. "But how could you understand? You have never lacked for anything. You could buy all the luxuries my mother devils my father for without so much as a thought." He stopped abruptly and turned away, as if ashamed he had revealed so much.

Catherine reached out and touched his arm, unwilling to let him retreat once again into silence. "It seems we each have what *the other most desires. That is some kind of bond, is it not? I feel you are my friend, Michael, more my friend than any other man I have ever met. You understand what no one else has—that I am a nurse first and foremost."*

Michael turned to her, his expression so intent she was almost frightened into retreat. He clamped his hands on her shoulders and drew her closer.

"Friends! You will deign to grant me your friendship, Miss Stanhope? You will descend that far, to take some jumped-up Scottish nobody as your friend because he is a doctor and you are a nurse?" His burning gaze stole the breath from her body.

Fear fled and pride took its place. Catherine raised her head and spoke with all the dignity at her command. "My friendship is never patronizing, doctor. It is the greatest gift I have. I thought if you understood nothing else about me, you would understand that." Her voice clogged with tears of rejection and regret, Catherine wrenched herself from his arms, turned, and headed toward the ladder leading below deck as fast as she could. She would not let him see her tears. She never let anyone see her tears.

"Catherine!" His despairing cry had echoed after her.

Chapter Three

Oh, if only she did not keep thinking of him, dreaming of him. If only she had something to do. The enforced idleness of her life had chafed her before, but now, after she had known the satisfaction of work, it drove her mad.

Her father noticed her nervousness, her silence when people came to call. He thought she was not fully recovered from whatever ailment had sent her home, so he insisted she see a doctor, who prescribed a tonic.

The tonic did not help, but long walks in the gardens at Kew did. She went in the early morning with only Betsy to lend propriety. The beauty of the site even in the dead of winter soothed her troubled spirit. One morning, as she strode down one of the paths trying to make her body as weary as her mind, someone called to her.

"Nurse Stanhope," the voice said. "Nurse Stanhope, is that you?"

She turned around, looking for the source of the voice.

"Here, on the bench," the voice said.

She looked over, and there sat a shabby figure in an Army greatcoat, one sleeve empty.

"You do not know me, do you?" the young man said sadly.

"Of course I do, Private Glendower," she replied, smiling and reaching out her hands. "How could I forget my very first patient?"

The first time she had worked with Michael.

She had been working at cleaning one of the wards when a scream of pain rent the air.

She and Rose Cranmer turned to the far end of the ward, where a screen had been set up to hide the operations taking place behind it from the sight of the sick and injured men lying nearby.

"Oh, my God." Catherine's hand flew to her mouth and she looked at Rose in horror. "We have to help, Rose."

"We cannot, miss. You remember what Miss Nightingale said about acting only on orders from a doctor." Rose's clear brown eyes were clouded with concern, but she held on to Catherine's sleeve when she took a step toward the screen.

Another shriek sounded. Then came the awful scraping, grating sound of a saw hacking through bone.

"There's nothing you can do, miss!" Rose shook her head. "The poor lad's got a bullet to bite on. There's nothing we can do to ease the pain right now."

An orderly lurched out from behind the screen, holding something wrapped in a bloody rag. There was a sob from behind the screen.

Before she was aware of what she was doing, Catherine had sprung to her feet and was headed to the "operating room," marching as fast as she could without actually losing her dignity and running. She did not know what she was going to say or do

*once she reached it, but she could not bear to be kept from giving
what help she could to those who suffered.*

*Miss Nightingale had warned them against giving the medical
officers any reason to complain, but as much as she admired Miss
Nightingale, she did not care what anyone said—if the man who
had screamed could be helped by anything within her power, she
was going to do it.*

*She rounded the edge of the screen and stopped short. Dr. Soames
stood leaning over a young man lying on a cot. The doctor's
white apron was spattered with blood, and, as she stood there, he
straightened up and stared blankly into space. The young man
on the cot groaned and the doctor reached out to him, gripping
his hand hard.*

*"I'm sorry, lad. There's no morphine to give you. The damn
supply ships haven't been unloaded." Sorrow and anger threaded
through his deep Scots voice. "I hate to move you, but I've got
others waiting."*

*"Can I help you?" Catherine spoke softly, but her question acted
as an electric shock on both men.*

*"You should not be here, ma'am." The boy on the cot spoke
with an effort, his voice a thread. "You shouldn't see."*

*"I am a nurse, soldier," she replied, then faced the now scowling
Dr. Michael Soames. "I could stay with him to make sure there
is no excess bleeding, Doctor." Her tone was deferential, as the
Sisters of Charity had taught her to be toward physicians.*

*"The chief medical officer decreed you were not fit to help us
with our patients. I cannot disagree with him. These are not sights
for a lady. You are too weak to bear them. I have told you I need
no help from you." He dismissed her with a curt nod and turned
back to his patient.*

"Have I fainted? Do you see me running off in hysterics?"

*Dr. Soames looked back at her impatiently. Catherine kept her
voice low, but she was aware that passion burned in her eyes and
her tone. She was a nurse! She could not bear to sit by any longer,*

unable to lift a finger to help because some man had decided she and her kind were useless. "I am a nurse. I have seen amputees before, Doctor. I know how to change bandages and make stump pillows and keep a watch for fever."

The doctor looked from her to the pale, half-fainting boy on the cot and the orderly who had returned and stood breathing alcohol fumes over the patient. After a sharp glance at the drunken orderly, the doctor gave a brisk nod in Catherine's direction. "Very well. Go with him, Miss Stanhope. Go. I'll make it right with the chief if you're caught."

"Caught ministering to the sick and wounded. What a terrible indictment that would be." Catherine moved toward the cot and motioned to the orderly, who seemed to be standing upright with an effort, to move the boy to a stretcher.

The doctor had raised his eyebrows at her sarcasm. He studied her for a moment, then turned away. "Give any report on his condition to the orderly and tell him to look until he finds me. Look for swelling around the stump as well as fever and bleeding."

"Yes, sir." Catherine stood ramrod straight and spoke as to a superior officer. "What is the proper way to address you? Is it 'Mister' or 'Doctor?' Are you a surgeon or a medical doctor?"

"Actually, I am both. I suppose it is natural that a lady would care about such niceties." His scornful glance swept over her neat, gray uniform as if searching for jewels or some other sign of her aristocratic birth. "For simplicity's sake, you may address me as 'Doctor.'" Was there a slight curl to his lip as he spoke? Catherine was sure she detected one, yet somehow it did not matter. He was going to allow her to practice her profession, and she was grateful.

"Yes, Doctor. I will report any change to you." She slipped away to follow the stretcher bearing the young soldier to a cot in the ward. She had triumphed! At last she was doing what she was born to do. Whatever she might think of Michael Soames as a person, she had seen on the ship that he was a fine surgeon and

a gifted doctor, and he realized the wisdom of allowing anyone who could to see to the wounded and sick.

Catherine seated herself beside the young soldier's cot and picked up his limp, white hand. His pulse was strong but fast, the result of the assault on his body, first by the battle and then by the amputation of his shattered arm. She felt his forehead for fever. His skin was cool to the touch; so far, then, so good.

"Nurse?" His voice seemed weaker than it had in the operating room.

"Yes. Is there something you need?"

"Write to my family, would you, ma'am? Tell them I died bravely." The boy's voice was thick with tears. "I don't want them to know about my arm. They don't need to know, do they?"

"I'll write them, Private Glendower," said Catherine, having read the name on the paper pinned to his tunic, "but I shall certainly not tell them you have died."

"But I'm going to, ma'am," he said, his fingers plucking at the thin blanket covering him. "I know it."

"You know nothing of the kind," she replied, her voice brisk. "Dr. Soames is a fine surgeon. You're going to get well and go home to your family, private." She took his hand gently in hers. "Now, what would you like me to say to them when I write?"

Private Glendower looked up at her, a fragile hope dawning in his eyes. "If you could write my mum, ma'am, I'd appreciate it that much."

She had written his mother and sisters and had seen him off when he sailed for home. Because he was her first patient, because it was the first time she had worked with Michael and sensed the rapport they had both in and out of the operating theater, she had often thought of Private Glendower.

Now she sat down beside him on the bench and took his hand in hers. "Tell me how you are going on, private."

She was almost unaware of a gasp from Betsy, who had a finely tuned sense of propriety. Daughters of baronets did not take the hands of shabby ex-soldiers. Resolutely, Betsy sat down on the other side of the private.

"Oh, I am fine, miss," the young man said.

"And your family?" Catherine asked. "Your mother, how is she?"

"Well, miss, I don't rightly know." The ex-soldier all but squirmed in his seat. "You see, I haven't quite enough money to take me home. I've managed to get a little, but not enough. I'd take to the road, but with only one arm I'm afraid I would be easy prey, and that wouldn't do."

"No, indeed." Catherine reached into her purse. "Here, private. You take this and go home. You can repay me when your crop comes in."

The private rose to his feet. "I don't take charity, miss. I'll earn my way, or I won't go."

Catherine looked at him in exasperation. "Really, private, this is not charity. It is a loan. I fully expect you to pay me back."

Stubbornly, he shook his head. "I earn my way."

Catherine's brow furrowed. She hated being beaten, especially by misplaced male pride. She rose to her feet and stared the young man in the eye. "Very well, sir. Report to the stables in back of Stanhope House in Grosvenor Square tomorrow morning, six o'clock sharp."

Without waiting for a reply, she turned smartly and marched back the way she came. After a moment, she heard Betsy hurrying to keep up on her shorter legs. Catherine paused and turned to the little maid.

"Well, Betsy," she said, "now I've gone and done it, haven't I? I have to go and speak to the head groom. Is it still Marston?"

"Yes, miss, Mr. Marston is still in charge of the stables."

Betsy's voice betrayed her disapproval of Miss Stanhope's engaging her in conversation and concerning herself with unemployed young men.

"I shall have to go see him and ask him to engage my friend, Mr. Glendower," Catherine said. She smiled a little. For some reason the sun seemed a bit warmer and the day brighter. She had a task, something concrete, that involved helping someone. It was a bit like nursing—like enough to brighten her day, if not to cheer her completely.

"I hear you went to the stables to ask Marston for a favor," the baronet said that evening at dinner. His tone held a question.

"Should I have asked you first, Papa?" Catherine said, putting down her fork. She looked at the baronet down the length of the polished mahogany table, past the silver candelabra and large epergne that lay between them. They had been served with slices of roast beef, potatoes, and several vegetables. That had been preceded by soup and would be followed by a sweet and cheese. She found the mere idea of so much food rather daunting, and her appetite tended to desert her after a few bites, though she labored on in order not to insult the cook.

"Not at all, my dear," the baronet hastened to reassure her. He was worried about his daughter. Nothing seemed to interest her anymore. He could almost wish for one of their arguments, just to see her blue eyes flash with indignation and know she cared about something. "I was just commenting, wondering who this young man is."

"He was a private and wounded at the Alma. I helped tend him when he came to Scutari." Seeing the interested look on her father's face, she continued. "He was my first patient. The first time a doctor allowed me to work. Now he is trying to earn enough money to get to his home in the north. I thought Marston could find something for him to do for a few weeks until he saves the fare."

"Very well, my dear. I'm sure we can find space for another able-bodied young man for the short term."

Catherine decided not to tell the baronet about Private Glendower's missing arm. After all, he was still able-bodied. She hoped.

Her father informed her he had decided what she needed was a party. He still wanted to welcome her home with a celebration, and Catherine was forced to accede when he told her that Julian's parents had no objection and would indeed attend.

If only they would leave her alone, it would not be so bad. She rather enjoyed solitude—when she could get it. At the hospital, there had always been people around. The men, of course, in beds and cots and pallets. Some just on the floor. But the nurses, too. They had shared two small rooms, and so night and day there had been people around her. Sometimes she thought she would give anything for one half hour of silence and solitude.

She had forgotten that in London she was seldom alone. There were always servants or callers or tradesmen, trips to the shops and the theater and the opera. Her father took her everywhere, insisted she have new clothes, bought her a pearl necklace and matching bracelet. Everywhere people were talking to her, chattering about nothing, demanding responses, decisions. What did she want to eat, to wear, to see, to do?

Nothing. She wanted nothing. She longed to retreat to her room, to sit in silence, to fold her hands and do nothing.

Peace. If only somewhere she could find a little peace.

If only she could stop dreaming.

Last night she had dreamed of their arrival at Scutari.

The hospital loomed at the top of the cliff exactly as it had that November day. Cold and weary to the bone, she and the rest of the tired little band of women had climbed the endless stairs. The dark, huge hospital, originally a Turkish army barracks, seemed to swallow the very sunlight. Entering it was like going through the gates of hell.

She felt again in sleep that awful sense of apprehension as they had gone in, smelled again the stench that had assaulted them, saw the dark and the dirt that had oppressed them, heard the scurrying of rats in the hallway. But most of all, there had been the men.

They lay on the floor, wrapped in whatever rags of clothes and blankets they had managed to salvage from the battlefield at the Alma River. Some of their wounds were so hideous Catherine had felt bile rise in the back of her throat. Yet despite their suffering, they had been brave and stoic and so grateful for any help they were given.

Catherine awoke with tears on her face and determination in her heart.

She would find something to do.

On the night of the party, which she vaguely understood was to be only a reception with music and refreshments, she allowed Betsy to deck her out in a new evening dress of deep rose pink with a pleated collar of blond lace at the low décolletage. She felt uncomfortable and out of place, but she knew the importance her father placed on her appearance and she wanted to please him in this. She had disappointed him enough already.

The baronet had not wanted her to be a nurse, had hated her going with Miss Nightingale. But now she was cast in the role of heroine, and he would enjoy watching her queen it around London society. Her lack of interest in what mattered so much to him could not help but be one more way in which she disappointed him.

So Catherine descended the staircase resolved to do her best to give the appearance of enjoyment. What met her eyes almost sent her back upstairs.

Far from a simple evening's conversation and music, Sir Everett had invited a select twenty friends for dinner, but another one hundred for dancing afterward.

"But, Father, I thought we said just a small affair," she protested when he explained what was in store.

"Oh, my dear, you know how it is. If you invite so-and-so you must invite such-and-such, and so it goes until the world and his wife are coming." He laughed and rubbed his hands. The baronet enjoyed people and was looking forward to showing off his beautiful daughter.

Catherine tried, but only Julian's parents, the earl and countess of Eversleigh, managed to penetrate the shield of glass that seemed to surround her.

"Oh, Catherine, please do tell me." The countess, a beautiful doll-like woman, hardly seemed old enough to be the mother of one of the heroes of Balaklava. "How was he when you saw him? We have heard nothing but a few most unsatisfactory scrawls from Julian and a long letter from someone named Hall that told us practically nothing except that Julian was alive and Hall was over-worked. Really! So provoking!"

The countess took Catherine's hands in hers. "I know you could not stay with him." She must have sensed Cather-

ine's instant stiffening, for she added, "I know you were
ill. Julian said that was why you left."

Bless Jules, Catherine thought. *As depressed and sad as he
was, he still tried to protect me.*

And then the thought that had hovered near consciousness ever since she had seen Julian carried into the Barracks
Hospital, more dead than alive, sprang into her mind. *I
will have to marry him now.*

As if she could read her mind, the countess went on, "I
am so glad you are to marry him. Despite the happy-go-
lucky tone of his letters, I know he is miserable. Tell me,
how bad is the wound?"

How to answer? On the cliff leading to the hospital, half-
conscious and looking more dead than alive after what
must have been a nightmarish voyage from Balaklava to
Scutari, Julian had stared at Catherine as if he had never
seen her before. She hardly recognized him. The filth and
the month-old beard hadn't changed him profoundly, but
the cold, hopeless look in his eyes turned him into a
stranger.

"His leg was badly injured when he fell at Balaklava. His
horse struck him as they both went down," Catherine said,
choosing her words with care. "I had to leave Scutari before
his condition was fully evaluated, but the doctor on his
case seemed to think there was every chance he would not
lose his leg."

"Lose his leg?" The countess all but fell into the satin-
covered fauteuil behind her. "Oh, no. He cannot. You
know how he loves the outdoor life, Catherine. It is impossible."

Catherine stared at her. She had forgotten how impossible most people found it to accept difficult truths. If Julian
did not want to lose his leg, if his mother could not bear

to think of it, why, he would not. To the countess, it was as simple as that.

"Oh, Catherine, thank God you will be with him, to help him. I do not think I can. I feel it so deeply—" The countess broke off. "I do not mean that you are callous, Catherine, not at all. But you are so calm and controlled. I am sure it is just what Julian needs."

She did not look sure at all. But, thought Catherine with a cynical inward smile, whatever his mother thought, Catherine was what Julian was going to get. She could not jilt a man who had been so horribly injured, nor would she desert her oldest, dearest friend.

Hours later, her head was beginning to ache abominably and the noise seemed to be getting louder. She had difficulty following the thread of what people were saying to her.

"It is wonderful to have you back, Miss Stanhope." A young man with luxuriant muttonchop whiskers stood before her, unable to do more than thrust a glass of champagne into her hand. Apparently, she unnerved him. She'd had that effect on a number of people this evening besides the countess.

He stumbled on. "And looking as beautiful as ever." He smiled for a moment, but it faded quickly. Catherine knew she must have stared at him with complete lack of comprehension. It still happened to her, this feeling that she was separated from the rest of the world by a sheet of glass and that on the other side they were speaking some language she could barely hear and did not understand.

He was still speaking. "Such a dreadful place. No one understood how you could bear it. You must be glad to be back here where you belong. You certainly did your best for the lower orders."

She tried not to look at him with the anger she felt but

something must have seeped through, for he all but turned tail and ran from her presence. Relieved, she turned away to stare out the windows. But instead of the darkness she sought, the wavering reflection of the crowded room behind her danced in the glass, as insubstantial and grotesque as it seemed to her in reality.

Her father's worried face floated next to hers. "So many people have remarked on how beautiful you look. But you do not seem happy, and they have noticed that as well. I must ask that you make an effort, my dear. I am sure it will be the best thing for you, to throw yourself back into the old life."

Something inside Catherine simply gave way. Tears she had thought she could not shed began to course down her face. "I do not want the old life! I never wanted it! And I cannot throw myself into it. I am surrounded by people, and I have never been so lonely. They are all talking to me and there is not one to whom I can say anything of importance!" She clutched her father's sleeve and stared at the floor, trying to get hold of herself, knowing she was embarrassing the baronet by her behavior.

Even if no one heard her, someone would see the tears and gossip would run like wildfire: *Something is wrong with Catherine Stanhope. Are you sure she was ill? Is that the real reason she came home when the outcome of the war is still in the balance?*

But Catherine could no longer play a part. No one wanted to hear the truth. No one understood.

She had kept the secret of her sudden departure from Scutari, but the weight of it oppressed her. If only Lucinda or Rose were there.

If only she could talk to Michael.

Her father's face showed both anger and fear at his daughter's outburst. She could tell what he was thinking.

This kind of behavior was so unlike Catherine, who was always so calm and—what had the countess called her?—controlled.

She was looking toward the doorway, gauging if she could possibly get there without anyone's noticing her tear-stained face, when Holden entered the room. He made his way to the countess and the earl and spoke to them briefly.

The countess cried, "Julian!" and slumped to the floor.

Forgetting everything but her concern for Julian and his family, Catherine hurried over in time to hear the earl say, "Thank God. Julian is safe." Catching sight of Catherine, he seized her hands and said, his voice choked with emotion, "Cardigan gave him use of his own personal yacht to make the trip faster. Julian has just arrived home, safe at last."

Chapter Four

Sleep was impossible. Catherine spent the night trying to come to terms with the situation. She had last seen Julian on the morning he had arrived at the hospital at Scutari. He had been lost on the battlefield for several days, and when found was half out of his mind with fever and was suffering from exposure as well as a badly shattered leg.

But the assault on his body had not worried Catherine half as much as his listless, withdrawn attitude. Julian was young and almost indecently healthy. His body had already started to heal. But when she had entered his room and bent over his cot to kiss him, he had turned his head away and told her to leave him alone.

"I can't do that, now can I, Jules?" She had taken his hand in hers. "We are engaged, after all," she'd added as a joke.

"Go away, Cat," he said. "I can't marry anyone now. Don't want to marry anyone."

"You can't jilt me," she said. "Not before the whole world."

"One look and they'll understand." He waved her away when she sat on the edge of his cot. "Do go away. I'm tired." And he had turned his face to the wall.

She would have stayed. She planned to help him out of his sadness. But she had been summoned to Miss Nightingale's office, where she had spent a great deal of time helping with the director's endless correspondence. This time she was not given letters to answer and there was no pleasant exchange of views. She was told her behavior was inconsistent with the rules laid down for the behavior of the nursing staff by Miss Nightingale herself.

"I cannot make an exception for you, Miss Stanhope," she had said. "You are a lady born and bred. If you cannot behave in a modest and becoming manner and I were to condone your conduct, there would be no hope of discipline among the others."

Catherine had not, at first, understood what she had been guilty of. She had protested, explained that Julian Livingston was one of her oldest and dearest friends.

"I understood you were betrothed to him," Miss Nightingale had said, her eyebrows raised.

The gossip mills have been busy, Catherine thought. Was there anyone at Scutari hospital who did not think she was engaged to marry Julian? Her mind skittered back to the scene with Michael on board the transport ship.

"It was more of a childhood attachment. Something our parents wished for." Catherine knew the words were weak. She hated the subterfuge that had seemed like such a lark to Julian.

"I see. In that case, your conduct in his room—kissing him and teasing a very sick young man—is perhaps understandable. He stands in the relation more of a brother to you?"

Catherine smiled in relief. Miss Nightingale understood. "Yes, something like that."

"Then that might perhaps explain why you were seen kissing Dr. Soames." Miss Nightingale's expression was unrelenting. "Whatever the case, Miss Stanhope, the two stories are probably all over the hospital at this moment. I have done my best to keep the tale about you and Dr. Soames private, but I cannot guarantee I have stopped young Lieutenant Featherstone's mouth. I cannot have my nurses behaving in that fashion with doctors on staff here. I am afraid you must leave."

She meant it. Catherine was horrified. The thing she had worked so hard for was to be snatched from her just when she was succeeding at it. That was the worst thing, far worse than any gossip or disgrace. To lose her chance to nurse, her place as a healer—that was intolerable. Not to be able to help Julian. Of all people, he was the one who needed her the most, the one she could help the best.

She tried to explain something of this jumble of needs and desires to Miss Nightingale, but she was immovable. Where the issue was the reputation of the Army nurses, Florence Nightingale was as tough as any general. She understood Miss Stanhope's dreams—she shared them. But the Army doctors—indeed, the Army itself—had not wanted female nurses. Nothing and no one was going to give them the slightest ammunition to use to defeat the idea of female nurses.

Catherine had given them ammunition.

Catherine must go.

So, heartbroken, Catherine had boarded the next ship bound for Malta and then England.

She had refused to think about Julian. Rose would look after him as a favor to Catherine and Dr. Soames would take charge of the case. Lucinda had promised her that, and Lucinda's gifts of manipulation and finagling were unsurpassed. Whether either man wished it or not, Julian would be under the care of the best doctor at Scutari.

But now that Julian was home, Catherine owed it to her oldest and best friend to marry him. He would need care and nursing for some time. The passage home might have worsened his condition. And Catherine wanted to be the one to care for him.

But to marry where she knew she could not love—was that fair to herself or to Julian? Surely, even with a shattered leg, he would not lack for young women more than willing to fall in love with a charming cavalry officer who was the heir to an earldom and handsome as sin as well.

Julian, however, was not going to give any of them a chance. He had been ready to give up when she saw him, and she doubted the arduous round of treatment in the hospital or the trip home had changed his mind. No, Catherine would have to do that. Only by marrying him would she be able to coax and persuade him to embrace life again.

And after all, was giving up nursing such a sacrifice? She would be doing what women had always done—be healers in her own family. Julian would be her only patient, but he was worth it. His recovery would be reward enough. And if she did not love him, she did care for him. It had been enough for couples from the dawn of time. It would be enough for her and Julian.

She would make it enough.

Exhausted, she fell asleep.

And dreamed of Michael.

                              * * *

*They were once again on the boat carrying them down the
Bosporus toward Constantinople and Scutari. They had spent a
week on a mission for Miss Nightingale and the War Office in
London, looking into conditions at the regimental hospitals, which
were every bit as bad as John Russell, the* Times *correspondent,
had made them seem.*

*Catherine and Michael had become friends over the course of
the trip. At least, she had told herself that friendship was all she
felt—friendship and, of course, admiration for his skill as a
surgeon and physician.*

*She had been delighted that he seemed to accept her as a person.
Ever since she had assisted at the operation on Jemmy Glendower,
he had, she thought, approved her as a dedicated and skilled
nurse—very flattering, since he was the most gifted doctor on the
staff at Scutari.*

*But she did not dream of the conversations they had or even
the laughter they had shared. No, she dreamed of the moment that
had shattered forever her illusion they were merely friends.*

*It was their last night aboard ship. Michael was smoking,
looking out over the railing, in the company of Lieutenant Featherstone, the cavalry officer who was also traveling to Constantinople. Catherine had been tending to the wounded, who were on
their way from the regimental hospital at Balaklava to the general
hospital at Scutari. Two of the men had taken a sharp turn for
the worse. "Dr. Soames," she said as she came up to the group at
the rail, "I must speak to you."*

"Miss Stanhope?" He bowed gravely.

*"It is Sergeant Euwan Jones, doctor," she said, "the Welsh
artillery man. His fever has risen, and I believe he is becoming
disoriented. Will you come?"*

*Michael nodded and followed her. The sergeant's leg had been
amputated in the regimental field hospital. The stump had become*

infected. Catherine had sat with the grizzled veteran and his protégé, a young private who had lost an arm. The private was trying to help old Euwan, but was himself somewhat frail, being only fourteen or fifteen and suffering from a recurrent fever. The two of them had become important to Catherine in the way particular patients sometimes did. She was upset at the turn for the worse the older man had taken.

As they bent over the restless figure of the sergeant, the first drops of rain began to fall. This late in the year, the rain was almost sleet and the wind cut like a knife. The sergeant and the boy huddled together for warmth and the boy put his thin arms around his mentor's shoulders in a pathetic attempt to shield him from the rain.

Catherine doffed her cloak and held it over the two men as she knelt over them. Michael swung his own Army greatcoat off and spread it over the three. He, too, knelt and made a cursory examination of both men. There wasn't much to be done other than what she was doing—offering companionship and comfort. It was clear to both Catherine and Michael's trained eyes that neither man would last even these final few hours to Scutari. Catherine refused to let herself recognize the certain end to her vigil. She could not afford to think of it, for she needed to give hope as well as comfort through her murmured words and careful touch.

It seemed to Catherine that they stood in the dark on the pitching deck for an eternity while sleet fell in never-ending streams. Or perhaps it was only minutes.

"You will become ill if you stand out in this weather," he said, his voice low but concerned.

"You should worry about yourself, Michael," she replied. She was relatively dry underneath both her cloak and his greatcoat, but the wind blew under their makeshift shelter and she knew he had to be cold.

He smiled at her, and it was reward enough. Michael's smile was rare, but it warmed her to her toes. It transformed his craggy features and customary remote expression to warmth and friendship.

It was not long before the young boy began to shake with a renewed onset of the fever. Shortly thereafter the sergeant roused himself from the fitful doze he had enjoyed.

"Look after young Ben for me, miss, will you? He's just a lad. Had no business in the Army. You take care." He clutched at Catherine and she smiled down at him and patted his weathered, calloused hand.

"I will, Euwan. I promise." Their eyes met and Catherine saw that they were in perfect accord. They knew the end was near. "And Dr. Soames will look after him, too."

"And you as well, sergeant," Michael said, unwilling to give up on any patient who still drew breath.

The old soldier shook his head. "No, doctor. I know better, if you don't." He smiled up at Catherine. "I don't think you'll have overlong to look after Ben either, miss. I think he'll be joining me soon enough." His voice faded to a whisper. "Thankee, miss, for everything."

A deep sigh, and he turned his head away, toward the private. "Good-bye, young Ben." His voice was a gasp. "You be . . . good and . . . remember to keep . . . your head . . . down. . . ."

It was the end, and Ben knew it. "Don't go, Euwan. Don't go. Please don't leave me, Euwan."

Ben tried to take Euwan's hand, but the older man's head fell back to the deck and he breathed his last. Ben turned his head away, his thin chest shaking with suppressed sobs. In silence, Catherine took his hand and Ben turned into her arms. She held him as a mother would a small child, her heart breaking at the waste of war. She tried so hard to succor and to help doctors like Michael cure. And yet this happened over and over. Ben stayed silent and struggling to breathe normally for only a few minutes before he, too, slumped forward and stopped breathing.

Catherine continued to hold him, unable to admit he was gone until Michael reached over and laid Ben on the deck.

"It is over," he murmured as he stood and raised Catherine to her feet. Tenderly, he laid her sodden cloak about her shoulders as she stood, barely aware of the world around her, but intensely aware of Michael. Then, as he covered her with his greatcoat, she turned and burrowed into his chest. Like a child seeking comfort, she had to be as close as she could to the source of all the warmth and light in the world. Her sun and moon.

But even he could not conquer their enemy. "It will never be over. Men will continue to die and we can do nothing about it."

He held her tenderly and stroked her back under the cloak. "It will end, dearest. Someday."

"Oh, Michael, if only they weren't so young. So many of them just like Ben and Davy Blankenship. So young." Her arms crept around his waist, and she held him as tightly as she could. He was her lifeline, the one sane and healthy voice amid all the privation and death.

"I know, dearest. It is the nature of war." Despite the sadness and desolation of the moment, he still sounded young and strong and fearless. Catherine was heartened. With his arms around her, she thought, she could do anything.

"But we can fight for them," he said. "And win sometimes, as we did with Davy Blankenship. And Jemmy Glendower. We can do it together."

Together. *His words intoxicated her. He bent and, with one cold hand, raised her head. For a timeless heartbeat, they gazed into each other's eyes. Then, slowly, so slowly she was afraid he would stop at any moment, he touched her lips with his.*

It was a moment of unutterable sweetness. Despite the sickness and death all around them, the freezing rain that fell remorselessly on their bare heads, Catherine knew they were right to take this exact moment to reaffirm the eternal truths of life and love. The

*only two things, she thought, that could triumph over the darkness
and death that lay all around them.*

*"Together," she repeated and hugged him closer as she gazed
into his eyes. She smiled faintly, though she saw him through a
haze of tears.*

*He bent his head once again and took her lips with his. At
first, he touched her gently, almost reverently, more in shared
comfort than passion. Then the heat that had always been there
between them flared like a torch in the night.*

*Passion underlay their companionship and the shared delight
they took in their ability to heal the sick and wounded. It always
had.*

"Catherine, I—"

*She felt too much to talk. There was no need for talk. She was
sure they both knew the depth and strength of their feelings. Now
she needed to feel. Just feel. "Oh, Michael, don't let's talk now.
Please, just hold me. Hold me."*

His arms closed about her tightly. "Yes, dearest, of course."

*She wanted to stay in his arms forever, here where no one could
see them and no duty called them. His warmth and strength
poured into her and happiness surrounded her.*

*After a few moments, he slowly released her, but she swayed
toward him. Taking a deep, shuddering breath, he put her from
him and said, "You had better go down to your cabin. No one
saw. We will pretend this never happened."*

*She could feel the soft glow that had suffused her face turn to
a fiery blush of mortification. Did he mean that? Was he so
concerned with propriety that his first thought was not of what
they felt but of what others would think? What did he feel? Just
what others had hinted at—that she was a nurse and therefore
a slut no matter what her birth.*

He was just like the others.

*Catherine fled down the ladder to the tiny cabin, tears streaming
unchecked down her cheeks.*

* * *

She awoke in her cozy room in London to find the same tears flowing from her eyes, her sobs buried in her pillow.

Michael was lost to her. Before he knew anything but friendship and passion from her, he had turned away, had told her to pretend those kisses had never happened. Her engagement to Julian was just an excuse to think what he already had decided on.

So Catherine arose and, with the clear light of dawn shining in her eyes, sat at her window, vowing to make a life with Julian.

Julian, however, was having none of it.

She had dressed in her most becoming cobalt velvet afternoon dress, a close fitting bonnet of matching blue, and a fur-lined cloak over her shoulders. When she arrived at the Eversleigh mansion, only a few squares over from her father's, she was shown in as an honored guest and greeted by the countess like a savior.

"Catherine, my dear, dear girl." The French-born countess's accent was completely charming, making Catherine want to agree with anything she said. Catherine was kissed on the cheek and seated next to the countess, who rang for tea. "You really are the only one who can help us now." There was real distress in the countess's brown eyes.

"He is still sad and depressed?" Catherine asked.

"Still? You knew of this?"

"He was withdrawn and silent the one time I saw him at Scutari," Catherine admitted. "But it is not an unusual condition when men are first brought in. I think perhaps it helps them."

"Helps?" The countess turned startled eyes to Catherine. "How can it help to refuse the love and care of those nearest to you? It is as if he does not wish to be well. He simply lies there and stares at the wall. He will say nothing. He eats if we feed him, like an obedient child." The countess's eyes filled with tears. "He was never obedient, Catherine. You know that. Not for one day in his life."

Catherine reached out and put her arm around the countess's shaking shoulders. This was worse than she thought. She had her work cut out for her, not only with Jules but with his family. "I know, ma'am. I know."

The tea arrived and Catherine poured the countess a cup, knowing she must calm and hearten his mother if she was to help Julian. "You must be strong and cheerful for Julian," she told the countess, who continued to cry softly. "I know how difficult this is for you, but Julian needs you to be strong for him now."

"I understand," the countess murmured. "You are right. I will stop this foolishness now." She straightened her shoulders and managed a watery smile. "You must go to him. Help him, Catherine," she said, grasping Catherine's hands in a demanding grip.

Catherine promised.

As she stood inside the door of Julian's room, she recognized all of the symptoms of those who have been badly wounded and brought back from the brink of death—the pallor, the wan, listless manner. She had knocked but was not surprised when she received no answer.

"Hello, Jules. It is your private nurse, personally trained by Florence Nightingale herself, who has come to take charge of your case." Her tone was light.

Julian did not even acknowledge her presence. He lay in bed, the covers tidily pulled up to his shoulders, and stared at the ceiling.

"Do you mind if I sit down and stay for a while?"

"I wish you would not." The tone was polite, but there was an undertone of desperation.

"I might be able to help."

He shook his head, one brief movement. "No one can help." He turned his head toward her. "Please leave. And make my mother and father stay away. They might listen to you. I don't want to see anyone." His eyes were bleak and despairing, but at least he was talking directly to her.

"If I try to keep the others from bothering you, may I come?" She smiled, expecting him to agree to the bargain.

"No."

"But, Jules, we're going to be married and I—"

"No," he said again. Just a simple word, dropped like a stone. There was a world of rejection in it. "No." He turned his head away.

"Jules, you cannot expect everyone who loves you to simply let you molder away in this room. Why, you have a whole life ahead of you. I am sure Dr. Soames told you there is every chance you will walk again and—"

"Leave me alone!"

She looked deep into a face distorted by despair. He meant it. Catherine thought for a moment that she had elicited rage or some strong emotion, which was what she had intended. But no, he subsided again, ignoring her. She decided to let him have his way—for the moment. "All right, Jules. I will visit again tomorrow."

"Please do not. What do I have to do to be left alone?" It was a cry from the heart.

She closed the door gently behind her.

For the next four days she doggedly continued to visit Julian. He continued to ignore her, each day sinking deeper into the melancholy that seemed to lap at his mind like a black ocean, a tide growing stronger each day, threatening to engulf him.

Finally, on the fifth day, Julian broke her. "If you do not leave me alone, I will send an announcement to the *Times* that our engagement is at an end." His eyes were hard and dull as stones. "Then I will shoot myself. I would like to do that. I think about it and long for it, and if you continue to badger me, I *will* do it. I will leave everyone to speculate on just what you did to drive me to it." He smiled, a chill, unpleasant look that changed his features into those of a satyr. "You would not like that. Nor would your father. Let me go. There are plenty of cripples around if you need to marry in order to have a patient to practice on."

Catherine recoiled, not from the icy venom in his smile but from the matter-of-fact tone in which he had announced his suicide. She knew he meant every word. She bowed her head, finally ready to admit defeat. Julian was supposed to save her from having to choose what her life would be. Without marriage to a man who needed her skills, Catherine had to decide whether to accede to her father's wishes and take up a life of socially acceptable idleness or try to carve out a new, untrodden path for herself as a professional nurse.

"I am sorry you are crying," he said, his expression remote. "But you are only sad because you are losing a job. You will find one somewhere else. Perhaps you and that tediously thorough Dr. Soames can work together patching up people who would rather die. I am sorry, Cat, but I simply don't care what you do. I do not want to see you again."

She left then, tears leaking from her eyes, and told the countess she would not be back for a while. Julian's mother took her into a warm embrace and kissed her.

"You did your very best. I understand, my dear."

They both cried a little then for the husk of Julian, all

that remained of the man they both cared for. The countess promised she would keep a careful but unobtrusive watch over Julian. To get that promise, Catherine had lied and told her Julian's wound might easily become infected.

And then Catherine left to try to find the courage to make some kind of useful life for herself, despite the fact that the men she cared for most had no use for her.

Chapter Five

After that, Catherine could not help but notice a number of men wearing threadbare Army greatcoats in the streets and particularly in the parks. Most of them were missing limbs and some had a lost look in their eyes. To Betsy's consternation, Catherine stopped to speak to them and several times shook hands with them, leaving several tightly folded bank notes in their hands.

"You mustn't be seen speaking to strange men, miss," Betsy remonstrated. "Not men like that, in any case. They aren't any of them the kind of men you should be speaking to. I don't know what the baronet would say if he knew."

"But he doesn't know, Betsy, does he?" Catherine said, a militant sparkle in her eyes. "And you are not going to mention this to anyone."

Betsy understood the warning. "No, miss. Not a word will I say to anyone. Not if they was to torture me."

Catherine laughed. "I don't think it will come to that,

Betsy. We haven't tortured anyone in Stanhope House for years! Not since I drove my governess mad by insisting on doctoring the kitchen cat instead of learning irregular French verbs."

Betsy looked at her, uncertain of how much to believe. "Yes, miss."

"Have you been looking in on Private Glendower, Betsy, as I asked you to?" Catherine knew Betsy viewed the private as a lesser being, but she had hoped Betsy would look on him more kindly if she were asked to take an interest in him.

"Yes, miss, since you asked me to. Looks a bit peaky but he's got a very smart tongue in his head." Betsy looked disapproving.

"Well, just keep an eye on him, will you?"

Betsy sighed, but her lips quirked in a tiny smile. "Yes, miss."

Catherine was satisfied.

The next morning was the happiest Catherine had known since she had come back.

Private Glendower was ill and she was useful again.

It was Betsy who told her. Worried that Jemmy—Private Glendower, that was—had a fever and insisted on working anyway, Betsy had come to Catherine. She twisted her hands in her apron as she explained how she just happened to be in the kitchen that morning and just happened to notice that the new temporary stable hand was flushed and admitted that the stump of his arm was hot and swollen.

"He's that worried he'll be turned off if he doesn't work, miss. Marston is a bit picky like about his stables. Jemmy, he's very knacky, miss, despite his only having the one arm, but Marston is hard on new lads. So he wouldn't listen and now he's fainted, miss." Betsy's face was tight with worry. "So, if you would come when you can—"

But Catherine was already up, choosing a simple blue dress, washing her face and pinning up her hair before Betsy could do more than lay out the brush and comb. Within ten minutes, Catherine was on her way to the tiny loft above the stables where Jemmy and the three other lads slept.

"Oh, miss, you shouldn't," said Betsy, who had followed along in her mistress's wake. "Don't you want your chocolate first, miss? We could bring Jemmy down. You mustn't climb the ladder, miss. 'Tisn't fitting."

Nurse Stanhope turned to Betsy and briskly set her straight. "Please do not preach propriety to me, Betsy, not when there is work to be done. Kindly ask Cook for a big basin of boiled water and some clean linen for bandages." Betsy looked at Nurse Stanhope and clearly saw someone she had never seen before—competent, brisk, accomplished. Someone who expected Betsy to be just as brisk and competent as she was.

"Very good, miss." Betsy set forth to become a nurse's assistant.

"The wound has gotten infected, Jemmy," Catherine said as she examined the wound with gentle thoroughness. "The stables are not a good place for you to work until the stump has healed completely."

" 'Tis the only work I know, miss. Animals and crops, that is." Jemmy grimaced at the streaks of pain that flashed through what was left of his arm.

"Well, temporarily we will find you something else to do."

Catherine bathed the arm and decided the infection was forming pus and would have to be lanced. She prepared a knife the way Michael had shown her, passing it through a candle flame, and afterward she bandaged the stump and gave Jemmy orders not to get up.

As she gave orders to Marston as to what duties Jemmy could perform, Catherine realized she felt alive and energetic. She gave some thought to this as she sipped her breakfast cup of chocolate, still savoring every mouthful. Chocolate was one thing that was fully as wonderful as she remembered it.

Nursing had been her dream and then, for a short while, her life. Was it any wonder that, cut adrift from the wellspring of her being, she was listless and unhappy? She had wanted to nurse Julian, but he had known nursing was all she was interested in and had refused. Nothing she had tried had changed his mind. She would have to find something else to give purpose to her life. Now that she had tasted the joy of work again, she was determined to make it her life. That was the answer: She would return to nursing. The method, however, was not so clear. How to evade her father's questions and Betsy's constant companionship?

"Betsy, I must ask a great favor of you," she said later that morning as she sat watching in the looking glass as Betsy dressed her hair.

"Yes, miss." The young maid's expression was still worried.

Good, that should make it easy. "I need someone to stay with Jemmy today in case the fever goes up. I would feel easier in my mind if you were to do it."

"You won't be needing me then, miss?" Betsy was doubtful. She knew where her duty lay. Miss Stanhope was not to go out alone. Sir Everett had been quite clear about that.

"No," Catherine said. "If I go out it will be in the closed

carriage, and I will go only to the Eversleighs. I shall be quite safe.''

"Very well, miss, since you ask." Betsy's face lightened. Unless Catherine was very much mistaken, Betsy had developed an affection for the young veteran.

The rest was easy. She slipped out of the house wearing her plainest dress and the gray cloak and bonnet from her Crimean days. She took a hackney to a hospital not far from the site of Miss Nightingale's nursing home in Harley Street.

It was small—no more than fifteen people could be accommodated easily within—but she felt she might be welcomed more easily than at one of the huge institutions where the poor were taken.

She was wrong.

The first person she saw was the doctor her father favored. He greeted her with effusive goodwill, telling everyone within earshot that here was a veteran of the Crimea—a lady veteran, he added with a broad smile that made everyone take notice and Catherine cringe.

"Have you come to look us over?" he said with great goodwill.

She took her courage in both hands. "No, doctor. I've come to apply for a job. Nursing."

He took it for a joke and his jowls shook with his laughter. When he saw she meant what she said, he grew instantly serious. "I cannot do it, my dear. Your father would have my head on a platter if I even considered it. You have had your adventure, more than most girls even dream of." He patted her hand in an avuncular manner. Catherine longed to box his ears. "Be content with that," he admonished her. "It is time to take up your real responsibilities. As I recall, you are to be married soon."

She smiled and allowed him to see her out.

It would have to be one of the rougher, charity hospitals where the poor went, usually to die. This time she took the coach, afraid of trying to find her way home by public hackney from such a locale.

Marston and John, the coachman, were horrified when she announced where she wanted to go. Catherine threatened them without compunction. "I will go without you, John. A hackney will take me. Of course," she added, allowing a slight frown to mar her brow, "I may have some difficulty finding one there to take me back here, but—"

They knew when they were beaten. The coach was ready in five minutes.

The hospital reminded her forcibly of Scutari as she had first seen it—a vast, dirty cavern with wavering wintry light filtering through windows set high in the wall. It was a rabbit-warren of corridors and rooms. The smells of illness and death had never been sufficiently washed away.

Catherine felt at home as she had not since she returned to England.

She searched for and eventually found the medical director's office. There was an anteroom with a small desk. No one sat behind it, and Catherine boldly knocked once and then entered the unknown director's office.

The high-backed chair behind the desk was turned away from the door. She addressed its back. "I have come to apply for a nursing position," she said.

The man rose from the chair and turned to face her. Craggy face. Auburn hair. Eyes that could be brown or hazel.

Michael.

"Slumming again, Catherine?"

Shock froze her body, and a mixture of love and anger roiled her mind and dimmed her eyes for a moment.

She said the obvious. "Michael. What are you doing here?" Her hand crept to her throat and she could feel her pulse there, hard and fast, as if she had been running.

"The same as you, I gather. I am applying for a post at this august bastion of British medicine." He stared at her, his eyes as hard as agates.

"You are no longer at Scutari? You have left?" She continued to state the obvious; she couldn't help it. She could not believe the truth of what she saw.

"So it would seem."

Michael was always impatient with stupidity, and she felt remarkably stupid at this moment. Her brain refused to move beyond the astonishing fact that Dr. Michael Soames, instead of being a continent away in Turkey, in the cold and stench and blood of an Army hospital, stood before her in London, England.

Michael Soames had shared the best and worst experiences of her life, had understood her as no one else ever had. Not even Lucinda or Rose, her closest friends among Miss Nightingale's staff, had perceived the fire within her that drove her to battle disease and death wherever she could.

But Michael had. He had kissed her once and changed her life. Kissed her and then told her to go away. It was getting to be very repetitious, this being told by men she cared for that they would be much happier if she would simply leave them alone.

She raised her chin. There might be some excuse for Julian, wounded and in pain, to lash out at her. But Michael Soames had no reason in the world to berate her. "Well, I trust I can count on you to recommend me to this hospital—and not to mention my father. I have lost a position already because of his name." She spoke as crisply as she could, ruthlessly suppressing the rage and pain of loving a man who despised her.

"So you have talked the baronet around. And the earl's son as well, I presume?"

She ignored the jibe. "Why are you in London? The reports in the *Times* have said that the Army is camped in front of Sevastopol and will likely stay there the entire winter. What made you leave?"

He shrugged and continued to stare at her. "Dr. Hall felt he could live without my presence, and there is a parliamentary commission meeting here. An M.P. named Roebuck has started looking into the situation in the Crimea. Miss Nightingale and I agreed I should take up Dr. Hall's offer to release me so I could come here and testify."

"I see. So you are seeking a temporary position until the commission is finished with you?" How long would she have to face the mingled pleasure and pain of seeing him? She had counted on not having to meet him ever again. Her defenses were not in place. She had not yet stiffened her spine.

"I do not know how long I will be here." He did not seem very interested in his future. Instead, he stepped closer to her. "I had not planned on ever coming to London, but I thought if I did I could avoid you. And yet here you are." His eyes were dark and stormy as she gazed helplessly up at him.

"I could look for work at another hospital, I suppose." Would it be easier to see him every day, perhaps to work with him, or to go somewhere else and think about him every day?

"Perhaps that would be—" He broke off and grasped her shoulders, his fingers hard and demanding. "No. No. Work here, Catherine. With me. At least let me have that."

Her heart pounding with the thrill of his touch, Catherine scarcely heard him. She had reached her own decision. "No. I will not go to another hospital. I want to work here."

With you. She could not say those words, knowing how ill he thought of her.

"Yes." His gaze turned molten, and Catherine could feel her knees begin to give way. "Here. With me."

She nodded.

The hospital administrator bustled in at that moment and wondered what he had interrupted, but he was too delighted to have two such eminently qualified persons drop into his lap to ask any questions. Once he heard where they had trained and what their experience had been, he hired them both on the spot.

Catherine walked out of the hospital with Michael. She offered to take him to his lodgings in the carriage, which had waited for her, but he declined. "We work together," he had told her flatly. "But that is all the contact I want with you. I will go to see your fiancé, if you do not object."

"Why should I?" she said with feigned indifference. "You were his physician in Turkey."

"And on the voyage home. Another reason I left so soon. As an earl's son, the Army wanted him to have medical care on the voyage. We saw quite a lot of each other. He should heal physically, if he wants to. But I am not sure he does. Your friend Rose told him he was a spoiled brat who wouldn't play the game if he were penalized. I think he threw something at her."

Catherine grimaced and drew her cloak closer around her, for the wind was bitter. "Yes, that seems to be a habit of his. I must go. The horses have been standing a long time."

"Of course that elegant vehicle had to be yours. I am

surprised you did not bring your maid with you." His sarcasm flicked her already raw nerves.

"I would appreciate it if you would refrain from making any mention of my circumstances to anyone in the hospital. The administrator did not recognize my name, and I would like to remain simply Miss Stanhope." She raised her chin and waited for another sarcastic remark.

Instead, he smiled. "I admire your spirit, Miss Stanhope, and I will keep your secret."

On her way home, Catherine found that instead of worrying about how she was to tell her father of her plans, she was reliving the afternoon with Michael and trying to convince herself that she could work with him without risking her heart.

She met her father in the smaller of their two drawing rooms for their usual glass of sherry before dinner. Before she could think of a way to broach the subject, her father said, "I missed you this afternoon, my dear. Over trying to talk Julian out of his sulks, were you?"

Catherine opened her mouth to explain where she had been, but the baronet did not give her a chance to speak. Instead, he began to hold forth on politics and the character of the prime minister, Lord Aberdeen, and Palmerston, the man who was soon to replace him.

"Aberdeen is an ass and must go. It will be Palmerston. No one else can form a government. Charming as the day is long, of course, but a slippery customer. No wonder Her Majesty doesn't care for him." The baronet smiled at his daughter. "I must say you look especially pretty this evening, my dear. More color in your cheeks and your eyes are brighter. Must be love."

He chuckled. Catherine had told him of Julian's rejection of her and of the decision she and the countess had reached to allow him to have his way. But the baronet refused to believe Julian meant the break to be permanent. He insisted on regarding the engagement as still in effect.

Catherine was horrified at his words. "Nonsense," she said, the crystal sherry glass slipping from her fingers to land with a thud on the cherry tea table before her. "Love has nothing whatsoever to do with it. It was the walk I took in the cold air that has brightened my eyes. And my nose," she added with what she hoped was a convincing chuckle.

Love? No. She cared for Michael, despite what he thought of her. But she was determined to break herself of it, to get over it—whatever one did to recover from a disastrous affection that was not love. Never love. It could not be.

After all, what did it amount to, anyway? A few kisses. Of course, it had been most improper, but aside from her father and others of his generation, would anyone think she had done anything so terrible? It was a tiny mistake, that was all. She would get over it.

"I trust Julian will pull out of his state of—whatever it is. It is too bad to fall into lethargy just when he is home and can enjoy himself and get on with his life."

Catherine, who understood only too well the wrenching sense of disorientation Julian was suffering from, said merely, "It is a great change, you know, Father, to go from the battlefields and hospitals of Turkey to life here in London."

"But it makes no sense to be sad when you come home. I could understand it if he had been afraid and run away during the battle—not that Julian ever would be a coward, of course! But to refuse to see his friends and enjoy his life now? Ridiculous!" The baronet's no-nonsense nature had no room for the subtlety of life's responses.

"Father"—Catherine groped for words—"perhaps it is hard for Julian to believe in his luck and even harder to believe he deserves it when so many of his comrades died before his eyes.''

Her father shook his head. Luck was to be savored, in the baronet's view, and debate about whether one should be alive was just a waste of time better spent living. He decided he would tell Julian that at the earliest opportunity.

"Maybe I will go with you tomorrow and give the lad a good talking to."

"No, no, Father. Let him alone for the time being."

Without consciously deciding to do so, Catherine let her father assume that she was going to the Eversleighs to see Julian the next day, when in fact she was determined to go back to the hospital to begin her job.

How to do it was the question. It absorbed her thoughts at dinner so much that several times her father had to recall her from what he called her "daydreams."

"Planning how to bring Julian to the altar, are you?" he joked.

Catherine managed a small smile. She did not believe Julian would respond to efforts on her part to convince him to marry her. But perhaps she owed it to him to try in any case. He was her friend, and it was to help her that he had conceived of the engagement. Should she not do her best to carry out her part of the bargain? She was better equipped to do so than the earl and countess, for she had seen the results of battle before and understood a little of what Julian was going through. She had faced it, too.

Later that evening, she dismissed Betsy for the night and sat at her dressing table brushing out her hair. It was a soothing, mechanical task that aided thought. And she needed to think.

Julian needed her—or someone—but did not want her.

In Turkey, she had noticed that men responded better to repeated quiet attempts to interest them in their surroundings. Why had she not remembered that when she saw Julian? Instead, she had chattered and been bracing and cheerful. No wonder he wanted to strangle her!

And then she had allowed him to drive her away. What kind of a nurse was she? She would try a quiet, limited approach—visit him every other day or so, see what he needed.

Meantime, how was she to work at the hospital without telling her father what she was doing? It was unfair to engage the servants in a conspiracy, for if he found out, the baronet might make them suffer for her actions. No, she would have to deceive them, too—or at least not involve them in her schemes. Slipping out of the house early and returning before her father got back from his daily trips to the House or to one of his clubs would be simpler than to outwit Betsy or Holden.

But she could simply carry out her plans with a high hand. The servants were not her keepers. They could tell the baronet the truth—they did not know where Miss Catherine went during the day. They had assumed she was with her betrothed. Her father could not blame them for not questioning her, for she was no longer a child.

Satisfied she had solved her problem, Catherine went to bed.

She got up before dawn the next day and, after donning her gray Scutari Hospital dress, she crept downstairs and out the front door.

To find Marston and John waiting at the door with the coach.

Catherine was touched beyond words at their loyalty, but she could not permit them to risk their positions by helping her. When she told them as much, Marston replied, "We'd be turned off without a character, Miss Catherine, and deserve to be if we let you go into that terrible neighborhood without us."

She sighed. She had reckoned without the intense personal loyalty the Stanhope servants felt toward her. "No, it will not do, Marston. I am going to be working at that hospital as a nurse. No one there knows who I am, and they are not going to find out, if I can help it."

The two men looked at each other, nodded, and looked back at her, mulish obstinacy clear in their faces. This was going to be harder than she had thought.

"I want you to be here so my father will not suspect what I am about. He would worry and fret himself, and I do not want that." She warmed to her task. "It would not do for him to overexcite himself, so you must—"

"Begging your pardon, Miss Catherine, but if you was to get in the carriage, we could have you to that dreadful place and be back before the cat could lick her ear." Marston grinned. "Just let me help you up, miss."

Leaning back against the velvet upholstery of the Stanhope town coach, Catherine smiled ruefully to herself. She had never been able to get the best of the servants. She always ended up doing exactly what they wanted.

"We will be outside at four o'clock." Marston hopped down from the seat next to John and opened the door for her with his usual flourish. "You'd best be here, or we'll be late to meet your father at his club."

And that, Catherine knew, would never do. She acquiesced gracefully. "Very well, Marston. I will be here at four."

"Mind you're not late," was his last retort as the carriage swung around the circular drive on its way back to Grosvenor Square.

She did not see Michael. Unsure whether she was happy

or disappointed not to have her heart twisted by the sight of him, Catherine threw herself into the familiar tasks of nursing.

The hospital was disorganized, its nurses untrained and unsupervised. Without being asked, Catherine began the task of bringing St. Luke's Hospital for the Deserving Poor into the kind of shape Miss Nightingale would approve of.

She remembered how they had started at Scutari.

For the first three weeks as a nurse in the Army Hospital at Scutari, all she did was scrub. Thousands of men lay wounded, but the nurses had been forbidden to tend them. Instead, they had become scrubwomen.

Not that that scrubbing wasn't needed. Blankets, clothes, walls and floors—everything in the huge barracks of a hospital had been filthy when the nurses had arrived. Despite three weeks of unremitting toil, Catherine thought they had barely begun.

Catherine and the rest of the nurses had been ready to see to the men immediately. After all, that was what they had come to Turkey to do—help the injured soldiers, ease their pain, and tend their wounds. Instead, Catherine thought rebelliously, they had been forbidden to do anything. The Army Medical Service had not wanted Miss Nightingale and her nurses and had flatly refused to allow them to do anything with their wounded. Orderlies and the untrained wives of soldiers had been good enough for the Duke of Wellington's victorious army forty years ago. They were, by God, good enough for the modern fighting men as well!

And Catherine had thought Michael Soames was rigid and unenlightened! He was the picture of modern, forward thinking compared to the rest of the doctors she had encountered. As one of the few ladies (how she hated that word!) among the nurses, Catherine had been taken aside and told, sometimes politely, sometimes with a sneer, that she had better take herself off home before she saw or heard something too horrid to be borne and lost forever the sweet bloom of her delicate nature . . . or words to that effect.

They sounded remarkably like her father. Catherine had long ago learned to ignore the baronet when he began ranting about womanhood and used words like "delicate." She would ignore the jibes of the Army doctors and quartermasters and look for ways to help the sick and wounded.

But Miss Nightingale had not been able to ignore their orders. So, denied the opportunity to do the job they had been sent to do, she set her nurses the task of cleaning up the huge, filthy barracks.

It was impossible. Catherine vaguely remembered her governess telling her about a Greek hero who was ordered to clean out a stable. He had diverted a river to run through the place as the only way to succeed. After weeks of scrubbing, she had begun to think perhaps the hero was right. Nothing else seemed to help very much.

As she bent her aching back once more to the task of scrubbing, she had heard a soft voice with a North country burr say, "Why don't you let me do that, Miss Stanhope? I'm used to scrubbing and don't get so tired."

Catherine glanced up to see Rose Cranmer looking at her with some concern. Rose was a born nurse, although she had never had any formal training. She had assisted her mother, a village healer and herbalist, and knew far more about how to treat illness and injury than any of the other nurses. Catherine envied Rose her experience and feared that Rose viewed her as a useless aristocrat who would be more hindrance than help. She was determined to pull her weight, so she smiled and lifted her chin as she shook her head.

"Everyone gets tired of scrubbing, Rose. And you must call me Catherine."

Rose shook her head and gave a tentative smile in return. "Well, then, I will scrub alongside you."

It had been the beginning of a friendship Catherine cherished.

*She and Rose and Lucinda had forged an unlikely bond, composed
equally of shared hardships and laughter and the certainty they
could depend on each other for understanding and help no matter
what the circumstances.*

Catherine wished she had her friends with her now.
Instead, she was faced with a gaggle of dirty, sullen women,
most of whom worked only for money to buy enough gin
to drink themselves into oblivion. Well, a lot of the nurses
who'd gone with Miss Nightingale hadn't been much better, and they had turned into capable, useful workers.
These women would, too.

"Ladies," Catherine began and was met with dull-eyed
stares and nervous giggles. "We are going to work together
to make St. Luke's the very best hospital in London."

"We are?" said one young woman, whose face was thickly
painted. "And how are we going to do that, pray?"

"The same way Miss Nightingale and the rest of us did
it in Scutari Barracks Hospital." Catherine stared straight
at each woman in turn. "Hard work."

"You was with Miss Nightingale?" one woman asked,
clearly awed by the fact. "In that hospital what we heard
tell of? You are a real nurse?"

To her surprise, Catherine saw her words had wrought
a change in the attitude of most of the nurses. They had
heard of Florence Nightingale, and they revered her. If
Catherine had truly worked with Miss Nightingale, she
deserved respect.

"Yes," Catherine said proudly. "I was. And she was everything you have heard and more. If we work hard, as she
does, we can make this hospital as fine as hers."

"How?" said the painted young woman, much less
impressed than the others with Catherine's credentials.

"Well, we will start the way we started in Turkey." Catherine paused for effect. "We will clean everything. Floors, walls, sheets, blankets, the patients." She smiled at them. "That is a great deal of scrubbing. We should get right to it."

And to her surprise, they did. Perhaps the sight of Catherine on her knees, scrub brush in hand, had inspired them or perhaps the magic name of Florence Nightingale. Whatever it was, no one quit and no one refused to work. Some were more enthusiastic than others, but they all worked.

So absorbed was she in the task that she was unaware of the presence of the hospital administrator until he coughed politely. She rose to her feet, one hand at her back to ease the discomfort.

"I do not think you should be doing this yourself, Miss Stanhope. I did not think—that is, Dr. Soames told me you were an expert surgical nurse, and I assumed you would devote yourself to that." He looked around, his rabbity little mustache twitching in distress.

"But, Dr. ...." She scrabbled for his name. It came at last. "Dr. Dinsmore, we must do this first, or we will not be able to care for the patients. And I will need to know about your laundry and special kitchen facilities—for beef tea and gruel and invalid diets," she explained when he looked blank.

"Miss Stanhope," he said, "I do not think you understand. I am very grateful for all you are doing and contemplate doing, but really, St. Luke's cannot even afford all this." He gestured to the kneeling women.

"All this being," Catherine asked, her eyebrows raised, "a few buckets and brushes and some soap? A matter of a few pounds at most. Surely—" She saw the set of his jaw. A weak man's stubbornness, she thought. She gave him an encouraging smile. "But if you say your funds will not run to it, I will understand. Consider it a gift."

"Miss Stanhope." The man clearly did not know what to say. "You cannot—"

"We found in Turkey that cleanliness seemed to cut down on mortality."

His mustache still twitched.

She tried the magic name. "*Miss Nightingale* believes in scrubbing. It will be much more successful here than in Scutari."

When he looked not awed but worried, she changed her tack. "Please let me do this for the patients."

"Miss Stanhope, it is clear to me you do not belong here. Look at our nurses. They are scum from the street. Not your sort."

"I say, guv, that's not very nice now, is it?" It was the cheeky girl with the painted lips who spoke.

"And it is not true," Catherine said. "I *am* a nurse and I *do* belong here at St. Luke's. And these women are nurses, too—or will be. Give us just a week, Dr. Dinsmore. I guarantee you will not know the place, and the patients will be better cared for. You will see. Just tell me where the laundry is and who is in charge of the kitchen."

"That is not the point, Miss Stanhope. You are certainly a wonder, and I consider St. Luke's lucky to have you. But you do not belong here." His tired eyes were surprisingly shrewd.

"I do not belong anywhere else," Catherine replied, responding to the kindness she sensed. "Only here, as a nurse, do I feel truly at home."

"But the fact remains, Miss Stanhope, that you are not at home here. I saw your carriage waiting to take you home as I came in."

Catherine gasped. She glanced down at the watch she

had pinned to her bodice. It was well after four. "Oh, dear. I must go."

"Yes, you must." The doctor looked at her as she rolled down the sleeves of her dark gray dress. "And I will understand if you find you cannot return. For truly, despite what you and Dr. Soames think, you do not belong at St. Luke's."

Chapter Six

Catherine *didn't* belong at St. Luke's, Michael thought as he strode briskly down the long, dark corridors of the hospital the next day.

But he wanted her there.

Ruthlessly honest with himself, he admitted he wanted to see her, to work with her even though she was betrothed to another man—a handsome cavalry officer who had been one of the survivors of the now famous Charge of the Light Brigade at Balaklava.

A brave man, a worthy man. Michael had gotten to know Julian Livingston, heir to the Earl of Eversleigh, at Scutari and later traveling together back to England. He admired the man. Even though he had been sunk in the depths of despair, Julian had been unfailingly polite and kind to those around him.

The gift of the upper classes, Michael thought. Had he himself been wounded so seriously that his way of life, if not his life itself, was threatened, he was sure he would have struck out at anyone who came near. But Julian reserved his contempt and anger for himself.

Catherine could do worse, Michael had to acknowledge, than to marry her childhood friend. Julian had told him only that Catherine and he had known each other all their lives. He had never alluded to the kiss Michael and Catherine had shared. To this day, Michael did not know if Julian was aware of it. Perhaps the fellow who had informed Hall and Miss Nightingale of the improper behavior of a doctor and a nurse had not told Julian out of some kind of aristocratic sense of honor.

Michael didn't know what the higher orders considered honorable and did not much care. He had a rooted aversion to the kind of meaningless social life among the rich and idle that his mother craved. Michael admired his father in all ways except the elder Dr. Soames's devotion to his selfish and demanding wife. It was a mistake Michael did not intend to make.

Avoiding matrimony had been his credo, and he had never found any reason to change his mind.

Until Catherine.

Beautiful, dedicated, strong, and gentle, Catherine Stanhope was everything any man could want—especially a man like Michael who was dedicated to medicine, for Catherine was as devoted as he was. She had changed his mind about females in medicine just as surely as she had changed his mind about females in his life.

One female, at any rate.

He wanted to have her near him, but she did not belong in his life. His father had been a successful doctor and was the son of a successful farmer, but Michael knew that though his birth was respectable, it would not do for a rich, socially prominent London beauty like Catherine.

Even though he had seen examples of it over and over, including the fact that she had sought out nursing when she returned home, he still found it hard to believe she would not be happy to marry or at least to live at home and be surrounded by luxury and ease.

His mother wanted that above everything else in life. The love of a husband and children had been far less important to her than an active social life in the highest echelons of Edinburgh society. And his mother was the only woman he had known well. He found it difficult to believe that a woman who already had everything his mother never ceased to strive for would give it all up. Michael knew very few men who were capable of that kind of sacrifice.

But contact with Catherine had eroded the certainty of his judgments. He loved her and was almost willing to believe that she would sacrifice comfort and ease in order to nurse. What he still could not ignore was that she should not marry as far beneath her socially as Michael was. She could have any man she wanted. She had the ideal man already in Julian Livingston.

Julian loved her, Michael was sure. How could he not? So even though Julian referred to her as his childhood friend and showed no emotion at the mention of her name, Michael was sure that was just a natural reticence. Julian did not know Michael well, so of course he would not choose to reveal his feelings for Catherine. The young cavalry officer had everything Michael thought a woman could want.

Since Julian and Catherine were so clearly made for each other, there was nothing for Michael to do but grit his teeth and get on with his life. Knowing her father and her fiancé both disapproved of her nursing, Michael had reached the decision that he should discourage Catherine

from coming to St. Luke's. Much as he would have loved
to see her, to work with her, he felt he should not encourage her to do something that her world could not understand or approve of. She would be ostracized, perhaps even
disowned by her father and repudiated by Julian if she
continued to work at a charity hospital in the near slums
of London's East End.

Having decided to do what he did not wish to do, Michael
wanted to put it into practice immediately. He went to the
administrator's office and strode in without knocking. Dr.
Dinsmore was seated at a desk covered with papers.

"Dinsmore," Michael said, "you must tell Miss Stanhope
she cannot return here. She is not needed."

The small, self-effacing administrator looked at his new-
est, most skillful physician in amazement. "But you told
me just yesterday she was the best nurse you had ever
worked with! Now you want me to let her go?" He looked
at Michael as if he thought the doctor had lost his mind.

"Yes. She should not be here. You know St. Luke's is
not like anything she is used to."

"She told me very little about her background," Dr.
Dinsmore said. "But of course I know a lady when I meet
one."

"She is a baronet's daughter," Michael said, wincing
inwardly as he remembered his promise not to tell anyone
at the hospital who she was.

"So her tale of being in the Crimea was a lie?" Dinsmore
asked. "She just made it up so she could pull a prank for
a day or two by working here?"

"No." Michael could not lie, even though it would have
made firing Catherine easy. "She was in the Crimea with
Miss Nightingale. That is where I met her."

"Umm." The little doctor stroked his weedy mustache.
"But she is only here to annoy and astonish her society

friends? She is not the dedicated nurse she pretended to be?"

"No, no." Telling the truth was getting him in deeper and deeper. But he could not let Dinsmore think Catherine was less than the devoted nurse she was. It was part of what he loved about her, and he could not deny it.

"Then I do not see why I have to fire her. She has inspired my nurses to work harder than ever before. She has ideas about improving the hospital. Her only flaw is that she seems to have no idea of how poor St. Luke's is."

Michael grimaced. "So you will not let her go. But I notice she is not here today. Perhaps she has decided she cannot work and live as she is used to."

Dinsmore smiled. "No, she has gone on an errand. Quite mysterious. She would only say she was sure you would approve. I will let you know when she comes—"

A knock interrupted them, and after Dinsmore called out for whoever it was to enter, Catherine appeared. Michael was always taken aback by her classic beauty. When she saw him she smiled, an impish grin that dispelled the idea that she was a serene goddess.

"Oh, good, Michael, you're here. I have brought you a surprise."

And she stepped aside to reveal a stocky woman with capable, work-worn hands, her sandy brown hair scraped back from her face. The woman smiled, and her shrewd blue eyes twinkled.

"Good morning, Dr. Soames. I don't guess you thought to see me here in London."

"Mary Ann Evans!" Michael grinned at her. "By all that's wonderful! It is you."

"Indeed it is. Our Catherine found me at the third employment registry she went to. She knew I would be seeking work after two weeks with my sister and her layabout husband!'' Mary Ann Evans took Michael's hands in her small, calloused ones and shook them.

"You are right. I never would have thought to see you here. But I am glad I was wrong."

Michael had to smile. Mary Ann Evans was one of the few people he had met in the Crimea whom he both liked and respected. Miss Nightingale he revered far too much to consider a friend. His feelings for Catherine were unlike any he had ever felt before. But Mary Ann, blunt, capable, and always cheerful, reminded him of the no-nonsense schoolteachers and hospital matrons he had known in Scotland.

They had met during the trip he and Catherine had taken to the battlefields near Balaklava for Miss Nightingale. Mary Ann was one of the wives of ordinary soldiers who had been allowed to follow her husband to Turkey, and she managed to stay with him until he was killed at the battle of Inkerman.

She had taken what work she could find, nursing at an Army regimental hospital. It was there that Michael and Catherine had encountered her first. Michael had liked her immediately.

She'd had tears in her eyes when he told her it was lucky for them that she had time to give them.

Amazing him, her lower lip had begun to tremble and those faded blue eyes filled with tears. "There is nothing for me to do anymore, sir, now that Evans is dead." Seeing his consternation, she made a great effort to pull herself together. "And truth to tell, it's that grateful I am to you for giving me something to do besides work here." She gestured around the room, where several men lay on threadbare blankets. She lowered her voice. "There's little enough I can do for them. I only wish there were more, but they'll all likely be gone by morning."

Catherine had gone to kneel beside the pallet of one young man who was groaning softly. She laid a hand on his forehead. When there were patients around to be helped, she became a nurse no matter what her role was supposed to be.

Now she looked up at Mary Ann. "Cholera?" She silently mouthed the word.

Mary Ann nodded. Catherine rose to her feet and went to stand beside the other woman.

Mary Ann said in a quiet undertone, "There's nothing to be done for them, poor lads. I can't even make them comfortable. We've no morphine."

Catherine nodded and then led the way outside, where the three of them stood in a cluster. There she smiled at the gunnery sergeant's widow and shook her hand warmly. "Those boys look clean and cared for. That is a great deal to have done for them under the circumstances. I welcome your knowledge and help, Mrs. Evans."

"Please call me Mary Ann, ma'am."

"And I am Catherine."

Mary Ann looked at the beautiful blond lady in the simple gray dress and cloak and said simply, "Oh, I couldn't, ma'am."

Michael knew exactly how she felt. Somehow he could never feel Catherine was just another nurse. She viewed herself that way, he knew, but there was an air of quiet elegance and self-containment that made him feel he would never really know her. Michael felt that it was a result of her sheltered upbringing. No one who had been brought up in the lap of luxury could have suffered any real hardship or disappointment. That was the reason, he thought, for that impenetrable calm that highlighted the vast social gulf that lay between them.

He was wryly amused that his reaction was not so very different from that of Mary Ann Evans. Catherine smiled warmly at the older woman and took her hand. "We are both nurses, Mary Ann.

Equals." She chafed Mary Ann's hand between both of hers. "You are cold." She looked at Mary Ann's dress, thin and almost worn through. "We will get you some warm dresses when we return to Scutari. Until then, I'm sure I can find you a warm cloak. That shawl doesn't keep you warm."

"I am fine, ma'am," Mary Ann said, clutching the faded woolen scarf tighter about her shoulders. "The sergeant give this to me when we was married. It keeps me warmer than you know." Her lip trembled again for a moment, but she conquered her weakness and set her shoulders.

"Now, sir, ma'am," she said, "let us get started. We've a lot to see."

They had indeed seen a great deal over the next few days. Yet in a sense they saw very little, for every field station was the same. There were no new wounded coming in, but even during the few days of their stay, it became clear that frostbite and cholera were going to claim even more men than the Russian guns if the Army had to maintain their camp here over the bitter Russian winter.

The few doctors were overworked and had even less to work with than Michael and Catherine had at Scutari. Some of the field hospitals had no one in attendance. As they rode in the ill-sprung carriage that was all that could be found for them, the three discussed what they had seen. Mrs. Evans, the seasoned campaigner, had some practical suggestions. Once she had overcome her natural reticence in the presence of two whom she clearly regarded as superior beings, she had been eager to share what she'd learned over a lifetime of campaigning.

"There ought to be some way of getting the boys down to where they can get help quicker. I do think sometimes if we could get to them faster they wouldn't have to go into hospital at all. Begging your pardon, sir, but it's hospitals as kill them."

"I'm not insulted, Mrs. Evans. You are right," Michael said, his brow furrowed. "Hospitals are the worst places for sick people to be."

"It does seem to be true," Catherine agreed, *"despite all that doctors can do. Although the cleaning we gave the Barracks Hospital has had a good effect. Perhaps what hospitals need is better housekeeping."*

"If we could have anything here," Mrs. Evans said, *"the best thing would be clean water. And soap. And morphine. With just that, we could do a great deal."* She smiled a little sheepishly. *"I know that's not a very big dream."*

"Oh, I don't know, Mary Ann." Catherine gave her an answering smile as the carriage swayed from one side of the cart track to the other. *"I've often wished for the very same things at the hospital. And when we got them, things were better."*

"So much for all my surgical skill, I suppose," Michael had said, joining in the discussion. *"Just hand me a scrub brush and a pail and I'll do more good than with my scalpel."*

That sobered Catherine. *"I have seen what you can do with your scalpel, Doctor. Nothing is more important for the wounded than your skill. Nothing."*

Michael remembered how Catherine and Mary Ann had agreed on the subject of hospital cleanliness.

"Have you come to help us reform St. Luke's?" he asked.

"Miss Catherine has asked me to come and try," Mary Ann said. She looked around and saw Dr. Dinsmore seated behind the large desk. She gave him a quick smile. "But I'm thinking it's you have the final say, sir. So I'd best be talking to you, had I not?"

Dinsmore gave a thin smile. "I am not surprised Miss Stanhope has already engaged you, Mrs. . . ."

"Evans, sir. Mary Ann Evans."

"Miss Stanhope is newly in charge of nursing here at St. Luke's," he said.

"I am?" Catherine was so pleased she could hardly find room for surprise. It was what she wanted, what she had always wanted. And now it was hers.

"Yes, Miss Stanhope. If you cannot be persuaded that St. Luke's is not the place for you, then we will make the best use of you we can," Dr. Dinsmore said. "And, Mrs. Evans, I have found that Dr. Soames and Miss Stanhope are miracles newly dropped in my lap. I have a feeling you may turn into one as well."

"Well, sir, I don't know about that," Mary Ann said, clearly pleased at the praise. "But I did look around a bit, and it seems to me there's not a lot of money coming in here. Can you pay the three of us, sir?"

Michael grinned. Mary Ann was nothing if not blunt. He noticed that Catherine's face fell. He'd been right. Money was not something Catherine was used to thinking about. She had believed it when she said money would come from somewhere.

"Oh, dear," she said. "I should have thought of that. But we do need a housekeeper, someone like Mary Ann and—"

Dr. Dinsmore cleared his throat. "But Mrs. Evans is correct, Miss Stanhope. St. Luke's cannot afford the three of you. I could barely scrape together enough to pay Dr. Soames. But for you and Mrs. Evans—well, we just do not have the money."

Catherine looked like a disappointed child at Christmas. "Oh, dear, I didn't think."

"No, how could you?" Michael said before he thought. "Money just grows on bushes where you live. Any bills you run up, why, Papa will pay them. Who cares how much you spend? And if you spend too much, you can hide the bills until the next month. If the shopkeeper's family goes short, too bad. Is that not the way of it, Miss Stanhope?"

Catherine looked at him as if he had physically struck her. "I—I do not know what you are talking about. I manage the household accounts when I am home, and I never exceed my budget." She drew herself up to her full, not inconsiderable height.

Michael felt like the worst kind of fool. The mention of money, and Catherine's admission she had not thought about it sounded so much like his mother that it had set him off like a rocket. Of course, his mother had not wanted to buy help for hospital patients but rather some furbelow for herself. If they had been alone, he would have apologized, but he could not bring himself to do so in front of Mary Ann and Dinsmore.

Dr. Dinsmore stepped into the breach. "I have a suggestion for Miss Stanhope, if she is disposed to listen."

Catherine sank into the chair facing the desk. It meant she no longer had to look at Michael. She faced only the administrator. "Yes, Doctor? I am disposed to listen to any suggestion of yours."

"I believe you must have a number of wealthy acquaintances through your father, the baronet," the administrator began.

Catherine turned in her chair until she fixed Michael with a cold, blue stare. "I wonder how you could have come by that information, doctor. I do not believe I mentioned it."

Michael was tired of being a silent fool. He might as well be hung for a sheep as a lamb. "You are right, you did not. I told Dr. Dinsmore why he was correct in thinking you did not belong here at St. Luke's."

"I belong wherever I choose to go," Catherine said, an angry flush staining her cheeks. She turned her back to Michael once again. "If you are suggesting I ask some of my friends for money for St. Luke's, I am willing to try. I know they do sometimes give when subscriptions are raised. Miss Nightingale has a large amount of money at her disposal to purchase what the Army cannot supply, a great deal of it from donations. The *Times* has raised a fund as well, and I believe she has some influence over how that is spent. And yes, now that I think of it, I believe Mr. Jeffrey Bancroft also raised a fund for use in the barracks hospital." She spoke stiffly and her back was ramrod straight. If backs could speak, hers would be telling Michael he was no longer among the people she considered worthy of any attention whatsoever.

"Yes, the English aristocracy is very generous when they are properly roused," Michael said from behind her. He was not going to be frozen out of the conversation. He would apologize to Catherine later. But now he wanted to prolong the time they spent together. It was bittersweet, knowing that their link would have to be only professional when he wanted so much more. Still, time spent with Catherine was worth it. He could not help his temper when she was so near and yet so far above him.

"Then perhaps you would like to come with me to a party my father and I are attending tonight." Catherine had that militant sparkle in her eye he had first noted when she had offered to help with the young private who had lost his arm.

Now she was challenging him again. This time he was not going to rise to it. In an operating room he knew no fear, but a drawing room was an entirely different matter—particularly a drawing room full of baronets' daughters and earls' heirs.

"Sorry, Miss Stanhope," he said with, he hoped, a sufficient show of carefree indifference, "but my dance card is full for this evening."

"What a pity," she said with a wicked grin. "But I suspected that might be the case.'' With that, she rose and, with a genuinely warm smile for Mary Ann, offered to show her around the hospital before they both got down to work.

She was late leaving the hospital that afternoon, and to her surprise she found Betsy waiting in the carriage.

"It's Jemmy, miss," the maid told her, a worried expression in her eyes. "He's telling me he has to get up and either work or leave. He won't stay longer if he isn't earning his way."

"I will talk to him when we get home." Catherine reached up to remove her bonnet and massage her aching temples. If she dared, she would have loosened her hair, but the servants would be horrified if she came into the house with her hair in disarray.

"Miss!" Betsy's tone was horrified. "Miss, look at your hands!"

"I forgot my gloves this morning," Catherine said carelessly, not bothering to look.

"But look at them! They look like you've been scrubbing something." Betsy grasped one of them and turned it over, staring at it. "Mutton fat, that's what you need. My mum uses it when her hands gets like this."

Catherine stared down at them. She seldom thought about her appearance, and never about her hands. But now she examined them, and she had to admit Betsy was right. They were red and chapped and two of her nails had broken off right to the quick.

"Oh, dear. You will have to do something very quickly, Betsy. I have decided to attend a party my father particularly wants me to go to."

Betsy shook her head. "What do you do at that hospital,

miss? That's what I want to know. The scullery maid looks better than this.''

The maid's scolding tone made Catherine smile. "I am sorry, Betsy, but I have been working at St. Luke's."

Betsy shook her head sorrowfully. "And your hair! You did not let me see to it this morning and it does look a sight, miss—begging your pardon for saying so."

"It is quite all right." Catherine bit back a smile. "I did not want to wake you so early, so I did it myself. I am not very talented."

"Well, all I can say is it's lucky you are so beautiful, miss, or I would never be able to fix it by tonight."

At that, Catherine's laugh broke free. "Thank you, Betsy. I think," she added, still chuckling.

She managed to soothe Private Glendower's fears of being beholden by telling him he could come with her to the hospital in the morning as a man of all work until he was able to return to the stables.

Chapter Seven

"Why, Catherine, you look lovely." Her father smiled with pleasure as she entered the small drawing room. "Are you planning on accompanying me this evening?"

Silently, Catherine gave Betsy all the credit for turning her into an elegant lady in less than an hour. The pink satin gown was much simpler than was the fashion. Months ago, before she had left for Scutari, she had ordered it from the dressmaker and had insisted on limiting the decoration to a few satin roses on the shoulders and embroidered roses around the hem. The neckline dipped low, and she wore a delicate necklace of rose gold filigree and tiny diamonds. At Betsy's suggestion, she had rubbed glycerin and rose water into her abused hands and had covered them with lacy mitts. Normally, Catherine scorned such ladylike accessories, but tonight she was grateful they were in fashion.

"Yes, Papa." She went up to him and kissed him on

the cheek. Despite their frequent disagreements and his stubborn insistence on knowing what was best for her, she loved the baronet. He meant well and wanted only what was best for her. He simply did not know what that was. "I have spent too little time with you recently, and since you will not stay quietly at home with me, I have decided I must gad about a bit with you."

"I am delighted to hear it, my dear," replied her father. "And tell me, how is Julian doing?"

Catherine paused for a moment to gather her thoughts. She had not seen her supposed fiancé for several days. While the earl and countess understood her reasons, she did not want to reveal her absence to her father, who would want to know where she had been.

"He is doing as well as can be expected. His leg is giving him pain, but he is going to see the doctor who cared for him at Scutari this week, so perhaps we will have news of a new treatment."

It was not a lie. She had not asked Michael, but she was sure he would want to see his patient. And Julian should be looked at by someone who understood what had happened to him mentally, as well as physically. She would see to it tomorrow.

"Good, good. Glad the fellow is around to see to our Julian. Can't have him languishing at home like some old lady with the vapors, now can we?" The baronet didn't bother to wait for Catherine's reply, but took her arm and led her into the dining room.

A few hours later, as Catherine looked around rooms crowded with people, her heart failed her. How was she to approach anyone in this sea of humanity with a plea for a hospital for the poor?

The answer came to her almost immediately. A tall, somewhat portly gentleman with luxuriant side-whiskers was introduced to her by her hostess, Lady Charles Bellamy.

"Mr. Henry Blankenship, my dear Miss Stanhope, has asked to be presented to you, and your father has consented." Lady Charles beamed approval at this encounter between wealth and beauty. "He is a widower," she added behind her fan.

"Miss Stanhope," the gentleman said. "I hope I am not mistaken in thinking you are the same Miss Stanhope who nursed my son Davy at Scutari."

Catherine took his hand with a smile of genuine welcome as remembrance swept over her. David Blankenship had been one of Michael's spectacular successes. "Yes, I am. And how is Davy, Mr. Blankenship? He was such a good patient. I am sure he made a marvelous recovery."

"He has, indeed, though he is not fully recovered as yet. I am sure he would love to see you, Miss Stanhope. He speaks of you often—you and a Dr. Soames." Henry Blankenship looked a little nervous for a moment. "Would you talk with me, Miss Stanhope? Would you tell me about my Davy's wound? He won't talk about it and I don't want to hound him, but I want—I need—to know what happened to my son over there."

"Of course, Mr. Blankenship. Would you care to come for tea tomorrow? I would invite you for dinner but my father does not like to hear about what I did in Turkey." Catherine looked at the man intently. He radiated power, and she was not surprised he was one of the wealthiest men in England.

"Could you—I mean, if you would sit with me over there, in that alcove, we could talk here. We would be in plain sight. It would be quite proper, if I understand the conventions that govern these things."

Catherine gave him a wry smile. "You are joking, are you not? Lady Charles has already paired us off. If we are seen deep in conversation, the world will have us betrothed before morning. And since I am already supposedly promised to someone, I do not think that would be wise."

"Oh, what nonsense! I am old enough to be your father. This is why I never go out into society—or at least not until recently. I have been trying to meet you, you see."

Catherine closed her eyes for a moment, as if gathering strength. "And have you mentioned to your hosts that you wished to meet me?" she asked, dreading the answer.

"Why, yes, I did ask once or twice if you were to be included among the guests." He looked a little shame-faced. "You think that might have caused gossip?"

How naive could a millionaire tycoon be? Apparently as guileless as a newborn when it came to society's ways. "Yes, Mr. Blankenship, I do. I most assuredly do." But Catherine remembered why she had come to this party to begin with. She straightened her shoulders. Why should she care more now for what polite society thought of her than when she had gone to Scutari with Florence Nightingale? "But why should that matter to us? We know the truth. Come and sit down, and I will tell you how Dr. Soames saved your son's leg."

They seated themselves, and Catherine took a deep breath before she began. She quickly decided to tell Henry Blankenship the whole story as she knew it.

"It was late one night when I was going through one of the wards. I saw Dr. Soames. He was bent over one of the straw pallets on the floor. He called me over and . . .

* * *

"They didn't take his leg at the field hospital" Michael said, his tone brusque. "The note they attached said they had no time." He clenched his fists. "And now look at it."

Catherine looked down at the young man who lay moaning on the pallet. He was young—absurdly young, as were many of the casualties. This one looked no more than seventeen. He must have enlisted just in time to be sent to the Crimea and end up in this charnel house.

His left leg was swollen and looked hot. She laid a gentle hand on his brow. He was feverish. At her light touch on the calf of his leg, the boy winced and moaned a bit.

"Hello. I am Nurse Stanhope," she said, her voice gentle and warm.

"He's unconscious, mercifully," Dr. Soames said. "Now I have to decide whether to take his leg or not."

"Do you have a choice after the weeks he must have spent on board ship getting here?"

He looked at her, and a tight smile twisted his long, mobile mouth. "I think we may have a choice." He nodded toward her. "If you will help me."

"Of course. But why did they not operate there? Was there truly no time?" An amputation did not take long. She remembered vividly the quick, clean job Michael had done the first time she had braved the operating area.

"No, of course not. But the lad is no ordinary soldier. He is, it seems, the son and heir of Mr. Henry Blankenship, the railroad builder and textile magnate. The doctors did not want to risk his wrath."

"And you?" she dared to ask, though she knew the answer. Michael Soames feared no one, least of all someone who might attempt to cow him through the use of money or power.

"I think it is possible to save his leg. The bones have been shattered, and there may be bullet fragments there as well." He gave her a challenging look. "With you to help me, I believe we may be able to remove the bullets and set the bones."

"You wish to operate now?" Catherine was amazed. "At night?" The light in the hospital was not bright at high noon. At night, with only oil lamps for illumination, it was deep with shadows, and the pool of light from a lamp was small and yellow.

"Dr. Hall has decided nothing can be done. He will report that the trip down the Black Sea killed him, thus absolving the staff here from blame." Michael's voice dripped with scorn. Catherine knew he despised cowardice, particularly medical cowardice.

"But you think we can save him?"

"Yes. The shock of an amputation might kill him, but if we can save the leg, I think he might survive. With careful nursing." He stared at her and there was a warmth in his gaze that set Catherine's heart beating. "I naturally thought of you."

"Thank you."

"It is a risk for you as well, Miss Stanhope. Dr. Hall does not admire you." He smiled at her and, for a moment, she felt wrapped in a cocoon of warmth and comradeship.

"I will take the chance, Dr. Soames. I am sure you will do it if anyone can."

He reached out and took her hand. Catherine smiled up at him and clasped his hands in both of hers. For a moment they stood in a pool of light in the darkened ward. Then, with a deep breath, Michael became once again the impersonal surgeon.

"Good. Then let us begin."

Catherine looked around her. "We will need more light, Doctor. If you will swab the wound with alcohol, I will find another lamp." She walked up the ward between the rows of pallets and cots. There was a light high on the wall. Her fingertips grazed the bottom of the iron brazier that held the lamp, but she could not grip the lamp itself.

Behind her she felt a sudden warmth, and then Dr. Soames's hand, with its long, blunt-tipped fingers, reached around her *and grasped the lamp. "Perhaps you should reconsider, Miss Stanhope." His voice stirred the wisps of her hair that had escaped the severe white cap Miss Nightingale had decreed for her nurses. "I do not want to cause you difficulty." He stepped away from her then, and Catherine found she could breathe once again, freed from his overwhelming nearness.*

"I have considered, Doctor." Her voice was steady, she noted proudly. "I will be proud to assist you."

Together they walked back down the ward and began preparations. The boy did not stir as Catherine began to swab the area with alcohol. She used it sparingly. They had so little of it that everyone tried to use it as carefully as possible. She adjusted the two lamps so as to throw the light onto the leg. Dr. Soames made ready to begin, laying out his steel surgical instruments in their fitted leather case.

"Would you mind wiping these with alcohol, Miss Stanhope? For some reason I work better with clean instruments."

"Of course." Catherine had noticed that Dr. Soames, unlike most of the other physicians, always wore an apron which he removed after an operation and that he washed his hands when they became covered in blood. Both Miss Nightingale and the French nuns Catherine had studied with stressed cleanliness and tidiness. Catherine approved.

Michael bowed his head for a moment and then picked up a scalpel. "Try to keep the blood sponged away, Miss Stanhope. I will need to see as well as I can to do this."

Catherine nodded and they began.

It seemed to take hours. Michael was painstaking and slow, yet at the same time Catherine was so absorbed the time passed in a flash. At last Michael looked up and said, "There. I think I have removed all the bullet and bone fragments and set the fractures. Now it is up to the young man's constitution—and to you, Miss Stanhope."

Suddenly, Catherine was aware that her back ached from being bent over the pallet for hours. She swallowed a yawn and said, "Of course, Doctor."

He looked down at the patient. "His color looks good. I think we may have done the thing, Miss Stanhope. I truly do." And one of his rare smiles had swept over Michael's face. "My thanks."

His smile warmed her. "I was proud to do it."

As they both came back to earth from the period of intense concentration they had just been through, Catherine became aware of her surroundings again. It was almost dawn, and soon the hospital would be stirring, the morning routine beginning. It was time she returned to the tiny room she shared with Lucinda and Rose and three other nurses.

As if he understood exactly what she felt, Michael stepped back and frowned, the physician again. "You can take pride in your work tonight, Miss Stanhope."

"I do, Doctor." She had never been prouder to be a nurse.

"Any reason why you two are standing in this corridor staring down the hall looking as if you have just performed an operation, Doctor?"

The sarcastic voice of Dr. Hall roused Catherine like a cold splash of water.

"I have just finished operating on Private Blankenship."

That remark redirected the Chief's thoughts. "You did what?" The little red-faced doctor was all but hopping, he was so angry. "Don't you know who that boy is? Now when he dies it will be our fault, and Henry Blankenship will have your medical license. You fool, Soames!"

"I do not believe he is going to die. I managed to remove the bullet and the infection and reset the shattered bones. I believe the boy has a good chance of surviving."

Dr. Hall looked torn between his desire to have the rich man's son survive and his equally strong urge to see Michael Soames fail. "I hope for your sake you're right, Soames. Because if he does die, I'll make sure the blame for it falls where it should." His

*furious gaze took in Catherine, as well. "I shall report you to
Miss Nightingale. If I am not mistaken, it is not the first time
you have disobeyed my orders."*

*"On what would you have blamed the young man's death,
Hall? The good marksmanship of the Russians or the stupidity
of the British?" Michael gave his superior a tight-lipped smile and
did not wait for a reply.*

"And that is how your son's leg was saved."

Lost in the past, Catherine was silent for a minute. When
she looked up, tears were running down Henry Blankenship's cheeks.

"I can never thank you enough," he said, grasping both
her hands in his. "Where is Dr. Soames, do you know?
The man should have the Victoria Cross at least. And a
reward. And you—Miss Stanhope, I had no idea the conditions you worked under. The hardships."

He paused for a moment and reached for his handkerchief. His expression hardened, and Catherine could see the
ruthless businessman, not the loving parent. "And as for Dr.
Hall, I shall certainly let it be known in the highest circles
that the man is an idiot. He had the temerity to write that
Davy was alive thanks to him. We will see about that!"

Catherine could not let the opportunity pass. Imagine
the help Henry Blankenship could bring to St. Luke's!

"If you really mean what you say about rewarding Dr.
Soames, I think I know what you could do," she said.

"Of course I meant it. Tell me what you have in mind."
Henry Blankenship looked eager to begin whatever she
might suggest.

Catherine considered for a moment. "I think it would
be better if I showed you. Why don't I take you and Davy
to see Dr. Soames where he works?"

"Very well, Miss Stanhope. I am in your debt and in your hands. I know Davy will be delighted to see you both again. He thinks the world of you two."

"You have a very brave son, Mr. Blankenship. He wanted so much to prove to you how brave he is. I hope he has succeeded." She remembered Davy's refusal to be treated as special and his tight-lipped stoicism in the face of the pain of recovery.

"He has, Miss Stanhope, he has. Many's the night I stayed awake until dawn worrying about Davy and regretting my hasty words. There's many kinds of courage in this world, and watching Davy trying to get better, the pain he has to endure, has made me aware he has more than enough for ten men!"

Catherine looked carefully into his eyes. She believed he did value his son, and he would find more courage to admire at St. Luke's. "I will come for you and Davy tomorrow afternoon at two o'clock, if that is convenient."

"I would be pleased to send my carriage round for you, Miss Stanhope, and to give you and Dr. Soames tea."

Henry Blankenship was organizing Catherine's party for her. That would never do. "No, sir. I shall gather you and David up and then take you to where Dr. Soames and I work."

"Work, Miss Stanhope? I understood from your friends that you are shortly to be married."

Was there disapproval in his tone? Would he reveal her secret before she had found a way to tell her father herself? Catherine could only hope that was not the case.

"I will explain everything tomorrow." At his nod, Catherine rose and left him, already planning how to obtain the largest donation possible for her hospital.

She attempted to find her father in the crush of people, but could not locate him. She looked about the enormous room crowded with people—women in gowns of every color in the rainbow with voluminous skirts and tiny bodices and men in the dark evening clothes that had become the norm over the past few years. For the first time since her return, Catherine felt no discomfort, only a great desire to go home to bed. Morning came early when one had a job to go to. Catherine found herself smiling in anticipation.

"Miss Stanhope, I never thought to see you here." The voice was slightly familiar.

Catherine looked up to see a tall, distinguished-looking man in impeccable evening dress. His breathtakingly handsome face was crowned with a wealth of hair so black it gleamed with blue lights, like a raven's wing. Despite his formal attire and polite manners, there was something about him that forcibly reminded Catherine of a pirate. She identified him without difficulty. It was a face no one would easily forget.

"You are Jeffrey Bancroft, are you not?" she said without waiting for him to present himself. "Lucinda's friend."

He grimaced. "Not at the moment, I am afraid—I mean to say, I am still Bancroft, but she was not speaking to me when last I saw her."

Catherine remembered. "I seem to recall her calling you an imbecile. That was directly before I left. The day before, in fact. I remember it well." She smiled reminiscently and, for the second time that evening, returned in memory to Scutari Barracks Hospital.

She had encountered Lucinda when she returned to their little room to snatch an hour's rest. Lucinda was already there, brushing her long ebony hair with vigor.

"What has roused your temper, Lucy?" Catherine asked, smiling. When annoyed with something, which happened frequently,

Lucinda was apt to attack some inanimate object and reduce it to shining cleanliness. If no such object presented itself, she brushed her hair. Catherine had often teased her that her temper had one good result—her hair gleamed from all the brushing it got.

"Just one of the TGs Miss N has put in my care."

TG, or "traveling gentleman," was the term the Army staff used to refer to civilians, usually wealthy and influential, who came to see the war and needed to be shown around by busy military men with better things to do. When they came to the hospital at Scutari, Miss Nightingale liked to send Lucinda along, for she knew the intricacies of the supply system better than the men of the Army Commissary Corps and could indicate where money was badly needed. More often than not, her smile opened pocketbooks wider than might otherwise have been the case.

"A more annoying gentleman than usual?" Catherine queried sympathetically. She often thought it was a shame Lucinda did not get to spend more time nursing, but her friend did not seem to mind.

"Very much more so. His name is Jeffrey Bancroft and he is arrogant, pigheaded, conceited, and an absolute ass!"

"Lucinda!" Catherine could never get over her shock at her friend's vocabulary. Lucinda said words other women would not admit having so much as heard.

"Well, he is." Lucinda turned to glare, but at the look of prim shock on Catherine's face, she burst out laughing. "Oh, close your mouth, Cat, do. You look like a trout!"

"Lucinda!" Catherine said again, but this time she, too, was laughing.

"You are smiling," Jeffrey Bancroft said. "You must be thinking of Lucinda."

"Yes, she makes everyone smile; she is so outrageous." Catherine looked at Jeffrey Bancroft. Lucinda had been very angry with him. It was food for thought. "She is my dearest friend. Do you know when she is returning home?"

"I offered her the use of my yacht to bring her home in comfort. She should come back. She is wearing herself ragged, doing all the administrative work and trying to nurse and show the TGs around." He sounded genuinely worried. Catherine hid a smile. This relationship would bear watching when Lucinda returned.

Meantime, she had a use for Mr. Bancroft. "Sir, I wonder if I might speak to you on a matter of some importance." Catherine had no idea how to go about soliciting funds for a charitable institution. She would just go straight ahead and ask.

"Why, of course, Miss Stanhope. I would be happy to call upon you at your convenience." If he was surprised at her abrupt request he didn't show it, except that one ebony eyebrow quirked briefly. "Would tomorrow afternoon at four be acceptable?"

Catherine frowned. She did not leave the hospital until four, and tomorrow it would no doubt be later because the Blankenships were coming. She reached a sudden decision. "Would you be kind enough to meet me at St. Luke's Hospital at four instead of Stanhope House?"

Again, Mr. Bancroft showed no surprise save that telltale eyebrow. "Of course, Miss Stanhope." He bowed slightly. "I am sure you have an excellent reason for preferring to take tea at a charity hospital not far from some of the worst rookeries in London."

Catherine could feel her face redden. "Actually, sir, I do. I work there." For the second time that evening she had revealed to a stranger what she could not tell her own father. Perhaps it was precisely because they were strangers that she could tell them. They had no stake, nor even any particular interest, in what she did with her life. They might have fixed ideas on the place of women—Lucinda had said Mr. Bancroft's were quite firm and old-fashioned—but they did not care about her in particular.

At her announcement, the eyebrow all but disappeared into Mr. Bancroft's hair. "I see. You are still the dedicated nurse Lucinda described. I salute you, Miss Stanhope. There are not many who would continue that work after having experienced Scutari."

Catherine flushed. He did not seem to be the stern upholder of the status quo that Lucinda had described. "Thank you, sir. I believe you have an interest in philanthropy. There might be a great deal to interest you in St. Luke's."

His expression grew wary. "I must warn you, Miss Stanhope, in case your friend Lucinda failed to do so. I have almost no patience with layabouts. The poor who are willing to work I will help, but not those who have their hands out while they sit on the doorstep doing nothing."

"Very few people in St. Luke's fit that description. I will expect you at four tomorrow, shall I?"

He smiled at her formal tone, but Catherine did not know how else to address someone she was going to ask for money. "Yes. I shall not look for a large tea, I suppose."

"We do not rival the spread I understand is put on at some of the elegant hotels you no doubt frequent," Catherine said, a little annoyed. "But I shall see to it you are not sent away starving." She made a mental note to tell cook to prepare a picnic tea and have it ready in the morning.

He grinned at her. "I am sorry I have annoyed you, Miss Stanhope. Lucinda says it is a bad habit of mine. I was trying to be on my best behavior, but, as usual, my opinions betrayed me."

She could not help but smile back. He was an engaging

rascal. "Quite all right. I am willing to put up with any number of opinions to achieve my ends."

He bowed and they parted. Catherine was happy to see her father approach her. Having accomplished her mission, she was ready to go home.

She could not wait for tomorrow. What a triumph she would be able to recount to Mary Ann and Dinsmore.

And Michael.

Chapter Eight

"What the bloody hell do you think you are doing?" Michael's face was scowling and his voice would carry all the way down the hall. "I am not coming to tea and perform like some trained dog so you can screw some guineas out of your rich friends!"

"Nobody is asking you to do anything but graciously accept Henry Blankenship's thanks for saving his son's life and acknowledge Jeffrey Bancroft's greetings. I am sure you two met in Turkey."

"I still say it is an absurd idea. No one is going to give money to this benighted institution, certainly not just because I am here. You must have lost your mind at that ball last night, whirling around the floor with all those millionaires."

While I was sitting alone in the dark picturing you and being eaten alive by jealousy.

Catherine flushed, and Michael's jealousy grew like a

weed. As he recalled, Jeffrey Bancroft was handsome in addition to being almost obscenely rich. He had thought when he met him that the man seemed to have his hands more than full with Lucinda Harrowby, but Catherine was so beautiful that Michael could easily understand why Bancroft would transfer his affections.

As Michael continued to glower, Dr. Dinsmore came into the large reception area where Catherine and Michael were talking. Catherine took the opportunity to tell him of her evening's work and, unlike Michael, he was delighted and wrung Catherine's hand in congratulations. The little man was almost speechless with gratitude. And that earned him the smiles that Michael could have had for himself—if, as he told himself, he were willing to grovel before a lot of wealthy bounders.

"I do not think I will be able to be there. I have rounds to make this afternoon."

Dr. Dinsmore looked alarmed. "Oh, I am sure you can find the time to attend, Doctor. In fact, I insist on it." The little man's face was red, and he seemed a little frightened at his own temerity in actually giving an order.

I have scared him, Michael thought. How absurd. He didn't intend to frighten anyone. Just to go his own way, that was all he wanted.

"Michael," Catherine said, and he could not tell if she was angry or not, "you have to come. You are the reason the Blankenships are coming. Davy will be hurt and disappointed if you do not."

"Davy! Davy is well enough to come?" That changed everything. If a patient was coming, then Dr. Soames would certainly be there.

"Yes. Mr. Blankenship said Davy has been working very hard and can get about on his own. He still limps, but he is walking every day. Mr. Blankenship said Davy is very eager to see you." Catherine's smile was wholehearted.

He didn't deserve it. She was being kind and openhearted while he, eaten up with jealousy and anger, was mean enough to sour milk. He vowed to do better.

By and large, he did, by refusing to think of either Jeffrey Bancroft or Henry Blankenship and concentrating on his patients. That system worked very well until the time came to go to the main hall. There he found Dinsmore, Bancroft, and an older man who had to be Blankenship circling Catherine like planets around the sun. She wore a plain black dress with white collar and cuffs and looked serene and beautiful enough to stop a man's heart. Though she wore a white cap on her blond head, it was lacy and becoming. She was smiling at everyone.

Michael glanced around and saw a younger figure on the edge of the group, leaning heavily on a cane.

"Davy!" he called, striding over to greet the young man. "It is wonderful to see you up and about. Tell me how you are progressing!" This he could deal with—less a social occasion than a medical appointment. And he had grown attached to the brave young son of a millionaire father in the hospital at Scutari.

David had brought him even closer than before to Catherine Stanhope. He remembered one night when they had both visited Davy at the same time. The light of Catherine's lamp had isolated them, making it seem as if they were alone in that huge, dreary place.

He remembered it as if it were yesterday.

For twenty-four hours after the risky operation that saved Davy Blankenship's leg, wounded from the battle at Inkerman poured into the hospital. Michael had scarcely a moment, yet he worried

*about Private Blankenship. He didn't give a damn who the boy's
father was, but he did want to see how he was doing.*

He stole a few minutes the next night and made his way into
the ward where the boy lay. He told himself Catherine had certainly
tended to the lad and would have sought him out if there had
been an emergency. Nevertheless, he hurried into the ward with a
nagging sense of worry.

A pool of light shone round Private Blankenship's pallet, illumi-
nating the wisps of pale gold hair around Catherine's face. She
was bending over the private. Michael hurried forward. He should
have come sooner, should have—

"You are sure, Davy? Dr. Hall has come twice while you were
sleeping to insist you be moved to a private room." Catherine's
soft voice was pitched low so as not to disturb the other patients.

"I enlisted as a private and I am determined to be treated as
one." The boy's voice sounded surprisingly strong for one who
had almost lost his leg—and his life.

"Very well, but I am sure your father would want—"

It was clearly the wrong thing to say. Michael could hear the
anger and impatience in David's voice as he said, "I do not care
what my father wants. He told me I could never stand up to the
hardships of the British Army, that all his money had made me
soft, not like him."

"Well," Catherine said, her voice matter-of-fact as she stroked
his brow, "he was obviously wrong, David. You've proven that."

The boy smiled up at her, adoration in his eyes. "Do you think
so, Nurse Stanhope? Truly?"

Catherine looked up then and smiled at Michael. It was a smile
that included him in the circle. "If you do not believe me, just
ask Dr. Soames. He will tell you I am right."

"Indeed, yes." Michael's trained eye took in the boy's color and
his clear eyes. "You have survived a battle and, worse than that,
an operation in this hospital. Only the stouthearted and tough

can do that. One would almost believe you were Scots." One of his rare smiles swept across Michael's face.

"My mother was from Glasgow." David Blankenship beamed up at him.

"Was she now?" Michael expertly felt along the bandages on David's leg. *"To be sure, my mother has always thought Glasgow could not compare to Edinburgh, where she was born. But she will admit you Glaswegians are tough as old boots."* He put a gentle hand on the boy's head and smiled back, full of confidence and courage.

This was a side of Michael Soames few people saw. He reserved this kind of warmth for his patients. Otherwise, he chose to walk alone, questioning authority, cherishing his independence.

David interrupted his thoughts. He was gazing intently at the doctor. *"And I will walk? Nurse Stanhope assured me I would."* His full lower lip trembled a little as he said, *"That's all I could think about on the boat down here. Whether I would walk or not."*

"If you keep on making the kind of recovery you are doing now, I have no doubt you will walk and ride again. Why, you may even have to go to dances, though if you are anything like me you would rather be hanged." Michael carefully uncovered the bandaged leg. There was no blood or oozing.

"Maybe I'll tell my sisters I have been forbidden to dance. You won't tell them, will you?" David said.

"My lips are sealed." Michael's eyes twinkled down at the boy. Then he turned to Catherine.

"You have changed the dressing?" he asked her, trying to sound businesslike and formal.

"Yes, Doctor. There has been no bleeding. The leg no longer appears warm or swollen." Catherine was every inch the deferential nurse.

"It looks remarkably good this early after such an extensive operation. You have the constitution of the proverbial ox, young

David." Michael was exhilarated. He had succeeded. He and Catherine had succeeded, he reminded himself.

"That is hardly the tone to take with Henry Blankenship's son, Soames." Dr. Hall had made his way to the private's bedside before anyone was aware of his presence. "Now, young man"—*he gave David a wide smile*—*"we are ready to move you to a room more befitting your status."*

"I have already explained and explained to Nurse Stanhope that I do not wish to be moved." David's tone was a mixture of the haughty tone he would take with a social inferior and the impatient whine of a tired child.

"But your father—*"*

It was again the wrong note to strike. "My father is not here. I am here, and I can make up my own mind. I am not moving." David looked up at Dr. Hall. It was clear from his next words that he had taken that man's measure. "Dr. Soames says I need not. If you force me to move, I will tell my father. He will not be pleased."

"Very well, if that is what you wish." Dr. Hall capitulated at once and turned to easier prey. "Nurse Stanhope, Miss Nightingale would like to see you at once in her office. And I need a few words with you, Soames." He turned and walked off, not bothering to see if his subordinates were following.

"If there are any repercussions because you assisted me in an unauthorized procedure, tell Miss Nightingale I requested your presence and could not have performed the surgery without you."

A becoming shade of wild rose pink suffused Catherine's cheeks. "I am sure she will understand, but thank you for your offer, Doctor."

And now the three of them were together again, at another hospital, but this time David looked healthy and vigorous, except for the leg that was still regaining its strength.

"Father," Davy called, his voice excited, a smile wreathing his face, "come and meet Dr. Soames!" He said it in a tone that would have been appropriate for introducing a saint.

Mr. Blankenship turned away from the group, interrupting Dr. Dinsmore in mid sentence. He, too, was smiling as if greeting a very important personage, when everyone knew that except for the queen and perhaps Lord Palmerston there was nobody more important in all of England than Henry Blankenship. Even Michael, who made it a point to know nothing about society, had heard of him before Dr. Hall had made such a commotion about his importance.

"I am a plainspoken man," the elder Blankenship said. "I don't mince words." He frowned for a moment and looked down at his shoes, his Adam's apple working. When he looked up again, there was a sheen of tears in his eyes. He took Michael's hands in a grip like a vise and swallowed hard. "Davy's mother died when he was but ten years old. I have tried to be both mother and father to him. Davy is my only son, Doctor, and you saved him after I was fool enough to goad him into joining up." He shook his head in remorse. It was not an emotion Henry Blankenship was well acquainted with, Michael thought, noting the man's erect bearing and level, steely gaze.

Without releasing Michael's hands, Blankenship once again looked down at his feet. This time his shoulders heaved and he took a deep, shuddering breath to compose himself.

At that point, Davy intervened. "I say, Father, enough. We are both very grateful to you, Doctor. Did I tell you, Father, that Dr. Soames's mother is Scots? You did tell me that, didn't you, Doctor? I was never sure if you really came to see me at night. The morphine made me so dreamy.''

Catherine came up and stood by Davy in time to hear the last remark. Davy turned to her with a smile. ''Nurse Stanhope came. Every night. I remember that. And Miss Nightingale would pass through carrying her lamp. The men in my ward used to kiss her shadow on the wall as she passed.''

Davy was lost in reverie. He didn't see the effect his words were having on his father, but Michael did. Henry Blankenship was turning whiter by the moment. It was clear that the idea that his beloved only son had spent time in any hospital without his father in attendance was bad enough. But an Army hospital in some outlandish place, and in a common ward, was unthinkable. Michael also thought the fact that Blankenship's hasty words had driven his son to enlist weighed on the older man's mind as well.

''Davy remembers your visits, sir.'' Henry Blankenship was still regarding Michael as if he were the archangel of the same name. ''It was most kind of you, most kind.''

Michael could stand no more. ''Please,'' he said, feeling his face turn red. ''It was a pleasure to meet you, sir, and to see you doing so well, Davy. You must come and see me in my office, where we can really talk. I want to know what you have been doing with that leg. Whatever it is, it has done you a powerful lot of good.'' Michael nodded approvingly as Davy beamed with pride. ''Remember, now, what I told you about being your own best doctor.'' He began to move toward the door, but Dr. Dinsmore interrupted him.

''I have promised Mr. Blankenship that you would show him St. Luke's before you left for surgery.'' Dinsmore's eyes pleaded with him, but Michael could not bear to spend any more time being regarded as some kind of plaster saint. He knew doctors who loved to bask in the adulation of their patients, but he was not one of them.

"Let Miss Stanhope do the honors," he said, still moving toward the door. "She will be far better at it." The door loomed ahead, its very bulk welcoming. He would be safe on the other side.

A soft, implacable touch stopped him just short of escape.

Catherine.

She waylaid him, and when he looked at her, she kidnapped his heart as she had from the first. He would never shake off that touch, never walk away from the woman who held his emotions in thrall.

"I think Mr. Blankenship would like it if we both went with him." She smiled, but underneath he could sense hurt and anger. He always seemed to hurt her when all he wanted was to keep her safe, to protect her—most of all from himself.

Always to yearn for what he could not have was torture. But always to yearn for what he could have but should not for the good of the person who would give it—that was infinitely worse, demanded infinitely more control. So he walked a tightrope, trying not to hurt the woman he loved either by repulsing her as he should do, or embracing her as he longed to do.

This time he was able to be strong. "I am sorry. I must go. Davy, come and see me in my surgery tomorrow. I will examine your leg and we will talk."

If David was disappointed, he did not show it. Blankenship senior looked not disappointed, but angry. The millionaire industrialist was not used to being rebuffed, Michael thought with an inward smile. He avoided looking at Dinsmore, but something made him take one last look at Catherine. The hurt he saw in her eyes vanished the moment his gaze met hers, to be replaced by a blazing anger. She turned away, and as he left he heard her say, "What would you like to see, Mr. Blankenship?"

"Where does Dr. High and Mighty operate to perform the kind of miracle he did on my Davy?" The door closed and Michael heard no more.

Catherine led the Blankenships down the dingy hallway that led to the pathetically underequipped surgery.

"He can operate here? In this—" Henry Blankenship broke off and looked around in horrified amazement. The walls were a dirty gray, the windows let in scarcely any light, and the oak cabinets of surgical instruments were almost bare. "Surgery such as he performed on Davy? In this place?"

For some reason, Catherine felt a proprietary pride in St. Luke's, though she had been there only a short time. "This place is a great improvement over Scutari, sir. There the surgeons operated on straw pallets on the ground or on the men's cots—if they had cots. There were no operating rooms. They operated in the wards. Miss Nightingale requested screens be placed to give the lads some privacy, but it was primitive." She spoke with pride. "Surgeons like Dr. Soames can save lives wherever they are."

"And Davy, my Davy—"

"Yes, sir, as I explained last night, conditions were primitive." She decided it was time to ask for money. "And compared to wealthier areas, St. Luke's is Spartan, I know. But wonders can be done here, as well. Of course, it is luxurious compared to Scutari, but if we had—"

She broke off as she saw Henry Blankenship, his face a sickly green, cling to his son. David managed to get an arm around his father's portly figure and gazed at Catherine, as if asking her what to do.

Contrite, she quickly looked around. Finding no chair in the room, she motioned Davy to seat his father on the floor. Then she shoved his head between his knees. "There, sir. I am sorry. I thought you had seen Scutari and knew of conditions there."

"No, no," Blankenship said, his voice faint. "Davy had been moved to the British ambassador's residence in Constantinople by the time I arrived. It never occurred to me—" He broke off and scrambled to his feet. Clearly embarrassed, he said gruffly, "I have never done that in my life, not even when my mum died in front of me, hit by a runaway dray. But as I told you, Davy's my only son, and I almost lost him."

"I understand. There is no need to speak more of it." Catherine understood that to a man of action like Henry Blankenship, pain to a beloved child that his power and money could do nothing to alleviate was far worse than pain to himself.

"No, no, I need to know about the conditions David was in. I was hoping Dr. Soames—" He broke off with a shrewd smile. "But he cannot bear to be praised, and I am afraid I overdid it." He paused, giving Catherine an appraising look. "You were there. You operated on David." Mr. Blankenship stared at her. "I cannot believe it. A lady like yourself. You look too young and refined. And slender enough that a good wind would blow you away."

She smiled. "I am stronger than I look, Mr. Blankenship. Do not let my appearance deceive you."

"I'll be plain, Nurse Stanhope," he said. "No price can be put on what you and Dr. Soames did for me. But whatever I can do for the two of you, you have only to name it. I know you have no need of money, and I can hardly add to the position of Sir Everett Stanhope's daughter. But I do not think the same can be said for Dr. Soames."

The shrewd businessman was very much in evidence as Mr. Blankenship spoke. He had taken their measure very accurately.

Catherine recognized a father's love speaking and was not offended. But she thought he might have misunderstood Michael, being too fixed on the doctor's financial and social status.

"I am not sure Dr. Soames would want to use his skills to enrich himself," she said after a little hesitation. "He knows how much St. Luke's, for instance, needs money, and he certainly thinks it is a worthy cause. But I do not think he would ever say so."

"But he should not be here in this back slum! The best doctors have lavish offices in Harley Street," Mr. Blankenship exclaimed. "I will build him his own hospital there, with every modern device at his disposal. I will ask you, Miss Stanhope, to become head of nursing. And with your record of service and my backing, Dr. Soames will have patients by the score before the cat can lick his ear. There is no reason why either of you should labor in this dreadful place when a clean, modern hospital can be there for you in only a few months—less, if I can find an existing building in the right location. Tell me, where do you think he would like his surgical hospital to be located?"

Catherine sighed. Was there something about the female voice that simply did not reach the male ear, or did their minds refuse to entertain an idea a woman had thought of? Whatever the reason, Henry Blankenship was reacting very much the way her father did—ignoring what did not fit with his ideas.

She tried again. "I am not sure Dr. Soames wants a Harley Street practice. He seems more interested—"

Mr. Blankenship smiled at her indulgently, as if, Catherine thought, he was about to pat her on the head. "He was top of his class at the Edinburgh Medical College. Father a doctor, too. No family money or connections that I could find. I can supply those. Any young man would be a fool to pass that up. You would rather work at a fine, clean place in a fine neighborhood, now wouldn't you? Not that you'll be working long, I'm sure."

Catherine felt like stamping her foot and screaming, but that had never been her way, and she wasn't about to start making scenes now. "No, Mr. Blankenship, I have every intention—"

"I knew it. Every intention of leaving this place when you marry."

"No, Mr. Blankenship. I meant I will be staying at St. Luke's."

"I told you, Dad." David Blankenship had been following the conversation with great interest. He had not said anything, and Catherine had begun to think he was under his father's thumb. But Davy was as brave about contradicting his father as he had been about undergoing surgery. "Nurse Stanhope and Dr. Soames aren't interested in being fashionable. They want to help people. You should give your money here, Dad. This is where they're going to work."

"Exactly, Davy. I'm so glad you understand." Catherine was more grateful than she could say. David had said what she had tried to say, and his father seemed to have listened.

"All right, Davy, all right. I had to try. I'll never understand them, but I guess you do." Mr. Blankenship sounded so baffled and disappointed that Catherine was tempted for a moment to comfort him. Making St. Luke's better did not have the appeal for a tycoon like Blankenship that creating a brand new hospital had.

"We would all be extremely grateful," Catherine said.

"Well, I want to hear it from the horse's mouth," Mr. Blankenship said, stubborn to the end.

"Why don't we go back and join the others?" Catherine suggested, and led the two gentlemen back to the main hall where the tea she had arranged for was being laid out by several of the nurses under the direction of Mary Ann Evans.

Jeffrey Bancroft was listening to Dr. Dinsmore and looking supremely bored. His eyes grew brighter when he saw Catherine enter the room with the Blankenships. If ever a man signaled *rescue me* with his eyes, it was Mr. Bancroft, Catherine decided. She introduced the Blankenships to Mary Ann, who plied them with tea and cakes. Then she made her way over to Mr. Bancroft, a complicit smile on her face.

"I fear I have been boring Mr. Bancroft with my tales of the needs of St. Luke's and its patients," Dr. Dinsmore said apologetically as she came up to them.

"And its staff," Jeffrey Bancroft said. Dr. Dinsmore's face fell and his ears turned a bright red, a sign, Catherine had already learned, that he was embarrassed.

"One thing he never mentioned, however," Jeffrey continued, "was what the administrator needed. No mention of a new desk or a bigger office or a rug on the floor to remind visitors of how important the administrator is."

Dr. Dinsmore looked confused.

"I find that very interesting, and I am tempted to write out a check to this most unusual hospital and its most unusual administrator right now."

Dr. Dinsmore looked stunned.

Catherine took pity on him. "We are indeed fortunate in our administrator, Mr. Bancroft. He is so modest that I fear he is even yet confused as to your meaning. Come,

Doctor, let me get you some tea while Mr. Bancroft retires to your office to write that check."

She smiled at Jeffrey with understanding and gratitude. Jeffrey's answering grin was boyish. "I had to have my little bit of fun, Miss Stanhope. Dr. Dinsmore, you are a most unusual man. I must introduce you to your polar opposite, one Dr. Hall, when he returns home full of pomposity and self-love."

Catherine had to laugh. Dr. Dinsmore at last understood that he was not being mocked, just gently teased. More important, in his view, he had not jeopardized St. Luke's chance to get much-needed help. He smiled happily. Jeffrey raised his teacup in a mock salute to them both.

It was on this scene of shared amusement that Michael entered, his brow like a thundercloud. He felt like a child who had cut off his nose to spite his face by refusing to go to a party and when he arrived, late and sullen, no one had missed him at all. He scowled and strode over to the happy group.

"Have they managed to dig any money out of you yet, Bancroft?" he said without preamble. "That is the reason for all these smiles and cakes."

"No!" Jeffrey replied in feigned surprise. "It was not my charm but my pocketbook? I am stunned and saddened," he said, turning to Dr. Dinsmore with a mock frown.

Not even the socially awkward Dinsmore could mistake the glint in Jeffrey's eye. "Indeed, it is not so, sir. We have heard of your wit and—and humor."

Catherine stared at Michael, as if torn between laughter and anger. "Dr. Soames," she began and laid a hand gently on his arm. It burnt like a brand and set the seal on Michael's anger.

"Do not attempt to humor me like a difficult child," he muttered.

"Then do stop acting like one," she replied, clearly goaded.

Jeffrey smiled benignly on both of them. "Children, children," he said. "I see you must be separated for your own good. Come, Soames, let us seek some refreshment that is more suited to gentlemen than this pallid stuff." He set down his teacup and, taking Michael's arm in a firm grip, led him out of the room.

Chapter Nine

"Just what do you think you are doing?" Michael was furious with himself for behaving like a damned fool and with Jeffrey Bancroft for rescuing him. "Let me go! I have to operate with that arm, damn it!"

"Sorry." Bancroft didn't sound at all sorry. "I was trying to keep you from making more of an ass of yourself than you already had. Though why I should care is a mystery."

He had directed Michael's steps toward the administrator's office. Once inside, he closed the door and pulled a silver flask from the pocket of his dark frock coat. "Must be because Lucinda thinks you're such a damned fine doctor." He unfastened and filled the silver top, which formed a cup. "Here, old man. A little of the nectar from the sod of Scotland to cool your blood. Or do you still have patients to see this afternoon?"

"No. I saw them while you all had tea and conversation. Patients I can deal with. Tea and conversation I cannot."

He reached for the small silver jigger Bancroft held out to him. A tot of whiskey might soften his rough mood.

"Good. Well, this should help. Cheers." Bancroft filled a second jigger and downed its contents in one smooth swallow. "Now tell me what you think you are doing by giving Miss Stanhope the rough side of your tongue like that. She is doing all this for you, you know."

Stubbornly, Michael shook his head. "She loves nursing. She is raising money for the patients." He held out his jigger for another shot.

Bancroft looked at him as if he were some sort of exotic specimen. "You really are a hardheaded Scot, are you not?"

The look of humor and commiseration Bancroft gave him, along with those plain words, disarmed Michael. "I fear so," he said gloomily. "Never have been able to hide what I feel. She is wonderful—kind and beautiful and brave—and yet it seems I always feel angry when I am with her." Perhaps Bancroft would be able to help him. "Why is that, do you suppose?"

"Women have that effect on a man." Bancroft filled his silver cup again. "Make us feel unworthy, clumsy. Angry at ourselves."

Michael considered as he contemplated his third tot. "You're right," he said at last. "Exactly right. Good for you. Angry because she is too good for me."

"All too good for us." Bancroft lifted his silver jigger. A little of the golden brown liquid spilled onto his pristine white cuff. "Worse"—he lowered his voice—"they know it." Bancroft poured Michael another drink.

Michael nodded sagely and drank. "Know what's worse still?" Bancroft shook his head and tossed back another jigger. "They forgive us." Michael shook his head. "Oops. Head going to fall off."

"Hold on to it," Bancroft advised. "Not all of 'em."

Michael looked puzzled.

"Forgive us. Not all of them forgive us. Some of 'em hold a grudge." Bancroft brooded for a minute. Then he shrugged and swallowed another jigger. "Hell with them."

"Hell with them," Michael echoed, obscurely pleased with the thought. "Hell with everybody." He took another drink.

The door opened and he peered at it owlishly. It seemed to be farther away than it had been only minutes ago. A beautiful, angelic figure with azure eyes and hair of palest gold appeared in the doorway. He knew who she was. "Angel," he said and nodded. Then he looked closer. "No. Angels do not wear black. And no wings." He looked over at Bancroft to see if he knew the nature of the apparition. But Bancroft had gone.

"You have been drinking," the apparition said. "No wonder Mr. Bancroft slunk out of here the minute the door opened." She shook her head. "How could you, Michael? We have guests."

"Catherine." Michael thought hard. "Was right. An angel." He felt satisfied to have solved the mystery. But the angel was angry. Catherine did sometimes get angry. "She will forgive me," he said to Bancroft, forgetting his friend had left.

"Not this time," Catherine said, and her eyes flashed fire.

"Like lightning." It was amazing how clearly he saw these things. "Your eyes are like blue flame when you are angry."

"Don't think to turn me up sweet by saying things like that." Catherine tried to look stern.

"You have a dimple!" Michael said triumphantly. "Trying not to smile, but it's there." He gently touched the corner of her mouth with his forefinger. "Beautiful." He allowed his fingers to drift over her face, memorizing its contours. "So beautiful."

"Michael." It was a whispered plea. "What are you saying?"

"Everything I cannot say."

"You smell like a distillery. It is most likely the whiskey talking."

He smiled. She was so lovely when she tried to be stern. "No," he said and traced her lips with his forefinger. "Whiskey makes me able to tell you. In whiskey veritas."

"Miss Stanhope, are you in here? I think the Blankenships are ready to leave and—" Dr. Dinsmore's voice stopped as if a hand had been clapped across his mouth.

Quickly, Catherine stepped away from Michael. "What have you made me do? Come along now." And she took his hand.

Did she feel what he did, that strange connection, as warm and real as if it were tangible that occurred whenever they touched? Michael sighed. "Very well. I'll be good, my angel. I promise."

"Well, start by not calling me that. Watch your tongue, please, Michael. Mr. Bancroft has promised Dr. Dinsmore a check, but Mr. Blankenship still thinks you want a Harley Street hospital."

Michael made a rude noise. "I don't want Harley Street. Unless"—he stopped abruptly—"do you want Harley Street, Catherine? It would be a nicer place for you. Your father would be happier." He peered at her intently. If Catherine wanted a fancy society hospital, Michael would get it for her.

"No, no, of course I don't." There were tears in her voice, and that Michael could not stand.

"I have made you cry. Oh, God, Catherine, I am sorry."

He raked a hand through his hair. Could he never do the right thing where she was concerned? "Don't want you unhappy. Ever."

"I am not unhappy. I promise you." She laid a finger on his lips. "Here we are. Now, try to say as little as possible. Perhaps we will be in luck and no one will notice if you do not talk."

"No talking." He put his forefinger and thumb up to his mouth and turned them. "Locked lips." His teacher at the village school had taught him that trick.

Catherine's laugh rang like chimes for a moment. Then she reached up and smoothed his hair and Michael felt as if the bottom had dropped out of his stomach. "You will do. Come on."

She led him back into the large reception area. Mary Ann Evans and David Blankenship were deep in conversation, but Mr. Blankenship was looking impatiently around him. When he saw Michael, he broke away from the little group and moved over toward Catherine and Michael.

"Where have you been, Doctor?" he said, a hint of impatience apparent in his crisp voice and the tapping of his patent leather shoe on the marble floor. "I want to talk to you about your hospital."

"Don't want a hospital," Michael said. "Catherine doesn't want one, either." He nodded toward his angel, who had dropped his hand when they entered the room. He felt strangely bereft, cut adrift.

"Why not?" Blankenship wanted to know. "All the best doctors have their own little hospitals."

"That's why." Michael was pleased that he had managed to explain it.

"What?" Blankenship seemed puzzled. Michael could not understand why. He thought he had explained it very well.

"The rich already have hospitals, sir. It is the poor who need good doctors." It was Mary Ann Evans who spoke. She had come up to them while Michael was talking. "And good doctors need the best equipment to do a good job."

"That's it," Michael said, admiring her good sense. "Exactly."

"Oh," said Blankenship, looking a little cast down. "I see. Thank you, Mrs. Evans. You have made everything very clear this afternoon, and I am grateful."

"Not at all, sir," said Mary Ann, her faded blue eyes twinkling. "It was a pleasure."

"And you plan to work here at St. Luke's?" Mr. Blankenship said.

"Well, as to that, sir," Mary Ann temporized, "I am not sure that St. Luke's runs to the kind of money it will take to hire Miss Stanhope and Dr. Soames and me."

"Expensive, are you, Mrs. Evans?" Blankenship's eyes twinkled back at her.

"Terrible, sir." They both laughed, though Michael saw nothing amusing about losing Mrs. Evans.

"We need you, Mary Ann," he said. "They don't. Those Harley Street places never get dirty. Patients are already well fed. They don't need broth and scrubbing and—and—"

"Quite." Blankenship studied his son's savior. "I take your meaning, Dr. Soames. May I say, sir, I hope you are not operating again this evening."

Michael was horrified. "Of course not. I have had a little whiskey. I never operate in that condition."

"I am happy to hear it." Mr. Blankenship turned to Mary Ann. "Very well. I will promise to pay the salaries of all three of you," he said. "Dr. Dinsmore." He raised his voice, and the administrator appeared at his side as if by magic. "Dinsmore, I will undertake to pay the salaries of these three for a year. As to the rest, we will see. I am leaving now. Pleasure, Dr. Dinsmore. Pleasure, Dr. Soames." He looked around. "Tell Miss Stanhope it was a pleasure. Mrs. Evans," he took the housekeeper's hand and bowed over it, "I thank you again for all your help in explaining things to me. Davy!" He looked around for his son, who came toward him, leaning on his cane. "Come, lad. We're for home!"

With that, he marched firmly out the door. It was as if a strong wind had blown through the room. "Salaries for a year." Dr. Dinsmore could hardly believe it. "All three of you." He looked as if he had been struck on the head by a fairy's wand—happy but disconcerted.

"Are you all right, sir?" Mary Ann asked Michael.

"Fine, fine. Nothing wrong with me that a brisk walk in the night air won't cure."

"In this neighborhood?" Mary Ann looked worried.

"Don't fuss. I will be fine. How are you going to get to your sister's? Can I call a hackney for you?"

Mary Ann laughed. "And how would I be paying for a hackney cab? Mr. Blankenship hasn't written the check yet." Her shrewd blue eyes took in Michael's disheveled state. "I am going to clean up the tea things and stay here for the night. I'd advise you to do the same, Doctor."

Assuring Mary Ann he was far tougher than he looked, Michael left the building. Outside, the air was damp and a fog had settled over the city. It must be almost six, he decided. He had started down the steps when he heard sounds of an argument coming from somewhere near the hospital gate. It was hard to judge distance in the thick pea-soup fog and winter darkness.

"No, let me go!" A woman cried out in pain.

Catherine! My God, someone was hurting Catherine!

Without a word to warn whoever was assaulting her,

Michael ran softly to where he thought the voice was coming from. The sounds of a scuffle pointed him a little to his left.

"No!" Catherine screamed.

Two steps more and he came upon them. There were two of them, and he judged in an instant both were young. One was short and wiry and the other tall and barrel-shaped. The short one had Catherine's reticule and both were dragging her toward the fence. What they had in mind, Michael didn't stop to consider.

He rushed at the big man and with unholy joy in his heart he swung a powerful punch—one that had won him many a fight in his youth in Edinburgh. The man's head snapped back, but he shook it and came at Michael again. This time he got in a punch of his own, and Michael could feel his whole head ring like a bell.

He reined in his anger and remembered the boxing lessons of his youth. He turned slightly, stepped forward, and put his whole body into a punch to the man's belly. The man doubled up and started to fall headfirst onto the pavement. Michael slammed the back of the assailant's neck with his fist. The pavement did the rest. The man dropped like a stone and Catherine was free.

"Michael, watch out!"

Her cry came just in time. He pivoted and struck the other, slighter man on the ear. The man got in a punch to Michael's chin. Michael hit him again.

When the man reeled back, Michael used an old street trick and stamped hard on his foot, then punched him solidly, first in the stomach and then on the chin. The second man crumpled and joined his companion. Michael stood over him, breathing hard, trying to control his impulse to stomp the man into the ground.

"Oh, Michael, are you hurt?" Catherine hurried over

to him, heedless of her torn skirt below the short, fitted coat she wore. Her bonnet was gone and her glorious hair tumbled about her face and down her back. Her blue eyes, almost black in the moonless evening, were huge with concern for him. She ran anxious fingers over his face. "Your chin. Your face. Here, take my handkerchief."

Tenderly, she held the square of linen to his chin. Michael took the handkerchief from her and their hands met for a moment. His knuckles were bleeding, and she took that hand in both of hers. "Your hands!" she cried. "You have hurt your hand. Michael, how will you operate?"

"My God, who gives a damn? Oh, my love, my love." He drew her into his arms and held her tightly. "Are you all right? They didn't hurt you? What happened? Why are you still here?" He didn't want answers to his questions; he just wanted to hear her voice.

"You saved me," she said, wonder in her voice. "Oh, Michael, you came just in time. I don't know what they were going to—" She broke off as he pressed hungry kisses all over her face.

"Catherine, my love, if anything had happened to you—" His voice broke. He couldn't bear to think of it.

"But nothing did, thanks to you." She smiled at up him and his heart soared. He almost failed to note the scurrying sound of the two men as they slunk away into the fog.

"Miss Catherine! Where are you?" a voice from the fog called out.

"I am here, Marston. We will try to find our way to you," Catherine called. She took Michael's hand in hers. "Lead the way, Doctor. Marston, you had better keep calling so we can follow the sound of your voice. That's how you found me, isn't it?" she said to Michael as she clung to him in the misty darkness.

"I would find you anywhere," Michael said simply. He

felt as if he were somehow floating. Catherine's danger, the fight to save her, had swept away his scruples and loosened the iron control he usually kept over his emotions.

"You beat those men," she said, a note of wonder in her voice.

"I used to fight a lot when I was younger." He pulled her closer to him, stopped and turned her into his arms. "Young men's student brawls. I'm afraid I did not always follow the Marquis of Queensbury's ideas of fairness. I didn't shock you?"

"No, Michael. *They* shocked me." She looked up at him. "They came from nowhere and grabbed at my bag and then at me. They never said anything. Silent violence. I was terrified. I screamed and—you came." She raised her face to his.

It seemed the most natural thing in the world to kiss her again.

"Miss Catherine!" Marston sounded frantic—and quite nearby.

"We are almost there," Catherine called. Reluctantly, Michael let his arms drop. They were almost back to the real world, where he was once again just Dr. Soames, the Edinburgh nobody, and she was Catherine Stanhope, the baronet's daughter. For a few minutes, he had felt like a knight riding to the rescue of a fair lady, like the stories his grandmother used to read to him before he got too big for fairy tales.

Just a few steps and the Stanhope coach loomed in front of them. Two worried middle-aged gentlemen peered into the gloom. When Catherine and Michael stepped out of the fog, their expressions lightened and they rushed forward.

"Miss Catherine! Look at you! Who did this? And who

are you?'' The groom glowered at Michael and moved to remove Catherine from his grasp.

"This is Dr. Soames, Marston. He saved me. Please help us into the carriage and take us home as fast as you can." Catherine refused to release Michael's hand. When he attempted to pull away, she shook her head. "You are coming with me. I want to be sure you are not badly hurt, and then I insist you stay and dine with us."

And Michael, knowing himself for a fool, followed her into the carriage and allowed himself to be swept along by Catherine and carried into her world.

Catherine had planned to whisk herself and Michael to the rear of the house, where the worst of their bruises and abrasions could be dealt with before meeting her father. She had even entertained the hope she could change from her incriminating black dress. But the baronet had been concerned when Catherine was not at home when he returned from his club. Marston and John Coachman had disappeared after bringing him home. This was most unusual, and the baronet was pacing the hall when Catherine and Michael entered.

"Where have you been," he began, "and why have you not been with Julian?" Then he saw she was dirty and disheveled, and his anger turned to concern immediately. "My dear child! How did this happen? Were you in an accident? Who is this gentleman, pray? Let me ring for Betsy. You should be in bed with a hot brick. And you, sir, did you help my daughter? Thank you, thank you."

"Papa, please. This is Dr. Soames. He is a friend of mine and, yes, he rescued me. Saved my life." Catherine still held Michael's hand.

"You have saved Catherine? Do you two know each

other?'' The baronet was clearly surprised. Michael could understand. His clothes, while perfectly proper, were not costly, and he wore no rings or other marks of wealth. Then the baronet understood. "*Doctor* Soames," he said. "Of course, you knew Catherine in the Crimea. Come in, do come in." He beamed at Michael. "You brought Julian back to us. You are very welcome indeed, Doctor."

Catherine closed her eyes as if in pain for a moment. "Papa, I was attacked by ruffians on the street. Dr. Soames rescued me at some cost to himself. I would like to take him to Mrs. Marston's rooms to see to his wounds. Then we will return and I, for one, would very much like a restorative glass of sherry."

The baronet bustled about, ringing for the butler and exclaiming over Catherine's danger, but after a few minutes, Catherine managed to break free. She took Michael behind the green baize door to the housekeeper's room, where she bound his hand and cleaned and bandaged a cut above his eye.

"If you don't mind," she said, laying a soft hand on his shoulder to keep him seated in the housekeeper's comfortable chintz-covered armchair, "I will go upstairs and wash my face and change. I will return in a few minutes. Meanwhile, Mrs. Marston can get you a cup of tea, if you would like."

A cup of tea and a few moments of silence sounded wonderful. Then perhaps he could persuade the coachman to take him to his lodgings, or direct him to the nearest well-traveled street where he could find a hackney. He certainly wasn't going to stay to be thanked for saving Catherine's fiancé's life. There was only so much a man could stand, and he had just about reached his limit.

"Here you are, sir," said the housekeeper, a plump, motherly woman, as she set a steaming cup of tea on the small table beside the chair. "I'd offer you a crumpet or one of my muffins, but I would not want to spoil your dinner."

Michael leaned back and closed his eyes. "I seldom eat dinner, Mrs. Marston," he said before he could set a guard on his tongue.

"Well, then, 'tis a good thing cook has roasted a joint of mutton with vegetables and a good mushroom soup to start and tipsy trifle for a pudding. That should fill you up and stick to your ribs." She nodded in satisfaction.

"I cannot stay," Michael said, but he made no move to leave.

"Oh, you must stay. You saved our Miss Catherine. Sir Everett wants to thank you." She moved a small footstool nearer to the chair, and somehow Michael found he had placed his feet on it. "So you work at the hospital with Miss Catherine."

That woke him up. "I thought no one but the coachman and the head groom knew."

Mrs. Marston chuckled. "Doctor, I have been married to Marston these thirty years. There's not much he does I don't know about—and sooner rather than later, at that. Besides, everyone in the house knows about Miss Catherine's employment—except her father, of course. Though I fear the secret is going to pop out tonight."

Michael sipped his tea. Catherine had said her father did not approve of her nursing, but he had assumed that after the triumph of the Crimea nurses, the baronet had changed his mind. Had Catherine really gone to work behind her father's back? Did she contemplate a career without her father's help and agreement?

Unless it was true that this was a temporary job, one she took to fill her days until her wedding. To Julian Livingston. It was absolutely impossible to stay and be thanked for saving the life of the man who was going to marry the woman he loved. Michael put his hands on the arms of the chair and attempted to rise.

For some reason, his legs did not seem to want to support him. He sank back. Delayed reaction. He had observed it in patients many times. During a battle a man would conduct himself with great bravery. Afterward, momentum would carry him for a few hours or sometimes even days, and then he would sit and shake for an hour or start to cry like a baby.

Michael now observed the phenomenon in himself. His hands were shaking, so he put down his teacup with a rattle. A few deep breaths brought him some relief, but he was still seated a moment later when Catherine returned. She looked at him with a nurse's eye.

"Is there sugar in that tea, Margaret?" she asked Mrs. Marston.

"No, Miss Catherine, but it is right here." The housekeeper stirred several heaping spoonfuls into Michael's cup, and Catherine picked it up and held it to his lips.

"Drink this, Michael." Her movements were the calm, practiced ones of a nurse, but her eyes were warm with concern. He could look into those deep blue eyes forever.

"Do you think we should put him to bed with perhaps a light dinner later, Miss Catherine?" Mrs. Marston leaned over to look at him, but Michael was still drowning in Catherine's eyes. "Miss Catherine?"

"Oh, yes." Her dark lashes swooped down and hid those magical eyes. "Yes, that would be a good idea. I don't think he is up to a full dinner with Papa. Could Holden help him, do you think?"

"Of course he could! I'll see to it." And the plump little housekeeper hurried away.

"I cannot stay here tonight," Michael protested. "I have to be at the hospital by seven."

"Yes, I know. I do, too. We will go together." Catherine smiled down at him and smoothed his hair back from his forehead. It was a gesture so tender it brought tears to Michael's eyes. He closed them so Catherine would not see.

"But how are you going to explain all this to your father? Mrs. Marston said you had not told him." He was worried that he had somehow caused this problem. He could see how much the baronet cared for his daughter, and Michael did not want to be the reason for a rift between them.

"Don't worry about that," Catherine assured him. "I'll take care of it."

She did not feel as confident as she sounded. Once Michael had been helped upstairs, Catherine took a deep breath and hurried into the small drawing room for her ritual predinner sherry with her father. She found him standing in front of the fireplace, looking worried.

"Catherine, I want to know exactly what happened to you. Where were you that something like this could happen? And where were John and Marston? Surely they could have protected you. Although I must say," he added in a thoughtful tone, "that doctor fellow did manage to get you free with nothing more than a lost bonnet and a torn reticule."

So he had noticed the damage. Somehow Catherine forgot from time to time just how observant her father could be. She had washed and changed into a simple evening dress and had Betsy arrange her hair. But her father was not to be fooled, and he would not settle for less than the full story.

Catherine took a deep breath and told him about the hospital, the tea party to raise money, the delay while she

waited for Marston and John Coachman, who had taken
the baronet home and then took the carriage out again.

After she had finished, the baronet sat speechless for a
full minute, staring into the fire. He looked stunned, as if
she had told him something so unbelievable that he
doubted her sanity—or his. Finally, he turned to look
at her, and Catherine was amazed at the expression she
thought she saw there. Hurt. Her father was wounded by
her confession.

"Does it mean that much to you, Papa?" she said softly.
"That I be the kind of conventional daughter all your
friends have? Have I hurt you by being so different, wanting
something so outlandish?"

Catherine found her eyes wet with tears. She had never
meant to hurt her father. But she had known with a deep,
sure instinct what was right for her, what would make her
happy. Had she really found what she wanted at the cost
of her father's happiness?

"You thought you could not tell me," he said at last. "I
never thought I was such an ogre that you could not talk
to me, tell me the important things in your life. I only
wanted you to be happy." He sighed. "And I wanted you
to be the kind of daughter your mother would have wanted
you to be."

"I know, Papa." Her voice was thick with tears. "I know
you loved me and wanted what was best for me—an easy
life, an indulgent husband. Just what Mama had. But,
Papa"—she rose and went over to kneel by his chair and
take his hands in hers—"what is easy is not what is best
for me. I am not Mama."

"Oh, my dear girl, I know that. I have always known
that. Marietta, your mother, was sweet and biddable and
had such a tender heart." He smiled into the fire, as if he
saw something precious there. Perhaps he did, Catherine

thought. "You were always brave and independent and clever—everything your mother wasn't. Everything she was afraid of in other people."

"I know, Papa. And I cannot be Mama, any more than she could be me." Catherine squeezed his hands. "I would if I could. I did try."

"I know." The baronet smiled at his daughter. "I remember your attempts to be obedient and ladylike. They always ended in some escapade on your horse, or some nighttime visit to a sick cottager on the estate."

Catherine tried to smile. She had the most awful sense that her father blamed himself for her failure to live up to her dead mother's standards. "You will have to accept me as I am, Papa. I am afraid I cannot be anyone else. Or anything else. I am happy when I am nursing, Papa. I feel as alive as you do on the hunting field or in a parliamentary debate."

"Catherine, my dear, that is not what has hurt me. It is that you hid yourself from me. You have taken a job and have involved everyone but me. Did you fear me? I know some men think that is the only way to govern their households, but I have never subscribed to that. Have you feared me?"

Catherine sat back on her heels, astounded. Her father was wounded not because she was a nurse but because she had not trusted him to love her enough to accept her choice.

"You have never been anything but kind and loving, Papa," she said. Then she gave him an impish grin. "A bit blustery from time to time, but I never doubted you loved me."

There was a long silence while the baronet looked deeply into Catherine's eyes. "You have chosen a difficult road," he said at last. "My money and influence will protect you from most of the gossip, but not everyone will be kind about your choice. Especially at St. Luke's. I confess I would be happier if you had some kind of normal life outside

your work. If you married. Are you sure you do not want
me to use my influence to get you a position at that Harley
Street hospital?"

Impulsively, Catherine threw her arms around her
father. "No, Papa, but thank you, thank you. I love you
very much."

"And I you, my dear." The baronet looked uncertain
for a moment, but then he smiled at her. "I would like
you to do one thing for me, though. It would ease my
mind if you would continue to attend some social events,
enough so people will not think you are some sort of
peculiar recluse. Please humor me on this. You know how
I love to see you shine at social events. Will you do it? Is
it a bargain, Catherine?"

"Of course, Papa. I will be in every way a dutiful daughter, except for that one area." She thought it might be
difficult to attend too many evening parties. Her work
drained her, and at night she wanted nothing more than
to eat a simple meal and sit with her eyes closed. But surely
her father would understand.

The baronet actually chuckled, reinforcing her sense
that he would be understanding about the demands of
her work. "We should rub along tolerably well together,"
he said, "now that I have decided to give in to you on
every point."

Catherine laughed. "You are right, Papa. That was all
it ever took."

Holden entered the room, looking as distinguished and
imperturbable as ever. Catherine's world had been turned
upside down and righted again in the space of half an
hour, but Holden knew what was important. "Dinner is
served, sir, Miss Catherine," he said, just as if he had not
been listening at the door for the past ten minutes.

Chapter Ten

After dinner, Catherine excused herself to her father and went up to the guest chamber where Mrs. Marston had placed Michael. It was smaller than some in Stanhope House, but comfortable, with a slightly masculine feel due to the heavy French-Empire furniture her grandmother had favored. The draperies and bedcovers remained the same Chinese chintz, slightly faded now, but still graceful and beautiful in Catherine's eyes.

Her mother had favored the gilt and velvet and ornate gathers and poufs that were still in fashion, and the baronet could not bear to change anything after her death. Catherine felt stifled in the formal rooms and had slowly stripped her bedroom and dressing room of the fussy ruffles and fringes and substituted simple designs and clean lines. The guest room, too, felt comfortable to her and, she hoped, to Michael.

A cheery coal fire was burning in the grate and Michael

was sitting up in bed. He flung the book he had been leafing through facedown on the counterpane.

"I really must leave, Catherine—Miss Stanhope," Michael said as soon as she entered. "I cannot bear to stay in bed when I am neither sleeping nor sick." His words sounded rehearsed and his eyes refused to meet hers.

He was embarrassed. Well, so was she. What had happened between them twice now was not something well-brought-up young ladies indulged in. Did he think, as many did, that because she was a nurse and had seen and cared for the human body—the male human body—that she was not virtuous and discreet? Did he? The very thought made her clench her hands into fists.

"Catherine." His voice was gruff. She looked up, and she knew he could see the anger and hurt in her eyes. "I should apologize for what happened this afternoon, but I find I cannot. I know it was wrong, but I cannot regret it."

"There is no need to apologize." *If you would only say you love me. Is that what you mean?*

"Yes, there is. To Lieutenant Livingston, as well as to you." He looked at her now, his expression serious, yet there was a light in his eyes that gave her hope. "My only excuse is that in the emotion of the moment, I let your—your beauty and your—" He broke off and grimaced at his inability to express what he wanted to say. "I—I—it was wrong of me to kiss you, Catherine."

"I kissed you, too," she interrupted, sure he was going to be noble and renounce her. *Men!* she thought rebelliously. They might run the world on noble principles, though it was hard to see anything noble about the war she had just witnessed, but those principles got in the way of happiness and common sense, as far as she was concerned.

"Not only because we are colleagues," he continued as if she had not spoken, "but because you are engaged to another man. A patient of mine," he added, heaping reason upon reason. "A hero."

Catherine's shoulders sagged. She knew she was not really engaged to Julian, but Michael was right. Julian was a wounded hero who needed help. Her help? She thought not, but she might be wrong. Perhaps not through marriage—after all, Julian had repudiated her. But she could not desert him for another man now. That would be regarded as unforgivable. Doors would be closed to Catherine and Michael that might not matter to them but would matter to her father. Julian might give up hope and retreat into despair permanently, thinking his oldest friend had deserted him.

"I do not think I can marry Julian now." She spoke slowly, feeling her way. Sure that she loved Michael, would never love anyone else, she was not sure what to do about it. "I have tried to talk to him, but he will not speak to me. Only tells me to go away."

"You have seen that before." Michael's voice was wooden and his face expressionless, but his fingers plucked at the coverlet. "Many men react like that at first. He will come out of it. You will help him."

Catherine shook her head. "Something tells me I am not the one who can help Julian. I would be happy if I could. He is my oldest friend—more like a brother than a friend, really. But I do not think I am what he needs."

"But you must try."

"Yes." He was right. Until Julian had recovered enough to seek a new life, she was tied to him by a lifetime of loyalty. It did not matter whether they were truly engaged to be married. He was Julian, and she owed him her care and concern.

Until Julian recovered, she could not even try to win Michael's love.

"Yes." He repeated the word, as if it were a curse.

"I am going to continue to work at the hospital. Julian does not want to see me, but you are right. I must try to break through to him. I will go to see him tomorrow. I would be grateful if you would come with me."

Michael stared at her, uncertain of how he felt. True, he had renounced her because of her betrothal to another man. But she had accepted it so easily, speaking of her lifelong devotion to Julian. A sister's love, she had called it, but did she really mean that?

Michael had never been in love before, and he knew himself to be highly ineligible. He also knew women lied in order to deceive men into giving them what they wanted— admiration, love, money. All the things his mother demanded—and received—from his father.

Catherine had lied to him at least by omission in not telling him she was engaged. When Michael had kissed her on the Black Sea transport ship, he had dared to dream there might be a future for them. Their mutual love of medicine, he had believed, and what he thought was their love for each other could overcome the artificial obstacles the world had put in their way. Now, for the second time, she had sacrificed him to her loyalty to Julian Livingston, a man from her world.

"You are asking a great deal of me, Catherine. I will see Livingston, but I would prefer to do it when you are not there." Her already pale face grew even whiter as he spoke.

"Why? We can be friends at least, can we not? Until we can be something more." She went to the side of the bed and took one of his hands in hers. She sat down on the side of the bed and smiled at him, a wavering, uncertain smile. "I am not wrong in thinking we care for each other, am I? That we want something more?"

"I cannot live on the expectation that one day I may

get some other man's leavings." Was it unreasonable, the jealousy that wrenched those words out of him? He didn't know. He didn't care. He could not stand by and play some sort of role until Catherine felt free to love him. Might she not let something else stand in their way when—if—Julian was removed?

Catherine's hand jerked out of his. "And that is what I am to you? Julian's leavings?"

He shrugged, refusing to look at her. "I have kissed you, yet you tell me we are to be only friends. Livingston is your fiancé. How am I to know what favors you have bestowed on him?"

"I should strike you for that remark." Instead, she turned and walked to the door. "Mrs. Marston tells me she thinks it would be wise for you to remain here overnight. I will look in on you to be sure you have not sustained a concussion or some other injury that might manifest itself during the night. If there is none, I will meet you in the entrance hall at six thirty. Holden will wake you."

She walked out the door without looking back at him, and Michael was left feeling as if his entire world had collapsed—the way he had felt the day his father had told him there was no money to send him to medical college, that his mother had spent it all. The helpless look on his father's face, as if to say he was sorry but his wife's frivolous desires mattered more than his son's needs, had roused him to fury. He felt the same way now. He loved Catherine and he knew she cared for him, but she had put someone else's needs above his, and the same unreasoning anger overpowered his mind now.

But it was not the same. His mother's social life should not have taken precedence over Michael's education. His father was an adult. He should have made the right decision, but he had not. Catherine had decided that Julian's needs, which were grave but hopefully temporary, took precedence for the time being over her feelings for Michael and her own happiness. Michael had lost respect for his father because of his decision. But Catherine was making the harder, principled choice and should have Michael's respect and help.

What kind of love was not willing to help the loved one? Whatever her feelings for Julian, and for him, Catherine had asked for his help, but he had refused it and rejected her. He had been wrong—stubborn and pigheaded and wrong. He would go with her to the Eversleigh home tomorrow, and whenever she needed him he would be there. He would offer every help, not just because Catherine asked him to but because his profession demanded it of him.

Having finally made the only decision he could live with, Michael fell into a deep slumber, only to be awakened seemingly seconds later by Holden shaking his shoulder and telling him it was already quarter to six.

"Thank you very much for coming with me," Catherine said late that afternoon when she and Michael mounted the broad white limestone steps to Eversleigh House.

"I told you, I will help you and Livingston to the best of my ability."

She had been both surprised and warmed by the change in Michael's attitude. She had forgiven him without hesitation when he had apologized for the unkind things he had said to her the night before. He had been under a strain, and she could understand why he would be angry and doubt her feelings for him. They had never discussed what they felt for each other. Their kisses had spoken volumes, but no declarations or promises had followed. Yet she believed—no, she *knew* they loved one another.

The countess received them in the small sitting room that she used as her informal reception room. The walls were covered with pale yellow watered silk and there were delicate watercolors in gilt frames on the walls. The furniture was all delicate French fruitwood, the chairs and a settee upholstered in blue flowered tapestry. It suited the small, exquisite countess perfectly.

The strain showed in her face, Catherine thought. Lines that had been almost invisible before now had etched themselves deeply into her forehead. Her eyes were dull and her shoulders drooped.

"Catherine! I am so glad you have come." The countess's look of relief made Catherine vow to visit more frequently, if only to take some of the burden from the countess. "And you are Dr. Soames!" The countess took both of Michael's hands in hers and looked up into the craggy face of the man who had saved her son. Tears sprang to her eyes.

Embarrassed, Michael forgot this woman was a countess and saw her only as a caring mother, worried to death about her child. "He's a strong person, ma'am," he said. "And with a naturally buoyant personality, I'm guessing. I think with care he will come out of this."

"Catherine told you? He will do nothing. He simply lies in his bed." The countess led Michael over to a small settee and sat down beside him, her hands still in his. "He will not try to get well. I am not wrong in thinking that he can recover the use of his leg?"

"No, ma'am, I believe you are right. But he must use the leg. Walk on it just a bit at first, but then farther and longer. Lying in bed is the worst thing he can do." Michael focused all his attention on the countess, and Catherine could see his concern and confidence were having an effect. The countess's shoulders lost their slump and she smiled slightly.

"I thank you, Doctor. You have relieved my mind. Now I must try to find a way to get him out of that bed. I have considered setting fire to the bed curtains, but my husband tells me he thinks that a little drastic." And, remarkably, she laughed a little.

"I think we might want to delay such a measure—for a time, at least." Michael smiled down at the little countess. "I think it is time I see this difficult patient, if you don't mind."

Julian's room was still so tidy as to be unnatural. Julian had been impetuous, careless, always dashing from one activity to the next. Now he lay motionless in bed, his eyes closed. Flowers were in a vase on a chest opposite the bed where his eye would fall on them. Books were near to hand and a small lap desk stood on a nearby table. A picture of one of his favorite hunters hung above the fireplace.

Julian ignored it all.

"Lieutenant." Michael entered the room and was immediately the complete doctor. "I have come to examine your leg." He went over to the bed and looked carefully at Julian's waxen complexion and flaccid muscles. "With your permission," he said as he lifted the covers from Julian's leg.

"You do not have my permission. Go away." Julian's voice was expressionless and he lay perfectly still, his eyes closed.

"See, Julian, it is Dr. Soames come to look at your leg," Catherine said. She hated the false cheerfulness she could hear in her voice. She was not like this with other patients. Somehow with Julian, she became self-conscious and sounded like a nanny talking to a recalcitrant toddler.

"I know who it is, Catherine." There might have been the slightest suggestion of impatience in Julian's tone, but his expression did not change and he still refused to look at his visitors. "And I would like you both to go away."

"That's hardly a polite way to talk to guests who have come—" That sickeningly bright voice. Her governess, whom she had never liked very much, had talked like that, and Catherine had wanted to kick her.

"Catherine." That was all Michael said, but Catherine sat down and said no more. "Now, lieutenant, you cannot expect me to report to the authorities at the War Office unless I examine you."

Catherine raised her eyebrows. There was no report to the War Office that she knew of. Apparently, Julian did not know that.

"Very well," he said. "If you must."

It took but a short time. Michael professed himself satisfied with Julian's progress. That caused both Julian and Catherine to look up at him in surprise. "Yes," he said. "The leg is healing admirably. You tore a good many muscles and some tendons and fractured both the tibia and fibula of your left leg. Those fractures are mending nicely, as are the muscles and tendons. You can begin using crutches in a few days. The difficulty is that by lying in bed all day you run the risk of other problems."

He sat down on the edge of the bed, his back to Catherine, and spoke directly to Julian. "One of them is that your muscles shrink and weaken with disuse. That includes your arm and back muscles as well as the muscles in your right leg." He lowered his voice and spoke impersonally as he looked at Julian's eyes and then turned Julian's head from one side to another.

As he did so, Julian grimaced.

"You see. Your neck is growing rigid from lack of movement. If you do not get out of your bed and off your aristocratic arse pretty quick, you will one day find you cannot do so."

Julian had begun listening to Michael's speech with the expression of passive boredom he used on everyone. By the time Michael finished, his patient's eyes were fixed on him. "So," he said at last, every word a victory as far as Catherine was concerned, "I will become an invalid. Just as I thought."

Michael had no patience for this kind of self-pity. "You will become an invalid only if you insist upon becoming one. You can have your mother and father tiptoeing around you, cosseting you and catering to you, afraid to call you to account for anything lest they upset their dear, invalid boy. They love you and will do that for the rest of their lives, if that is what you seek."

"You don't understand. I do not want to be catered to, and that includes being wept over. I do not wish for anything. I just want to be left alone." Julian once again sank into his state of torpor.

Michael could have shaken him, kicked him. A young man with all the advantages, lying in stubborn refusal to pick up his life—his very fortunate life—and go on, made Michael furious. Too angry to speak, he got up abruptly and walked over to the window. He stood looking blindly out, his hand convulsively clenching and unclenching a fold of the bottle green velvet curtains that draped the tall casement windows.

Catherine rose and went over to Julian. She did not see what Michael saw. Instead, with the eyes of an old friend, she saw the furrows etched in his brow by pain and disillusion. His eyes were the eyes of a sad old man. There was no light in their depths at all. Julian, Catherine could see, wanted nothing, cared for nothing except to somehow make the pain go away.

"Jules," she said, "I know you do not want me here and I am willing to stay away, but on one condition only."

"Anything." The word sounded heartfelt. Catherine suffered a pang, knowing that Jules, her childhood friend, wanted only to be rid of her.

"Promise me you will not take the easy way out." Her eyes held his, and she knew he could read fear in hers as she could read a kind of dull despair in his. "Promise me, or I will set a guard on you."

"I promise." There was defeat in his voice and Catherine closed her eyes, thanking God he had given his word. For she knew he would keep it no matter how much he might want to break it.

"Thank you, Jules, for we could not do without you, you know."

Michael had turned away from the window in time to hear her last words. He looked at her sharply, as if unsure exactly what she meant.

"I will look in on you again in a few days," Michael said. "And I will hope to see you up in your chair."

"Why?" Julian's face was again turned, unseeingly, to the ceiling. He had given his word not to kill himself, but he was not going to do more. He was not going to live.

Michael made a disgusted noise and let himself out of the room, but Catherine paused and kissed Julian's forehead before she left.

Once they were in the hallway, Catherine put a hand on Michael's arm. "You must try to see him the way you would any other soldier," she said. "You have to see beyond the good looks and title and money to the man beneath. He is suffering the way that poor young man was who could only sit on his pallet, shivering and crying. Remember?

You never showed impatience with him. You spent hours with him, talking gently, encouraging him. You have to do the same for Julian."

"I did nothing for that boy. I don't think he heard one word I said. It wasn't I who helped him. It was your friend, Rose Cranmer."

"Rose? I had no idea. She never said anything. But then," she added thoughtfully, "Rose never talked a great deal. There was something about her, though, as if she was at peace with herself but it had been hard won. Perhaps that's why she could help soldiers who had lost themselves."

"Do you seriously think Julian Livingston has lost himself?" Michael sounded unconvinced.

"Yes. I think he wants to stop living. It is more than the injury to his leg," she added. "Something happened to him over there. I don't know what, but it was something profound. It made him lose whatever reason he had to go on living."

Michael was silent as they began to walk again, down the corridor covered with bright Turkey carpeting in shades of red and blue. As they descended the stairway to the hall below, the countess came out of the door of her reception room and stood looking anxiously up at them.

"What should we tell her?" Catherine asked, worried lest she mislead Julian's mother, who had been like a mother to her during her childhood after her own had died. "I do not want to worry her unduly, but he is—"

"My lady," Michael said and bowed over the countess's hand. "I wish I could give you an unequivocal answer to the question of your son's injury. It seems to be healing nicely, but there is a question of the pain and the lassitude engendered by his prolonged exposure on the battlefield.

I think, in short, we will have to wait and carefully monitor his situation.''

The countess looked a little puzzled. As well she might, Catherine thought. Never before had she heard Michael use the sort of pompous, all but meaningless verbiage other doctors employed as a matter of course.

She taxed him with it when they had left the Eversleigh mansion. "You sounded remarkably like Dr. Hall," she teased him. "Lassitude, engendered, carefully monitor. You learned from a master.''

He gave her a small, wintry smile. "I did not like doing it. But I could hardly tell the fragile little woman that her son was lying upstairs in a black fog of mental pain, unable to so much as sit up. She would have been beside herself, and we would have two patients instead of one.''

Catherine shook her head. "You really do not understand women, Michael. The countess is far stronger and of more practical use than you could imagine. When Julian fell and broke his arm and was knocked unconscious, the earl was quite useless, stalking about and berating the governess and the gamekeeper who did not keep his son from climbing a tree! The countess took charge, got Julian home on a makeshift stretcher, and sat up for two nights to make sure he had no serious brain injury.''

Michael gave an ironic little bow. "My respects to the countess.''

"You have a very skewed and peculiar attitude toward my sex," Catherine said. "I do not understand it, but I have been the recipient of enough unfair judgments from you that I know it to be true.''

Michael knew it was true as well. But he was not going to go into details. The subject was too painful, and he did not understand his own feelings. He resented his mother and thought of his father as weak. Yet, perversely, he loved

the woman who had given him birth and respected his
father as a dedicated and gifted physician who had never
let his wife's needs and his love for her to threaten his
care of his patients.

In a sudden insight, Michael admitted to himself that
despite the fact that his view of women had been shaped
almost entirely by his mother, the one person he had ever
met whom he admired without reservation was a woman—
Florence Nightingale, the intrepid fighter against disease
and death, and, he admitted, against masculine pride and
bureaucracy. The woman he loved bore more than a passing resemblance to Miss Nightingale—but none at all to
his selfish, flighty mother.

Chapter Eleven

"Tell me again why I am here," Michael said under his breath to Catherine two nights later as they stood at the entrance of a glittering ballroom. Michael was a striking figure in the black and white evening clothes that society decreed. His lean figure showed off the long frock coat and trim-fitting trousers perfectly. For once, his thick auburn hair was brushed into gleaming order. Taller than most of the men in the room, he was a figure of elegance and dignity.

"You are here because Davy and Mr. Blankenship invited you," Catherine replied, smiling.

The room seemed to be lit by a million chandeliers holding a thousand lights each. The walls were draped in what Michael thought was at least three acres of crimson silk and miles of tasseled gold cords. There were mirrors everywhere, reflecting the crowd of brilliantly dressed women and the starched and pressed gentlemen who'd brought them. It was like nothing so much as a huge jewelry box.

Henry Blankenship did nothing by halves. When he gave money to a hospital, he gave lavishly. When he entertained, nothing was too much or too costly. And when he gave his friendship to a struggling doctor, he included the young man in all his social activities.

"And why in the world would they do such a nonsensical thing?" Michael asked, his grip on Catherine's elbow increasing in intensity as they passed into the glittering inferno.

"Because you saved Davy's life and because they both like and admire you." Catherine's smile was serene.

"I hardly fit into the picture of such a lavish social event." His cravat was strangling him. Where was an operating room or a hospital ward, where he might feel at home? "I do not add to his consequence. Though I must thank him for sending me to his tailor. Without the clothes, they wouldn't even let me in the back door tonight."

"When you are as rich as Mr. Blankenship," Catherine replied, her eyes scanning the crowd for their host, "you already have consequence. You can invite whom you like. You do not need to concern yourself with petty social distinctions."

"Right you are, Miss Stanhope," said a hearty voice from behind them. They turned in unison to see the beaming face of Henry Blankenship. "It is one of the best parts of being rich, being able to have the friends I want and watching society swallow their objections."

"I am glad I can provide you with a source of amusement," Michael said, but he could not help smiling.

"The trouble with you, my boy, is you haven't had any champagne as yet. Softens up the hard edges. And you have a good many of those." Henry Blankenship's eyes twinkled. "All these overdressed snobs will look a lot more appealing after a glass."

The industrialist snapped his fingers and a waiter appeared with a tray of glasses sparkling with the bubbling, straw-colored liquid. "Here, now, both of you must have some. Miss Stanhope," he said, giving Catherine a slight bow as he presented her with one glass, "you are looking lovely this evening, my dear."

Catherine was strangely exhilarated. She had not truly enjoyed a party in years. Before she had gone to Turkey with Miss Nightingale, every social occasion had been overshadowed by her father's relentless pursuit of a husband for her. If she danced more than once with anyone, the baronet was inquiring into the young man's prospects. Since her return, any event had been overshadowed either by her own sense of dislocation or by the shadow of Julian's illness. Even the last party had been the occasion of her seeking money for St. Luke's. She had not simply enjoyed herself in what seemed like years.

And tonight she was here with Michael, who looked handsome and had smiled down at her with warmth and something more. She gazed at Henry Blankenship and at Michael. Then, as she looked around, young David Blankenship made his way over to them and Jeffrey Bancroft smiled and saluted her with his champagne glass.

She had friends. For the first time since the informal dances at their country house when she had first made her debut, she had a group of people she was genuinely glad to spend time with. She knew she looked her best. Betsy had seen to that. Her dress was satin in the same clear blue as her eyes, with a tiny waist and a low décolletage that made the most of her creamy shoulders and bosom. Betsy had done her hair in smooth curves and twists and had placed several blue satin roses among the waves. It had been a long time since Catherine had cared what she looked like. Indeed, she had usually sought to play down her looks with sober dresses and a modest demeanor in order to convince her father that all she wanted was to nurse the sick and to discourage any young men from seeking her out.

But now she was at a party with Michael and she felt like a giddy schoolgirl. She laughed at Henry Blankenship and gave him a tiny curtsy. "You flatter me, Mr. Blankenship. But I thank you for it."

"Not at all, my dear Miss Stanhope. You always know exactly what to wear for any occasion, unlike many of our young ladies, who look as if they tried to wear everything in their wardrobes at once."

Catherine looked around. It was true. A good many of the young ladies wore dresses so trimmed with flowers and flounces and furbelows that the fabric could scarcely be seen. "I think they wanted to wear their very best tonight, sir," she responded diplomatically. "This is sure to be the very best party of the year."

Mr. Blankenship laughed. "They all wanted to see the inside of my house and sample my food and drink. And the young ladies would all like to catch the eye of Davy here." He opened his arm to include his son in their group. "Come along, Davy, and join us. You are safe here. Miss Stanhope has her eye on another fellow."

David Blankenship was a good-looking man, still young enough to have the fresh coloring of youth, yet with that interesting limp and the sober look of a man tried in the crucible of war. Catherine was so used to thinking of him as her patient that she had never really looked at him. Now she had to agree with his father—all the young ladies were very likely looking at him. "You have a very handsome son, Mr. Blankenship," she said.

Davy blushed a little and bowed to her. "Miss Stanhope, I hope you will consent to sit out a dance with me, ma'am. I'm afraid I am not ready to dance again quite yet." He gestured to the ornate Malacca cane he was leaning on. Although he looked at ease, Catherine could see a slight tightening of his hand on the cane and knew Davy hated the fact he could not dance. Though Michael had told him the chances were good he would recover completely, for someone as young and active as Davy, having to sit while others whirled around the floor with pretty girls in their arms could not be easy.

"I would be delighted to sit out with you, sir," she replied.

"That's all very well," Henry Blankenship intervened, "but I think you should do a little dancing as well, Miss Stanhope. Doctor, I trust you will ask the lady for a waltz."

Michael looked blank for a moment, as if he thought his host was addressing someone else. Then, to Catherine's dismay, he gazed at the floor in apparent embarrassment. "I—I—"

He doesn't know how to dance, she thought, equally embarrassed for him. Then he looked up and met her agonized gaze. "It would be an honor, Miss Stanhope. May I?" He offered his arm, and Catherine took it and allowed him to lead her into the adjoining ballroom and onto the dance floor. Neither noticed Mr. Blankenship gesturing to the leader of the small string orchestra. It seemed a waltz had been ordained just for them.

Catherine stepped into Michael's arms and was enfolded in magic. He held her as if she was the most precious thing in the world, but there was leashed passion in the steel bands of his arms, and Catherine gave herself over to the thrill of dancing with Michael.

"You did not think I knew how to waltz, did you?" he murmured as he swung her around the floor.

"You always portray yourself as unfit for polite society. It surprised me you knew how to use a fork." Catherine allowed herself to tease this gruff and touchy man. She knew from the touch of his hand in hers that this evening she would not be misunderstood.

Michael actually laughed. She met his eyes in surprise. "Yes, I can laugh at myself," he said with a grin. "You didn't believe that either, did you?"

"You are full of surprises," she responded.

"Tonight I am ready to give in to all the impulses I usually force myself to ignore," he said. "I find that the sight of you and the feel of you has melted every ounce of moral fiber I possess."

"And what impulses might those be?" she responded, smiling up at him. She knew her heart was in her eyes, but she didn't care. Michael knew how she felt, and she understood his heart as well. The fact that so much stood in their way did not matter tonight.

"Keep smiling at me that way and you will find out, my blue-eyed witch." His answering smile warmed her to the toes of her dancing slippers.

For a few minutes more, they swept around the floor to the strains of the waltz, and then the orchestra fell silent and Michael gently twirled her to a stop.

"That was wonderful," Catherine said, as she fanned her flushed cheeks with the swan's-down fan she carried attached to a bracelet.

"You are wonderful. It does not take a ballroom or champagne to make magic when you are near."

"You have never talked like this, Michael."

"I have never felt as if life contained as many possibilities as I do this evening," he replied, leading her back to the group of comfortable chairs in the reception room where Mr. Blankenship was holding court. "Is your father coming? I have not thought to ask where he is."

"The House is sitting late this evening. He told me to go without him. I was to come with my aunt, who is visiting London for a few weeks, but she begged off at the last minute, so I brought Betsy, my maid."

"Perhaps it is the lack of a glowering baronet that enables me to speak freely," Michael said, only half joking.

They reached the group, and Catherine noticed that Mary Ann Evans was in attendance. She was dressed very plainly but becomingly in a black silk dress. Catherine greeted her as one more friend in a warm circle of friends. It seemed to her as if at last she had a group of people with whom she could feel at home. If, like Mr. Blankenship, they had not known her at Scutari, still they were the sort of people who might have been there, sensible and humorous and able to turn their hands to whatever might need to be done.

"Mr. Blankenship asked if I would come and oversee the catering," Mary Ann explained. "I had nothing to wear so he sent me a length of this silk and I found a seamstress. He is very forceful, is he not?" she added.

"Yes, indeed, but always in such a kindly way," Catherine said.

"I don't know how kindly he'd be if you told him no," Mary Ann said with her habitual shrewdness. Then, looking around, she added, "I've only been in London for a few weeks and here I am at a fancy party and I even know some of the guests. Who would have thought that plain Mary Ann Evans, with hardly a penny to bless myself with, would end up so fortunately placed? I owe it to you and

Dr. Soames, Miss Stanhope, and I hope you know I don't forget it. You are a blessing to me, and I thank you for it every day."

Catherine was so touched at this forthright declaration of friendship that tears misted her eyes for a moment. "Mary Ann, you have earned every good thing that has happened. I did you no favors. You were the best hospital matron anyone could wish. St. Luke's is fortunate to have you."

At that moment, Henry Blankenship spoke up. "Miss Stanhope, my boy has waited patiently for a chance to take you to the supper room. I am assured by Mrs. Evans that all is in readiness. Will you give him the pleasure of your company?"

Catherine thought perhaps Mr. Blankenship was doing a little too much speaking for his son, but she was more than happy to fall in with his plans. "Of course. David, I would love some supper. I ate very little dinner." She looked around before taking Davy's free arm and saw Michael across the room, deep in conversation with Jeffrey Bancroft. *What do those two have to talk about?* she wondered.

"You seem quite at home here, Soames," Jeffrey was saying. "Has Catherine Stanhope managed to coax you out of your shell? Or did Henry Blankenship simply order you to appear?"

Perhaps because the magic of having danced with Catherine still lingered, Michael could not resent Bancroft's plain speaking. "A bit of both," he said, "plus Dr. Dinsmore pleading with me to represent the hospital. He has quite taken to the idea of raising money among society— of course, that is probably because no one expects him to do any of it."

"While you are caught. Too wellborn to be excluded but not rich enough to be comfortable."

"Well, that is plain speaking," Michael said, not sure whether he should feel insulted or pleased that Jeffrey Bancroft thought him equal enough to be open with.

Jeffrey shrugged. "Blankenship comes from the poor end of Manchester. I myself—well, let us simply say I was not born to wealth. If I were poor, I would be excluded. You are a member of the middle class and have a respectable profession. The world is changing. Money need not be inherited any more, but certain standards remain. You will be accepted. You know how to dance and eat lobster patties, so you needn't be rich. I have never learned."

"I cannot imagine anything easier than eating lobster patties," Michael said. "And it seems to me money is a better door opener than dancing lessons. I can feel half the people here wondering who I am and then when they find out, wondering what I'm doing here. A poor doctor from Edinburgh."

"Blankenship has already told at least half the people here that you saved his son's life and that you are undoubtedly the best surgeon in London, if not in the entire British Isles." Jeffrey gave him a quizzical look. "If you wish it, you could have a very lucrative private practice just by saying the word to Blankenship."

Michael hunched his shoulders under the fine broadcloth of the suit Mr. Blankenship had insisted he order from his tailor. "I do not wish it. The rich can have their pick of surgeons and doctors. It is the poor who suffer and have no one. There are only a few hospitals, and those are charnel houses. No, Bancroft, I would rather take care of those who really need my services."

"I thought you would say so. Lucinda told me you were the most dedicated doctor she knew in Turkey. Miss Nightingale shared that opinion." Jeffrey nodded. "I am prepared to help underwrite St. Luke's, provided you and

Miss Stanhope are there to oversee medical care and Dinsmore stays as administrator."

Michael was stunned. Here was one of the richest and most sought-after men in the kingdom letting him know he thought Michael his social equal—if not his superior! More important, he was willing to back Michael's medical undertaking just on the strength of Michael's reputation as a doctor. That more than anything warmed him and filled him with a sense that he was among people who understood and valued him for exactly who and what he was.

"I am grateful. And I am sure Dinsmore will be dancing tomorrow when I tell him what you have said." Michael smiled, thinking of the little administrator's glee when he learned what Bancroft had promised.

"I doubt that. Dinsmore strikes me as being as unfamiliar with dancing as I am." Jeffrey smiled wryly and said, "We have discussed enough business for one evening. Let us go to the supper room and see if we can find some of those lobster patties."

Catherine saw them enter the room, laughing together like old friends. She had ceased to be surprised at Michael's behavior this evening. Friendship with the rich and handsome Jeffrey Bancroft was no more startling than the fact that he waltzed marvelously, laughed easily, and looked every bit as distinguished as Jeffrey. They came over to the small table where Catherine and David were seated. David had commanded a waiter to bring "one of everything for my special guest," and the man had done as he was bid. As a result, Catherine's plate was heaped with food. She had managed to eat more than she usually did at affairs of this sort. The food was marvelous, but fashion decreed that even one as slender as Catherine be laced into a corset that deprived her of breath and appetite so that her waist would appear tiny. She was eying the large serving still awaiting her when Michael and Jeffrey asked if they could join them.

If David was disappointed at having his tête-à-tête with Catherine interrupted, he was too polite to give any sign. Dr. Soames was his hero, in any case, and he commandeered two more enormous plates for him and Mr. Bancroft and two glasses of champagne.

"I am happy you could come to our party," he said to Michael. "I was afraid you would scorn such a frivolous evening."

Michael shook his head. "I am not so foolish as to decline an evening that includes food and drink such as this, nor a chance to see one of my prize patients looking as fit as you. Tell me how you managed to recover so quickly, David. I would like to pass your secret along to others."

"No shop talk this evening, Doctor," Henry Blankenship said as he came up to stand behind his son's chair. "David can come to your hospital and you two can talk about it as much as you like. But tonight Davy is to enjoy himself. There is a young lady over by the potted palm in the corner, my boy, who has been casting glances at you all evening. I have discovered that her name is Emma Carpentier. Her father is on the board of the railroad I have recently bought into. Come and meet her. We will see you later," he added as he shepherded his son off to meet the well-connected young lady.

"I hope that boy is allowed to draw breath for himself," Jeffrey said as he looked after the Blankenships. "His father seems to do everything else for him."

"I wouldn't worry too much about David," Catherine said. "He enlisted in the Army over his father's objections and insisted on being treated like every other private. That takes courage. He could have had a much easier time if he had traded on his name."

"A wound such as he suffered tends to stiffen the weakest spine," Michael said. "The fact that he has worked so hard to recover as fast as he has also speaks well for his mental toughness." He looked at Catherine and then added, "Not everyone who is wounded responds with such courage and fortitude. Some people will not make the effort to remake their lives."

"Or cannot." Catherine met his gaze. She knew he was speaking of Julian. While she agreed with Michael that Julian was not working at recovery, she did not judge him as harshly as Michael. She knew Julian and realized that for someone one as basically lighthearted and devil-may-care as her childhood friend, it was devastating to find everything he had taken for granted yanked away in one tragic, painful moment. The way one coped with tragedy was sometimes not within one's control. Julian's passivity was the result of the battle he had been in, not a sign of a weak character.

"Not everyone reacts to adversity the same way." She didn't mean to sound defensive, but Michael's eyes narrowed. She did not want this evening to end with another discussion of Julian. She determined to lighten the mood.

"Will you dance with me, Mr. Bancroft?" she dared to ask, hoping the tycoon would enjoy the friendly joking tone of her invitation.

He rose abruptly and said simply, "I am sorry, Miss Stanhope, but I do not dance." He left them then, and Catherine stared after him, appalled.

"Did I offend him?" she wondered. "I know women are not supposed to ask, but I thought—he is Lucinda's friend and I thought he knew that I—"

"Don't worry about it. Come and dance with me instead." And Michael rose and offered his arm.

Once again, Catherine was swept into the magic of the dance, and once again she realized she was falling deeper and deeper in love with Michael Soames. It was a very foolish thing to do, but for this one night, she did not care if she was foolish. She was happy.

As she swirled about the floor, she caught sight of her father at the edge of the ballroom, watching her with a somewhat grim expression. He was engaged in desultory conversation with a man who seemed to be doing most of the talking. Catherine could not recall ever having seen him. She smiled at her father over Michael's shoulder and then lost sight of him as the movement of the dance took her across the floor.

When the dance ended, Catherine and Michael found themselves on the far side of the floor, surrounded by dancers neither of them knew. Catherine took Michael's arm, and they began to wend their way back to the table where the Blankenships had been seated. Almost as if he had appeared out of nowhere like an evil genie, a figure appeared before them.

"Why, Nurse Stanhope," a falsely genial voice proclaimed, "and your faithful swain, the good doctor."

Catherine struggled for a moment to put a name to the gentleman's face. It was a classic, upper-class English face—long, with a thin nose and eyes of a pale blue that seemed almost glacial. His thin lips wore a perpetual sneer, and he gave Catherine an insultingly long stare.

"Have we met?" she said, her voice as frosty as she could make it. How dared this man stare at her as if she were a joint of mutton in a butcher's window?

"Indeed, yes, Nurse Stanhope. At Raglan's headquarters

in the Crimea. I am St. John Featherstone," he added as
she still looked blank.

"You were one of Lord Raglan's aides?" she said.

"Yes, from the Heavy Brigade." His pride was evident.
He clearly expected Catherine to remember him.

Actually, she did remember him, and not very happily.
He had given her the same sort of insolent stare when she
and Michael had met him during their visit at Lord Raglan's headquarters in the Crimea.

*They had been taken to the forward camp where Lord Raglan,
the commander in chief of the British forces, made his headquarters,
as soon as they had landed at the little port of Balaklava. Lord
Raglan had greeted them and introduced them to his staff.*

*He was white haired and seemed a little frail. His face showed
the lines of age, which was not to be wondered at, as one of the
aides had remarked later when the general had left. Raglan had
been the Duke of Wellington's secretary and had been at the Iron
Duke's side at the battle of Waterloo forty years before, where he
had lost an arm. Catherine was regaled by tales of long past glory
as she sat in a large tent, sharing the officers' evening meal,
conscious always of Michael only three seats away.*

*Raglan's deficiencies as a general were already the subject of
rumors. As commander, he had issued the orders for the tragic
charge by the Light Brigade at the battle on the heights above
Balaklava. But most of the men present seemed to blame a Captain
Nolan, who had carried the order for the charge from General
Raglan to the commander of the cavalry, Lord Lucan. It appeared
that Nolan had told Lucan to order a charge to take the Russian
guns, when Raglan intended that the Light Brigade ensure the
British guns were not captured by the Russians.*

*When Catherine had asked what was to become of the man who
had made such a terrible blunder, one of the officers, St. John*

*Featherstone, had shrugged. "Dead," he replied. "He was in front
of the charge and was the first man down."*

*Michael had been incredulous. "He didn't know the difference
between Russian guns and British? The man must have been an
idiot. What was he doing on the general's staff?"*

*Featherstone had bristled. Whatever he might think, he did not
take kindly to criticism from an outsider. "Bruising rider, Nolan,"
he said, as if that excused such a monumental error. "Knees like
steel. Held him in the saddle till his horse was out of the way after
he'd been shot dead."*

*Michael was silent, but his sardonic smile told Catherine he
was not much more impressed with their acquaintance's intelligence than he was with Captain Nolan's. She knew from their
shipboard conversations that Michael detested waste, and to his
mind war was nothing but a colossal waste of lives and treasure.
Even a great general might not have commanded Michael's
respect—and Raglan was hardly that.*

But whatever General Raglan's deficiencies as a commander,
he was a gallant gentleman and was clearly delighted to have a
beautiful young woman from the highest echelons of society in
camp. He wanted Catherine to accompany him on his early morning rides in the area around Balaklava. He offered to point out
the sites of the various battles and was visibly disappointed when
she gently told him she was not there as a tourist but had been
sent by Miss Nightingale as part of the mission to study medical
conditions at the front.

"But my dear Miss Stanhope," he protested, "I cannot believe
you and Miss Nightingale have really undertaken to help these
brutes. The Duke, you know, would have said that the British
enlisted man is fit for nothing but to take a bullet. You would
not want to soften them with kindness, I am sure. Then they
would be fit for nothing."

Catherine had to bite the inside of her cheek for a moment to
keep from uttering her instinctive protest. It would do her mission

no good at all to antagonize the commander in chief, so she forced herself to smile and speak softly. "But, sir, surely it is simple economy to save a trained soldier so he may fight again another day."

Lord Raglan seemed to consider the idea for a moment. Catherine thought he might actually be entertaining a new idea. Then he shook his head and smiled at her. "Oh, my dear Miss Stanhope, you are jesting with me. How you would have amused the Duke. He did love a pretty face, particularly when it was allied with a pretty wit." He bowed to Catherine, who ignored Michael's derisive snort.

Now they had met again in a London ballroom, and the lieutenant had clearly not altered his view of her. He addressed her as "Nurse Stanhope" and it was plain he meant "nurse" as a synonym for "slut" or "doxy."

"You have given up your . . . profession," the lieutenant said, his voice heavy with innuendo. "Here in London you have found other . . . diversions."

Catherine could feel Michael stiffen at her side. "We have had words about your attitude toward Miss Stanhope, Featherstone. She is a healer. She would even attempt to save your worthless life, should the occasion ever arise."

Featherstone raised his hands in mock surrender. "Oh, please, Doctor. I have nothing but the highest esteem for Miss Stanhope and the others of Miss Nightingale's intrepid little band. I must admit I find all the official blather about her a bit overdone. But if I seemed just a bit dazzled by the sight of a nurse dressed for her night off duty, well, you must forgive me." He bowed to Catherine.

She inclined her head in a cool little nod worthy of Queen Victoria herself. "I accept your assurance that you meant no insult either to me or the profession I am honored to belong to."

"Oh, of course, Miss Stanhope. Or may I call you Catherine, now that we are certain to become such good friends?" His smile was all salacious glee.

Catherine stiffened. For a virtual stranger to call an unmarried woman by her given name was unheard of. It implied that, for whatever reason, she was not considered marriageable—or even quite respectable. "No, sir, you may not. In fact, I would be much obliged if you would call me nothing at all. Ever. I have no wish for your acquaintance, sir."

She turned and would have walked off, but Michael was leaning close to Featherstone and she could hear his menacing whisper. "Be very careful what you say, Lieutenant. This house—indeed, all of London—is full of Miss Stanhope's friends."

"Oh, of course, my dear fellow. Discretion is my watchword." And with a little bow and a slight hesitation in his turn, Featherstone walked away.

"What a horrid man!" Catherine said. "I will never get used to people's attitudes towards nurses. It is appallingly ignorant and in the lieutenant's case—"

"In the lieutenant's case, he was hoping to lure you into his bed," Michael said bluntly.

Catherine could feel herself blush. Of course she knew about men and women. One could hardly train as a nurse without having learned a certain amount of practical anatomy. But to hear Michael refer to it was a shock. A delicious, forbidden shock!

Just then the familiar voice of the baronet cut through the sensual tension that Michael's words had conjured in Catherine's mind. "Catherine, my dear, I managed to get away from Parliament at last." He came forward and kissed his daughter on her cheek. "Soames," he said to Michael, his tone dismissive. "Tell me, Catherine, was that St. John Featherstone I just saw walking away? Did you know him in the Crimea? Dashed popular fellow, though I'm damned if I know why. Doesn't have a penny to bless himself with."

"I met him in the Crimea, yes," Catherine said. "He was one of Lord Raglan's aides. I met him at headquarters above Balaklava."

"Yes, yes, I thought as much." The baronet pulled on his long, curling mustache. He was clearly uncomfortable talking about Catherine's work. "At any rate, that is neither here nor there. I wish to present someone to you." He stepped aside, and the tall, burly man he had been speaking with earlier bowed over Catherine's hand. "Allow me to present Sir Ronald Bolton, Catherine, my dear. Sir Ronald, this is my daughter, Catherine Stanhope."

"Miss Stanhope." The man bowed respectfully over Catherine's hand, and his voice had a pleasant, deferential tone that was soothing after St. John Featherstone's encroaching manner. "Your servant."

Yes, he seemed perfectly polite and unexceptionable. So why did Catherine feel as if a cold wind had blown over her soul when she looked into his eyes?

Chapter Twelve

Catherine sat in the carriage with her father and Betsy on the drive home from the Blankenships and stared out the window with unseeing eyes. She did not want the evening to end.

As they drove through the dark London streets, she relived it moment by moment. It had been magical. With Michael she would not have a great many evenings of waltzing and champagne. Medicine came first for them both. But that would make the rare occasions when they could enjoy a frivolous evening with friends that much more precious.

"What did you think of Sir Ronald?" her father asked.

"Hmm?" Catherine did not want to think about Sir Ronald. The tone of her father's voice was the one he used when he had introduced her to some young man he wanted her to favor.

"Sir Ronald. He is newly arrived from the country. Somewhere in the north, I believe. Not very well known, but he has won a safe seat in the House, so the party favors him. He has all the right opinions. A good, sound man." She could feel her father's eyes on her.

With a sigh, Catherine gave up her reverie. "What do you wish me to think of him, Papa? I said scarcely two sentences to the man."

"He was very taken with you," the baronet replied. "Asked to be introduced. Never been married," he added.

"Really?" Catherine's eyebrows rose. What was her father up to? As far as he knew, she was engaged to Julian. Why was he introducing her to some supposedly eligible gentleman from the north? She was not sure she really wanted the answer to that question, and she could not ask with Betsy sitting beside her.

When they arrived home, Catherine was about to follow Betsy upstairs when her father stopped her. "Come into my study for a moment, Catherine."

Surprised, Catherine paused, her hand still on the banister. "Is it important, Papa? I must arise early tomorrow." It was the first time she had alluded to the fact she worked at St. Luke's.

Her father grimaced as he remembered why she had to arise early. "It will take only a few minutes. The House will be sitting late all this week, and I don't know when I will have a chance to talk to you."

With a sense of resignation, Catherine preceded her father into his study. She seated herself in the low chair before the fire and folded her hands in her lap. "Yes, Papa?"

The baronet stared into the smoldering coal fire on the hearth. For a moment he said nothing. Then, without turning, he said, "I went to see Julian today."

"Oh. How is he? I have not seen him for a day or two."

She kept her voice neutral, though she was surprised. Her father did not like to visit the sick. Whenever Catherine had suffered from a childhood illness, he had always inquired after her and made sure she was well taken care of, but he could bring himself to visit her only on rare occasions.

"I had to see how ill he really was. The countess has canceled all her engagements, and the earl looks as if he has aged twenty years since the boy has been home." The baronet turned from the fire and went to the mahogany chest on which several crystal decanters and glasses were placed. He poured himself a generous brandy. "Would you like a brandy, Catherine?"

"No, thank you, Papa. How was Julian?" she repeated.

The baronet sat down in a leather-covered wing chair facing Catherine's chair. They had spent many hours seated just this way, Catherine thought, not always talking, sometimes just reading quietly. When it seemed as if all conversation turned to argument, they sometimes tacitly agreed to avoid talking. "I must say, despite what you told me, I was surprised to find him still in bed. Not even sitting up. He was always such an active lad. I could not believe he would still be malingering. Well, I talked to him, Catherine. Told him he had to pull himself together. For you, for his parents. Just get out of bed and bite the bullet, I said. If you are in pain, we can get the doctor to do something for you."

Catherine sighed. In her experience, exhortations to be a man and bite the bullet rarely had a beneficial effect on a patient. "And what did he say?"

"Nothing. Not a dam—dashed word could I get out of him. He just lay there and let me natter on." The baronet leaned forward, a worried frown creasing his brow. "I told him again he was being unfair to you, lying around like an invalid, instead of getting up and getting married. 'People will think you've jilted my girl,' I said. I wasn't serious, you know. Just trying to get a response out of him. And do you know what he said?"

Catherine thought she probably did. "That we were no longer engaged and that I could do whatever I wished?"

Her father stared at her. "You *knew* he considered your engagement at an end?"

"He told me that, yes." Catherine was not prepared to tell her father that her engagement had been a fraud from the beginning. "But I think it was just to keep me from coming around too often. I am not sure he truly feels that—"

"No, it won't do." The baronet got up and poured himself another brandy. "I won't have that young coward making a laughing stock out of my daughter! People will talk—probably already are talking. It simply will not do."

"But, Papa—"

"I know you have always cared for Julian, but this time I am not going to allow you to wait on his convenience. I told him that as far as I was concerned, if he did not get up out of bed and at least take you for a carriage ride, be seen with you somewhere, that I would send a notice to the *Times* that the engagement is at an end." The baronet nodded his head decisively. "Thought you should know what I have decided."

Catherine rose, her sapphire satin skirt belling out around her. "Papa, do you not think you should consult me before you make these arrangements? First you insist I become engaged to Julian and now you decide that the engagement must end. Am I never to have anything to say in this matter?"

The baronet's face turned red and he shrugged his shoulders in a gesture Catherine recognized. He was embarrassed and a little guilty. He knew he had acted precipitously, and in his own maladroit, prideful way he was asking for her approval of what he had done.

"I do not know what to say," she said, moving about the room as she thought aloud. "I am afraid that even though he insists he does not wish to marry me—which I believe, by the way—Julian still needs me. And now I am not sure the countess will welcome me. She will see this as a repudiation of her son. I do not think you should have done this, Papa. Not at this time. I will go tomorrow to see how the countess feels."

Catherine went over to her father and kissed his cheek. "You really should let me decide my own future, Papa."

"Nonsense. You know nothing of men or of money. It is my duty and my right to decide for you what is best."

Catherine smothered a yawn. Hopeless to discuss this further now. A battle for another time. "Good night, Papa."

Could he possibly believe all that nonsense? After nursing soldiers in an Army hospital in Turkey, could he truly think his daughter could not look after herself, knew nothing of men? He wanted to believe it, Catherine decided as she mounted the stairs to her room, and therefore he did.

Betsy helped her off with her dress and underthings and then, in her long white nightgown and matching robe, Catherine sat at her dressing table while the maid brushed her hair. The reason for introducing her to Sir Ronald was now explained. Papa was on the hunt again for another prospective husband for his difficult spinster daughter.

For a while, when he had been so hurt because she had not told him of her work at St. Luke's, Catherine had thought her father at last understood and accepted her as she was. But old habits die hard, and he wanted to see his only child safely married and at home with a husband and, if all went well, several children gathered round her knee.

Then she would be safe. Then and only then he would consider his job done. When he could turn her and her affairs over to another man, he would feel he could relax and stop worrying about her.

Catherine slipped into bed, aware she would have to tell her father that even if she were to consider marriage, it would never be to Sir Ronald Bolton. There was only one man she could marry.

As Catherine slid into sleep, she dreamed of waltzing in his arms.

The next afternoon after leaving the hospital, Catherine stopped at Eversleigh House. The countess greeted Catherine with an air of quiet reproach. "Did you send your father to scold and harass Julian?" she asked as they seated themselves over the tea table in her little French reception room. "Surely you could have spared him that."

"No, countess, I did not. That is why I came today, to assure you that nothing my father said and nothing Julian said—to me or to him—will change anything." Leaning across the little fruitwood tea table, Catherine took one of the countess's hands in both of hers. It was cold, and Catherine chafed it gently. "I will always care for Julian, always be near when he needs me."

The countess withdrew her hand and looked at Catherine in surprise. "My dear, what has happened to your hands? They used to be so lovely, and now—" She caught Catherine's hands in hers and turned them over, examining them. "You have been nursing again, have you not?" The countess shook her head. "You have not given it up, have you? You are working as a nurse here, in London?"

Catherine nodded and waited for the usual condemnation. Instead, the countess leaned forward and kissed her cheek. "You have always had that dream, have you not, my dear?"

"Yes, always, ma'am."

"And where does my Julian fit into this dream, Catherine?" The countess studied her guest gravely. "I do not believe he does, or that he can. Julian needs someone for whom he is the sun and the stars. I sometimes think he needs a woman he can rescue in some way. He has a bit of the knight errant in him." She smiled, a charming, rueful smile. "I do not think you have ever needed rescue, have you, my dear?"

Catherine thought of the times at Scutari that she had felt as if she could not go on, had been foolish to think she would ever be a nurse, when Michael's presence had steadied her, his faith in her had sustained her. "No rescue Julian can provide, at any rate. And he knows that. Our feelings for each other are those of a brother and sister."

She took a deep breath and decided to make a clean breast of their deception. "We have always known that. And we have also known that my father in particular strongly wished our feelings to be warmer than that. So when we both wanted to go to the Crimea, we agreed to pretend to be engaged. That way, my father would let me go with Miss Nightingale."

"I confess, Catherine, I had wondered. I thought you did not love Julian in a way that would lead to marriage, but I hoped perhaps I was wrong. I would so love to have you for a daughter." She smiled again, that charming, rueful smile that accepted the vagaries of the world with amusement and resignation.

"And I could have no kinder mama-in-law than you, ma'am. It would almost be worth marrying Julian to gain you." Catherine smiled. She was telling no more than the truth.

But the countess shook her head. "No, it will not do. But you will have my affection, Catherine, just as you always have." She sighed and took a small sip of the tea that had sat untouched in her cup. "But I must ask a favor of you, as a friend. Please do not desert Julian now. If you and Dr. Soames fail him, I do not know what will become of him. And I ask that you think of whatever you can that will help him. My poor boy is so sunk in despair. He cries out at night in his sleep—great, wrenching cries as if his heart is going to burst with pain. If you can think of anything—or anyone—that can help him, please tell me. We will do anything. Any amount of money or time or effort— nothing is too much. Please."

"I will try, countess. And I will ask at the hospital as well. Someone else may have an idea that will help."

The countess sighed. "I suppose I will have to be content with that. And I do thank you for being honest about your betrothal. I can understand why you did not tell your father of your tiny fraud. It has kept him from trotting out any more candidates for your hand, has it not?"

Catherine smiled. "I confess, I was enjoying the sensation of not having Papa try to find someone who would marry his odd daughter."

"His beautiful, gifted daughter!" the countess corrected her.

"I fear Papa does not see me in that light. Or perhaps he just realizes that the world does not. Never mind," Catherine said, stifling a weary sigh and stiffening her backbone once again. "Soon I will be old enough to be considered eccentric and Papa will stop looking at every man he meets as a candidate for my hand."

"He will never give up, my dear," said the countess, judiciously studying the macaroons on the tea tray. "When you turn ninety he will simply limit himself to men who have white hair and palsied limbs."

Catherine laughed, relieved that Julian's mother did not blame her for failing to love her adored son. Catherine rose regretfully to her feet. She would love to sit in the countess's lovely room, sipping tea and talking. But her father would be at home for dinner, and if Catherine was to fulfill her part of their bargain, she had to be there, dressed elegantly and ready to converse on a variety of light, unimportant topics.

When she descended the staircase an hour and a half later, she was not as tired as she had anticipated. The bath Betsy had waiting for her, the brass cans of water warming on the hearth, had revived her, and she found changing into a pretty dress was good for her spirits. Perhaps now that her father and the countess knew and apparently approved of her continued work she felt able to express that feminine side she had ruthlessly suppressed for so long. She could picture having dinner with Michael, looking at him across the table, candlelight glinting on the silverware and—

"My dear, how lovely you look. And see here—I have brought a dinner guest home with me." The baronet gestured to a figure standing behind him. Catherine recognized Sir Ronald Bolton and her heart sank. She wondered why her father was making such a point of throwing her together with this man he had just met.

"Sir Ronald." Her innate social sense came to her rescue. Not for anything would she be less than gracious to a guest in her home. "I am happy to see you again."

Sir Ronald was everything that was correct. His evening clothes were perfectly fitted and made of the finest materials. His conversation was pleasant, and he voiced all the opinions that would find favor with her father. In fact, Catherine had almost decided his very conventionality was the reason she did not care for him very much. He was a bit of a bore.

"Yes, I agree, Sir Everett," he said halfway through what seemed to Catherine a very long dinner. "Disraeli may yet prevail and stop free trade. He is a powerful orator, and the old idea of the landed gentry and aristocracy as guardians of English civilization is powerful as well. If the reformers continue as they have, who knows what will be next—universal manhood suffrage?" Sir Ronald laughed at the absurd thought. He turned to Catherine. "I hope we are not boring you with all this talk of politics, Miss Stanhope. Tell me, have you been to the theater often since you have returned from your trip? I would very much like to take you and your father some evening, if you think you might enjoy it."

"We would both enjoy it immensely," replied Sir Everett before Catherine could politely decline. "Name the day and we will be ready, won't we, Catherine? You have missed many diversions since you returned." He beamed at his daughter, who was strongly tempted to decline the invitation and leave her father to listen to Sir Ronald prose on about trade laws during the intermission.

But her father looked so pleased, as if he was eagerly anticipating an evening with her, that Catherine did not have the heart to beg off and murmured some polite acceptance, making it as tepid as she could consistent with good manners.

After Sir Ronald had taken his leave, Catherine sank down into the low chair in her father's study and said, "Papa, I must warn you that if you hope to make Sir Ronald Bolton my husband, you are doomed to disappointment."

"But, my dear, he is not very old, is possessed of a fair fortune, and seems to admire you prodigiously."

"I do not return his regard." She looked sternly at her father. When it came to prospective sons-in-law, Catherine felt she had to take a strong line from the outset. Otherwise, her father would be negotiating marriage settlements while she was still dancing her first waltz with the lucky fellow.

"But, my dear, what fault can you possibly find with him?" The baronet looked genuinely puzzled, and Catherine could only wonder at the vagaries of the male mind.

"He is the most boring man I have ever met." She crossed her arms across her chest, all but daring her father to contradict her. "I would fall asleep over the soup every night."

"I am sure he will grow more interesting in time."

"So you admit he's boring now." She would not give up the point. "Which makes me ask, why have you decided I need a husband and that this one will do?"

"I met St. John Featherstone today." Her father paused as if waiting for some telltale reaction of hers. She merely looked inquiringly at him. "He said the story was all over London that you were sent home from Turkey by Miss Nightingale not because you were ill or could help with the presentation of her written testimony to the Sanitary Commission."

The baronet stared at his daughter in sorrow. He bowed his head and spoke in a heavy voice. "He said he felt it his duty to tell me you were caught kissing not one man but . . . but two in the hospital there and that Miss Nightingale dismissed you for light morals." He looked stricken, as if the world had fallen on his head. "I will not ask you about the truth of these stories. I am going to assume that there is an explanation though I do not ask you for it. It is important for your reputation, however, that you marry, and marry as soon as possible. Featherstone may be a light-minded gossip, but he is received everywhere. That story will be told over every tea table with many embellishments, you can be sure of that."

Catherine was stunned. She had not thought about Featherstone since she and Michael had run into him. She knew he did not like her—indeed, he regarded her as a veritable slut—but she had never considered he would ruin her reputation among her father's friends. For herself, she was furious because the story, while true on its face, was wrong in the interpretation it put on things.

"Well, if he is ruining me in polite society, I shall simply have to marry Dr. Soames and live in poverty doing good works at St. Luke's. Or perhaps in Scotland." She pretended to be speaking in jest so she could gauge her father's reaction. In truth, she did not need to think about life with Michael. She would take him on any terms.

"Marry Soames? My God, Catherine, you cannot be serious!" The baronet's voice and shocked expression made it very clear what he thought of that suggestion. "A middle-class professional man! From Scotland! Such a mésalliance would be the end of our social life and perhaps even of any influence I may have in the House. Do not ever say that, even in jest."

Catherine was horrified. She had known her father would not instantly approve of her marrying Michael, but she had been sure he would judge the marriage on its merits—and that, of course, meant he would approve it eventually.

"But—but—Papa," was all her surprised brain could manage to think. "Did you bring Sir Ronald because he would salvage my life—or yours?"

"Nonsense, my dear girl. I just thought someone so obviously reputable and even a little stuffy would be the perfect antidote to a story like this."

"The Blankenships like and admire Michael. He

attended their party the other night." She had not meant to bring this up. She did not want to plead Michael's case. For all she knew, he would never ask her to marry him. After all, he basically agreed with her father. "Jeffrey Bancroft is a friend of his. They do not regard him as—as a social outcast."

"Because they are very close to being social outcasts themselves. For Heaven's sake, Catherine, have your wits gone begging?" She could see her father was beginning to grow angry at her blindness where the nuances of social behavior were concerned. "We have held our lands since the days of Henry VIII, and the title, though modest, is an old one. Jeffrey Bancroft and Henry Blankenship are wealthy, no doubt. They could probably buy and sell me many times over. But they have come from nowhere, while Sir Ronald inherited a large estate in the north somewhere and moves in the highest circles. He is regarded as a coming man in the party and may even have a cabinet post one day."

Catherine hardly knew where to begin. "I think you are not looking around you carefully enough, Papa. The Blankenships and Mr. Bancroft are accepted everywhere. They know how to manufacture goods and how to ship them across the world. I could see in Turkey how much the Army depended on that and could have used their services. I think you will find some father is going to consider himself very fortunate to acquire Jeffrey Bancroft or David Blankenship for a son-in-law. They are every bit as well bred as Julian or Ronald Bolton—and rich, to boot. Good night, Papa."

She kissed him on his cheek, which was still ruddy from anger. "I still say Sir Ronald is an enormous bore." She smiled at him as she opened the door. "I would far rather spend my evenings with you."

Chapter Thirteen

"You look as if you have not slept in a week. There were times even at Scutari when you did not look this tired. What have you been doing?"

Startled, Catherine turned and saw Michael approach her as she walked down a long corridor at St. Luke's on her way to one of the wards. Michael's gruff words were belied by the look of warm concern in his eyes.

"If those circles do not go away soon I shall order you a tonic."

Catherine laughed a little, feeling better by the minute. "No, I do not need a tonic. I am just a bit overtired."

"Davy Blankenship said he saw you at the theater a few nights past with some political gentleman, a friend of your father's." It was a question, though not phrased as such.

Catherine seized on the opportunity not to talk of Sir Ronald Bolton. "You have seen Davy? How is he faring?"

"He is doing very well, walking better each day." Michael

returned like a compass to the subject of her health. "He said you looked tired, and I can see he is right."

Catherine pushed a wayward tendril of soft blond hair back from her forehead. "Yes, I confess I am. I promised my father I would try to keep up my social responsibilities to him while working here, and it is more difficult that I imagined. He has some affair that I simply must attend almost every evening."

"And do you enjoy them?" Michael said as he fell into step with her.

"I think I would enjoy some of them if I were not so fatigued. But others are just tedious—dinners with political friends of his. I used to go to all these entertainments, and they chafed me terribly because I thought they were a waste of my life. It was all I did, run the household and assist my father. But now it is different. I have work that I love, so these affairs are merely recreation, and for me they are not particularly entertaining."

Michael thought for a moment as they walked. "So most of these dinners and parties are really connected to your father's work. For him it is part of his job. Perhaps you could make it part of yours."

Catherine stopped at the door to the men's ward. "You mean ask them for money?"

"Not just that, though God knows Miss Nightingale could always use more. The Army has plenty but won't spend it for the men, and St. Luke's is still run on a penny and a prayer. You could arouse interest in hospitals, in medical care, in the Army. These friends of your father's are politicians, after all, and I know there is great concern about the conditions in the Crimea. It is why I have returned, to testify and try to talk to some of them privately, the way Miss Nightingale would do if she were here." Michael touched her hand briefly and Catherine could feel the warmth of that touch spread all through her. "I cannot do that, because, as I told Miss Nightingale when she insisted I go, I do not have any acquaintances in those circles. But you do."

Catherine thought for a moment. "I am not sure they would listen to me. But they would certainly listen to you." She looked up at him with new resolution. "I will see to it you are invited to the next reception where members of the government will be present." She saw refusal in his eyes. Before he could speak, she said, "It would help the men, Michael."

"You know just what to say to convince me. Very well. I will attend if you can somehow procure an invitation for me." He smiled a little, and Catherine could tell he thought she would fail and he would not have to go.

Later that day, Catherine was inspecting the hospital laundry to see what could be done to improve it. It was a vast, dank underground room with a huge copper boiler and a number of cast iron tubs. Mary Ann was scrubbing at one tub, up to her elbows in soapsuds.

"What would you say to the idea of whitewashing this room and installing more gas lamps?" Catherine said after greeting the housekeeper.

"I would say ask Dr. Dinsmore and see if he thinks he can spare the money from all the other projects he has." Mary Ann smiled. "He is like a child at Christmas. Mr. Blankenship told him the other day he would pay to outfit a new operating room, and the little man was speechless!" She laughed and bent over her scrubbing again.

"You see Mr. Blankenship as well? Dr. Soames was saying he visited a day or so ago." Why did she feel a vague pang of envy? Because she would far rather be taking tea and talking with her friends at the Blankenships' than enduring another boring evening of politics with her father and the ever-present Sir Ronald.

"Yes, he asked Dr. Soames and me to stop by at teatime on Sundays. Davy cannot get around well even yet, so his father has people in for tea from time to time. He says he cannot entertain in the evening because he lacks a wife." Mary Ann finished scrubbing the nightshirt in her tub and gave it an expert twist to wring out the water. "He has a sister who comes when his daughters are home, but she hates London and won't live here. So he limits himself to teas and the occasional enormous ball he can host alone."

Without thinking, Catherine took the nightshirt from her and put it in the next tub for rinsing. "It sounds like a nice afternoon," she said, unaware of how wistful she sounded.

"It was. Dr. Dinsmore came by with his wife, as well."

"Quite a medical convention. I wonder Davy wasn't bored." Catherine wrung out the shirt and put it in the basket with the wash to be taken to the drying yard.

"If he was, he did not show it. He is a nice lad, with nothing but gratitude for those who helped him save his leg." Mary Ann gave Catherine a shrewd, sideways glance. "I am sure they would love to see you on Sunday—or any time."

Catherine shook her head. She could not simply arrive on the Blankenships' doorstep without an invitation. Though she had broken society's rules in large ways, when it came to the small social niceties, Catherine tried to conform, to spare her father any more social anxiety on her account.

"You must have an invitation?" Mary Ann did not seem surprised. She had told Catherine she had once worked in a large country estate and often served as a lady's maid to officers' wives to earn money when she traveled with the regiment. Very little about upper-class social rules surprised her.

Catherine nodded. "Let me help you with this basket. It looks heavy."

"Now, Miss Stanhope, I can carry this as easy as can be. Besides, Davy said you was looking a bit fatigued, and I think he is right." Mary Ann hoisted the heavy basket with ease and together they left the laundry room.

"Does everyone take stock of my looks?" Catherine said, half exasperated.

"No, miss," Mary Ann said, with a touch of starch in her tone. "Only those as cares about you."

Catherine followed Mary Ann out to the enclosed garden at the back of the hospital where clotheslines had been set up at Mary Ann's instigation. No use trying to dry anything in the damp air of the laundry room. At least outside, the washing had a chance of getting dry before spring.

"You are right, Mary Ann. I am just overtired from too many late nights and it makes me a bit hasty-tempered. Forgive me." Catherine began to hang the heavy linen shirts and sheets in neat rows alongside the ones Mary Ann was hanging.

Mary Ann's smile broke out, making her look like the young country lass she must have been not so very long ago. Catherine was always strangely comforted in her presence. Mary Ann had taken everything life had handed to her and was still cheerful and grateful for friends and an opportunity to earn her bread.

"You take on a heavy load," Mary Ann said. "All of your hospital work, plus the parties and dinners. You must feel as if you lead two different lives and nobody to care about the both of them." Mary Ann patted her hand and reached for another sheet.

"Thank you." Catherine felt as if a burden had been lifted from her shoulders. Mary Ann understood. "I must see to the wards now."

That night, at a large reception, Catherine and Michael found themselves in the midst of a circle of politicians. Catherine had procured an invitation by telling her hostess, a woman avid to become a noted political hostess, that a doctor from the Crimea would attend if she but asked him. Within the hour, a card of invitation was delivered to the hospital.

Now questions flew thick and fast, and the two beleaguered medical workers tried to answer them as best they could. As the circle grew ever larger, with more and more members of parliament and cabinet ministers trying to get information, Michael began to feel as if he was the star attraction at a bear baiting.

Some members were angry at the disclosures of inefficiency and waste in the quartermaster corps. They thought it was a disgrace for Michael and Catherine to speak of such things—it was bad for morale in the service and gave ordinary people the wrong idea about the army.

Others were avid for details of Florence Nightingale's life and work. What did she look like? Did she carry a lamp everywhere? Was her touch magic? Was she a saint?

"No, no, not a saint," Michael said. "She has done more good than twenty saints. If it were not for her, there would have been a complete breakdown of supplies and food. Chaos would have resulted."

"And to what do you attribute this breakdown, doctor?" It was the smooth baritone rumble of the man Catherine had introduced as Sir Ronald Bolton. Michael had not liked the man, perhaps because he had laid a proprietary hand on Catherine's arm and had thanked her for dinner at the Stanhopes'. Warning him off, Michael thought. Laying claim. No matter what Sir Ronald thought, neither of them had a claim on Catherine. But Michael knew it. So now he smiled blandly and answered.

"The Army's archaic system of supply is at fault. And the obstructionist tactics of Dr. John Hall." Michael's voice was clear and strong. Catherine tugged on his sleeve. He was about to be cross-questioned mercilessly by Hall's allies—of whom there were many. Miss Nightingale had said before he left that Hall was a consummate politician. He had many ways of making Michael's life uncomfortable.

"I believe Dr. Hall has been knighted," Sir Ronald said with a chilly smile. "He is now *Sir* John Hall."

Michael inclined his head. "I stand corrected. The difficulties are attributable to the Army's archaic system of supply and the obstructionist tactics of *Sir* John Hall, M.D."

"Are you not perhaps overstating your case, Doctor?" The new voice was smooth, but the face was one of startling plainness. Almost, Michael thought, like that of the fairy-tale frog.

"No." He had not told them the half of it, and he was not going to recant a single word.

The homely little man's face split into a smile. "I do like a man who says exactly what he thinks."

"As do I, sir." Michael smiled and the tension in the air dissipated. As the crowd began to disperse, Michael said, "I do not believe we have met. I am Michael Soames."

The little man bowed. "And I am Benjamin Disraeli. Your servant, Doctor."

There was a quality of humor and intelligence beyond the ordinary in Mr. Disraeli that attracted Michael. Before long, they were deep in conversation.

Unfortunately, that left Catherine standing alone just as

Sir Ronald came up to her, a tight smile on his face. "Your doctor friend is certainly outspoken, Miss Stanhope. I fear Sir John's friends may take this amiss and make trouble for your friend."

The repetition of the phrase "your friend," coupled with Sir Ronald's cold little smile, made Catherine stare at the man her father had held out as such a paragon. Sir Ronald was angry.

"Dr. Soames tells the truth as he sees it," Catherine said, two bright spots of color burning in her cheeks. If Michael could be fearless, so could she. "At Scutari I saw a great many similar incidents of waste and of callous indifference to the suffering of the men. Too many to believe they are accidental, or that Dr. Hall—excuse me, Sir John Hall—does not know of them." She turned and her skirts swirled as she walked proudly away, leaving Sir Ronald standing alone.

"What have you said to him, Catherine?" The baronet seized her arm and walked with her around the room until they stood in a relatively secluded corner. "He looks furious."

"I told the truth, father. Apparently, that is a grave error in these times."

"Dr. Soames started it. And that busybody Disraeli fanned the flames! That man is a menace to the country, not just his own party. He will never be prime minister if I can help it." Sir Everett glared at her. "And I expected you to smooth the rough edges and pour oil on troubled waters. Instead, you are Joan of Arc, making enemies and telling truths with no thought of the consequences."

Catherine beamed. "Joan of Arc, Papa? Am I really? I am most sincerely flattered."

"You shouldn't be. Think for a moment of what happened to her!"

* * *

That Sunday afternoon, Catherine was putting on her gloves in the hall while she waited for Betsy. She had been invited to the Blankenships for tea. Since she was not to be accompanied by an older friend or relation, she took her maid. Her father had insisted that she live up to her role as a baronet's daughter and that meant no unaccompanied drives, except those early morning trips to St. Luke's.

In what she thought of as her "real life," she cared for patients, planned the nurses' time, and oversaw all the practical workings of the hospital in conjunction with Dr. Dinsmore and Mary Ann. In this, her "other life," she had to behave like a delicate flower and not be left alone for a moment, lest she go astray.

Her father came out of his study and consulted his pocket watch. "Where are you going, Catherine? I have no engagements and had hoped to have a quiet evening alone with you."

"That is very unlike you, Papa. Recently you are always going somewhere, doing something." Catherine smiled. "I am going to the Blankenships for tea."

Something must have revealed to the baronet how much she was looking forward to the outing, for he frowned and said, "I do not know that I can approve of your visiting them, Catherine. They are two single men, after all. It would be most improper." He spied Betsy hurrying downstairs. "I do not think your maid is enough of a chaperone for a bachelor establishment."

She was not going to give up tea with the Blankenships. "Why do you not come with me, Papa? You always like meeting new people, and I am sure you will be welcome.

Mr. Blankenship asked me if I thought you might enjoy it, but I assumed you would be otherwise occupied."

The baronet frowned. She could see he was torn. He did not want to go and yet he had just said he had no engagement for the evening. It would be churlish to deny Catherine her party just because the hosts were not of his choosing. Unlike a good many men of his acquaintance, the baronet prided himself that he did not say no to his daughter without a good reason.

He did not know the Blankenships well, though he had met them. Usually, he avoided closer acquaintance with the *nouveaux riches*, for they had a tendency to hang on anyone with a title. Still, once he had given them a chance and disliked them, as he surely would, he could deny her their company much more easily.

"Very well, my dear. If you will wait a few minutes, I will be happy to accompany you." He turned and hurried up the staircase to change his brocaded smoking jacket for the dark suit one wore for a formal call.

"I will not be needing you after all, Betsy," Catherine said. "You may as well spend the evening with Jemmy. How is he doing, by the way?"

"He has almost enough money to get home to his mother, miss," Betsy said, her eyes downcast.

"That is good news indeed!" Catherine said, thinking to make Betsy smile. The girl had been looking a bit glum recently, but Catherine had not had time to inquire as to the reasons. "Perhaps I can give him a little help and let him leave that much sooner."

Betsy threw her one anguished look and, picking up her skirts, fled to the back of the house. The baronet arrived just as Betsy ran through the green baize door to the servants' hall.

"What is the matter with your maid, my dear? Surely

you did not speak unkindly to her. I have never known you to do so."

"No. I think I know what the trouble is. Betsy may be leaving us before too long." Catherine sighed. She would have to arrange for Betsy to marry Jemmy, if that was what they both wanted. She could manage a small dowry out of her allowance. Every girl should have a dowry. But she would miss Betsy's devotion and cheerful presence every day.

"Shall we go, my dear?" The baronet offered Catherine his arm.

Tea at the Blankenships was not what the baronet expected. He had thought that Henry Blankenship wanted to make his way socially and was using Catherine to do so. Sir Everett was determined to extend no invitations to the newly minted millionaire.

Instead, he found himself treated very much as if he were not as important as his daughter. Catherine was welcomed for herself and because she had helped save David Blankenship's life. The Blankenship house was enormous, and the decorations tended toward velvet draperies and upholstered pieces in deep tones of crimson and cobalt. Although the colors and materials were formal, the sofas and chairs were wonderfully comfortable. The tea service, which Catherine had been asked to preside over as the honored guest, was heavy Georgian silver, but the tea was strong, black Indian tea, not the pale Chinese version preferred by the socially knowledgeable at least in the afternoon.

As for the guests, there were several fashionably dressed young ladies in the room along with their parents. None, the baronet was surprised to see, were known to him. There were no daughters of impoverished peers. All the young ladies, though well dressed and well brought up, were of

the wealthy merchant class. Henry Blankenship took pains
to arrange for his son to spend time with each one of
them. It could not be more obvious, the baronet thought
to himself as he made a hearty meal of savory sandwiches
and good strong tea. Henry wanted his son to marry one
of these rich industrialists' daughters in a few years, and
David was chafing at his parent's interference.

"Makes a wonderful tea, doesn't she?" Henry Blankenship said as he sat down in a comfortable chair next
to the one Sir Everett sat in.

"Yes, indeed. I don't know when I have enjoyed one
more." The baronet was surprised to find it true. The food
was much simpler than he was used to, but it was delicious.

"It's Mary Ann Evans who does it for me," Blankenship
said, just as if Sir Everett was supposed to know who that
was.

"Your daughter's friend," he continued. When Sir Everett still looked blank, he added, "They met in the Crimea
and Miss Stanhope helped Mary Ann get home and find
employment."

"Oh." Sir Everett was never comfortable talking about
Catherine's activities in the Crimea. "Well, I do not know
much about her nursing."

Mr. Blankenship smiled over Sir Everett's shoulder at
someone and waved whoever it was to come over. "Come,
you will meet her now. Mrs. Evans," he said with his beaming smile, "I want you to meet Miss Stanhope's father. Sir
Everett, Mrs. Mary Ann Evans."

If Mrs. Evans was nervous about meeting a baronet, Sir
Everett could not detect it. "Sir," she said, giving his hand
an unexpectedly firm handshake, "I have never met anyone I admire more than your daughter. She is as brave as
she is beautiful."

Sir Everett did not at first know what to say. He had

always found his daughter lovely and charming, and he loved her very much. But there was an entire part of her personality that had always puzzled him—indeed, he had been a little ashamed of it. Now someone was telling him the very part of Catherine's character he found so difficult was what made her remarkable. He did not quite know what to say.

Mr. Blankenship took pity on him. "You know, Sir Everett, I have had generals tell me my Davy is the bravest lad they know, that he did things in that godawful battle that were far beyond the call of duty. And it makes me proud to hear that, of course. But I have to tell you, I don't really recognize my Davy in that talk."

"Yes, I suppose it is difficult for parents to see their children as the world does." He could take a little comfort in that, he supposed. But still he wished he were in his home where his word was still law to Catherine. *In most things,* he amended.

Catherine came over to him, and beside her was the tall, craggy Scot, the doctor who had saved her from the attack by those ruffians. The one who had made friends with Disraeli at the reception. What was his name?

"Papa," Catherine said, "you remember Dr. Soames."

The baronet did not rise but he did speak as warmly as he could around a large bite of éclair. "Yes, of course. I am forever in your debt, Doctor."

"It is a pleasure to see you again, sir," Dr. Soames said. Having seen to the pleasantries, Catherine moved off to talk to one of the pretty young girls.

The baronet was surprised to realize the young doctor did not mean a word of what he said. He was almost bristling with dislike and, unless Sir Everett was very much mistaken, disapproval.

The baronet did not encounter disapproval very often,

and he found he did not like it. Ordinarily he would not have remarked on it, but he had been thrown off his stride by all the people here he would not usually encounter. He could read men easily after years in politics, but that did not lessen his sense of discomfort.

"Why do you disapprove of me, Doctor?" The words were out of his mouth before he was aware he was going to say them.

"I do not have the right to approve or disapprove of you, sir." Dr. Soames straightened. From his considerable height, he looked down on Sir Everett with a frown.

The cut and thrust of debate was something Sir Everett felt at ease with. "I agree," he said, taking a sip of his tea, "you do not. But that does not alter the fact that you do. I want to know why."

Dr. Soames placed his hands behind his back and thought for a moment. "Because you do not value your daughter's work, and thus you do not value her as you should."

He had expected to hear something similar, but it did not make it any more palatable. "I see. I do not value her work because it seems to me a very precarious and difficult existence for a woman. I think women are better served if they remain always under a man's protection. Catherine does not agree."

"Still, she lives at home, with you." Dr. Soames still gazed down at him with what Sir Everett saw as a judgmental frown on his face.

"Oh, do sit down, Doctor, and stop glowering down at me." The baronet picked up another éclair as they were passed and set it down on his plate.

"Catherine loves and respects you, sir. And I know you love her. But I think you must learn to respect her as well."

That was plain speaking and no mistake, but the baronet

did not take offense. Something in the doctor's tone, something so sure of the rightness of the judgments he made, caused the baronet to at least consider what he said. "You know my daughter very well."

"We have worked together here at St. Luke's and in Turkey. That is a bond that cannot be explained. David Blankenship shares it, as does Mrs. Evans."

"Are you in love with her, Doctor?" That was suddenly very clear to the baronet, but he needed to know if the doctor had admitted it to himself.

"With all due respect, sir, I do not think that is any of your business. I am aware Miss Stanhope is betrothed to another man."

"Ah." He liked the young doctor, despite his views of the medical establishment. But he did not think he would do for a son-in-law. Should he tell him of the obstacles in his way—the obstacles Catherine's father would place in his path if the need arose?

"I do not think of her in that way. So there is no need to discourage me." Dr. Soames stood once again, ramrod straight.

"Then we understand each other." The baronet extended his hand and, after a moment's hesitation, Michael took it.

"Yes, sir, *we* do, but that is not to say that Catherine sees it as we do." There was an ironic curl to the young doctor's mouth, and the baronet understood.

"She has always been extremely stubborn," the baronet said. "Always."

"I am not a bit surprised to hear it, sir." And Dr. Soames smiled.

"I am glad you two have had a chance to talk," Mr. Blankenship said as he came up to them.

"Yes, I think we understand each other perfectly," the

baronet said, on the whole not displeased with the afternoon's visit.

Michael said nothing but bid his host good afternoon and left, the baronet was pleased to see, without speaking to Catherine again.

"I wonder if either of you understands Miss Stanhope," their host mused as he looked at Michael's stiff retreating back. He smiled as David came up to him. "Davy, boy, have you said hello to Miss Melton as yet?"

David sighed. "Yes, Dad, I have said hello to everyone. But why did you invite her? She has not a single idea in her head. And she giggles."

"But her father is in business with me on a number of projects. I had to invite them when they learned you were home. Really, Davy, is it asking too much for you to be pleasant to the girl?"

"I *am* pleasant, but she wants to flirt with me!" David was clearly revolted.

The baronet was enjoying his host's discomfiture after his remark about understanding Catherine. "A little young to be thinking of matrimony, surely?" he said to Mr. Blankenship after Davy had strolled off to be polite to another young lady.

"Oh, I don't think of it!" Mr. Blankenship replied. When he saw the baronet's raised eyebrows, he had the grace to look a little guilty. "Well, you know, I want David to meet the kind of girls he should be considering in a few years' time. I don't mean to speak out of turn, Sir Everett, but a number of gentlemen with titles before their names but nothing in their bank accounts have been throwing their daughters in Davy's way. It won't do, it won't do at all. I would like my son to meet a girl and fix his interest with her, even though marriage cannot be thought of for some time."

"Hmm." The baronet confessed to himself that he was a little surprised. Surprised and pleased that Blankenship knew his place in the world and wanted his son to stay in that same place.

"I know, I know," Blankenship hastened to add, "Some of the peers I meet are as fine as any fellows I know. But too many of 'em have no sense at all about money. They think it beneath them to earn any, yet they spend it like drunken sailors. I'll not have Davy with a whole family of wastrels draining my purse. You'll pardon my plain speaking, sir, I know."

Sir Everett did not know whether he was insulted or amused. To have his snobbery turned on him was disconcerting, but he thought his daughter, for one, would think he deserved it. Perhaps he was not as knowledgeable about men as he thought he was. It was an unsettling notion.

"Papa, you are looking very thoughtful," said Catherine as she came up to his chair a few minutes later. A few minutes, the baronet noted, after Dr. Soames had left. "Would you mind if we left now? I fear I am a bit tired."

The baronet would not mind at all. He had been given much to think about.

Chapter Fourteen

Catherine took a day of rest the next morning on Dr. Dinsmore's orders. He had caught her yawning over a list of supplies to be purchased for the kitchens and ordered her to take the one day per week that she was entitled to—*now*. Too many late nights with her father and early mornings at St. Luke's had sapped her strength.

Reluctantly, she took a hackney home, Marston and John Coachman having already left her for the day. Once there, she found that a leisurely morning looked very inviting. She rang for Betsy and ordered a bath, relaxed in the hot water, and then dressed in one of her prettiest morning dresses of dark green crepe with a wide white lace collar and lace insets in the wide skirt.

The day stretched before her, ready to be filled with any sort of frivolous pleasure she could think of. There had been times at the hospital when she had thought she would give anything for a chance to sit down and read for an hour or two. She retreated to her father's study and picked out a copy of the newly released novel by Charles Dickens, a writer she had enjoyed. It had come out serially the year before, but she had missed it. The very title promised a more somber story than some of his earlier works. "*Bleak House*," she murmured. "Interesting title."

She tried to immerse herself in the story, but somehow problems with the hospital, Julian's difficulties, and most of all Michael and her father's horrified reaction to her joking suggestion of marriage all jostled for a place in her thoughts. She could not seem to settle down to anything.

Just as she was about to give up and call Betsy to go for a walk, Holden appeared at the door. "There is a young lady to see you, Miss Catherine. She is not known to me and she did not wish to leave her name. I don't know what you wish—"

"Catherine! I did not mean to startle your butler, but I wanted to surprise you!" The brilliant blue eyes and blue-black hair of her best friend came into view just after her voice had brought a smile to Catherine's face.

"Lucinda!" she cried, all her boredom forgotten. "Is the war over? Why did you not warn me you were coming back?"

"I didn't know myself I was coming until I was bundled aboard a transport ship bound for Malta. I had a fever and could not do anything but lie about and shiver, so they sent me home." Lucinda shrugged off her illness but Catherine could see she was thinner and her complexion had lost its strawberries and cream bloom. She seemed pale and drawn, but still sparkling with mischief and vitality.

"Let me look at you," Catherine commanded, leading her friend over to her father's desk, where a large lamp burned continuously.

Obediently, Lucinda sat down. "Do not fuss, I beg you,

Catherine. I have had enough fuss to last me a lifetime since Malta. I was on a ship with the wives and daughters of officers serving in the Crimea. When they learned I knew Miss Nightingale, had actually worked with her, they could not do enough for me.''

"You do not look ill, Lucy, but you do seem sadly out of frame. Would you like to stay here with me? I can't promise to be here much of the time, but you will be spared the Harrowing Harrowbys."

They laughed together. That had been Lucy's name for her annoying relations. "No, dear. I thank you, but the harrowing ones have actually improved. They realized while I was away that they cannot manage without me. Add to that, the newspapers have painted Miss Nightingale and the rest of us as heroines. So at least for the moment they are careful not to offend me." Lucy laughed a little at the vagaries of her relatives.

Catherine rang for tea and sat smiling at her friend. She was so happy to see her. In the rush of life in London, she had felt an emptiness, and now that Lucinda was back, Catherine remembered how much that friendship had meant to her.

They were opposites in many ways, Lucinda's irreverence and sharp tongue contrasting with Catherine's more measured temperament. But that only added to their friendship. It had been forged aboard the ship that took them to Turkey, and nothing that happened afterward had altered it.

Although both their families were of the highest echelons of society, they had not known each other before joining Miss Nightingale. Catherine's father moved in the political world, while the Harrowbys' circle comprised the wealthy, more frivolous elements of London society. Lucinda was an orphan and had been taken in by her aunt and uncle. Going with Miss Nightingale had appealed to her sense of adventure and a desire to help others. Though very different, she and Catherine shared a determination to make their own lives. Most of all, for Catherine, Lucinda was a friend with whom she had shared a profound experience.

"Tell me everything that happened after I left Scutari," Catherine said as Holden entered with the tea tray.

Lucinda reached for a buttered scone and said, "Well, things were not the same after you and Dr. Soames left. Miss Nightingale told me the quality of care went down by half with your departure."

"She said that?" Catherine was as thrilled as if she had received a medal from the Queen's hands. "I have always felt that I let her down, that she must despise me. Misbehaving like a schoolgirl. She must think—"

"I explained that Lieutenant Livingston was a childhood friend, and I think she understood about Dr. Soames. She said she knew it was difficult to keep your equilibrium when you work as we did, in the worst circumstances and with very little space or time to ourselves. It breeds emotional outbursts, she said." Lucinda looked at her friend over the rim of her teacup.

"I don't know if that makes me feel better or worse," Catherine said. "I—I don't think it was that, Lucy. It was more than that, but I do not know exactly what."

"Well, I think Miss N. understood that. And she did remark on your abilities as a nurse. I knew you would want to know that."

"Yes, yes, that takes a burden from my mind. Now tell me the rest of what went on after I left."

"Well, Rose and I looked after Lieutenant Livingston for you. And then Mr. Bancroft flitted off on some quest or other, without a word." Lucinda frowned, and for a

moment Catherine wondered if she did not care more for
the handsome Mr. Bancroft than she let on. Then Lucinda
tossed her glossy black curls and continued. "That left just
Miss Nightingale and her friends the Bracebridges and me
to run the entire enterprise. I was beginning to enjoy
myself—going into Constantinople to discuss business with
the ambassador and organizing the hospital store—when
I fell ill. And that was that. Miss N. unceremoniously packed
me off home and here I am."

"And though I am sorry you were sick, and it is too bad
to leave Miss Nightingale shorthanded, still I am so happy
to see you." Catherine's heart was lighter already. She had
a friend with whom to share her thoughts and feelings.
With a sigh of relief, she poured them both more tea and
began to tell Lucinda of her life in London.

"I am working at a charity hospital near the Marshalsea,"
she began.

"Your father consented to let you work, and in such an
area?" Lucinda's surprise was understandable. Catherine
had told her about the baronet's stubborn insistence on
a conventional life for his only daughter.

"Papa and I seem to be in a state of armed truce."
Catherine bit into a macaroon. "He has decided Julian
won't do for me." She realized that she now had a resource,
someone who could help her. "I am worried about Jules,
Lucy. Would you go and see him? He doesn't respond to
me at all, but when the doctor saw him, I thought he was
a little more cooperative. You saw him at Scutari. Could
you go to visit? Just now and then. I am at my wit's end to
think how to help him."

"Of course. But are you sure it is not because you don't
love him that he is so distressed and listless?"

"Oh, no. Julian has never thought of me that way. Whatever it is that he cannot rid himself of has something to

do with Balaklava, not me. Julian has never been in love in his life. But if you go to see him wearing that saucy little bonnet in that particular shade of blue, that may change!"

Lucinda laughed and promised she would visit Eversleigh House that very afternoon. "And I will look in on St. Luke's. Are you the only Crimea veteran to work there?"

"No." Catherine studied her teacup. "Mary Ann Evans, one of the Army widows, is there—and Michael Soames is also there, at least for the time being. He is here to testify before the Sanitary Commission, you know."

"Ah." Lucinda leaned back in her chair and studied her friend over the edge of her teacup. "So you and Dr. Soames are working together again."

"Yes, and it is wonderful, but very difficult. Michael still thinks he is not good enough for me, and unfortunately my father agrees with him."

"Oh, dear. Well, we will think of some way to convince Sir Everett that Dr. Michael Soames would be the paragon of sons-in-law." Lucinda got up and went around the tea table to kiss Catherine's cheek. "I have not yet decided how we will bring this about, but rest assured we shall."

Though she doubted her father would ever be reconciled to anything less than a socially stellar marriage for her, Catherine nevertheless was much cheered by Lucinda's visit.

Lucinda lived up to her promise and visited St. Luke's a few days later. "It is a great relief to be in a true hospital again and see some people lying in bed who really are sick, instead of suffering from some imaginary complaint." Lucinda's aunt was subject to frequent palpitations and other ailments no doctor had ever been able to diagnose, but which kept the entire Harrowby household dancing attendance on her. Lucinda had escaped to St. Luke's, as she told Catherine, before she dumped a pitcher of water over her aunt's head and precipitated a real crisis!

"Show me everything, and tell me all about your plans."

No one would ever take Lucinda for a nurse in her brilliant green wool walking suit trimmed with black soutache braid in a military scroll design on the sleeves and the skirt. She looked like the picture of a fashionable young lady as she greeted Dr. Dinsmore and Mary Ann Evans with a charming smile. But her questions revealed a depth of knowledge surprising in one so young and seemingly frivolous.

As they sat in the reception area, Catherine looked up, a sixth sense telling her when Michael was near. He greeted Lucinda with a smile. "So you have returned to us, Miss Harrowby. Mr. Bancroft will be surprised. He seemed to think you would remain at Scutari until the end—whenever that occurs."

The smile seemed to freeze on Lucinda's face. "Mr. Bancroft? You have seen Mr. Bancroft?"

"Yes, he comes here often. He has made great contributions to St. Luke's." Michael looked a little surprised at the change in Lucinda's expression. The next minute, however, she was smiling as charmingly as ever and finished her tour of the hospital without mentioning Jeffrey Bancroft's name.

Catherine had arranged to take Lucinda home in her carriage so the Harrowbys would not be inconvenienced for even a few hours. As they sat on the well-cushioned seats and were whisked across the city, Lucinda said, "Well, you might have told me, Cat. For goodness sake, I had no notion Jeffrey was a friend of yours here."

"We meet at parties occasionally, and I asked him for a donation to St. Luke's. He came to look around before he actually agreed to make a contribution." Catherine looked at her friend. "You have to keep me informed of your conquests, my dear. I was not aware Mr. Bancroft was one of them. There were so many men buzzing around you I could not keep track."

"Nonsense. Any men around me just wanted to see if I would let them have extra soap from the hospital store." Lucinda blushed a little. "I suppose I should have told you that Jeffrey Bancroft and I had a falling out of sorts before he left. He never approved of me. I had met him in London, and even then he managed to find fault with me. Horrid, disagreeable man!"

Catherine waited but Lucinda said no more. "Very well. I will do my best to be sure you do not both visit at the same time."

"Thank you, Catherine."

"You do not wish to tell me more about this—falling out?"

"No." And Lucinda sat back, an expression of unmovable silence on her face. Catherine was sure there was a great deal more to be said, but Lucinda was not going to say it.

"Very well. My father has insisted that I appear at one of his endless series of political receptions this evening. Palmerston will be there and possibly Sidney Herbert. I will probably be grilled by one or another of the guests as to the status of things at Scutari. Could you bear to come and help me fend off the wolves?"

Lucinda shook her head. "I think that is exactly the kind of party Mr. Bancroft would attend. I think I will spend the evening with my aunt and her ailments. You cannot know what a sacrifice that is!" Laughing, Lucinda changed the subject and regaled Catherine with her aunt's latest foolishness until the carriage stopped at the Harrowbys' house.

They bid each other a fond farewell and promised to meet again in a few days, when Catherine had her next day off. Catherine rode on to Stanhope House wondering what Lucinda's quarrel with Jeffrey Bancroft was really all about.

The party that evening was as formal and stiff as Catherine had thought it would be. The talk was of politics, and Catherine found it difficult to concentrate. Sir Ronald Bolton dogged her every footstep and spent his time in heavy-handed attempts to convince onlookers that he stood in a much closer relationship to Catherine than she thought appropriate. He took advantage of her refusal to make a scene in public by touching her hand, taking her arm, and calling her his dear Miss Stanhope with an indulgent chuckle whenever she expressed an opinion.

At last, goaded beyond endurance by this display of supposed possession, Catherine waited until the group around them had drifted away. Then she turned on her tormentor. "Sir Ronald," she said through clenched teeth, "I would appreciate it if you would stand at least two full paces further away from me. I would also appreciate it if you would not interrupt me when I am speaking and if you would not speak to me as if you were talking to a small child or a dog."

If Sir Ronald had apologized or even shown himself to be in the slightest degree embarrassed, Catherine would have forgiven him and made light of the incident. Instead, he gave that same irritating, indulgent chuckle and said, "Now, Miss Stanhope, that is simply my way. I am sure your father would say you are being rude. I treat you as any man of a certain age and experience would treat a young, unmarried woman in whom he had evinced a serious interest. Like any such young woman, you need guidance, my dear, and I am prepared to provide it."

He positively beamed at her in fatuous self-congratulation. "I had not meant to speak so soon, but your father has given his permission, and indeed went so far as to say he favored my suit. So I do not scruple to tell you I wish to make you my wife. I am sure we will suit admirably."

It was not unexpected, but the fact that he chose to speak in the middle of a crowded social event put her at a disadvantage. She tried to rein in her emotions, but he had infuriated her.

"I am not a young untried woman, Sir Ronald. I am a trained nurse and I have served my country in a war in a far-off country. That hardly makes me a childish creature who needs guidance." Catherine spoke in a low voice, since they were still within sight, if not within earshot, of a number of guests. "And while we are speaking frankly, let me say that if I were to seek guidance or a husband, I would not seek either from you. We will not suit at all!" And with that, Catherine turned and moved away from Sir Ronald, rejoicing in the idea she had finally ended his ridiculous courtship.

But no one else seemed to think Sir Ronald was going to go away. He must have told her father with the speed of a carrier pigeon, she thought as she and the baronet were being driven home later that night.

"Catherine, I do not know what I have to do to convince you that you need to marry," her father began.

"Papa, I simply cannot face another scene tonight. If you wish me to marry, then you will have to find someone I can bear to be near, not Sir Ronald, who persists in treating me as if I were a rather backward child." She sat back and firmly looked out the window, refusing to continue the discussion.

The baronet said only, "Neither Sir Ronald nor I have any wish to make you unhappy, my dear."

"Then keep him away from me. He is impossible."

The baronet wisely said nothing further.

However, the next evening, when Catherine came down to dinner expecting to find the baronet ready for their ritual glass of sherry, there was Sir Ronald, smiling as fatuously as ever. Catherine stopped in the doorway and considered simply leaving. But good manners, as always, carried the day.

"Good evening, Sir Ronald," she said, her smile frosty as she went over to the mahogany cabinet and offered him a glass of sherry or brandy.

"Neither, my dear Miss Stanhope," he replied, the smile still fixed on his face. "Your father has given his consent for me to ask you to be my wife," he continued.

Catherine felt her knees go a little weak and she sat down, her midnight blue evening dress spilling in shimmering folds to the floor. This man and her father were taking on the quality of a nightmare, she thought—one where she spoke and cried out and everyone continued to act as if she had made no sound whatever. No matter how often or emphatically she told them she did not wish to marry Sir Ronald, neither paid the slightest attention.

"No," she said, giving the word as much force as she could.

"I beg your pardon?"

"No, I will not marry you, Sir Ronald." There, that should take care of the problem. Surely no one could ignore that refusal.

Sir Ronald paused, but then his smile appeared again. "I am not going to take that answer as final, my dear Miss Stanhope. I really do think you need my help and guidance. Your father, an estimable man but very much inclined to spoil you, has allowed you to indulge in behavior that is simply not to be tolerated in polite society."

As the speech went on, Catherine began to see another Sir Ronald, one who was not the placid, conventional suitor she had seen up to now. "And you are going to reform me, Sir Ronald?" Catherine said with deceptive mildness. "Do, pray, tell me how you are going to accomplish this."

"You will leave your work immediately, which is unseemly and completely ruins any woman for a place in decent society. I can only think that it has coarsened you already or you would not object to the advice and correction of an older, more mature man." Sir Ronald's smile had not faded, but there was a steely glint in his eye.

"I am not going to resign from St. Luke's and I am not going to marry anyone who would want me to do so." Catherine rose and stood facing him. Drawing herself up to her full height, which put her nearly on his level, she said, "Surely that fact alone should convince you I am totally unsuited to be your wife."

She began to leave the room, too angry and upset to eat—or to care that her father would think she was being rude. But Sir Ronald took her arm and held her where she was.

Catherine was not frightened. She did not for one moment believe that a guest in her father's house, a suitor for her hand, would have the monumental stupidity to try to restrain her by force. And Sir Ronald's grip on her arm was not hurtful. But as she looked into his eyes, she saw something disturbing, something more than the stubborn belief in the superiority of his sex.

"Let go of me, sir." She met his eyes with a message of her own. He had gone too far. He saw it and dropped her arm.

They stared at each other without moving for a long moment. Then Sir Ronald spoke. "I will have you. Make no mistake about it, my dear Miss Stanhope. I mean to marry you and I will have you."

It was the voice of a man who did not admit defeat and, most disturbing of all, his face had never lost that fatuous, beaming smile. She had to get away.

"No," Catherine said for the third time and swept out of the room.

She was more shaken than she had thought. The intensity of the confrontation had kept her nerves at bay, but once in her room she found herself shaking. When Betsy brought her a light repast, she could not eat it. Nervous activity kept her pacing her room all evening, unable to read or write a long overdue letter to Rose Cranmer, still with Miss Nightingale in the Crimea. Instead, she decided at ten o'clock to seek out her father and request him to bar Sir Ronald from the house.

She found Sir Everett in his study, staring into the fire when she entered. He looked grave when she made her request. "Catherine, I was concerned when you did not come down to dinner, but Sir Ronald explained your absence."

"Did he, indeed?" The man's effrontery knew no bounds. "And what exactly did he say?"

"Why, that he had been so overcome by your beauty and charm that he proposed to you without properly leading up to such a profound subject. And that you were overcome with maidenly shyness and ran away."

"Oh, Papa, really! How could you believe such a tale? You know very well I have never been overcome with maidenly shyness in my life!" Catherine was not sure whether to laugh or scream in vexation.

Her father looked less amused than she would have thought. It was curious that he even liked the man. Ordinarily, her father spent his time with men at the top of the political world, men who might be shortsighted and pompous but who were certainly not stupid.

"Why do you favor this man, Papa?" she asked bluntly. "He really does not seem to be up to your usual standards. Admittedly I do not know him very well, but you do. What do you see in him? Am I so old and eccentric that the only man you can find for me is someone I dislike?"

"I have told you," the baronet began to bluster, "he is a fine man, a coming man. He is rich, which is important."

"Why is it important that I marry a rich man?" Catherine sat down. Suddenly, she began to feel uneasy. Something was wrong, and it involved her father. It was as if the ground had begun to shift beneath her feet. No matter how angry she had been with him, still he was there, a presence in her life, someone she could always count on. He was the rock against which she had hurled herself all her life. Now she felt the rock shifting, giving way, and it frightened her.

"It is not—not precisely, anyway," he said, looking steadfastly into the fire.

"Papa, why do you want me to marry Sir Ronald? Please!" she said when he opened his mouth with what she knew would be more evasions. "I do not want to hear about what a fine man he is. There is more to it than that, isn't there?"

"I am in business with him," the baronet said at last.

"So you said. Some sort of investment in shipping, wasn't it?"

"A large amount of capital was needed to start the business, and Sir Ronald offered to lend me the money to buy in at a very favorable rate of interest."

A sense of foreboding possessed Catherine. "And the investment was lost?"

"Not precisely, but the profits are slow in coming. Sir Ronald assures me that they will come, and soon, but until then, of course, I have to keep up the interest payments which, on top of the rest of our expenses . . ." He trailed off. "It would be different if he were my son-in-law. Then the entire debt would be forgiven. It would be in the nature of a wedding gift from Sir Ronald."

He could not meet her eyes. Catherine sank back into the low chair she habitually sat in and tried to make sense of it.

The long and the short of it was that her father was bartering her life for his fortune. He had never made a secret of the fact he wanted her to marry and marry well, but he had never tried to use her as if she were a parcel of land or a factory. Yet when that was suggested to him— and she was sure that it had been Sir Ronald's idea—he did not refuse.

It was not unusual for marriages to be arranged for the advantage of the family, but the baronet did not have half a dozen children to provide for. He had only Catherine. If he had paid the slightest attention to Catherine's needs—

"I will not do it, Papa," she said. "Sir Ronald told me I would stop work immediately, that he knew what was best for me and for our children. He thinks you have spoiled me."

"What?" It was one thing for the baronet to entertain the idea that Catherine was headstrong and stubborn and needed guidance. It was something else entirely for another person to suggest there was the slightest fault to be found in her. "I will have a talk with him and tell him that my daughter is the bravest and most beautiful girl in England!"

"Why, Papa, thank you!"

"He is an intelligent man. He will see the advantage to treating you with kindness and considera—"

"No, Papa. Believe me, Sir Ronald will never see anything but what he wants to see."

"But, Catherine—"

"No, Papa. You can sell one of the smaller estates if you have to, or use my dowry. I will not need it. But you cannot expect me to marry just to make your life easier. There must be another way to pay Sir Ronald." She did not want to hurt her father, but she was not prepared to sacrifice her life for his. "You cannot use me."

Catherine turned away, pain and resolution mingled in her heart. Every step she took away from the conventional life of an upper-class young woman seemed to drive her farther from her father. But in this, as in her need to nurse, she had no choice. She had said everything there was to say. She had thrown down the gauntlet and her father knew exactly where she stood.

As she opened the door, her father said, "Catherine, you cannot—"

But she could. She walked out and closed the door.

Chapter Fifteen

Sleep had not made Catherine any happier. She knew she was doing the right thing in refusing to let her father marry her off as if he were selling livestock. No matter how he tried to convince himself she would benefit, Catherine knew better.

Still, as she made her rounds in the hospital the next day, she could not help but worry about the debt her father owed to Sir Ronald. Something about him told Catherine he would not react reasonably to her father's "little talk." Sir Ronald Bolton thought he knew best about everything. He had revealed that he had as little respect for her father as he did for her.

What could he do to either of them? The nagging mystery tugged at her mind. She told herself Sir Ronald had never done anything but talk a lot of stuffy nonsense and get her father involved in a questionable investment. But somehow she could not manage to reassure herself.

For the next several days, nothing happened. Catherine and her father lived in a state of armed truce. They talked about the weather, politics, and the queen's growing dissatisfaction with politicians of both parties because they refused to listen to her beloved Albert. But they did not talk about the topic uppermost in their minds.

Then one evening the baronet requested Catherine's presence at a dinner and large reception where he hoped to have a chance to talk privately to Lord Palmerston, the newly appointed prime minister. Catherine reluctantly agreed. She and her father had maintained their fragile peace by not spending much time together. In the past, that had allowed them both time to reflect. When they did talk, they had managed to smooth over their differences. This time, Catherine was not sure that was possible.

After dinner as Catherine was circulating around the room, talking easily with one group and then another while her father met with Palmerston in a small library, Sir Ronald entered the room. She had been relieved to note he had not been invited to the dinner. A number of additional people had been invited to the reception, however, and he was one of them.

He did not see her at first, and Catherine had to repress a craven desire to flee, or at least hide behind a potted palm somewhere. Sir Ronald was looking around as if searching for someone in particular. The room was crowded and people were constantly moving from one group to another. He apparently did not see the person he was looking for. He stood apart for some time before moving off in what looked like a particular direction. Catherine was curious as to who he was looking for. It was not her; he had not so much as glanced in her direction.

Instead, he headed toward a long table on which refreshments had been set, and there he paused beside a figure Catherine recognized.

St. John Featherstone.

Sir Ronald wore what Catherine thought of as his mask—the smiling and affable look that hid a will of iron. As he led Lieutenant Featherstone off to the side and engaged him in earnest conversation, Catherine had a feeling she knew what they were discussing.

Her. Her dismissal from the Crimea by Miss Nightingale because she had kissed Michael on board a ship with no one to see them but St. John Featherstone. And then she had very publicly kissed Julian, who had been announced as her fiancé. A ship had been leaving for Malta and England immediately, and she had found herself on it, with no time to see either Michael or Julian to say good-bye.

She had not known that Featherstone had spread the story beyond Miss Nightingale until her father had mentioned it. Catherine had heard no further whispers, and she had thought the story too tame to interest anyone. Her life in London had been almost that of a nun in its simplicity. Her only social life had been in her father's company. She had assumed where there was no smoke, society would decide there was no fire.

Was Sir Ronald trying to rekindle that fire? To what end? So gossip would compel her to marry wherever she could? Sir Ronald little knew her, or he would not have miscalculated so badly. Anyone who knew Catherine knew she would be far more likely to declare that she would never marry than to marry someone she disliked because she had been coerced into it.

Catherine decided she'd had enough of standing by watching while these two men talked about her. Taking her courage in both hands, she strolled slowly over to them, pausing to chat with first one group and then another as she made her way across the room. She did not want to look as if she were pursuing either man.

She did not have to finish her stroll, for once he saw her, Sir Ronald himself came over to the group she was talking with. He smiled in the kind and patronizing way that set Catherine's teeth on edge as he greeted her. Then, with great affability he said, "I hope you will not mind if I take Miss Stanhope away with me for a while. Too much political discussion is not good for women's brains. Causes them to overheat." And he laughed heartily while Catherine longed to box his ears.

As he guided her steps toward a small bow window that would afford them some modicum of privacy, Catherine gritted her teeth and did not pull away. She did not want to call attention to their quarrel, even though that desire played into Sir Ronald's hands. She knew Sir Ronald arranged to speak to her at social events to avoid a confrontation he could not control.

Before she could speak, he leaned close to her ear and said, "I would not wish anyone to overhear what I am about to say to you, dear Catherine."

She pulled away a few steps. "I have not given you permission to use my given name, sir."

"But, my dear, as I keep trying to explain to you, since your father has given his permission for me to pay my addresses to you, it is only proper that I begin to take those, shall we say, liberties to which my status as your betrothed—"

"I am not betrothed to you," Catherine said, her teeth clenched so tightly her jaws ached. "I will never be betrothed to you. I do not understand why you cannot accept that idea. Perhaps when you are left waiting at the altar—"

She had never seen such a change in a man take place
so quickly. Gone were the affability and the endless smile.
There was something dark and a little dangerous in his
gaze now. He grasped her arm, and this time it hurt. "You
would never make a laughingstock out of me. Never. If
you even tried—"

If she had not seen it with her own eyes, Catherine would
not have believed it possible. It was as if two separate men
had stood in the same spot only instants apart. The change
that had swept over him was just as instantly gone, and the
affable, stuffy country squire was back in his place.

"I hope to persuade you to change your mind," he said.
"I was talking to Lieutenant Featherstone just now, and
since he has just returned from the Crimea, your name
came up. It seems he encountered you there. You and that
Dr. Soames. Featherstone believes you and Soames were
something more than friends. Of course, I do not for one
moment believe that. You are too delicately reared, your
father too zealous in teaching you the correct behavior for
a female for such a thing ever to be true."

He paused, if only for breath, and Catherine interrupted. "Sir Ronald, I do not choose to discuss my personal
relations with you. Lieutenant Featherstone is almost
unknown to me. He was on the transport ship that took
Dr. Soames and me from Balaklava to Scutari when we
returned from a medical mission for Sir John Hall and
Miss Nightingale. What he saw or thought he saw during
the course of that voyage I do not know, nor do I choose
to know."

There! she thought. *I can sound every bit as stuffy as you.*

"You may take that tone if you choose, Catherine." Sir
Ronald's affability was unimpaired. "But unless you agree
to marry a man of substance and probity—a man such as
myself"—he laid a hand on his breast in a gesture both

falsely modest and self-congratulatory at the same time— "if you are not able to attract such a suitor, I fear the lieutenant's story might gain credence. I, of course, would make it my first concern to convince the young man, by whatever means necessary, to stop such baseless, vicious gossip."

From the moment she had seen him with Featherstone, the idea he would try to hold Featherstone's threat over her head had tugged at the corners of Catherine's mind. She was coldly furious but not shocked, and she had her reply ready. "Then you think you could stop him from spreading that unkind and untrue tale?"

"Of course. I am not without influence here, for all I have just recently come to take my place in the capital."

"Why, thank you." Catherine beamed at him, a smile as false as his. "I knew I could depend on one as truly chivalrous as you. For a moment, I thought you implied you would only correct the dastard's insinuations if I agreed to marry you."

She was sure that was exactly what he meant, but she had decided her best course was to try to make Sir Ronald live up to the exaggerated ideas of men's honor he espoused. She enjoyed watching his reaction to her remarks play across his face. A sort of baffled anger was replaced by the affable expression he habitually wore.

"My dear, of course you may depend upon me to do what I can. However, without the status that will be conferred when I have the right to call you my own, I am not sure how much success I will meet with."

A new voice interjected, "Ah, then you can but try, can you not?"

"Michael!" It was a cry from the heart.

"Yes, Bancroft dragged me along so I could discuss the work of the Roebuck Commission with some of these august chaps." Michael grinned down at her and then turned to Sir Ronald. "We have met, have we not? Sir Ronald Bolton, isn't it?" He extended a hand.

Catherine was surprised at the smooth aura of manners and charm Michael exuded. Where had he learned the ways of the world—to be both polite and cutting at the same time? To pretend to scarcely be able to remember another, more prominent person? She did not know. She was only glad he had come when he had, not to make a scene but to beat Sir Ronald at his own game.

Sir Ronald cleared his throat, and for a moment Catherine feared he would refuse to accept Michael's offer of civility. But the moment passed and Sir Ronald gave Michael a perfunctory handshake. "Dr. Soames, I believe." He stood a little straighter, and the white satin of his evening waistcoat pulled a bit against its buttons.

"Yes, I have been looking for Miss Stanhope. There are some people over there that have questions about Scutari that I am afraid I cannot answer. We need you to set us straight, Miss Stanhope." He smiled dismissively at Sir Ronald and, with a firm hand, led Catherine away. Catherine could feel Sir Ronald's angry frown burn her back, though she did not look around.

When they reached a gap in the crowd, Michael led her out through a glass door into a small room that looked like a miniature version of the famous Crystal Palace in Hyde Park. The many panes of glass glittered in the starlight. Though there were only a few oil lamps set about, it seemed very bright. It was clearly a conservatory, with many plants set in pots about the room. Several other couples sat in bamboo chairs in the style made popular forty or fifty years before by the prince regent.

"Now, tell me what that man has been saying to you. I could tell from across the room he was behaving like an encroaching toad and you were mad as fire about it." Michael's smile was tender and took the sting out of his words.

"I did not mean to convey to people that I was angry," Catherine said.

"Oh, you didn't. Only someone who knows you as well as I do would notice."

The idea of Michael watching her from afar, able to read her moods, warmed her heart. He was the only man who cared about her without wanting to change her. The only one who understood her.

"Michael," she said, "do you think I should give up nursing?"

"What? Is that what that idiot wants you to do? What an absurd idea! You are a gifted nurse. It would be criminal not to use that talent." Michael frowned down at her. "You are not seriously thinking of marrying that fool, are you?" He grasped her hands and pulled her a little closer. They stood a little apart from the other couples and could not be overheard. "If I thought he was going to get hold of you—"

"No, of course I am not going to marry him. If only I could convince him of that. Both he and my father seem to think it is a perfectly splendid idea, and the more I protest, the more thoroughly they ignore me."

Michael's clasp on her hands tightened. Somehow, unlike Sir Ronald's grip, this possessive hold was very welcome and felt warm and reassuring. "You do not have to marry anyone. You are over twenty-one and, in any case, the bride's agreement is an essential part of any valid marriage."

Catherine laughed, a little breathlessly. She had hoped for something more, another kind of rescue—the kind his earlier words had hinted at. "You sound like a solicitor."

"My best friend from school became one. We used to talk when we were in school, and later when he read English law here in London he would fill me in by letter. Said writing it down made it stay in his mind."

Catherine smiled. "I will try to remember that when they browbeat me. But I am beginning to feel a bit cornered. Sir Ronald is a relentless sort of man, and he is beginning to alarm me a little."

"What has he done? If he has threatened you, I will—"

"He hasn't threatened us precisely. He is too devious to do anything that crass. He has lent my father money and involved him in a business transaction that seems to be strangely unprofitable. And he told me that Featherstone had been gossiping about me. Which, of course, Sir Ronald could stop instantly were I to become affianced to him." Catherine looked down at her hands, still held in Michael's. "You see, no threats."

"The b—dastard!" Michael said. "Well, I don't know about business partnerships and loans and such, but I know those who do. And I can shut Featherstone's mouth without any difficulty." There was a look of anticipation on his face, and his hands tightened around hers.

Catherine remembered the way he had fought the two cutpurses outside the hospital and was a little concerned. It would do her reputation no good at all to be brawled over. Such conduct would be regarded as beyond the pale, and all who engaged in it—including any young lady unfortunate enough to be the cause of such behavior—would be ostracized by polite society.

"Michael, you threatened Featherstone before. It would not do then, and it certainly would be disastrous here in London."

"You underestimate me, my dear." It was the London sophisticate who spoke and gave her that heart-stopping grin. "I have other, more subtle weapons. Fear not. It will not be necessary to so much as graze the man's jaw to reduce him to permanent silence."

"What do you intend to do?" Catherine was intrigued. Michael seemed so sure of himself.

"I will tell you once I am certain of exactly how to go about it." Michael gave her a reassuring smile and then turned once again to the door back to the reception room. "I have had you in the conservatory for upwards of ten minutes. If we do not return forthwith, you might have to become betrothed to me. Perhaps preferable to becoming linked for life to Sir Ronald in your eyes, but a fate worse than death in your father's."

"Pooh! My father will learn to value you as he ought if we give him a chance to do so. I'm quite sure of it." Although she hoped she sounded confident, in truth Catherine thought the baronet might never come round to her point of view.

"Soames. Miss Stanhope. I have been looking for you both." Jeffrey Bancroft came up to them and offered each one of the glasses of champagne which he was carrying in his white-gloved hands. "I have been carrying these all around the room, fending off thirsty guests as I go."

"It is nice to see you again, Mr. Bancroft. I do not believe I mentioned to you that Lucinda Harrowby is back in London." Catherine watched the gentleman with an eagle eye. She was certain she was not mistaken in detecting a spark of interest in his expression. A moment later she was sure.

"Why has she returned? I was under the impression she intended to remain at Scutari until Miss Nightingale herself returned to England." There was a note of anxiety in his voice that warmed Catherine's heart.

"She was taken gravely ill with a fever and it was thought best for her to return, lest she run a risk of serious harm."

Michael looked at her then, and she thought perhaps she had overdone the note of concern in her voice. But she *was* concerned. Lucinda did not look as well as Catherine would have hoped. The look on Jeffrey's face was bland, but she thought she saw a gleam of worry in the pirate's green eyes. She was well satisfied.

"I would call upon her, but I do not think my presence would add to her peace of mind." Jeffrey's voice was sardonic.

"If you could spare me a few moments," Michael said to him, "there are a few things I need to consult with you about."

"Certainly." Jeffrey looked a little surprised, and Catherine supposed she did, too. Not often did Michael think he needed anyone's advice on any topic.

At that interesting moment, just when Catherine was hoping Michael would begin the discussion, her father bore down upon them, a frown on his face and Sir Ronald trailing smugly in his wake.

"Come, Catherine, it is growing late. Sir Ronald will see us home." He looked at the two men his daughter was talking with and gave them each the minimum bow required by courtesy. "Soames. Bancroft. Your servant. Come please, Catherine."

And with that, he stood aside to let his daughter precede him out of the room.

Michael looked after her with a longing he knew he could not hide. Catherine spoke to his heart in a way no one else ever had. She stretched him in ways he knew were good for him. Because of Catherine, he had dredged up memories of parties his mother had dragged him to in Edinburgh where polite conversation and waltzing had been the order of the day. He had discarded those days as thoroughly as if they had never been, just as he had discarded any idea of love.

Until now.

Until Catherine.

He had learned compassion was not just for patients lying in hospital beds. Catherine's compassion extended to the families of those who were wounded and ill. She spent as much time with Julian's mother as she did with Julian himself. Michael had extended his concern to David Blankenship's father and in return had made a friend.

"She is beautiful," Jeffrey Bancroft said, pulling Michael back into the present. "You are a lucky man."

"Yes, she is beautiful. And she is as beautiful inside as she is to look at." Michael looked at Jeffrey and saw a look of mingled commiseration and humor on his face. "But I am hardly lucky. I am making a fool of myself, am I not?"

"Not at all," Jeffrey said. "It seems to me she has some powerful adversaries and could use as many friends as she can find. Why does Featherstone want to ruin her, do you know?"

"I'm afraid that is my fault. He made some rather warm remarks about her within my hearing and I took strong exception. After that, he included Catherine in the circle of his dislike, and she has fewer weapons at her disposal and is more easily damaged."

"How did you all meet?"

"It was at Balaklava. Catherine and I had gone there from Scutari at Miss Nightingale and Dr. Hall's request to see what needed to be done to improve the regimental field hospitals."

Michael's voice grew softer as he remembered.

Upon landing at the crowded little port of Balaklava, they had been taken to the farmhouse that served as the commander in chief's headquarters. Lord Raglan himself had greeted them, and afterward Michael and Catherine had visited the nearest regimental hospital. It had been a horrific sight. The one doctor was working around the clock, but men still waited for days out in the winter cold before they could be tended. Michael and Catherine had quickly changed their mission from observation to temporary surgical help.

Returning to headquarters late that afternoon had been like returning to an unreal world. Men in impeccable uniforms sat about as if they had nothing whatever to do.

Later, at dinner, Lord Raglan had told Catherine he saw no need for additional regimental surgeons and that, like his hero, the Duke of Wellington, he disapproved of spending too much time and effort taking care of enlisted men, since their major contribution to any battle was to die at the orders of their officers.

Catherine had protested. Michael could remember the real horror in her eyes as she remembered the men lying outside the regimental hospital, waiting patiently for the one doctor to take care of them.

Michael had been seated near her at the table and he could see her twist her napkin in her lap as she spoke. Her voice was low and reasonable. She was taking out her emotions on the napkin. It dawned on Michael that she wanted not to voice a protest but to convince Lord Raglan she was correct and he should change his views.

What a woman! he had thought at the time. Ready to take on the commander in chief of the Army, a man who fought with Wellington at Waterloo, and certain enough of her cause and her abilities to think she can convince him.

One of the aides-de-camp, a Lieutenant St. John Featherstone, had intervened, smiling and using that upper-class English drawl that made a Scotsman like Michael long to bloody his nose. "Really, ma'am. Miss Stanhope, is it?" Though Featherstone pretended not to remember her name, Michael had seen his eyes widen at the sight of Catherine, blond and beautiful even in the midst of an Army in the field. "I am afraid I have forgotten your name. It is so difficult to remember the names of the lower ranks."

"Yes, Lieutenant, it is Stanhope." Catherine had smiled a chilly little smile, the kind a baronet's daughter uses when being patronized by a mere soldier.

"Sir Everett Stanhope is her father," Lord Raglan remarked. Featherstone looked blank. "Sir Everett is a member of the government," Lord Raglan remarked. "The government, which is deciding whether to vote to remove Lord Aberdeen as prime minister."

Featherstone still looked puzzled, but he did seem to recognize that annoying the daughter of a crown minister, however minor his post, would not be a sensible course of action. Catherine recognized that Lord Raglan was trying to signal to Featherstone that Sir Everett might be a political ally if he backed installing another prime minister, one who would be more enthusiastic about pursuing the war than Lord Aberdeen had shown himself to be.

Catherine inclined her head in a tiny bow to the tactless lieutenant and then gave him one of her best smiles, thus making him even sorrier he had offended her.

After dinner, Michael went outside and stood thinking. Catherine Stanhope was a miracle of a woman—beautiful, intelligent, intrepid, devoted, and the daughter of a baronet who was also a member of parliament. And he, Michael Soames, surgeon and physician, had fallen in love with this paragon of creatures. How stupid could he possibly be? No one could consider him an eligible suitor for Catherine Stanhope.

Just as he was about to go back inside to face Lord Raglan and his overbred, underbrained staff, Catherine drifted out onto the terrace.

"It is a beautiful evening," she remarked, "although cold. I worry about the men out on the hillsides with nothing but camp fires and thin blankets."

She was as good as she was beautiful. If there were not something wistful about her, something that told him she needed a friend, Michael could have found her too good to be true. Then he might have wanted to find her fatal weakness, her flaw. As it was, he had fallen in love with her.

"Perhaps we can encourage Miss Nightingale to ask some of her friends in the government to do something about that."

"Perhaps. But when you listen to the staff here—" She broke off as Lieutenant Featherstone came outside.

He paused when he saw them, then bowed to Catherine. "I am sorry if I caused you any embarrassment or pain, madam," he said. "I did not realize who you were."

"I hope that does not mean if I had not been Stanhope's daughter, you would have behaved as rudely as you did but felt no need to apologize."

Even in the silver starlight, which bleached most of the color from the world, Featherstone's angry flush could be clearly seen. He bowed again stiffly and then took out a cigar case, which he offered to Michael.

"If you do not mind, Miss Stanhope?" Michael said. Featherstone had once again failed to observe the elemental courtesy of asking Catherine if she objected to men smoking in her presence.

"Not at all. I was about to go inside. Pray excuse me." And Catherine glided away, leaving Michael to wonder if he could

*endure any more of the cavalry lieutenant's company. He had
agreed to smoke a cigar with the man to give Catherine an excuse
to leave. She was clearly eager to get away.*

*And he could hardly blame her. He might not have the back-
ground and breeding of Baronet Stanhope's daughter, but he
certainly knew how to behave toward a woman who looked to him
for protection. The least he could do, he decided, was to give her
an opportunity to leave Featherstone's presence. So now he was
condemned to a half hour of the fatuous lieutenant's company.
And since he was smoking the man's cigar, he could hardly tell
him what he thought of him.*

*It was his penance, he thought with grim humor as he listened
to more of Lieutenant St. John Featherstone's tedious tales of the
cavalry. He even had to enter into the conversation, more's the
pity.*

*He recalled something from the dinner table discussion and
tried to pretend to an interest he did not feel. "And so Lucan
actually ordered the infamous charge?" he said. "Gave his hated
brother-in-law, Cardigan, the order to ride into the mouths of the
enemy cannon?" Dear God, it was a wonder the British Army
ever won a single battle, let alone a war!*

*He looked around at the camp and the plains beyond, dotted
now by a few campfires here and there against the chill and the
dark. Only a few more minutes and he could bid the lieutenant
good night and good luck.*

*"There was nothing personal in it," Featherstone was saying
stiffly. "Lord Lucan is an officer and a gentleman." He gave
Michael an appraising look. "Speaking of gentlemen and ladies,
what is Sir Everett Stanhope thinking of, allowing a beauty like
that to travel about the battle fields with no one but an Army
doctor as escort?"*

*"She is one of Miss Nightingale's most trusted assistants,"
Michael said, keeping his voice neutral, though his blood was*

starting to boil at the avid look in the man's eyes. "Without them, I don't know what we would have done at Scutari."

"But still—to allow a gently bred, unmarried woman to travel halfway around the world to tend to the bodies of perfect strangers—perfect male strangers at that—well, my father would shoot my sister before he would let her do anything like that." Featherstone leaned a little closer and lowered his voice. "Unless—is she so wild her father had to send her away?"

"Miss Stanhope, like Miss Nightingale, is devoted to nursing," Michael replied coldly, tossing his cigar into the night, unwilling to discuss Catherine with this fatuous idiot.

Featherstone shook his head and grinned. "She's far too pretty to have to traipse around a battlefield to find a husband, even if she did blot her copybook at home."

Fury swept through Michael. "I have told you, Lieutenant. Miss Nightingale sent Miss Stanhope, her trusted assistant, to look at what was needed at the regimental field hospitals." Michael was holding his temper in check.

"I wouldn't mind getting a saber cut or two if it meant being nursed by that little beauty." The lieutenant grinned. "D'you think she needs a cavalry escort? She's a bit beyond your touch, right? Might as well give the gentlemen a chance at her."

Michael's fists clenched. He was sorely tempted to smash one into the "gentleman's" face. But it would hardly help Catherine's reputation to be brawling over her with some idiot in spurs.

"Miss Stanhope is as much of a lady as Miss Nightingale," he said through clenched teeth. "To suggest otherwise is to give offense to me and to everyone who knows her."

"No insult intended, old boy. Truly." He spoke casually, but the lethal glint in Michael's eye must have told Featherstone the doctor was spoiling for a fight. He hastened to apologize further. "Very well, don't get quarrelsome. I was merely admiring the lady. Can't expect a mere doctor to understand such things, I suppose."

That was the end. "I can understand an insult to a lady when

*I hear one. If you ever so much as suggest Catherine Stanhope is
anything other than a chaste, sincere, devoted nurse, I will personally thrash you within an inch of your life."* Michael turned and
strode off inside with a curt, *"Good night, Lieutenant."*

"So you threatened the lieutenant, did you?" Jeffrey
could not help grinning. He was sure the sight of the
surgeon, who topped him by a good four inches and out-
weighed him by several stone, must have caused Featherstone's heart to sink just a bit.

"I suppose he could have regarded it as a threat. I
thought of it as protecting a young lady's reputation from
undeserved harm."

"Of course." Jeffrey looked at his friend's stiff expression and guilty eyes. "And that's all that happened? You
never saw him again?"

"Well, not exactly."

"What then?" Though Jeffrey thought he knew.

"I—I kissed her. It was on the ship going back to Scutari
from Balaklava. And Featherstone saw."

"And?"

"And made some remark about whether she was as good
as she looked, and he would try his hand with her, since
she had already stooped to take a doctor for a lover."
Michael's face darkened as it had that night on the pitching
deck of the transport carrying them back.

Two men had died that night, and Michael had comforted Catherine, who had cared for them tenderly. The
kiss that had followed was one of the great moments of
his life. He would live on the memory of that kiss—or so
he told himself. And then Featherstone had tried to sully
it.

"What did you do?"

Michael shrugged. "I choked him a little, and when he complained, I told him if he spread any sort of story about Miss Stanhope, I would kill him."

"Oh, well, I don't think anything that drastic will be necessary. I think I may be able to help you silence that little jumped-up gossip once and for all."

Chapter Sixteen

Catherine tried to throw herself into her work and forget about the threat to her reputation posed by St. John Featherstone. The threat to her life's happiness posed by Sir Ronald she found harder to ignore.

There had been an outbreak of fever amid the slums, and Catherine was working long hours. She and her father saw little of each other. By the time she got home from the hospital in the evening, he was ready for John Coachman to take him out to the evening's party or dinner. He no longer insisted she accompany him.

A week after her encounter with Sir Ronald, Catherine arrived home tired and hungry after a long day in the wards. They were shorthanded, several of the nurses having been taken ill. She had scarcely removed her bonnet and cloak when a knock on the door heralded a caller. Thinking it might be Lucinda, she told Holden she would wait in the library to see who their untimely guest might be.

She had not thought to tell the butler not to admit anyone but Lucinda. When she heard masculine voices, her head began to pound. If she had to undergo another scene with Sir Ronald or her father, she was not sure she could survive without screaming at them. Catherine could not contemplate that without self-blame. Brought up to present the world with a smooth, unfailingly well-behaved façade, she was ashamed at how close she was to the breaking point.

She stood and faced the door with the same emotions with which she would face a firing squad. But instead of her father or Sir Ronald, Jeffrey Bancroft and Michael strode into the room. Between them, however, looking smaller than before, was her other nemesis.

"Lieutenant Featherstone," she said, her heart sinking. Though not as formidable as Sir Ronald, the soldier was even more unpleasant.

"*Mr.* Featherstone has something he wishes to say to you," said Michael.

Silence.

"Don't you, *Mr.* Featherstone?" Jeffrey added, pushing the smaller man into the room.

"Yes, yes." Featherstone was actually flinching. "Miss Stanhope, I have come to beg your pardon for anything I may have said or done to cause you embarrassment."

Another silence.

"And?" Michael prompted.

"And I have written your father and Sir Ronald telling them that I know nothing to your detriment. That your reputation in Scutari Hospital was excellent. That I was advised of that by Miss Nightingale herself. That—that—"

"That you will actively quell any gossip you hear. That you will report, to any and all who ask you, the truth: Miss Stanhope was an excellent nurse whose efforts saved many lives." Michael glared down at Featherstone, as if daring him to contradict a single word. "And if asked for particulars, what will you say?"

"That David Blankenship is only one of many who can attest to Miss Stanhope's care and devotion." Featherstone looked up as if seeking approval for repeating a lesson well learned.

"And skill," Michael added.

"And skill," Featherstone quickly agreed.

Silence.

"You may go," said Jeffrey. "*Mr.* Featherstone."

Featherstone turned and left without another word.

Catherine stood, speechless, looking from Michael's triumphant face to Jeffrey's. "What in the world did you do to him?" she asked at last. It was the only question she could formulate. Her mind was in a whirl, and all she could think of was what threats or promises these two had made in order to obtain the extraordinary speech she had just heard.

"Nothing," Michael said, holding his right hand up as if taking an oath. "Bancroft here just happened to remember something he heard in Constantinople. From Sir Stratford de Redclyffe himself."

"Something the British ambassador told you?" Catherine said. "Please, sit down. Let me pour you a glass of sherry. Or brandy?" she offered. Even at this moment, she was still conscious of her social duty. Guests must be offered refreshment.

Both men accepted, and the three of them sat down. "Tell me," Catherine said once each had taken a congratulatory sip.

"It seems a certain young cavalry officer was shipped home in disgrace. Sold his commission. Affair of honor. Hushed up for the sake of the regiment and all that."

Jeffrey took another sip. "I just happened to be there when the news arrived. Seems the officer in question was a friend of Sir Stratford's nephew. Sir Stratford was all in favor of having the young man sell out and leave immediately for home. But nothing would be said, of course."

"And the young man was Featherstone?" Catherine could hardly believe it. "What did he do?"

Jeffrey drew himself up and assumed a posture of outraged dignity. "Why, Miss Stanhope. That is something that no well-brought-up young lady would even think to ask."

"Indeed, so," said Michael, wearing a very schoolmasterish expression. "In fact, she would not even think to *think* it. I am astonished at you, ma'am, I truly am. Actually," he said, falling back into his normal tone of voice, "I think it had something to do with cheating at cards. Or a woman."

"I imagine it was cards," Jeffrey agreed. "A woman isn't usually that important. Unless it was the commanding officer's daughter. Or wife."

Catherine shook her head. The vagaries of the male code of ethics were beyond her. "So you told him if he did not agree to retract his misstatements about me you would let it be known why he was home when the war is still going on?"

"Something like that," Michael agreed, not wanting to tell Catherine of the foul things Featherstone had hinted at when first approached. It would do her no good to know of them, and she was looking so relieved, as if a large weight had been rolled from her shoulders. He felt as if he had received a medal when he saw that look on her face. "It is the kind of thing that makes you wonder why they still allow idiots like that to become officers simply by purchasing a commission."

"One would hope," Jeffrey added, helping to defuse the moment, "that the idea of a fabulously wealthy fool like Cardigan able to lead men to their deaths because he could buy a general's commission would convince them of the folly of the system. Yet I hear he is regarded as a hero."

Michael sighed. This was the delight of friendship, having someone who agreed with your positions. He could remember making a similar remark in the Crimea and being stared at as if he had grown a second head. He was just relaxing, ready to enjoy a few moments of pleasurable gloating with his friend and the woman he loved, when there was a commotion in the hall. He heard the butler's voice raised in protest and then a sharp retort and a heavy tread across the marble floor.

Before he could wonder whether it was the baronet, home and annoyed to find his library occupied and his sherry being drunk by two men he clearly regarded as beneath him and his daughter, the door was flung open and the red face and barrel-chested figure of Sir Ronald Bolton came into view.

"Catherine! What is the meaning of this?" The man's outrage was palpable.

Michael was about to come to his beloved's defense when Catherine sprang to her feet. If she had been tired when he came in and happy a few moments ago, now she was the picture of boiling outrage.

"How dare you burst into my home as if you own it, browbeat my servants, and shout at me?" For once, Catherine was too angry to be careful of her words or her tone. She knew she was shouting, and it felt wonderful. "You are not welcome here, sir. Get out!"

She might as well not have spoken. Sir Ronald, disregarding her as was his custom, turned his anger on more worthy opponents. "What are you two doing here alone in the evening with my affianced wife? I must ask you to leave."

"Affianced wife?" Catherine shouted. "I am *not* affianced—to you or to anyone else!"

"First I've heard of any betrothal, old man," Michael said, with a cheery smile. "And I would have heard. Miss Stanhope and I work together, and she would have told me had she done anything as foolish as to become engaged to you."

"My engagement is no business of yours. But, Catherine," Sir Ronald turned to her with an expression of bland concern on his face, "you should not be entertaining gentlemen alone in the evening."

"Sir Ronald," she replied, keeping her voice down with immense effort, "whom I see and when I see them is no concern of yours. Please leave this house and do not come back."

"I'm afraid I can't undertake to do that, my dear," he said, a smug smile quirking his lips. "Your father and I are in business together, and we have a great deal to discuss. It is usual for business partners to spend time together outside of business hours. Especially, as in this case, when our investment hangs in the balance."

"Just what business are you in, Bolton?" Jeffrey inquired. "I don't think you have ever said. It sounds a bit speculative. It seems to me I've never heard what part of the country you come from, either. Is your family estate listed in any guidebooks?"

Sir Ronald turned a mottled shade of red. Anger snapped from his eyes, but he still maintained that bland smile. The effect was rather chilling, as if he had forgotten he was still trying to hide behind his smile and had let the underlying anger gleam through.

"I do not have to answer to you! Sir Everett knows me,

and he is the only one who matters." He turned to Catherine, and she shrank away from the rage in his eyes. "You need to be taught manners, madam. And I am the one to teach you. You will learn or—" He seemed to suddenly recollect himself and snapped his mouth shut. Without another word, he stalked out of the room.

Catherine found herself shaking. Her knees felt like jelly, and she sank gratefully into the low chair she habitually used. For a moment, the room swam before her eyes and she thought she might faint.

"Absurd," she whispered, "I never faint."

She felt a warm hand between her shoulder blades and gratefully let her head fall to her knees. Michael's hand gently rubbed the back of her neck. "Breathe deeply and slowly. You'll feel better in a moment. If you would like, I have some spirits of ammonia in my bag."

She shook her head. She wanted only to feel his hand and know that, for the moment at least, she was safe. "I will be fine in a moment. Just a moment." She relaxed for a few deep breaths.

No longer dizzy, Catherine slowly sat up. She could feel the flush of embarrassment mount her cheeks. Reluctantly, she looked up at Michael. But there was no pity in his face. Concern, yes, but not that patronizing air of sorrow for her weakness.

"You have been working too hard and going to too many social gatherings in the evenings. I prescribe a few nights at home reading in front of the fire and a glass of hot milk or chamomile tea in bed at ten o'clock." He was smiling. "I will prescribe the same for myself. Bancroft here has had me trotting about all over the city. I shall need another tailcoat if he does not stop."

She managed a weak smile. "Bed at ten with a book sounds like heaven."

"Well, neither of you is going to enjoy it quite yet, I'm afraid." Jeffrey had been leaning against the mantel, but now he advanced on them both. "I received a very distinct whiff of chicanery from our friend Sir Ronald. I could stand to know a good bit more about him. Arrived rather suddenly on the scene, did he not? Doesn't much want to talk about the past. In my experience, that usually means he's hiding something, and that usually means a skeleton somewhere in the cupboard." He grinned a little wolfishly. "I expect I shall enjoy finding out what that something is."

"But, Mr. Bancroft," Catherine said, "I cannot ask you to do that for me or my father. My father most particularly. He has not been—" She broke off, realizing too late that what she was going to say reflected poorly on her parent.

It was Jeffrey who flushed. "I am not acting in order to earn your gratitude, Miss Stanhope. I do not hope for your father's goodwill. I had hoped I had already earned yours."

"But that is exactly it!" Catherine realized to her horror she had tears in her eyes. "You have already done so much. I am so much in your debt. Your donations to St. Luke's, your kindness to all of us there—I can never repay you. And now to take an interest in my difficulties—you are much too kind."

"Never let Lucinda Harrowby hear you say such a thing. She will have you clapped into Bedlam." He smiled a little crookedly. "No, Miss Stanhope, I just do not like men like Bolton—men who use their money and position to bully others. I received such treatment in my youth, and I vowed then to do what I could to pull the fangs of any other such men I encountered."

"You have already saved me from St. John Featherstone. Both of you—I have always thought I could get along without friends. Well, I had to do so for the most part because my tastes and interests were so different from

other girls." Catherine rose to her feet, still a little shaky
until she felt Michael's hand under her elbow. She turned
her face to his and gave him her heart in her smile.

"Now you know that friends are the greatest riches in
the world," Michael said. "It is a hard lesson for those of
us who think to travel through life alone." He smiled back
at her, all the love she could ever want shining in his eyes.
"But one well worth learning."

"Now, now, you two. You are going to make me feel
terribly *de trop,* when I am absolutely necessary to confer
any hint of propriety upon this gathering. I am afraid your
father would not approve of this meeting of the Crimean
Friends' Society." Jeffrey grinned at them both. "I think
we had better go and let Miss Stanhope finish her evening
in a more peaceful style."

Michael looked at the brass clock on the mantel. "Good
lord, yes. We are keeping you from your dinner. Your
father will have me barred from the house."

He and Jeffrey had moved toward the door when it
opened and Holden's worried face appeared. "Sir Everett
has returned home, Miss Catherine. He is asking for you."

"In here, are you, my dear?" Her father's jovial tones
preceded him into the library by only a few seconds. He
stopped on the threshold of the room and a monumental
frown replaced the welcoming smile that had wreathed his
face. "What are you doing in this room alone with these
gentlemen, Catherine?" he asked, his voice carefully calm.

"These gentlemen have been saving me from scandal
and possible social ostracism, Papa." Catherine went up
to him and took his arm. "It is time you realized Dr. Soames
and Mr. Bancroft are two of the best friends we have. I do
not know what makes you so blind, but I want you to know
wherever I am, they will be welcome."

"What are you talking about? Scandal? Ostracism?" The

baronet was outraged. "The Stanhopes would never be subjected to that."

"You forget St. John Featherstone," Catherine said.

The baronet's face fell. "You are right. I had forgotten the little toad."

"You will be receiving a letter from him in the morning, attesting to your daughter's character and kindness." It was Michael who spoke.

Jeffrey and Michael had been moving toward the door, but the baronet's stocky little figure still barred it. He looked up. "You managed to still the little beggar's tongue? I think Catherine overestimated his influence, but nevertheless I thank you, most sincerely. If I have not been as welcoming as I should be, I am sorry. I have had a great deal on my mind lately. Between Palmerston and the queen, I shall never have any peace."

"She still opposes him, even now that he has taken over?" Jeffrey smiled. "She never forgets and never changes her mind, does she?"

The baronet shook his head. "No, she doesn't. Palmerston is light-minded and too popular for her, and he does not take every word out of the prince consort's mouth as if it came direct from Mt. Sinai." He stopped and then, with a somewhat forced smile, added, "But why are we standing here when we could be in the drawing room, having a glass of sherry in front of the fire? I daresay we might run to an early dinner tonight, eh, Catherine? Mrs. Marston up to that, do you think?"

Catherine smiled in relief. She had been afraid her father might not be able to overcome his longstanding social prejudices, and that would have posed a greater problem in some ways than their disagreement over her marriage.

Her father would never force her to marry a man she

could not love, but he might make it difficult for her to entertain those he considered his social inferiors, and that could lead to a real estrangement and to Catherine's leaving her father's home. Fortunately, he seemed ready to at least give the appearance of cordiality to these two who had helped his daughter avoid a nasty bit of gossip.

Michael and Jeffrey both demurred, insisting they could not trouble the Stanhopes, but at Catherine's insistence they agreed to stay. She had a feeling both regarded dinner with her father as more of a penance than a treat. Knowing the baronet would be unhappy if she dined in her drab hospital uniform, Catherine slipped away and washed and changed into a soft blue silk dress. She wore a collar of pearls and a matching ring that had belonged to her mother.

When she returned, she found the three gentlemen chatting amiably over sherry. At the dinner table, politics became the topic, and Catherine and Michael found themselves listening, fascinated, to the opinions and ideas of Jeffrey and Sir Everett. They were both well-informed, and their ideas were just different enough to inspire a spirited discussion. One thing they agreed on was that Benjamin Disraeli was never going to be prime minister. Too many enemies, too few friends. Unlike Palmerston, who had regained power because he had so many highly placed friends and could work with anyone, Disraeli had only his intelligence to recommend him.

After listening for some time to the discussion, Michael spoke up. "I met him the other night," he said mildly as he cracked a nut between long, strong fingers. "I thought him formidably intelligent and quite fascinating. If he were a woman, one would call him charming. But very determined. I would not bet against him. It may take him some time because of the rupture with the Peelites, but I think one day you may be surprised."

Sir Everett looked at Michael with shrewd eyes. "It is interesting to hear you say that. I have known Dizzy for some years, so I perhaps lose sight of the force of his personality. You may be right, doctor, though I sincerely hope you are wrong. The man may be charming, but he has no principles!"

Jeffrey said, "He is very clever, but his fight with Peel has guaranteed a Whig government for years to come. I do not think his party will forget that. No, Doctor, I think you are mistaken."

Catherine had not excused herself, deeming the gentlemen's conversation more interesting than a solitary cup of tea would be. She was fascinated to see how men tested themselves by exchanging views on an impersonal topic. If three women had been getting acquainted, they would have talked of family and fashion. Well, some women, she amended. She and Lucinda had made friends while holding basins for seasick nurses on the crossing to Turkey.

She arose at last and excused herself, not to drink tea but to go up to bed. Michael had recommended an early night and she was only too happy to comply. A few minutes later, as Betsy brushed her hair, a part of her bedtime ritual, Catherine heard the front door close, and she smiled.

It had been a very eventful day, but in the end a positive one. St. John Featherstone sent packing, Sir Ronald routed again, and her father reaching out, however tentatively, to her friends. A good day.

She had particularly enjoyed losing her temper. It was a wonderful, light, liberating feeling to shout at someone who deserved to be shouted at. She must try it more often.

Having resolved to show her anger frequently in the future, Catherine fell asleep with a smile on her face.

Chapter Seventeen

Michael found himself actually enjoying a little of the social life that acquaintance with Jeffrey Bancroft and Catherine had forced on him. He found he had friends and a crusade. He and Bancroft were going to free Catherine from Sir Ronald. He would personally enjoy administering a good thrashing or at least a duel, but unfortunately modern life did not permit such direct methods.

Bancroft's methods might prove to be just as effective, but they were taking a devilishly long time. They seemed to involve a great deal of talking with Henry Blankenship and other men of affairs over brandy and cigars at the kind of clubs Michael had never been inside. They were not the exclusive, secretive domains of the aristocracy. According to Bancroft, men like him, self-made and in many cases far wealthier than those with old titles, had formed their own establishments.

"Never even been inside White's," said Jeffrey one evening as he and Michael sat in luxurious comfort in his club's smoking room. "Much prefer this. I hear we have better food and much more comfort." He grinned. "Blankenship said he might drop by if he has any information. He's not fond of clubs unless they are useful to him."

"It is very good of you both to take such an interest in Catherine's difficulties. I am involved because I— because—" Michael floundered to a stop. He found it impossible to actually put into words how he felt about Catherine. He realized with a start he had not even told her.

"Because you are in love with her," Jeffrey finished for him. "Well, Blankenship thinks you and she saved David's life. If you wanted the Prince Consort's head on a pike, I daresay he would make a push to get it for you."

Michael grinned. "Prince Albert may keep his head. I would much prefer Sir Ronald Bolton's, thank you very much."

"Well, lad, I think I may be able to help you with that." With that remark, Henry Blankenship came around from behind the high backs of their chairs and drew up another one for himself. "I finally found the chap I was looking for, a clerk in the office of a shipping concern Sir Ronald has an interest in. Came from the same village as me, so he was willing to talk to me—for a small consideration, of course."

"And?" Michael could not hide his impatience. He really did not care to whom Blankenship had spoken. Only the result of the conversation interested him.

"The ship Catherine's dad invested in landed safe as houses some two months ago, loaded to the gunwales with Indian spices." Henry leaned back and surveyed his companions with a grin.

"Ah." Jeffrey Bancroft nodded sagely and grinned back at the older man. "So that's his game."

"Yes. A neat little swindle, but it only works with them as trusts you. He wouldn't get very far with the likes of you and me, Bancroft."

Michael couldn't stand it any longer. "What are you talking about? If the ship returned and the cargo was unloaded, what is the difficulty? Why is Sir Everett still under the impression that it—" He broke off as a small ray of light began to dawn.

Henry Blankenship had seen the awareness break over Michael's face. "That's it, Doctor. Sir Ronald just doesn't tell him the ship has returned and there are profits to distribute. Instead, he sends the ship out again under another name, perhaps this time to the Caribbean. In a few weeks, I imagine he will report it sunk."

"And he can get away with it? Won't his partners want to see the books?"

"Not if he has mostly men who pride themselves on the distance they keep between themselves and any kind of business." There was no bitterness in Jeffrey's voice, but there was a wealth of cynicism. "It's not difficult to fleece men who want the fact of their investment kept quiet."

"Why would he do it?" Michael wondered. "If the scheme is exposed, he stands to lose more than money. He would have to leave London, I would imagine. People would cut his acquaintance. To a man like Bolton, that would be a terrible fate."

"Money?" Jeffrey said, as he carefully rolled a cigar between his fingers. "Have you been able to learn anything about him, Blankenship? I have run into a stone wall. From what I can tell, he seems to have sprung to life six or eight months ago when he arrived here. Before that, I can find no trace of him, and no one I have met seems to know anything about his past."

"Apparently he tells everyone the same story about coming from the north and inheriting his father's lands and title not long ago. I have friends in Manchester and Liverpool. I've asked them but have not yet had a reply." Henry frowned. "I must say I am puzzled. I have talked to people who know who everyone is and what all their secrets are, and still nothing."

Michael really did not care where Sir Ronald came from, as long as he could be made to return there—without Catherine. "Surely we have enough to send him packing back to wherever it is he comes from and to get Sir Everett's money for him. What more do we want?"

Henry stirred in his chair, as if suddenly uncomfortable. "I never like to leave a scorpion with a sting still left in his tail. If he is keeping something so carefully hidden, then I think it is worth knowing."

"But in the meantime—" Michael could not hide his impatience.

"In the meantime, lad, we will convince Sir Ronald that his ship has just made a miraculous appearance and profits due and owing Sir Everett can thus be paid forthwith. Never fear, the lady's father will be saved and she will be free to marry you." Henry was carefully gazing at the brandy swirling in his glass and thus arranged to miss the embarrassed look on the young doctor's face.

"Is there anything I can do?" Michael asked.

"If you could, lad, I would appreciate it if you could visit Davy. He is still limping, and his sisters are home from school and about to drive him distracted with all their fluttering around and sympathy. If you could think of something he could do—something real, not a made-up job." The worried look on Henry's face belied his carefully casual manner.

"Of course. I do have an idea, but I would like to discuss it with Miss Stanhope first."

"Ah, yes, lad, wouldn't do to decide anything without you discuss it with Miss Stanhope!" And Henry chuckled. His own children were not yet old enough to marry, and he did enjoy watching the love affairs of other young people. "When are we going to have the pleasure of wishing you happy?"

"I don't think she—that is, we do not really inhabit the same world," Michael protested.

"Seems to me you do pretty well at the chat-and-drink routine. And you work together. What more do you want? Don't tell me you don't think she's beautiful. Why, Miss Stanhope is the prettiest thing in three counties!"

"Yes, yes." Michael wanted to explain, but it was so embarrassing to confess one's social shortcomings. "I know all that. But I am a Scottish doctor with no pretensions to social standing."

"Not even a hint of the aristocracy?" Jeffrey wanted to know. "An aunt who married a duke or something similar? Doesn't take much, you know. Just a whiff will do it." He saw the arrested look on Michael's face, as if he had suddenly thought of something. "Well, is there? Perhaps you have thought of a duke?"

"Not exactly," Michael replied. "But now that I think of it, my father's second cousin married the Earl of Bothwell. We don't see them—they live off in some drafty castle in the Highlands. My mother tried to get her to sponsor us in Edinburgh society, but I gather her cousin Althea is a bit of a rebel and wanted no part of it."

"And you never thought of this when Sir Everett was treating you as if you should go to the servants' entrance?"

Jeffrey shook his head. "I guarantee you, once you drop that bit of news in his ear, Miss Stanhope's parent will embrace you happily."

"But it is not a close connection. Besides, the Countess Bothwell is known as at best an eccentric and at worst a lunatic. Rides all over the countryside in breeches and opposes the railroads as the work of the devil."

"All the better. The aristocrats love eccentricity, particularly if it never shows its face. You have the winning trump in that cousin. Use it." Jeffrey nodded decisively.

The three friends parted soon afterward, with Michael walking home wondering how to work the countess of Bothwell into his next conversation with Catherine.

As it happened, the thought of his aristocratic connection was far from his mind when he saw Catherine the next day. She was in one of the wards, with a group of nurses gathered around one patient's cot. A training lesson was going on, he realized as he entered the large, high-ceilinged room. Catherine was giving the patient, a fever victim from the nearby slums, a sponge bath.

The group looked very different from the way they had when Michael had first seen them. They were tidy now and clean, in uniforms of dark blue with white caps and aprons. But they exhibited more than mere physical change. They stood straight and walked with pride and purpose.

Not all had changed completely, however. Michael noticed the youngest and best looking of the group still painted her face and fluttered her eyelashes at any male who was conscious. He waited quietly for Catherine to finish the lesson.

"Now, ladies," she concluded, "I want you each to take

a basin and two cloths and wash one of the patients. I will come by to check your work. After that, it will be time to take the broth and claret around to those on special strengthening diets.''

Michael was, as always, delighted by the sight and sound of Catherine. But he also noticed that the little painted nurse was blatantly trying to get his attention. Catherine noticed, too.

"Nancy," she asked, "why do we give strengthening diets to patients?"

"Account of we wants 'em to get their strength back," Nancy shot back. "And beef broth and claret and eggs and such are strengthening," she added with an air of stating the obvious.

"Very good, Nancy." Catherine beamed approval, and Nancy visibly bloomed.

Catherine caught sight of him and, with the smile that always caused his heart to stumble and then start beating twice as fast, she began to make her way across the room. She was stopped by nurses with questions and patients with complaints, so it took her a good few minutes to reach him.

"Good morning, Doctor," she said, dipping a small curtsy. Catherine was meticulous about observing all the deferential niceties that protocol decreed between doctors and nurses, but her eyes were warm.

"Good morning, Miss Stanhope." As the head of nursing, Catherine was addressed as *Miss* rather than *Nurse* Stanhope. It was peculiar to St. Luke's, for titles varied greatly from one hospital to the next. "Might I hope for a word with you?"

"Of course, Doctor." Catherine proceeded with him out into the corridor.

Michael wanted to share the good news about her

father's investment, but did not have Henry and Jeffrey's permission. They wanted to be certain Sir Ronald did not have a means to retaliate before they sprung their trap.

"I wanted to ask about David Blankenship. His father mentioned to me that David was becoming impatient at not having recovered completely. He took a chill, I think, and his sisters are driving him mad with cosseting." Michael looked at her profile as she passed under the high clerestory windows that marked the hallways. It was etched with pure morning light and was perfect. One of those Italian fellows could have painted her as a saint or an angel, he thought. The shimmer of gold that the light made of her hair almost resembled a halo.

Having Catherine walk beside him was one of life's small but important pleasures. He wanted to prolong it, so he waited a moment before he said, with a certain amount of diffidence, "I thought perhaps he could visit Julian Livingston. He has done so well recovering from somewhat the same injury. Perhaps it would help. What do you think? I did not want to suggest it until I had discussed it with you."

She was silent for a few moments, and Michael's heart sank. She hated the idea. She thought him an encroaching fellow for daring to suggest anything where her old friend Julian was concerned.

Just as he was about to tell her that it had been a stupid, foolish idea, she stopped and put her hand on his arm. She was smiling. "Of course, David and Julian. That would be perfect! Jules is still sunk in gloom, and is spending his days being perfectly horrid to everyone. David would be wonderful for him. He can tell him practical things—get him started on crutches, perhaps! Jules won't want to be caught sulking by someone so much younger. He'll have to get well so he won't be shown up!"

By the time she finished, Catherine was practically dancing, she was so enthusiastic, and Michael's heart was once more beating solidly in his chest.

"I am glad you think it is a good idea," he said, though that hardly began to express how he felt—relieved she had not minded and happy they thought alike on the subject.

"Shall you broach the subject to David?" she said.

"Yes. I have to see his father this evening on another matter, but I wanted to be able to set his mind at rest about a task for David. Would you want to stop and see Livingston and his mother this afternoon, to see if it meets with their approval?"

"I suppose I might as well, though the countess will agree to anything that might help Julian. And he will not think anything is worth trying. I have almost given up on him, he has become so unpleasant. But the countess says he keeps having nightmares and calling out in his sleep, so we cannot give him up to the darkness. I do not think I help him much, but Davy might."

Her visit that afternoon with the countess went very much as her prior visits had. Catherine was saddened to see the countess's face drawn and pale, attesting to the difficulty she was having sleeping and eating. Her worry for her son was like a fog surrounding her formerly bright spirit.

When Catherine brought up the subject of David Blankenship, the countess threw up her hands and cried, "I should not. Julian's father will be horrified. He will never associate with *les nouveaux riches*. But for the sake of my son, you may bring this chimney sweep or weaver's brat—"

She stopped short when Catherine burst out laughing. "My dear ma'am, David Blankenship is a product of Harrow. His upbringing has been of the strictest. Your only

fear should be that he might be led astray by some of
Julian's stable language!"

A little affronted that her scruples were brushed aside
so lightly, the countess said, "One cannot help but think
that you have been coarsened by your adventures with the
Army! I had heard as much, though of course I do not get
about much these days."

"Then perhaps you should, ma'am." Catherine's feath-
ers were a little ruffled by the countess's words. More of
Featherstone's insidious work, no doubt. "I think it would
be good for you to go about your usual pursuits. You know
it does no one any good for you to sit in here and get
sadder and sadder. Please, ma'am?"

"Oh, none of the invitations that have arrived appeal
to me. I wish for fresh faces and interesting conversation."

The countess's fretful words caused Catherine to think.
Her father and now the countess had voiced prejudices
about the industrial tycoons who were newly come into
their wealth. She knew several of these men and found
them to be interesting and well-mannered. Suppose she
arranged a soiree and included denizens of both worlds
in a setting intimate enough that conversation would be
possible? Might she not enable both sides to see the virtues
of the other?

"You know, ma'am, I have been thinking. Papa and I
have enjoyed a great deal of hospitality these past few
weeks." Here Catherine had to exaggerate. In truth, she
had found very little to enjoy about most of their attendance—except the waltz with Michael, of course. But that
seemed months ago.

"And," Catherine continued, "it would seem only polite
if Papa and I were to give a party in our turn. Nothing
elaborate, you understand, since both of us are so busy.

But a dinner and then perhaps a reception. What do you think?"

The countess was famous for her entertainments. People vied for invitations to Eversleigh House, for the food was always French, the music often German, and the hospitality English. At Catherine's words, she began to visibly brighten.

"Ah, Catherine, that is a splendid idea. You could perhaps have a little music after dinner. Perhaps invite a few additional people to come to listen. And then a late supper. Would Mrs. Marston or your cook be insulted if you borrowed our chef for the evening, do you think?" The countess's little half smile appeared for the first time in weeks.

"I think they would both be most grateful. At Stanhope House, we all know our limitations, I most of all. I hope you won't think our entertainment too paltry, ma'am, for I know I haven't your knack." Catherine looked down at her hands, which were neatly clasped in her lap.

"I could perhaps help a little?" the countess suggested, a smile still tugging at her lips. "If you would not mind, of course, dear Catherine."

"Oh, would you, ma'am?" Catherine exclaimed. "But no, I could not ask it of you."

"Minx! As if you had not planned this all along!" The countess got to her feet and came over to put her arms around Catherine's shoulders. "Very well, you and I will give a party. And I warn you, *ma chère*, I shall exhaust you all before we are through!"

The countess was as good as her word. She took over the planning and execution of the Stanhopes' soiree before the baronet could do more than voice a weak protest. Catherine maintained control only over the guest list, which she insisted on drawing up by herself. She wrote most of the invitations, leaving the countess in some doubt as to who was coming.

"It is going to be small, as we agreed," Catherine said. "No more than twenty for dinner and twenty more for the music. Have you managed to secure the chamber ensemble you talked of?" she added when the countess looked as if she might ask who the guests were to be.

"No, but instead we are to have the pianoforte. But how will I know who I can talk to about it if I do not know who is to be invited?" she complained.

"I think you should have your own party a few days later—a large one—and then you can talk to everyone about that." Catherine tried to look bland and not laugh at the countess's expression.

"You do not fool me. I am going to be surprised by your guests, am I not? All Crimean veterans, perhaps? Or doctors and solicitors and other grubby *bourgeois*?" She frowned. "I like my prejudices, Catherine, and I will not welcome having them overturned."

"Mr. Disraeli told me once that most people never think, they just rearrange their prejudices," Catherine said thoughtfully. "I would like people to do more than that. Perhaps I should send a card to Mr. Disraeli. What do you think?"

"That you must ask your papa. I know nothing of politics and I absolutely refuse to learn anything whatsoever!" And the countess left Catherine to her invitations while she herself went down to the kitchen to preside over the meeting between her chef, Jean-Pierre André, a student of the great Royer, who was even now on his way to the Crimea to teach the army how to cook.

"It is worse than the Congress of Vienna, you two," she said as she parceled out who was to cook what. "You must each do what you do best. Jane," she addressed the Stanhopes' cook, "you must roast the capons and make the trifle. Jean-Pierre, you will do the vegetables and the accompanying side dishes.

"For everyone knows," she added to her chef in rapid French, "that the English cannot put a vegetable on the stove without turning it to gray mush."

She beamed at everyone. "It is going to be wonderful. You will all outdo yourselves!"

Catherine managed to persuade Michael and Jeffrey Bancroft to come by appealing to their chivalry. She was afraid, she said, that she might have difficulty filling her chairs if they refused. She had had no time to reanimate the friendships she had enjoyed before the Crimea. She needed them.

Of course, they said they would come.

She went to the Harrowbys' house one night after work. Catherine was reluctant to cause her friend any trouble by appearing in her plain hospital dress and thus prove to her relations that Lucinda's friends were as strange and déclassé as Lucinda herself. Catherine thus took the time to change into a rose colored twilled silk afternoon dress with matching bonnet. She wore a sealskin cape to ward off the late winter chill.

Lucinda greeted her in a small, shabby drawing room at the back of the house. Obviously, this was the room set aside for Lucinda to receive her guests in, as opposed to the Harrowbys' guests, who were received in style in a large, opulent room overlooking the square. Catherine frowned. She wished Lucinda would come and live with her, where she would be treated as she deserved. When she said as much to Lucinda, her friend laughed.

"But I am not going to be here much longer," she said. "So you needn't worry. I am going to be married."

"You are! But how marvelous, Lucy. But why have I heard nothing of any fiancé or wedding date?" Not only was Catherine surprised, she was a little hurt that Lucinda had not shared her happiness before now. "Who is the lucky man?"

"Oh, I haven't got as far as that yet!" Lucinda said, and went off into another peal of laughter when she looked at Catherine's face. Catherine was sure she looked as astonished as she felt.

Lucinda's next words left her in no doubt she was correct. "Shut your mouth, Cat. You look like a trout."

"Well, of all the ridiculous plans. Don't you think you ought to find the man you want to marry before you announce the event?"

"No, silly. Not if you are intelligent about it. The important thing is to make up your mind you wish to tie yourself to a male for life, and then you find the least objectionable one around and that's that." Lucinda poured tea for them both. Catherine could not help but notice that the pot was a simple Staffordshire set ornamented with roses, not part of the family silver, as would have been the case had she been taking tea with the Harrowbys. Thus, Lucinda was made to understand at every turn that she was a poor relation.

"Well then, my errand will serve your purposes nicely. I have come to ask that you grace us with your presence at a dinner we are giving next Tuesday night. I have to tell you, however, that I have asked Jeffrey Bancroft."

Catherine took a deep breath and eyed her friend warily. Lucinda had a temper, and Catherine wasn't sure how she would react.

She hurried on. "He has done me a great service recently

and we have become friends. I want him to come, along
with Michael and the Blankenships, to meet and mingle
with my father and the countess—and you. I want this silly
prejudice on both sides to end, and this will be a start. I
need you there, Lucy. You have been to the Crimea, yet
you move in the first circles. You can cross the lines. Please
say you will put aside your dislike of Mr. Bancroft for one
evening. Please?''

Lucinda could see she was serious, so after a few
moments she said she would come. "But only if there are
a few rich and handsome men around as well. Not just
politicians and older couples, but some entertaining and
eligible gentlemen.''

Catherine promised to do her best to bring some new
gentlemen to her friend's attention. Privately, though, she
thought Mr. Bancroft probably fit the requirements better
than almost anyone else in London.

Two days before the event, Catherine was well pleased
with the results of her efforts. The countess was in and out
of Stanhope House a dozen times a day, leaving everyone
with a thousand new things to do. She was in her element
and looked younger and happier than she had since Julian
first announced he was going to the Crimea with the 11th
Hussars. Catherine had hoped Julian himself might deign
to come, but the countess said he had turned his face to
the wall and refused to speak when she mentioned it.

Despite that setback, everything seemed to be going
smoothly until her father arrived home that evening and
remarked that he was looking forward to seeing Sir Ronald
at the event.

"But I did not invite him, Papa," Catherine blurted out
before she could think of a more tactful way to put it. "I

told him when he burst in here the last time that he was not welcome in our house."

"Not welcome!" Sir Everett seemed thunderstruck. "But I have just had the most splendid news from him about our investment."

"Truly?" Catherine was skeptical. Sir Ronald would stop at nothing to get what he wanted, and for some inexplicable reason he wanted her. Telling her father a lie to gain an invitation to a party would be completely in character.

"Yes, the ship he thought had been lost in a typhoon limped into port, her cargo intact, not a week ago. I have more than doubled my investment." Her father was as happy as a child on his birthday.

"That is wonderful, Papa, but it does not change my aversion to him. I do not necessarily receive everyone you do. There are members of your club and even members of parliament you would not wish me to know."

Catherine hoped that this appeal to her father's sense of what was fitting for women would trump his desire to please his wealthy business patron, for the baronet had made it clear that there were men, rakish fellows of loose morals, who were quite acceptable for other gentlemen to know but completely inappropriate for their wives, sisters, and particularly their daughters. If possible, Catherine wanted the baronet to see Sir Ronald in that light.

"I understand how you must feel. I have explained to the fellow that you simply cannot be brought to see what a splendid chap he is and that I will not force you to marry where you cannot feel affection. But he seems to think you will change your mind." The baronet shook his head. "He is a most stubborn man. But as I said, he has befriended me and I have already received him in my home. I am afraid I cannot now refuse to receive him."

"But I can, Papa, and I do. I simply will not have him

in my house, standing next to me, calling me 'my dear Catherine,' and insisting he will marry me whether I wish it or not.'' Catherine was becoming more and more agitated the more she thought of Sir Ronald. "I simply cannot bear it. You mustn't invite him. Please, Papa.''

"Well, but you see, my dear," her father said, looking a little shamefaced, "I am afraid I already have.''

Catherine sat down with a thump. "Oh, Papa, no. Well, then, you must keep him away from me. I simply will not be responsible for what I might do if he pursues me!''

The baronet promised to do his best, though privately he wondered whether anyone could thwart the iron-willed Sir Ronald.

Chapter Eighteen

As it happened, the baronet need not have worried.

Catherine had mentioned to Henry Blankenship when she went to tea at the Blankenship mansion that evening, as she tried to do every Sunday when she was free, that Sir Ronald was coming.

"He is a very difficult man to divert," she said, willing to confide in the shrewd financier but hoping to hide from him how threatened she felt. "I would be obliged if you would attempt to engage him in conversation, sir. Apparently, his venture with my father succeeded after all. He reported to Papa that the ship they backed had come in and Papa made a handsome profit. That is why Papa thinks he cannot refuse to invite the man to a dinner."

"My dear Miss Stanhope, I think I can assure you I will keep Sir Ronald very busy on Tuesday evening!" Henry Blankenship's eyes twinkled and he chuckled. "We businessmen are always eager to learn new tricks and tactics.

I'm sure Sir Ronald has a few I would be interested in, and I believe I have a few tricks to show him, as well.''

"Mr. Blankenship," Catherine said earnestly, "far be it from me to tell you how to conduct your business, but I do know Sir Ronald, and I do not think it would be wise to go into any venture with him. Papa is delighted with him now, but I cannot trust him. I introduced you to him, and I would feel responsible if you were to lose because of it." Catherine placed her hand on her host's arm and looked at him with real distress in her eyes.

"I can promise you faithfully I will not go into any business venture with Sir Ronald. If I may ask, Miss Stanhope, do you think your father is going to go into another venture with Sir Ronald?"

"I have asked him not to, if only because it makes it necessary for him to invite Sir Ronald to our home. He has said he will not, but Sir Ronald seems to have some strange power over my father. I do not understand it. Perhaps because he is a businessman and Papa is not. He has convinced Papa that he can make money almost by magic."

"And does your papa need this magic money, Miss Stanhope?" Mr. Blankenship's eyes were gentle. He hated to see Miss Stanhope, in his opinion the most wonderful young woman in the entire world except for his daughters, unhappy for any reason. And he simply could not understand how any father could make his child unhappy for the sake of money.

Mr. Blankenship had the knack for making money grow, but unlike many men who had worked their way up in the world, he did not value money for its own sake. He cared about it only because with it he could protect his children, and his wife if he was lucky enough to have one, from the grinding poverty he had been born into.

He had joined the conspiracy with young Bancroft and Dr. Soames, the most wonderful young man in the world (next to his Davy, of course) because of his deep-seated conviction that to protect women and children was the highest duty of every man.

Catherine had to think about her answer. "I do not think he has debts he cannot pay, Mr. Blankenship." Her father had never talked much about money and it had never seemed to be a problem, but now she tried to put her finger on what drove the baronet. "I think it is because so many of the politicians he deals with are so very rich. It makes him feel poor, even though he is far from being so." She shook her head. "I do not know if that is it. It is just what I sense from seeing him in the company of other, wealthier men."

"I think you are very likely right. Now come along and say hello to Davy, who has been waiting this age to greet you." He took her arm and led her over to the settee by the fire where Davy was sitting, a silver-headed cane by his side.

"Miss Stanhope, how glad I am to see you!" Davy called out as she approached. "I can walk almost halfway across the room without my cane. What do you think of that?"

David Blankenship had fought and been wounded and suffered greatly while the wound was healing. Through it all, he had been brave and steadfast. Yet now that the danger was over, he was regaining the infectious high spirits of his youth.

Mary Ann Evans stood beside the tea tray, which had been placed on a table near the fire. She was arranging plates of sandwiches and teacakes. At the sound of Catherine's greeting, she turned with a smile.

"Miss Stanhope, may I pour you a cup of tea?"

Catherine glanced about the cozy, homelike room where

she had known such warmth and friendship. She only hoped she would still have these people as friends after Tuesday night.

"Miss Stanhope," Henry Blankenship said later as he saw her to the door, "I have a favor to ask of you. I will understand if you feel you cannot grant it, but . . ."

Tuesday evening was one of those rare winter nights when a breeze that was almost balmy gave a hint of spring to come. Catherine had dressed with unusual care, allowing Betsy to dress her hair in a more elaborate style than usual, with curls and a soft chignon wreathed with flowers.

Betsy looked suspiciously woebegone and Catherine was afraid the maid had parted from Jemmy with no promise of future meetings. As she stood looking at herself in the mirror to be sure she looked her best, she heard a sniff and turned to see Betsy in tears.

"Why, Betsy, my dear, what is the matter?" Catherine took her maid's hands in hers and looked into her face. "What has happened? Is there anything I can do?"

"Oh, miss, you are too good to me!" And Betsy flung her apron over her head and sobbed.

"Good heavens, there is no need to cry about it." Catherine was torn between laughter and tears herself.

"Oh, Miss Stanhope, Jemmy wants me to come north and meet his ma-ma-mam and ma-ma-marry h-h-him." Betsy's wails broke out in earnest.

"Well, Betsy, I still do not see what you have to cry about. You love Jemmy and he loves you, and now he has asked you to marry him! It is wonderful. Why are you crying?"

"Because I'll have to leave you, Miss Catherine, ma'am. And I can't hardly bring myself to do it." Betsy wiped her eyes and looked at her mistress with a teary smile. "You gave me my chance and are so good to me. And to Jemmy. Why, we'd do anything for you."

"Thank you, Betsy. You will be difficult indeed to replace. But I could never be happy knowing you had stayed with me and sacrificed your own happiness. You must go to Jemmy. I think that as a going-away and bridal gift, a dowry would be appropriate. No girl should be married without one—particularly if she is to live with her mother-in-law. Now dry your eyes and tell me if I look presentable."

"Oh, miss, you look beautiful. That color makes you look like a queen."

Catherine had once again refused to choose the usual pastels deemed appropriate for blonds, especially unmarried blonds, no matter what their age. Instead, she had chosen a rich cobalt blue that made her eyes look like sapphires and her hair like spun gold. It was cut in her usual simple style, with line and fabric instead of trimming making the statement. Catherine smiled. If Betsy thought she looked right, it must be so.

She descended the staircase to find the earl and countess of Eversleigh had arrived before her. The earl took Catherine aside. He had aged since Julian's return, the lines in his forehead more deeply etched, the silver in his hair more visible.

"I have to thank you, my dear," he said in a soft undertone. He looked with deep affection at his wife, who was hurrying from one room to the next, her honey-colored taffeta skirt belling around her as she moved. "She has brightened so much thanks to this party. And she has followed your suggestion and is giving a much larger soiree of our own next week. I think it is the first time I have seen a real smile on her face since we learned of Julian's wound."

"Oh, it was an entirely selfish act, my lord." Catherine returned his smile. "The countess has always been my social arbiter. I only hope she does not lose all patience with me after tonight."

"That is not likely, my dear. The countess told me she is sure you have invited some entirely unsuitable guests and she is prepared to welcome them with open arms." He looked down at Catherine and she thought, as she so often had, that Julian and his father might almost be duplicates of each other. "We both are a little unhappy still that you and Julian cannot make a match of it. But we will always love you, my dear, and support you in anything you choose to do."

"Thank you, my lord. Thank you." Impulsively, Catherine reached up and kissed his cheek. She felt as if she had taken the first jump in the hunt. The rest would be easier. She had feared that the Eversleighs would balk at the nature of some of her guests, particularly since she should have warned them beforehand.

"You are flirting with my husband again, Catherine." The countess was smiling as she floated over to them. "I have always known that you had a *tendre* for the earl, and he for you. Alas, I am but second best to you in that glorious dress." And she looked at Catherine with real affection. "I trust you will present all your guests to me. I can be trusted to behave with proper decorum, I do assure you."

She reached up and patted Catherine's cheek. "I am French, after all. I must believe in *liberté, égalité, fraternité* or lose my right to claim the nationality. So bring on the chimney sweeps, *ma chère.*"

Catherine's smile slipped a little. There were no chimney sweeps among the guests, but several came from origins that would raise eyebrows. She raised her head and took a deep breath. They were her friends, and must be accepted as such.

The dinner guests began to arrive then, and Catherine and her father greeted them at the top of the staircase that led to the formal drawing and dining rooms. Sherry and lemonade were available, and since there were so few guests, Catherine was soon free to mingle and move people from one group to another.

The Blankenships arrived with a distinguished-looking woman. It took Catherine a moment to recognize Mary Ann Evans. Her invitation had been the favor Henry Blankenship had asked on Sunday and Catherine had agreed, although she was a little afraid Mary Ann would feel out of place and ill at ease. But to look at her in her elegant dark brown silk twill dress with black lace trim and a black lace cap on her smooth brown hair, she seemed quite at home.

"Mary Ann," said Catherine, giving her a welcoming kiss, "I am so happy you could come. You look wonderful."

Mary Ann smiled serenely. "Thank you. It was good of you to have me. The Blankenships have gotten in the habit of including me, but I did not expect you to do so."

"I am delighted to have you. This is an evening for all my friends who are in London." Catherine turned to David, who looked handsome but heartbreakingly young in his evening clothes. His open, unlined countenance contrasted with the cane he still used. "David, I am so glad you could come. I wanted to ask you if you had yet seen my friend, Julian Livingston."

"Yes, Miss Stanhope, and I am afraid it was not a success." David's face was red and he looked very embarrassed. "He was not very happy to see me. Asked if I was there on behalf of all the Crimean cripples and told me to get out and tell you he did not need anyone to talk nonsense to him about getting better.

"So I tried to tell him he *could* get better. That I had. But not if he did not try. Then he told me to leave. I'm afraid that made me angry—he wasn't very nice about it, you see. So I said Nurse Cranmer would make him get out of bed if she had to hide the chamber pot and bellpull. He told me I wasn't Nurse Cranmer, and then I'm afraid I got fed up and left." Davy looked at her beseechingly. "I am sorry, Miss Stanhope, but he does have a way of getting up my nose—pardon my plain speaking."

Catherine laughed. "Yes, he certainly does. So Rose Cranmer nursed both of you at Scutari?"

"Yes, ma'am. She saw to most of the surgical patients. Had a way of making us try to get better. She'd make short work of the lieutenant's sulks, she would."

"Well, unfortunately, she isn't here, so I suppose you and I will just have to continue to do the best we can. Will you try again with me, David?"

"Of course, Miss Stanhope. Whenever you wish."

"Good. It's a bargain then." She extended her hand and Davy took it and gave it a firm shake. "We'll try to do whatever Rose would do. Maybe she would consent to take a look at him when she comes home."

"I don't know, ma'am. She said she wasn't coming to London. She wasn't sure where she was going. Someplace new, she said. Maybe America."

"Good heavens." Catherine was astonished. She and Rose had been friends, yet she'd had no idea that Rose considered emigrating. A quiet, country-bred girl with beautiful eyes and a hint of sadness about her, Rose was a wonderful nurse. Catherine wasn't surprised Rose got the best results with the surgical patients. But never to see her again? "I must write to her. If she does decide to go abroad, I would love to have her stay here while she arranges it."

She made a mental note to write to Rose, and then went to make sure that Lucinda and Jeffrey Bancroft were not left alone together long enough to exhaust their supply of polite small talk. They had already encountered each other, and Catherine thought they had been like two wary cats circling each other. She could practically see their backs go up and their fur rise.

"Lucinda," she said as she approached, having noted the heightened color in her friend's cheeks, "I have just heard Rose is thinking of emigrating to America."

"Which America?" Lucinda asked. "Canada? The United States?"

"How should I know?" Catherine sighed. When Lucinda got snippy, it could only mean someone had annoyed her, usually by saying something Lucinda thought was stupid. "I only heard it this minute, from David Blankenship." She turned to Jeffrey Bancroft and smiled. "Hello, Mr. Bancroft. I am delighted you could come this evening."

"And I am delighted to be here." He bowed. "Particularly since I have learned you are not going to request that I give you any money this evening."

Catherine laughed, but Lucinda snapped, "That is typically materialistic and rude."

"While you are being the soul of tact and charm," he responded with a grin that clearly inflamed Lucinda further.

She flushed and opened her mouth to annihilate him, but Catherine forestalled her. "Lucinda, dear, I believe we are ready to go in to dinner. I have asked Mr. Blankenship to escort you. Mr. Bancroft, if you would take Mrs. Evans?"

She had spent some time over the seating arrangements,

and was satisfied she had done a good job of mixing the old with the new. Michael, who had been talking to the earl for some minutes, was seated next to the countess with her father, at the head of the table, on the countess's other side. It was a dangerous move, but Catherine wanted Michael to know and like her friends—and her father, if that was possible.

Catherine held her breath, but at least at first all seemed to be going well.

"You have mixed an interesting brew, my dear," the earl said. As the highest-ranking guest, he was seated at his hostess's right. Catherine was delighted that protocol had given her such a pleasant partner and was looking forward to a pleasant meal.

Then the earl brought up her erstwhile suitor. "I notice Sir Ronald is not a guest this evening. You have decided against him?" At Catherine's nod he nodded back. "I am not surprised. A very strange fellow, that one. But your father seems very taken with him, so perhaps I am mistaken."

"Yes, my father likes him and cannot understand why I cannot." Catherine smiled. "And he *is* coming this evening. He will be here for the music."

Dinner seemed to go very well. As she looked about the table, Catherine did not see any guests who were silent or, conversely, having too lively a conversation. The countess and Michael appeared to be interested in each other's thoughts, and her father was talking to a political wife on his other side.

After dinner, the remaining guests arrived. Sir Ronald, whom Catherine had dreaded encountering, apparently wanted to avoid her, too. He went over to her father and engaged him in low-voiced conversation.

"My dear Miss Stanhope." Michael's voice came from beyond her vision, over her left shoulder. "I have been sautéed, grilled, and flambéed by your friend the countess of Eversleigh. I may never be the same again."

"That does not sound like the countess. What did you do to provoke her?"

"I told her her son was a spoiled brat and she should stop catering to his every whim. She said I was unfeeling and did not understand a mother's heart."

"Oh, dear. She adores Julian and has difficulty recognizing that he may have a tiny flaw or two." Catherine smiled. "What did you say then?"

"I said I might not understand a mother's heart but I understood a boy's, and her boy was having difficulty adjusting to a world that isn't going to give him everything he wants just for the asking. We all have to learn that, sooner or later." Michael grinned at her. "I think she was beginning to see my point by the time we reached the puddings and jellies stage."

"I am glad. I wanted you two to understand each other."

"Why? I have been wondering all evening. Why did you invite me here to meet the Eversleighs and your father socially?"

Catherine had finally discovered her underlying reason. Dare she tell him? Why not? A little champagne with dinner had done remarkable things for her courage. "Because I may want to marry you, and I want you to know and get along with my family and my old friends."

Michael stood and stared at her as if he had turned to stone.

"I had best make sure everyone has found seats. They are

tuning up. The pianist is about to begin." And Catherine turned to leave Michael and resume her hostess duties.

"I don't think so," Michael said, taking her by the arm and leading her out of the room. "They can find their own seats." He hurried her along the hall until he saw a fire and chairs inside one of the doors they passed. "In here."

He was not so lost to propriety that he closed the door completely. He left the requisite inches of space, but he led her, unresisting, over to the fire. There he stood, staring at her, running his hands up and down her bare arms.

It was as if he had been hit in the stomach. His breath came harshly and his head seemed to spin. "I feel as I used to after a street fight. Exhilarated but light-headed. Now tell me again. I was to come here tonight because . . ."

Catherine tried to pull away from him. "I should not have said what I did. It was completely out of—"

"Did you mean it?"

She met his gaze, and what he read in her eyes had Michael reeling. "Yes," she said.

"Then there is—" But he didn't want to talk. She was beautiful and she wanted to marry him. Fire raced through his veins. That must mean she loved him. A woman like Catherine would not say that otherwise.

He pulled her into his arms and set his lips to hers. Unlike their other kisses, this was a leisurely exploration of tastes and textures. He teased open her lips, and she responded with a sigh when he deepened the kiss, his tongue tasting the honeyed sweetness of her mouth.

This kiss was a declaration of intent. He wanted her. But that was not all he wanted her to read in his caress. The time had come. He could be as brave as she.

"I love you," he said. "God only knows what we can do about it, my dearest, but I do love you. I was afraid perhaps you didn't know. Yet I thought surely you must know." He kissed her again and felt he could never get enough of kissing her. "But I had not said the words." He trailed kisses down her neck. "I love you, Catherine. I love you."

He stepped back a half pace and, with his arms still loosely around her, said, "I still think your father will object, as will your friends. The countess was very kind to me at dinner, but she wants nothing less than perfection for you, and I do not think she sees it in me."

"Do you know, I think you refine much too much upon that topic. They all like you well enough. And I," she added, suddenly losing courage, "like you very much myself."

He threw back his head and laughed. "Such a weak declaration from the redoubtable Miss Stanhope!"

"Well, you had not said the words and now that I have heard them, I find I will need to hear them again before I can say them myself." She grinned up at him, a carefree, impish look he had not seen before. What a creature she was! The most serious nurse, braving untold dangers and difficult doctors to help her patients. A social reformer even in a small, personal way—teaching the hospital nurses, bringing different groups together tonight. And now a loving witch, weaving her spell about him.

"I love—"

"So this is where you have gone, my dear Catherine."

"Sir Ronald." It was a nightmare. Was she never to be rid of this man?

"Your father will be most displeased when he finds out you have been in here alone with a man—and not a man he can approve of." Sir Ronald's voice had the hectoring, pompous note she knew so well.

"Sir Ronald," she began again. But what, after all, was there to say?

"Sir," Michael said, gently releasing her and walking over to stand before the other, shorter man. He gazed down on Catherine's tormentor.

Sir Ronald stepped back a pace. Catherine had long thought he was a physical coward, for all he tried so hard to intimidate her. He dared attack only those weaker than he was.

"Do not threaten Miss Stanhope and do not hope to tattle to her father. He is learning not to trust you, or your investments." Michael's voice was a low growl. His fists were clenched, and Catherine knew he longed to strike Sir Ronald but that he would not do so in her home and in her presence.

In any case, he seemed to have taken some of the starch out of Sir Ronald's backbone. "I—I don't know what you mean. But I had better go to find him, before he hears the vicious, untrue rumors you and your lowborn friends are spreading." With that, he beat a hasty retreat.

"What did you mean about my father learning not to trust him?"

"Your father will tell you when he is ready to do so. In the meantime, Sir Ronald was right. We must return to the music now."

As the strains of a Chopin nocturne died away and the guests politely applauded, Sir Everett got up and made his way to the nearest tray of champagne that waiters were carrying through the room at a signal from the countess.

He was not a music lover, and when he listened he liked orchestras and choruses. Handel, now there was a composer. Or that German fellow—Beethovel or some such. But this romantic tinkling he found annoying, feminine, and unrewarding.

Henry Blankenship had asked before dinner if he could have a word with the baronet at some point in the evening. His expression had been grave and Sir Everett was disturbed, in part because he did not know what Blankenship wished to speak to him about. He very much feared the industrialist was going to try to persuade him to propose Blankenship to his club. The very thought made him uncomfortable.

In their conversation at Blankenship's home, the baronet had thought that the industrialist did not particularly wish to move in higher social circles. He had apparently realized the only way he could climb higher would be through marrying one of his children to the child of a peer, and he seemed more than reluctant to do so. But in the baronet's experience, men did want to ascend the social ladder once they realized they had the money to do so. If not for themselves, these self-made men wanted it for their children.

With these thoughts in his head, he began to wonder whether Blankenship did not have some shrewd scheme in mind to use the Stanhopes to advance his social standing. Blankenship approached him and asked if there was someplace they could talk uninterrupted. Sir Everett led him to his study at the back of the house.

A fire burned brightly and a few lamps burned, the gas set low. The baronet motioned his guest to a seat and awaited Blankenship's next move.

Mr. Blankenship looked a little worried. "I do not know how to approach you with this, Sir Everett."

Sir Everett's heart sank lower. This man was a friend of his daughter's, and while he might deplore the connection, Blankenship seemed a good enough fellow and the baronet was not looking forward to declining to aid his ambitions. "Please say whatever you think you must."

"Well, for the sake of your daughter, I must warn you about a business fraud I fear has been perpetrated upon you."

Sir Everett stared at the man, astounded. "Business?" he said at last. "You wish to talk to me about business? To help me?" *Aha*, he thought. *Now I have my answer. He will help me and I will owe him my patronage.* He stiffened his resolve to resist. "I am already advised by Sir Ronald Bolton."

Blankenship looked pained. "Yes, I know. That is the help I wish to give you. In a manner of speaking."

The baronet looked puzzled. "You wish to help me with Sir Ronald?"

Blankenship swore softly under his breath. Then he began again. "You see, I have made inquiries, and I have discovered Sir Ronald Bolton has a bad habit of losing money on his shipping ventures. He has a tendency to report ships as being lost."

"The habit? The tendency? What do you mean, sir?" Sir Everett was still off balance from discovering that Blankenship seemed to want to do him a favor. But, of course, he did not need any additional help with his investments. "It may interest you to know," he said somewhat huffily, "that Sir Ronald told me earlier this week my investment was saved. The ship he believed lost had been found."

"Yes," Blankenship said, a smile tugging at the corners of his mouth. "I know. Mr. Bancroft and I paid him a little visit, after which he 'discovered' the ship."

Sir Everett shook his head. "I am afraid you will have to explain."

"Of course. I'll try, but it is complicated. Following these twisty fellows takes someone with a long career in business. Hard for someone not used to it to get to the bottom of it. I daresay," Blankenship added, with the air of someone who sought to reassure, "I would feel the same about a bill or whatever in the House. Lost as a lamb, I'd be."

"It is kind of you to say so," Sir Everett replied. He didn't know whether to smile or frown in anger at being so transparently patronized.

"What happens is," Blankenship continued, "he reports the ship sunk, takes all the cargo for himself, collects on any insurance, repaints the hull, and sends it out again under another name."

Sir Everett was stunned. "But that's fraud!"

"Yes, sir. Bancroft and I got a whiff of it and tracked it down, Miss Stanhope being very upset about it."

"Catherine talked to you about it?"

"Just about your being in a business dealing with the man and that she did not trust him. I had heard a few things—got a whiff, as I said. I checked into it a little more, asked some friends of mine, and what I learned was that no one I know will do business with the man."

"But he paid me." Sir Everett stuck to the important point.

"Yes. As I said, we paid him a call and he decided he would rather pay you off than be sued for fraud. So that is what he did." Blankenship frowned a little. "But I would not have any further dealings with him, were I you. These are hard charges to prove, record keeping being as haphazard as it is in some business concerns. I don't doubt but what we'd see a real basket of snakes if we were to look at the books of Sir Ronald's company. But you're out of it with a whole skin, and that is what matters."

"You spoke to him. That is why he suddenly was able to pay me?" Sir Everett was chagrined. He felt like a small child who had to be protected by a knowledgeable older comrade.

"Well, you see, sir, I have a certain reputation in this

area. Shipping, manufacturing, goods in general all come in my way a great deal more than they come into yours."

"Sir Ronald is a fraud?" That was a blow to his self-esteem. He had invested with the man, but more than that, he had invited him to his club, his home. He had wanted him to marry his daughter! Anger began to overtake his embarrassment.

"Did he ask you to invest in another shipping venture? Another ship, perhaps?"

"Yes, yes, he did, but Catherine had asked me not to do so because she did not want to have to meet him again." Sir Everett's anger was growing by the moment. "He is a fraud and he thought to marry my daughter, my Catherine?"

Henry Blankenship smiled a little. The baronet's fondness for his daughter was a saving grace in the industrialist's eyes. It was for Catherine that he had involved himself in the baronet's troubles, but now he thought he would take an interest for the man's own sake.

"Sir Everett, I could put you in the way of an investment that would be much safer than anything Sir Ronald would put your way."

"You could? But why should you do that, Blankenship? What could I do for you?"

Henry Blankenship drew himself up as tall as he could. "Well, you could start by going to see that hospital your daughter works at. She all but runs it, you know. Davy and I stop by to see Mary Ann and Miss Stanhope from time to time. But you never have." He looked defiantly at the baronet, who was staring at him as if he were the most amazing man of his acquaintance. "Well, it is what I want. Will you do it?"

"Of course. I never thought—I have never really approved. Thought she'd grow out of it, you know."

"She has a talent for it. You should be proud of her." Blankenship looked earnestly at the baronet and shared with him the profoundest truth he knew. "Family is everything, you know. It is the only thing that matters when all is said and done."

Sir Everett stared at this man, so rich and powerful and yet so simple and good. "I should be grateful to have your investment counsel whenever you can give it, sir. And I will certainly visit Catherine's hospital. Tomorrow, by gad. And, sir," he added, extending his hand, "I should be proud to call you friend."

"Done, sir. Just don't be inviting me to any of those fancy clubs. I've had my fill of them this past week, tracking down rumors of Bolton's tricks. Waste of time better spent at home. But friends, now, I'd like that." And Henry clasped the baronet's hand.

Chapter Nineteen

Sir Everett felt vaguely shamed and thrown off balance by his encounter with Henry Blankenship. He had misjudged both Blankenship and Sir Ronald. He seldom made that kind of mistake. Had he also misjudged his daughter?

As he went to bed in the early hours after the musicale, he vowed to go in to the hospital with Catherine in the morning. Unfortunately, he asked his valet just what time Miss Stanhope arose in the morning. When the answer was five thirty, he quickly changed his mind.

"Good God," he said. "That is incredible! After going out with me in the evening, she arises with the sun and goes to work?" He shook his head in amazement. "I don't see how she does it."

His valet, Jennings, who had been with him for twenty years, presumed upon that long acquaintance. "She has been looking a bit pale recently. We've been noticing in the servants' hall."

Sir Everett flushed. The servants had noticed what her father had not. He had made Catherine promise to attend social events with him, and she had lived up to her promise. But he had still pushed Sir Ronald upon her as a husband and had barely tolerated the work she loved.

"I need not arise before seven," the baronet said. Jennings's eyes widened. His master had not arisen before eight at the earliest in years. "I will surprise her by visiting," the baronet murmured, and his valet nodded as if he understood the cryptic reference.

As indeed he did. He reported to the servants' hall that the master was going to visit Miss Catherine's hospital. There were nods of satisfaction all around the table. It was about time. They were not entirely sure they approved of the quality working—it upset the proper balance of life—but they adored their Miss Catherine, and anything she chose to do was fine by them. Besides, Holden read them bits from the newspapers at dinner, so they had followed the war and knew what Miss Nightingale and her nurses had done at Scutari.

She was a true heroine, and no mistake about it.

The baronet might have decided another day would do for his visit, but his valet decided otherwise. Jennings ruthlessly opened the window curtains and let the pale winter sunshine into the room. Then he pulled aside the covers and smiled down at the baronet. "You said seven, sir."

Sir Everett burrowed his face back into the pillows.

"You were wishful to visit Miss Catherine's hospital, I believe."

Sir Everett gave up. "Oh, yes," he said. "So I was."

Barely two hours later, the coach pulled up in front of the frowning gray stone façade of St. Luke's Hospital for the Deserving Poor. Sir Everett descended and started up the shallow limestone steps leading to the hospital without paying much attention to the group of people ahead of him. They were three shabbily dressed working men, and they were carrying another who was covered with blood.

Without thinking, Sir Everett moved to go in front of them into the hospital. Men of his rank and fortune always took precedence.

Not here. Not today.

"Look 'ere, guv," one of the bearers said. "We've got a wounded man 'ere. Stand aside."

And with that, the group pushed past him and entered the building, leaving Sir Everett standing flat-footed. Well, it was a hospital for the poor. Perhaps it was right that they go first, particularly when one had clearly been badly hurt.

Once inside the cavernous entrance hall, he did not know where to go. There was a big desk in the center of the room, but no one was behind it. Instead, a woman in a navy blue dress and white cap was hurrying over to the group of working men and seemed to be directing them to go down one of the corridors that radiated off the central room. As he watched, the door opened again to admit two more groups of men carrying others who looked unconscious and were bleeding profusely.

The groups began milling about, calling out for help and asking, in plaintive tones, what they were to do with Max and Sam. Three more men, these less seriously injured, walked in under their own power. Sir Everett was wondering what to do and where to go when onto this scene of incipient chaos came another figure in a dark dress and simple white cap. She spoke first to the other nurse who had been there in the beginning, then to the two groups. She laid gentle hands on the injured and spoke softly to the men carrying them. Within a minute, everyone had begun to move under her direction.

Catherine. He recognized her at last. This calm, capable woman who was managing everyone with kindness and skill was his daughter. He stood and watched her, an unfamiliar emotion squeezing his heart and causing his eyes to brim. When she had directed everyone to their proper place, she turned and began to move swiftly down one of the corridors. Sir Everett moved after her, thinking to catch up to her but reluctant to interrupt what was clearly a crisis.

She went into one of the large rooms along the corridor. Sir Everett looked in to see her standing by the bed on which one of the injured workmen now lay. Beside her was Dr. Soames. They both looked grave and were bent over the man, still talking. They were oblivious to everything else going on around them, so focused were they on their patient and each other. Then Dr. Soames touched Catherine lightly on the arm. She looked at him and nodded, smiling a little. He moved on to another bed and Catherine bent over the patient, talking to him as she carefully sponged the blood from his face. She had washed his hand, which her father could see was torn and bleeding, and was beginning to bandage it when he felt someone approach the door behind him.

"Excuse me, but may I help you?" a familiar voice he could not quite place said.

Sir Everett turned around. It was the Blankenships' friend, Mrs. Evans. He was embarrassed to be found skulking about. "I—I came to see Catherine, but there was some sort of accident, I believe, and I hesitate to bother her now."

Mrs. Evans smiled at him. "She will be very glad you

came. Perhaps you can come and wait with me in the office. I have some forms to fill out.''

He went along, though he would have liked to stay and watch Catherine as she worked. It was a revelation. He knew, in a general way, what she did, but this was the first time since she was a little girl he had seen her do it.

"She was always bandaging the workers on our estate," he said to Mrs. Evans as they walked. "Not her dolls, mind you, but real people. From the time she was five or six, she would watch as the village doctor did it, and then the next time she would insist on helping him. The third time, she could do it herself.''

He smiled, thinking about those days. At the time, he had to admit, he had thought his daughter should be playing with dolls or riding across the countryside. A tomboy he could have understood, but a quiet, devoted healer had been beyond him.

And so he had forbidden her to go out to the fields for any reason, hoping to curb her strange hobby. He found out later that the workers simply brought the injured to the stable yard, where she was permitted to go.

"Nothing I tried stopped her." He spoke almost to himself, but Mrs. Evans heard and nodded.

She ushered him into the director's office, where she and Catherine shared a small desk in the corner. Dr. Dinsmore was out helping where he could in light of the extra work the accident had caused, so they were alone in the room.

"Sit down, sir," she said. "I'll brew us a pot of tea. I keep a kettle on the hob." She went over to the cast-iron stove in the center of the room and took a kettle from the shelf at the back. It was steaming, and she soon had a small china pot steeping fresh tea.

"You were saying Miss Stanhope always liked nursing?

I remember hearing Miss Nightingale herself took to it early on." She poured two cups of the fragrant tea and seated herself at her desk, turning the chair to face Sir Everett.

"Yes. She always knew what she wanted to do. It was such a strange thing to want, to be so set on. I never understood it." And not understanding it, he had forbidden it.

"It really does no use to oppose a child, I think, when they have their heart set on something that early and never swerve. My Evans, he wanted to go for a soldier from the time he could pick up a branch and pretend it was a rifle." She smiled at him, as if they were companions sharing memories over a cup of tea. It made him feel strangely comfortable, talking to this worn, tired-looking woman.

"You met Catherine in the Crimea?" he said, ashamed he did not know or, if he had been told, could not remember.

"Yes, she found me helping at a regimental hospital and took me with her to Scutari and then home. There's not place in the regiment for the widows of enlisted men." She did not complain, she stated a fact. "She found me through a registry, knowing I would be looking for employment."

"And what do you do here at St. Luke's?" Again, he was ashamed he did not know. He was sure someone had told him, but he could not remember. Had his daughter's life been so unimportant to him?

"I am the housekeeper. I try to keep things running smoothly so they don't even know I do anything at all."

He laughed. "That is a real calling, Mrs. Evans—to make the necessary things in life run so effortlessly that no one even knows they are being run."

She smiled in delight. "That's it, sir. That's it exactly. Would you like more tea?"

"No, thank you. If Catherine is going to be busy, perhaps I had better come back another time." He rose, realizing he was keeping Mrs. Evans from her unobtrusive but essential work, and that Catherine was likely to be busy for some time to come.

"Tell her I was here, if you would, Mrs. Evans," he said, a note of humility in his voice.

"Of course, sir. She will be sorry she missed you, but glad you came all the same," the head housekeeper said.

Sir Everett left the hospital with a great deal to think about.

When Catherine arrived home that evening, she was tired and sore. Her feet ached, and she longed for nothing more than a hot bath and the book that Michael had prescribed. Somewhere in her weary brain was the memory of her father telling her of a party they were to attend that night. Her spirits sagged at the thought.

Mary Ann had told her of her father's visit. She entertained a vague hope that he was canceling their engagement and for some reason wanted to tell her of it in person. Or perhaps he had another party to add to the agenda. She simply couldn't. Not this evening. They had worked over the four shop-accident victims in the morning and a woman bleeding from a botched abortion in the afternoon.

She came in the house and gratefully gave her cloak to Holden, who told her Sir Everett was waiting for her in the study. "Oh, dear," she said, "I suppose I am late again."

"No, miss. I think it is something else."

Catherine found her father waiting with a glass of sherry

for her. He informed her he had sent their regrets to the hostess of tonight's party. "We will be dining in, my dear. I thought we would have an early dinner and then just read for a while here before the fire. Would you like that?"

Like it? It sounded like heaven.

"Finish your sherry, and then you should have time for a bath before dinner."

This was unheard of luxury. Ordinarily she was only able to snatch a quick sponge bath before donning her evening clothes and making ready to leave again for the second half of what she thought of as her double life.

"That sounds wonderful, Papa, but I thought the party tonight was important to you."

"Not as important as your rest is to you, my dear. Go along now, and take your time. Dinner will be ready when you are." He beamed at her, and Catherine could not help but wonder what had come over him.

But a few minutes later, as she lay back in the tub with her eyes closed, she was grateful. She dressed with care and went downstairs for dinner feeling more cheerful than she had in the evening for quite some time.

Dinner was simple but delicious. Mrs. Marston had told her that Jane, the cook, was trying out some of the recipes Jean-Pierre, the Eversleighs' chef, had given her while they collaborated on the party.

"My compliments to Jane, Holden," she said as he removed her plate. "That was a wonderful dinner."

Her father smiled at her. He had taught her to praise the servants when they did their jobs well. "Come into the library, my dear. We will both have tea in there." He escorted her into the cozy room and after she was seated said, "Catherine, I went to the hospital today, but you were busy. I saw you at work and I wanted to tell you—I thought I should say—"

Her father floundering? Talking to people, persuading them to do what he wanted, was his stock in trade. "Yes, Papa. I am sorry I missed you. There was an accident nearby and we got the victims."

"Yes, I know. I saw you work on them. You and Dr. Soames." He cleared his throat and paused when Holden entered with the tea tray, but did not take up the thread of the conversation when Catherine poured him a cup and extended it to him with a smile.

"You are a beautiful woman, Catherine."

"Thank you, Papa."

"But more than that, you are doing work that needs to be done, and even I can see you do it well."

"Why, Papa, thank—" The words clogged her throat. He had never said anything about her work. He ignored it when he couldn't prohibit it, but now he seemed to want to talk about it.

There was a long pause while the baronet obviously searched for words. "I am very proud of you, Catherine."

Tears threatened to overwhelm her at those words she had never thought she would hear. "Oh, Papa," she managed to whisper past the lump in her throat. "Oh, Papa."

He cleared his throat again. "Now I must read a report that will come up in the House tomorrow. You should find something soothing to read. Not that Dickens book *Dreary Hall* or whatever it's called. Full of lawsuits and secrets. Too dark by half. Don't we have that new book by Mrs. Gaskell? Nice and relaxing, I'll be bound. Try that."

And Catherine, her heart overflowing, complied.

The next day was bright and sunny for a change. The air was still winter-sharp, and Catherine all but skipped up the hospital steps. Could life get any better? Her father had said words she had never thought to hear. Her work was going well. With a few more donations, the hospital's finances would be on a firm footing, according to Jeffrey Bancroft. She smiled at every member of the staff she met on her way to the administration office.

There she leafed through the mail and messages that awaited her. Most were unimportant but one, written on heavy cream-colored paper in a delicate, feminine hand, looked interesting. She slit the envelope.

> *Dear Miss Stanhope,*
>
> *You and I met once several weeks ago at Lady Dalrymple's reception. We spoke briefly of your work. I would like to aid that work in any way I can. Please come for tea this afternoon at five so we can discuss how I may best help.*
>
> *With my compliments,*
> *Cassandra, Lady Peter Mitford*

Catherine furrowed her brow in thought. Lady Peter Mitford. The name rang a faint, far-off bell. Lord Peter Mitford was the second son of the Duke of Blanford. She did not recall having met his wife, but she might well have. As for talking of her work at the hospital, she did that with everyone who would listen, and sometimes it meant a donation from one of the people who had listened to her. One more donation! Wonderful.

"Tea this afternoon?" she murmured. "Very well. I'd best send a note home that I shan't be needing the carriage. Five o'clock will make them too late for Papa. I shall order a hackney."

Plans made, she turned to her work once again. At five o'clock, she gave the hackney driver the address. It was in Belgravia, but a bit on the fringes, which surprised her. However, the second sons of dukes were not always wealthy.

Perhaps the Mitfords could only afford a lesser neighborhood. The driver asked her if she was sure of the address, which struck her as odd, but she shrugged it off. A middle-class home would not bother her if Cassandra Mitford could give her a check. They were hoping to start a ward just for children soon. Catherine began to think about the advantages of being able to isolate children from adults' illnesses, and before she knew it they had arrived.

The house looked prosperous, the door painted a shiny black, the brass knocker polished to a mirror shine. She paid the driver and watched him leave as she mounted the carefully scrubbed steps. As she waited for the door to be opened, she looked up and down the street. The other houses were not as well-kept as this one, but they all seemed nice enough. She raised the brass knocker again and let it fall as a carriage pulled up in front of the house and Sir Ronald got out.

He was beaming at her as he reached the door and raised the knocker. The door opened before he had tapped twice. A maid in a black uniform and white apron smiled at Sir Ronald. "Good day, Sir Ronald," she said. There was something disturbing about her. Catherine could not put her finger on it for a moment. Then she realized that, like Nancy at the hospital, this maid was wearing makeup, and her uniform was a little different as well.

She did not have time to finish the thought. Sir Ronald had her by the elbow and was leading her into a small reception room. He closed the door firmly behind him.

"Sir Ronald, I do not quite understand. Is Lady Peter going to meet us here? Is she a friend of yours?" There was something vaguely disturbing about this scene, something she had been too intent on her quest for Lady Peter's donation to take in.

Now she looked around. The small parlor was opulently

decorated in crimson velvet and gold brocade. There was a tête-à-tête settee and a chaise longue but no upright chairs. Something was wrong with this place. She could not put her finger on it, but a trickle of unease slipped down her spine. She perched nervously on the end of the chaise longue and said, "What are you doing here, Sir Ronald?"

He smiled, that same inappropriate fatuous grin that so grated on her. "I have come to have tea with you, Catherine."

"Where is Lady Peter?" A premonition caused her heart to clench in her chest.

"Actually, you know, my friend Peter Mitford is not yet married." And Sir Ronald sat down beside her on the chaise longue.

Catherine rose and walked to the door. As she grasped the knob, Sir Ronald said, "I do not think you want to go out there, my dear."

He was trying to frighten her, she told herself. What could he do to her in the middle of Belgravia? Resolutely, Catherine opened the door. And slammed it again.

In the second she viewed the scene, she saw all she needed to. Catherine had led the sheltered life common to upper-class girls until she had gone to Paris to study nursing. At that point, she had come into contact with people who lived on the fringes of society, though she had not known their environment. She recognized *filles de joie* when she encountered them. In the hall, half-dressed girls wandered. All had painted faces and carefully blank expressions.

A brothel. She had come to have tea in one of the high-class, discreet houses of prostitution that existed next to some of the best neighborhoods in London. It had been the same in Paris when she had worked with the Sisters of Charity.

She turned and faced Sir Ronald, her back against the door. "Why have you done this? To ruin me because I won't marry you?"

"Ah, you recognize the location? Your work as a nurse, no doubt." His nose lifted in faint distaste.

He had never approved of her profession, she remembered, and stifled a burst of semi-hysterical laughter. A fraud and a cheat and he sneered at her. She had never before appreciated the depths of his hypocrisy.

"Yes," he continued, "if it became known you had come here, you would be ruined. This place also serves as a house of assignation for bored wives and their lovers. You, as a nurse, might be expected to have tastes that are, shall we say, out of the ordinary. No one will find it strange that you chose to meet me here."

Of course he was wrong. Many, if not all, of the people who knew her would find it not only strange but unbelievable. The trouble was, Catherine knew, that gossip was spread by the people who did not know you, and thus were free to believe anything they wanted to.

"You have made your point. I have come here. I would like to leave now." She gave him a level look, trying to show no fear.

She could not marry this man, but she could not see her father's career and reputation ruined because he was thought to have an out of control, sexually promiscuous daughter. She did not know what to do, but she could not stay here with this man. She risked becoming truly hysterical with rage if she had to look at that smug, oblivious face much longer. She needed to think.

"Before we have had our tea? No, I must protest. They provide a very fine tea here. I will take you out through the secret entrance—but later. First, I must first introduce you to my friends. Come." He rose and came toward her, his hand outstretched.

It was too much. "No." She shook her head. She must not stay here. There was no telling what he might do to her. Fortunately she had not taken off her cloak, and she still clutched her reticule. Now she opened the door and started into the hall. But Sir Ronald was faster than she had thought. He was beside her, pulling her roughly back into the little parlor and slamming the door. He rested his fist against the door and kept his other hand firmly on her arm.

"Now, now. You are spoiling my little surprise. Come along, my dear." His smile was as bland as ever as he added, "Or I might be tempted to do more with you than drink tea with whores."

She froze. She would not risk being raped. She would go with him to the parlor. If no one was there, if he had lied, then she would run for the door and hope she could find help or a hansom cab.

His grip was like iron as he pulled her through the door. The hall held only two girls this time. They were dressed in a sort of parody of afternoon costumes. The fabric was crepe and the colors subdued, but the bodices were cut low in front and the skirts were skimpy and ended above the ankle. The girls were young, Catherine thought, though it was difficult to tell because of the makeup they wore. Beside them stood a man dressed as if he were a banker going to the City for a day's work.

Sir Ronald greeted them with his usual beaming smile and introduced Catherine to them. The man was Lord Peter Mitford. He flashed an embarrassed smile. "How do?" he said, looking down at the floor.

Catherine ignored him and turned to the women. "I

have been brought here under false pretenses. Whatever these men tell you, I am not here for an assignation with him. I detest him and he is determined to ruin me. Please do not help him. If you need help to leave this life, please come to me at St. Luke's Hospital. My name is Catherine Stanhope." She realized she had just handed these young women evidence that she had in fact been at this house. It was a risk. But she could not leave without giving them some means of contacting her if they ever decided to leave this kind of life.

Sir Ronald laughed uproariously. "Catherine, Catherine," he said, shaking his head. "Really. You are so simple. You must know that whores like whoring. These girls wouldn't know what to do if they stopped making the easy money here at Mona's."

"I want to leave now." She did not want to discuss the girls in front of them. She had looked in their eyes. They did not look as if they liked their work.

"No." He had planned this and he wanted it the way he had seen it in his mind's eye. He wanted her to have tea with two whores and then he wanted to take her, demoralized and shaking, weeping at the loss of her reputation, at the unspoken threat of how much more he could have done, home to her father.

The real point was Sir Everett, not his daughter. Sir Ronald knew she would never marry him without pressure from dear Papa, and Papa held Sir Ronald's reputation in his hands. So he had thought and thought and come up with a way to get the daughter and ensure the father's silence—and the silence of those two rich, meddling friends of theirs.

He had done it just by getting her inside the house and introducing her to Mitford. He had made his point. He could let her go now. But he didn't want to. She had led him a dance, made him look foolish. Her friends had come and told him what they knew, what they could prove about the ships. *Give back the money,* they'd said. Easy for them. They had more than they could ever spend or even use.

But they understood power and how to use it. They had made him give Stanhope back his money. Damn them! But they wouldn't ruin him if it meant ruining Catherine Stanhope. They would have to keep silent to keep him silent.

So he could let her go now, his point made. But he liked watching her sitting so prim and proper, drinking tea with prostitutes. The maid came in with the tea and set the tray before one of the other girls.

"You should pour," she said to Catherine, clearly unnerved at having such an obvious lady there.

"No," Catherine said, her smile encouraging, "this is your house. You pour the tea."

And then, damn her, she had proceeded to ignore him and Mitford and make polite, tea-table conversation with a couple of prostitutes. He could hardly believe it. By the time she had drunk a cup of tea, she had those two whores eating out of her hand. He could kill them! She was supposed to be shivering in her shoes with shame and fear and they were supposed to be laughing at her.

Instead, they had practically become fast friends!

"Come on," he said, "we're leaving. I want to tell Papa where his saintly little girl has spent the afternoon. Then we'll see about posting the banns."

He was happy to see Catherine turn white at that reminder that she might have her innings but the match would be his in the end. But still she did not flinch. She thanked the two girls for the tea, bade them a polite good-bye, and left with her head high.

Sir Ronald's carriage had been waiting at the other

entrance, which was through a flower shop on the next street. They sat in absolute silence. After they had taken Lord Peter to his home, Catherine moved as far away from him as she could get.

"Oh, stop clutching the door, Catherine." He smiled. "I am hardly going to ravish you now. It isn't necessary."

When they arrived at Stanhope House, Sir Ronald demanded to be taken to Sir Everett immediately. Holden began to tell him that the master was not available.

Sir Ronald could feel his hackles rise, and Catherine quickly intervened. "It is important, Holden. Go and fetch Sir Everett."

Holden looked at his mistress and went without another word.

"Well done, my dear. You adapt quickly. That is good."

Stony-faced, Catherine started up the stairway. On the second step she paused and turned back. "I am going to my room. I will not see you again."

"Perhaps not this evening, but soon." He beamed at her.

He had won.

A half hour later he was not so sure.

The baronet had kept him waiting for ten minutes, come in without greeting him, seated himself behind his desk, and listened impassively to Sir Ronald's story. He must know his daughter had not been physically harmed and did not seem to be hysterical or otherwise distressed. Holden would have told him that.

Sir Ronald had not counted on that. He had thought Catherine would be visibly shaken and upset and that her father would be so concerned for his daughter's well-being he would hardly bother to negotiate. He would care only about saving face.

Instead, Sir Everett had stared at him almost without blinking and without uttering a word while Sir Ronald recounted his activities.

"So you see, Sir Everett, if I cannot still the tongue of my friend, your daughter's reputation will be ruined." He paused, waiting for a reply, but none came. "I am, however, willing to marry her and make an honest woman of her. And you will, of course, not want your son-in-law's reputation sullied with accusations of business fraud. So you will tell your friends to stop their investigations of me, and you will tell them you are well pleased that your daughter has seen fit to accept my hand and my heart."

He stopped, sure he had won the day.

Sir Everett steepled his hands and looked long and hard at Sir Ronald, who began to feel his collar tighten around his neck. This was not the Sir Everett he knew, but someone harder and stronger.

"I do not think so, sir," he said at last. "I do not think you can afford to tell this story unless you wish to be even more unpopular than you are beginning to be now. Ravishers of virgins do not have many friends in parliament, or in the City."

"But that is nothing compared to what your daughter will suffer. She will not be received at many people's homes. She will never be able to marry."

Sir Everett smiled. He actually smiled! "Well, you know, then it is very convenient she does not wish to marry and will regard not being received as a treat. I have had to beg her to come with me to the parties we attend." He sat back, smiling and at ease.

"But your career!" Sir Ronald protested. He could feel himself losing control of the situation. Where had he gone wrong? Why were these damned Stanhopes not reacting as they should? "You will be pilloried by people who think you should keep a tighter rein on your daughter. By marrying her to me, you will avoid that. You can keep your position in the party."

"Well, Bolton, I find that the rough and tumble of politics has lost some of its savor. One has to meet and socialize with so many undesirable men. I have been thinking of retiring. Writing my memoirs, perhaps. *Rogues I Have Known.* You are earning a prominent position in that pantheon." And still the man smiled.

Thwarted at every turn, Sir Ronald said, "I'll ruin you both. You deserve it."

"And ruin yourself in the process?" Sir Everett's eyes sharpened, but he continued to smile as if Sir Ronald had given him a present.

"You are doing that now. Soon I will have nothing left to lose."

"I can save you."

Sir Ronald ground his teeth. "Of course you can, you fool. That is what I have been telling you!"

"No, you have been threatening me and trying to blackmail me." Sir Everett leaned forward and fixed him with a shrewd gaze. "Now I will tell you what will happen. Neither you nor your friend will speak of what happened this afternoon, in exchange for which I will tell my friends you have made full restitution for all losses which you mistakenly thought had occurred when you got the false news of your ship's going down."

Sir Everett rose and came around the desk to stare down at Sir Ronald. "You will never file another such false claim or I will have investigators on you like flies on a dung hill. An apt simile. Agreed?"

Sir Ronald considered trying for more. But did he really

want to marry Catherine Stanhope? It meant a lifetime with a woman who made him feel like a slug, a woman he could not beat into submission because she had powerful friends who were unconventional enough to take her in regardless of his matrimonial rights.

Was there anything worse than a woman with ideas of her own?

"Very well, Sir Everett," he said at last, getting to his feet. "We have an agreement. No hard feelings, I trust."

Sir Everett stared at his extended hand as if it were a snake. "We have an agreement. And there is one last thing. If you ever again come within ten yards of my daughter, I will horsewhip you. Now get out of my house and do not come back!"

Chapter Twenty

Catherine managed to hold everything inside her until she reached her room. Still standing and wearing her cloak, she rang for Betsy and told her to fetch her father before he went to see Sir Ronald. God only knew what that man would tell her father. She had to show him she was all right.

The baronet came upstairs. She was still standing at her doorway, holding on to the frame so her knees would not give out.

"Papa," she said, holding her voice even by sheer willpower, "that man lured me to a house of prostitution this afternoon. He and a friend, Sir—no, *Lord* Peter Mitford. They did not do anything to me, but Sir Ronald said he would ruin me if you did not cease your investigations and marry me to him." There. She had managed to say it all.

Sir Everett had turned pale as she began to speak, but as she went on his face hardened. A threat to his child brought out all his fighting instincts.

"I don't know what to do, Papa. I don't want ruin. It would ruin you as well. I don't know what to do," she repeated, her brow furrowed with worry.

"Never mind, dear child. I do." He kissed her gently on the forehead, his lips conveying all the comfort and love he could not tell her of just then. "I will take care of everything. You just rest now."

He left. Catherine felt all the strength drain from her now that she was safe at last. She made her way across the darkened room like an old woman, bent over with stomach cramps that threatened to bring up the cup of tea she had drunk a bare hour before. She sat on her bed, and shivers wracked her body as she rocked back and forth, her teeth clenched so they would not chatter.

She had never been as frightened as she had been in that awful house. Every minute she had expected to be knocked unconscious and raped or drugged and thrown into some dark hole to await Sir Ronald's pleasure. Why he had not done more to her, she did not know. Perhaps he really did think he could still marry her. She would run away to America—but no, that would not help her father.

Catherine put her head in her hands. She could not think. She was so tired and cold and still so frightened that she could hardly move. She needed—she needed to be held and comforted and kept safe. She needed someone who could think while she could not.

She needed Michael.

The moment the thought formed, she knew that seeing Michael, being with Michael, was the only thing that would keep her from dissolving into hysterics. And she could not afford to break down while her father was still under threat from that man.

Without conscious volition, Catherine, her cloak still wrapped around her and her reticule clutched in her hand, moved to the door and crept down the hall and the stairs, expecting at any moment to see Sir Ronald emerge from her father's study in triumph. She did not dare pause long enough to ask John to drive her to Michael's rooms. Instead, she slipped out the front door while Holden was elsewhere and hurried to the corner where hackneys sometimes loitered.

It had started to rain, a cold winter downpour, but luck was with her. She got wet, but found a cab and gave the driver Michael's address. The cab was cleaner than most, and she leaned back against the leather seat, her eyes closed, her hands clasped, white-knuckled, in her lap. Michael had taken rooms in a widow's house not too far from the unfashionable middle-class neighborhood where the Blankenships resided.

She was never sure how long the drive took, but it seemed both very short and far too long. She had begun to shiver from the cold and wet. She did not know what she would say to Michael when she saw him. He had taken the entire first floor, with the idea of in time opening a surgery in the back. In the meantime, it ensured his privacy—and tonight hers as well. Standing in the cold steady rain as she waited for the bell to be answered, Catherine's resolve never wavered. She had to see Michael. That was still her only thought.

The door opened and Michael stood there in his shirt-sleeves, a book dangling negligently from his hand. "Catherine, what—"

She tried to smile. "I—I—came—" She couldn't find the words. Instead, she flung herself into his arms. "Oh, Michael, hold me, hold me. Please don't let me go." She waited only to feel his arms close around her like steel bands, and then she let go. All the fear and tension flowed from her as she found release in a storm of weeping. Her tears were silent and all the more devastating for that.

Michael pulled her into the house and closed the door with one foot. The book fell to the floor unheeded while he gently whispered in her ear, "There, there, my darling. Come along, darling girl. Into the parlor." His arm still around her, he led her into the cheerful room that served as both living and dining room. The lights were low except for the lamp beside the deep leather chair where he had been reading.

Without letting go of her for a moment, he gently took off her soaking cloak and let it drop. "Here, dearest, sit down by the fire. Your feet are soaked." He knelt before her and took off her sodden shoes. Then he sat back on his knees and looked at her.

"I—I got wet looking for a cab." She managed to speak, but tears continued to flow down her cheeks. It was as if she were letting go of so much that had troubled and hurt her. Now she was with Michael, it would be all right. She could let go.

"Sweetheart, sweetheart, it is all right. You are safe with me. I won't let anyone hurt you."

"Oh, Michael, it was awful. I was so frightened, so frightened. But I pretended I was brave, just as I used to do at Scutari, and I don't think he knew." She was coming to the end of her tears, and he pulled a large white handkerchief from his pocket and gently blotted her face.

Then he took her face between his hands and studied her carefully. "My darling, what happened? Who has frightened you? Was it Bolton?"

She turned her face away, suddenly afraid. Would Michael think what happened was her fault? She knew some men blamed women for any assault on their persons or insult offered them, on the grounds that if they had not invited such licentiousness it would not have occurred. She had never believed that. She had passionately insisted it was not so when the daughter of a tenant had been raped and the girl's father felt himself disgraced.

She had known even then, at fourteen, that men were not logical creatures. They blamed women for their own sins. But Michael was not like other men. She took a deep breath and plunged into her story. When she finished, she looked up, trembling, her heart in her eyes, waiting to be judged.

Michael did not hesitate for a moment but crushed her to his chest. "My darling, I am so glad you came to me. And you will stay here where I can keep you safe. I don't want you in the same house with him for an instant. Shall I kill him for you? Believe me, I would like to. The beating I gave those robber boys who tried to steal from you is nothing compared to what I would like to do to him." He kissed her then, tenderly, with no demands made upon her.

Catherine sighed. It was healing. She had known Michael to be a healer, but she had never thought of herself as needing to be healed. If that was contrary to the image she had entertained of herself as a strong and self-reliant creature, then so be it. Right this moment, she needed to be cared for by the man she loved.

Michael understood, as she had instinctively known he would. He held her safe and stroked her back, long, soothing strokes that relaxed her and at the same time made her feel warm and alive.

He pulled her to her feet. "I would tell you to go into the bedroom to change into my dressing gown, but I cannot let you go." He smiled down at her. "Come along and let me play lady's maid. You have one, do you not?"

"Y—yes. Betsy." Leaning on his arm, she allowed herself

to be led into his room. "Th-thank you for coming with me. I don't know if I can stand right now."

"You don't need to, dearest. Let me." He turned her around so he could deal with the long row of buttons at the back of her dress. "Just close your eyes and pretend I am Betsy."

She closed her eyes, but he was not Betsy. Her back tingled where he had bared it. At his direction, she stepped out of her dress and then her petticoats.

"Now I think we had better remove your stockings. Then I will lend you my dressing gown and a pair of my slippers." Suiting the action to the words, he knelt before her and began to unfasten her garters. His hands were warm, but as they touched her it seemed to Catherine they trembled a little.

Catherine gasped. A thrill unlike anything she had ever felt before seemed to run from the tender, incredibly sensitive flesh of her thighs where his fingers touched her to someplace deep inside her body. She felt a sort of melting, and at the same time every nerve ending cried out for more of his touch. She looked down at the top of his head and bent to kiss his thick auburn hair.

"Oh, God, Catherine, I should have known once I touched you—" His voice was thick and muffled now in the thin linen of her chemise and the softness of her abdomen. "I am lost."

"Oh," she moaned as his breath, warm and soft through the chemise, brought the melting ache inside her to all parts of her body. "No, my darling," she murmured as she slid down onto her knees to face him. "We have found each other."

Her lips found his and her hands tunneled through the soft waves of his hair, as she had often thought of doing. His mouth opened and his tongue caressed her lips, teasing and enticing. Awash in sensation, she clung to him, sure that if she let go she would fall.

His hands were all over her now, and everywhere they left a trail of fire. She pressed herself closer to him, moving restlessly, wanting to be closer still.

He broke their kiss and held her away from him. He was gasping, and she could see a fine sheen of sweat on his face. "Dearest, we must stop. If we don't stop now I— I don't think I can." His face was taut with effort. "Please, dearest, now."

But she knew better. "No, no, I can't. I don't want to." She pressed closer to him. "I need you. Please."

"Oh, God, I can't resist you." He buried his face in her neck.

"Good." It was heartfelt. "I am glad." She raised his head and kissed him, opening her mouth under his as he had done and teasing his lips. It felt exquisite.

His arms closed around her and he groaned. Then he picked her up and moved a few steps. She paid no attention to where he was taking her. Her attention was all on him. Her love, her life. With infinite care, he laid her down on his bed and she looked up at him.

"Come," she said and smiled up at him. He was disheveled now and his eyes were dark with passion. She watched, fascinated, as he stripped off his clothes.

When he was naked, he paused. "Do I frighten you?" he asked.

Without a word, she reached up and stroked the length of his shaft. He gave a strangled cry and fell on the bed beside her. "Catherine, dearest, I have dreamed of this. I love you and I want you more than I have ever wanted anything in my life."

"Then take me." She opened her arms and drew him to her. At this moment she felt stronger and surer than she ever had before. She had thought when the time came she would be embarrassed or afraid of the huge step into the unknown she was about to take. But she had been wrong. With the right man—this man—she was eager to share her love.

He did not move to complete their union immediately. Instead he proceeded to arouse her in every way he could. He used his lips and his hands, and as he stroked and kissed he removed the last thin barrier of her underclothes.

When she was as naked as he, he gazed down at her with flagrant adoration in his eyes. "You are exquisite. So beautiful, dearest. I never could have imagined how beautiful you are."

She was quivering now with anticipation, and she arched closer to him until every inch of her body was touching his. He groaned and, after touching her to see if she was ready, he slid into the depths of her.

There was a moment of fullness, almost of pain, and then the most incredible feeling of mingled completion and anticipation. This was wonderful, but her body knew there was more.

She reached up and traced his features with gentle fingers. "Love me, Michael."

"I am afraid of hurting you." He looked down at their joined bodies—hers long and slender and white and his brown and muscular, sprinkled with auburn hair.

"I won't break. I'm strong." She squeezed her arms around him then and moved her body against his.

That was all he needed. He began to move, and she was whirled to a new state of consciousness, one that made her feel as if she were climbing a rainbow. Then, suddenly, when she thought there was no more, the rainbow splintered and she could feel the iridescent pieces all through her body.

It was the most shattering, beautiful experience of her life. She knew there were tears in her eyes as she reached up to urge his mouth to meet hers. He saw them, and his face betrayed the fear he felt.

"I did hurt you. I was afraid—I tried—are you all right?"

"I am so far beyond all right there are no words to describe it."

He kissed her again, still softly, making no demands on her, and then held her against his hammering heart. He whispered gently, "I am so glad you came to me. I will keep you safe. You knew that, and so you came to me. I love you, Catherine, so much." He tightened his hold. "You should not be here, of course, but I am not letting you go just yet. Just for this little moment you are mine. Stay with me for a while."

"Yes." She could hardly speak. "Forever." His words had moved her. She had known he loved her, but somehow she had thought of his love as a sort of bloodless mixture of respect, understanding, and a perfect sort of friendship born of their mutual love of medicine.

Now she knew better, and it thrilled her. He wanted her as a man wants the woman of his dreams, as she wanted him. She had not recognized the sizzle of awareness that ran along her nerves when he was near for what it was. She loved and admired him—and she desired him.

She was not sure how long they lay in the aftermath of love, entwined still, languorous and happy. At last, though, Michael moved to separate them. He kissed her then and got out of bed. He came back with a silk robe in a dark paisley design. Carefully, he helped her into it.

"This is what I was going to give you to wear." He smiled. "I was going to be very gentlemanly. I was sure I could resist you."

"But why should you? I didn't want you to." She rose

to face him and knotted the belt of the robe around her. "I made it happen, too."

He had put on his trousers and a soft blue sweater. Now he picked her up again and carried her into the parlor, where he sat down in his leather chair with her upon his lap.

"I can walk," she said. "Not that I don't prefer traveling this way, but I can walk."

"We need to talk, dearest," he said. "About Bolton. What do you think your father has done about him? He wouldn't give in to Bolton's demands, would he?"

"I don't know. I don't think so. I believe Papa will stand up to him. But what can I do, if he threatens to ruin Papa as well as me?" She sniffed a little. "I do not mind being ostracized—at least not very much. I have my work, and nurses are not very highly regarded in any case. I do not have very much to lose. But I cannot let Papa's career be ruined because of me."

"Let us think for a moment. Your father has probably convinced Bolton that he has as much to lose as you do, since his reputation as a sound man in politics will disappear in the wake of this kind of scandal." He paused and looked down at her, a tentative smile lurking at the corners of his mouth. Smoothing back her hair, he said, in a diffident voice unlike any she had heard him use before, "In a case like this, do you not think any marriage would do?" He drew back so he could look into her eyes.

She nodded, a little doubtful as to what he meant. "You mean I must still marry? You really think I have to do so?"

He shrugged and kissed her nose. "No. You do not have to do anything you do not wish to do. You are right. You can live a full and rewarding life with your friends and your work. But I love you and I want to spend my life with you. Why not simply marry me instead of Sir Ronald?"

Michael smiled at her and kissed her again. "See what an easy solution that will be?"

"Michael, I know you do not want to marry me, and I did not mean to force you to." Honor demanded that she refuse him. She loved him. If marriage meant being with Michael all the time, then she wanted marriage.

But she understood he did not feel the same. "I love you too much to force you to marry me. I should not have come. I didn't think of the position I was putting you in. I just had to see you. I had to." She began to struggle out of the sanctuary of his arms, but he refused to let her go. "And then, I wanted us to be together." She disdained euphemisms. "To make love together."

"I know, dearest, but it was wrong of me to take advantage of the state you were in. I have compromised you. In the eyes of the world, we must marry."

The words were like stones in her heart. After what they had shared, he still thought of her as damaged goods, as needing a saving gloss of respectability. Didn't he care for her? Yes, she knew he did, but not enough, evidently, to wholeheartedly want her as his wife.

"Is that how you feel?" she managed to say at last. "That you owe me your name?"

"No, not that. I love you, but I do not have the fortune or the family that your husband should bring you. Just ask your friend the countess if you do not believe me. She will certainly tell you how ineligible I am."

She twisted in his arms until she could glare into his eyes. "I am not going to tell you again. I do not care what anyone thinks. You are the finest man—the finest gentleman—I know. I love you, and that is all I have to say. I have already thrown myself at you, and I am not going to propose to you."

He laughed at the sudden release of tension. "Oh, please

do. I would so like it if you would get down on one knee. Best you do it before you put that confounded dress back on. I'm not sure you could get up or down in that."

"I am sure you find this very amusing, but I have really ruined myself this time. I came to see you at night. There can be no possible excuse for it. So if you are still thinking you are not good enough for me, you should think again. I am going to be an outcast, not you." She again tried to struggle free of his arms. "If I leave now, it is possible no one will know I have even left the house."

But Michael was not going to let her go. The feel of her in his arms, the sight of her with her hair disheveled and her lips swollen and red from kissing had fanned the flames of his desire for her. He had always found it hard to resist her, and now it was impossible.

"I am sorry for teasing you. It is just that I am so unsure of myself, and so very much in love." He traced her mouth with his forefinger. "I think I have loved you almost from the moment I first saw you, looking so cool and refusing to be intimidated. Then I looked into your eyes when we worked on that first case in Scutari, and I saw you were afraid but you wouldn't be conquered by it. And that was it for me. I had found the love of my life."

"And yet you would let me go?" She leaned toward him and kissed the edge of his mouth that so often quirked into a smile while the rest of his face remained grave. She loved that secret little smile.

"I love you," he said simply. "I want what is best for you."

"*You* are what is best for me." She kissed him again. She found that she liked initiating a kiss. "And I am not nearly as unselfish as you are." She smoothed the unruly auburn hair back from his forehead and smiled into his eyes. "I'll marry you even though I had to seduce you to make you propose."

"You did no such thing. There was no seduction involved. There was love. Just love."

Catherine's heart was soaring. Michael loved her. Just being here in his cozy chair, with his arms safely around her holding the world at bay, made her feel almost drunk with euphoria. She could do anything, dare anything, try anything as long as Michael loved her.

"What will happen to me if you do not marry me? I will not marry anyone else, so I will eventually turn into an eccentric old lady."

"You will run seven hospitals and start a school of nursing," he said.

"I could do that so much better if I had you to talk to and share things with. Think if we could work together all the time and live together as well." She snuggled closer.

"Catherine, I love you so much. I think you should marry me." He kissed her. "I *know* you should marry me."

"Then all we have to do is convince my father and the rest of the world," she said. "The way I feel right now, that should take a matter of moments."

Then she kissed him, and Michael found himself almost believing her. "Perhaps we had better talk to him before my courage seeps away and I remember how completely unworthy I am."

Chapter Twenty-one

After Sir Ronald had left, the baronet sat for almost ten minutes without moving. He was seeking some way to prevent the ruin of his career and his daughter's reputation.

The first answer, the one Sir Ronald had proposed, he rejected out of hand. He had no right to compel his daughter into a distasteful marriage, though many parents did so every day. If he had ever thought he could, he knew better now. Catherine was a rare and beautiful young woman, and he was proud to be her father. In the last few weeks and days, he had begun to see that clearly.

So, having discarded the easy, conventional answer, he had to come up with something else. Riding out the storm was a last resort. He had meant what he said to Sir Ronald—losing his career and seeing his daughter's name muddied would be difficult, but not nearly as difficult as giving in to Bolton's blackmail.

Martha Schroeder

Having analyzed the two extremes of giving in or bra-
zening it out and finding them both distasteful, he tried to
think of a third way. Enough people had seen Catherine's
distaste for Bolton. If another explanation could be found,
it could be made to stick. With the help of the Eversleighs
and Blankenship, he should be able to say—what? What
would seem plausible?

"That she wanted to marry someone else and that Sir
Ronald in a fit of jealousy kidnapped her in some bizarre
bid to make her change her mind?" He tried the thought
aloud. It did not sound too outlandish.

But who could be persuaded to marry Catherine under
such a cloud? Julian? No, she had already dismissed that
idea, and after his visit the baronet was inclined to believe
she was right.

"The doctor." Why hadn't he thought of it first? It was
the perfect answer. He was not much of a catch. No money,
but didn't the countess or someone say he was related to
the Bothwells? That would carry some weight in social
circles—not that Catherine cared much for society and its
judgments. If he was not mistaken, she and the doctor
would probably be too busy saving the world to go out
much.

Could the doctor be persuaded to marry Catherine?
Could Catherine be persuaded to marry anyone under
such circumstances? She would want to be desired for her
own sake, not because someone was feeling chivalrous and
would agree to save her reputation.

"Blankenship!" He would ask the industrialist if he
thought Soames would be a good husband for Catherine.
He had to talk to him about Bolton's threats in any case,
since he and Bancroft had both participated in the scheme.

"Bancroft?" Would he be a better choice as husband?
No, the baronet knew instinctively that Soames and Cather-

ine would be a perfect match. "If you disregard everything that matters and just think about how well they would deal with each other, it becomes easy."

When had he thrown away the lessons of a lifetime and begun to think that love was important?

He had married where his father had indicated it would be prudent. He had grown fond of Catherine's mother, as he always thought of his wife, and she of him before her untimely death, but it was not a love match. Where, then, had he gotten the idea children should have some voice in their fate?

"Blankenship!" That was what it was. When he had faced Sir Ronald, the voice had been his but the words, the bluff—all about retiring from politics and Catherine's not caring about her reputation—had been Blankenship's. Because Bolton had not called him, he had begun to believe in some of his own words. Yet even Blankenship, who had urged him to look at Catherine through her work, still believed he could direct his own son's affections.

Now the baronet was beginning to wonder. He had better go to see Blankenship now. They needed to discuss what to do about Bolton. The industrialist was bound to have some ideas, and perhaps his own crumbling sense of the importance of parental guidance could use some bolstering.

Without thinking about dinner or Catherine, he called for the carriage. When Holden asked, the baronet told him not to worry. He remembered how white and shaken Catherine had looked, despite her sensible behavior, and he told Holden she was not to be disturbed. As for dinner, he waved a careless hand. "Tell cook that the servants should enjoy it." He thought for a moment. "Seems to me my daughter told me her maid is leaving to marry. You should have a celebration, Holden. Surprised you didn't think of it yourself. Do it this evening!" And off he went, leaving Holden openmouthed behind him.

As a result of the baronet's kindness, no one thought to look in on Miss Catherine.

The Blankenships were just about to sit down to dinner when the baronet arrived. The baronet, who was never rude, thought to take himself off to his club and return at a more convenient time but Henry would not hear of it.

"Nonsense, come in, come in. It will give you a chance to meet my daughters, Emily and Sarah. They are home from a most excellent seminary for young ladies in Bath and this will give them an opportunity to practice their deportment lessons." Beaming, Henry led Sir Everett into the parlor. There, awaiting dinner, was the entire Blankenship family. Henry introduced him. "My sister, Mrs. Mendenhall, and of course David you remember, I'm sure. And here are Sarah and Emily. Make your curtsies, girls."

Two fresh-faced young ladies who looked to be fourteen and fifteen gracefully curtsied. The baronet bowed gravely to them both. They had already let down their skirts and put up their hair, signaling their transformation from children to young ladies. It seemed a bit young to him to be leaving the schoolroom.

Henry Blankenship explained. "Sarah must always do what Emily does, and Emily is so shy that she always wishes her sister's company. When she is in school, Emily is still a young girl, since she is only fifteen. But my sister believes a little polish is not amiss, so while she is home, she dines with us and puts her hair up. Of course, that meant Sarah had to grow up, too."

They were pretty girls, with soft brown hair and hazel eyes, fresh complexions, and excellent manners. The baronet approved. Sarah had a bright, inquisitive light in her eyes, while Emily's look was sweeter and quieter. The affection between them was plain, but the light of everyone's life was David. He took the kind but slightly patronizing tone brothers were apt to take with adoring sisters, particularly brothers who have fought in a war and been wounded.

Henry Blankenship's sister, Mrs. Mendenhall, was a little butterball of a woman who made no secret of the fact that she hated London and longed to be back at Bath with her friends and the waters she was sure did her no end of good. Despite her negative attitude, she looked after the girls and took charge of the household.

"Though why they think they need me, I'm sure I do not know," she confided to Sir Everett over an excellent baron of beef stuffed with oysters. "That Mrs. Evans has organized the entire household so there is nothing to do but approve the menus. She has not been here since I have come, but I've heard about her knack for housekeeping and keeping the servants smoothed down. And the girls are so well-behaved that taking them to buy new dresses and such is a real pleasure. For a while. But truly, I can never get used to the fog and the crowds and the chill—and the strange people everywhere I go. I do miss Bath." And she sighed a little and inquired as to whether he was sure he had enough mushroom savory.

After dinner, the baronet felt compelled to listen to the girls play for a half hour or so before he could ask his host for a few minutes of his time in his study. Henry Blankenship suspected Sir Everett had some bee in his bonnet, so he was more than happy to bid the children and his sister good night and repair to his study with his guest. Once there, he seated his guest in a deep armchair, poured him a splash of a truly superior brandy and sat down to listen to what the baronet had to say.

"Now, what has brought you to my door unannounced?" he inquired. "No, no, none of that 'so sorry' nonsense. I only meant that it is very unlike you. Something must have happened. What is it? Bolton?"

"How did you know?" Sir Everett was astonished at the man's quickness and grasp of things.

"It has been on your mind of late, and Bancroft and I have been stirring the coals. What has happened?"

Sir Everett hesitated for only a moment. As he told the sordid tale, it occurred to him there was no one in the group of men he saw at his club or in parliament, whom he had always thought of as friends, he would have told this particular story to, no one he would have trusted without question as he did Henry Blankenship.

After he had finished, Henry sat for a long time with his head resting on his hand. Sir Everett now took a deep sip of his brandy, but Henry did not touch his.

At last he spoke. "So you sent him off with his tail between his legs. Good. He's a cur and will slink away if he's shown the stick. But show weakness and he will go for your throat. You did the right thing."

"I think I have convinced him he would rather have silence than Catherine." The baronet was still not convinced that this was true. He got to the main problem. "But that does not solve my main problem. I think she should marry. That would insulate her from any malice of his later on."

Henry Blankenship nodded slowly. "Yes, I think you are right. She would have a hard enough time living as a single woman and working where she does. But with any whiff of scandal, she would find herself ostracized, would she not? I do not know all of the intricacies of your world, but I believe it is very unforgiving to women who do not behave exactly as society decrees."

Sir Everett nodded. "I am afraid you are right. So long as I am here to stand behind her and let the world know I approve of her and everything she does, I believe she can brush through life tolerably well. My estate is not entailed—only the title and the London house will pass to my heir—so I will leave her very well provided for when I die. But she will not be fabulously wealthy. I fear that at that point the people who have never understood her and regard her as somewhat beyond the pale will begin to circle like jackals."

"So you believe marriage is her only safeguard in the long term?" Henry nodded, but whether in agreement or simply to indicate he understood Sir Everett could not tell. He wished he knew what Blankenship was thinking.

He continued. This was the difficult part. He knew how he felt, but he was not sure it was the right answer. For some reason, he believed Henry Blankenship would know. He took a deep breath. "Yes. But it must be the right marriage."

"Ah!" Henry's eyebrows lifted. "Someone socially acceptable and rich, like Sir Ronald?"

Sir Everett looked down at his hands. "Yesterday, in all likelihood, I would have agreed with that. But now that I have seen Catherine at the hospital I realize the kind of man I favored will not do for her."

"And why is that?" Henry's face was expressionless, his eyes hooded.

"Because she would not be happy. Catherine needs someone who understands her calling." As he said the words, Sir Everett realized they were true. "If there is no man who can value her for who she is, then she would be better off not marrying. She has friends. Even after I am gone, she will have people she can rely on."

Blankenship stood up abruptly and came across the

space between the chairs to grasp Sir Everett's hand. "You are a brave man! You are willing to let your daughter follow her heart, first to the Crimea and then to marry Dr. Soames."

Sir Everett's jaw dropped. How did this man know everything? It was uncanny. "How did you know I had selected Dr. Soames? I have scarcely decided it this evening before I came here. I have told no one."

Blankenship looked as if he were about to sneeze. His cheeks puffed out alarmingly and his face turned red. Finally, he gave a sort of explosion and turned aside for a moment to wipe his eyes. "Forgive me, my dear sir. I have simply observed the two of them together, and you *did* say you were going to let her follow her inclination. It seems to me that is the way her inclination leads her."

Sir Everett looked at him suspiciously. Had that been a laugh instead of a sneeze? The baronet had endured a good deal this day, and was prepared to endure more—a Scottish nobody to marry his beautiful Catherine. He was not inclined to put up with being laughed at.

"I have spent a certain amount of time at the hospital where I have seen them both. It is clear to me Dr. Soames loves Miss Stanhope dearly, but he does not think there is a chance for him. I think you will make them both very happy when you suggest a betrothal."

"I hope I am doing the right thing. There are other, safer choices for her." Choices most fathers would make for their daughters, not a choice that was simply a ratification of her own inclination.

"You are. She is a most superior woman, Sir Everett. She has character and strength and she cares for people. She is rare and needs a rare man to stand beside her." Henry smiled a little smugly. "My two girls are as ordinary as can be. I love them both, but they are not superior beings and they will need a father's guidance. Of course, it will be many, many years before they are ready to consider matrimony. And then I'm sure they will listen to me."

It was the baronet's turn to smother a chuckle. "Wait and see," he said. "And you do not have so very many years to wait, or I miss my guess. Then we will see how much guidance Miss Emily and Miss Sarah think they need!"

Their father looked a little startled for a moment.

When he arrived back at Stanhope House, the baronet immediately asked Holden if Miss Catherine had eaten anything or if she had been too upset to eat. Holden maintained the expressionless mien required of butlers, but his surprise was evident.

"No, Sir Everett. You instructed me not to disturb her." Holden drew himself up to his full height and looked reproachful.

"Yes, very well. Perhaps she does need sleep. But I do not want to let this go unfinished. I am of a mind—" Sir Everett became aware that he was confiding his plans to his very interested butler. "Well, never mind. There is no need to discuss it with my daughter first, in any case."

He nodded decisively to his butler and turned to make his way to his study when there was a rapid knocking at the front door. The baronet paused, unable to conceive of who would be coming to see him so late in the evening. When Holden opened the door, he was amazed to see Dr. Michael Soames on the doorstep.

"I have come to see Sir Everett," he told Holden. "Please convey my request that he spare me a few moments, though I realize it is late."

Holden was about to give the young man a pithy lecture on the proper hours to call upon important people. Ten-thirty at night was not that time. As he opened his mouth, Sir Everett called out, "Let him in, Holden, and show him into my study."

Gratefully, Michael followed the ramrod straight back of the butler to the small room Sir Everett preferred to the larger, colder reception salons. Michael and Catherine had decided that for them both to appear together at this hour of night would shock Sir Everett gravely. It could only harm their case, for it would reveal she had visited a man alone, and in the evening, too. So while Michael called at the front door, Catherine slipped around to the servants' entrance and then took the back stairs to her room, where she tried to find the perfect dress to wear while convincing her father to allow her to marry Michael.

There wasn't such a dress. Instead she found a sober but pretty dark blue crepe the same color as her eyes. She dressed carefully and, unwilling to ring for Betsy at this late hour, contrived to put her hair up in a very creditable chignon, drawn simply back from her face. It looked a trifle stark, so she put on the pearl necklace and bracelet her father had given her when she returned from the Crimea. Perhaps that would soften his implacable opposition to Michael.

Meanwhile, the baronet ushered Michael into the study and gestured to the most comfortable chair in the room. The baronet took his customary chair behind the desk that dominated the room.

"I very much want to speak to you, sir," Michael said.

"I would have sent for you if you had not come," Sir Everett said.

"I wish to ask for your daughter's hand in marriage." Michael felt as if his tongue had swollen to twice its normal size. *Now he will throw me out of the house,* he thought apprehensively.

"You do?" The baronet managed not to smile. No use giving the young man the idea that Catherine did not have her pick of eligible suitors. The man wasn't eligible at all, and Sir Everett did not want him to forget that. So he frowned a little and sat back, staring at Michael over his steepled fingertips. "What makes you think I would grant my daughter's hand to a nobody like you?"

"We love each other," Michael said, his heart sinking. He should have known that no matter what Bolton had done to compromise Catherine, the baronet would still hope for someone richer and more socially prominent than Dr. Michael Soames. "Catherine does not care that I am never going to be rich." He studied the baronet's stony face. Oh, God, it wasn't going to work. "We both want to spend our lives healing the sick. Together."

"You would let my daughter work?" the baronet said, apparently astonished at the idea. "Are you that poor, Doctor?"

"No, sir. It is not that. Catherine wants to nurse, needs to nurse. I would never stand in her way." Michael decided to throw himself on the baronet's mercy. "I know I am not worthy of her, sir. No one could be. But I do understand her and I do love her. I think that should count for something. It does with Catherine."

He looked so worried and strained that Sir Everett had almost decided to put him out of his misery when there was a discreet knock at the door and it opened immediately afterward. Catherine, looking beautiful as always, entered the room.

"Papa, has Michael told you we have decided to be married almost immediately?" She walked over to where Michael sat and took his hand.

"Dr. Soames has very properly come to ask me for permission to court you. I have not yet given my consent."

The baronet felt a twinge of regret that he was not going to play the part of the domestic emperor longer. He had quite enjoyed it.

"Well, that was proper but not necessary. We love each other, Papa. There is no reason why we should not be married, is there? Except perhaps the incident with Sir Ronald this afternoon." Her face had taken on a streak of crimson across her cheekbones. She was suffering from acute embarrassment. Her father could not allow it to go on.

He rose from his chair, his face wreathed in smiles, and came around the desk to the front of the desk where Catherine and her fiancé now stood as stiff and unsmiling as if they faced a firing squad. "No, my dear. The reason I give my blessing without reservation to this marriage is that you are a rare person and you need a rare marriage. I think with Dr. Soames, you have a chance of making that happen."

The relief in both their faces was almost ludicrous. Sir Everett smiled at them then. "It is strange. I have never met a young woman who did not need her father's permission to marry. But you, dear Catherine, do not. You have your work and can pay your own way even if I were mad enough to cut you off. But I thank you, Doctor, for asking for my permission nevertheless. I'm afraid I would feel more than usually useless if you had not."

"Papa, you are hardly useless." Catherine wasn't sure she liked her father in this new, humble guise. It was so uncharacteristic. She was used to arguing with him about everything, and now he was telling her she was wonderful and special and she should make her own decisions—all the things she had always wanted to hear from him.

She looked at her father and her betrothed standing side by side, speaking in low tones and nodding in agreement. That was even more strange. She went over to the embroidered bellpull and tugged. Within moments, Holden knocked on the door. He had undoubtedly been standing there for at least five minutes.

"Holden, you are very quick this evening," she murmured as he came in.

"As are you, Miss Catherine," he said with a frosty smile. "Considering when you arrived."

"Hush, Holden," she said, her cheeks flushing. "We will need some champagne in here. As soon as you can, please, Holden."

"Of course, Miss Catherine. And may I be the first to offer my congratulations?" And Holden, correct, ramrod-straight Holden, a stickler for rules, bent down and, in complete contravention of every rule of deportment ever laid down, kissed her cheek. "May you both be very happy."

There were tears in her eyes. "Thank you," she whispered. "Dear Holden."

Once Holden had left the room, she began to wonder again just what Michael and her father had to talk about.

"You are absolutely right, sir," Michael said. "She is absolutely too good for me. I know that. But, sir, she is too good for anyone else, as well."

The baronet nodded sagely. "I daresay you are right. She is certainly too good for Sir Ronald Bolton. I won't tell you what happened to Catherine—to my Catherine—" Tears sprang to his eyes. When he thought what could have happened to his darling girl at the hands of that unprincipled villain, his blood ran cold.

"I know," said Michael without thinking. "She told me."

"She did?" said the baronet. "When?"

That was a poser. He could hardly tell him the truth. Before he could come up with a plausible lie, Catherine came up and took his hand in hers. "Michael knows Sir

Ronald has fleeced a good many investors beside you, Papa. I am not sure we can trust him not to try to fleece more now that the threat of exposure has been removed. I almost wish I could just tell him to publish and be damned—like the Duke of Wellington.''

"Catherine, such language!'' Her father was shocked. So shocked that, as she had intended, he forgot his earlier question. "I do not know where you have learned to speak so.''

"But, you see, Michael is *not* shocked. Which just demonstrates all the more how perfect we are for one another.''

"You have convinced me,'' the baronet said, holding up his hands in mock surrender. "Now we must decide when the wedding is to be. Would you prefer to be married in the country or here in London, my dear?''

Catherine thought for a moment. "Here, I believe, Papa. So all our friends can come.''

"It will be a bit of a scandal, I'm afraid. I hope the two of you realize that.'' The baronet peered deeply at both of them. Apparently reassured, he gave a wintry smile and said, "I think you will be happy. You truly appreciate the treasure you are getting, Soames, and that is what matters to me. I am going to leave you alone for precisely ten minutes. After that, you must leave and Catherine will go to her room. I daresay I am the only one of the three of us who will get a fair night's sleep tonight.''

The baronet had scarcely closed the door behind him when Michael swept her into his arms. He buried his face in the satin softness of her hair and breathed in deeply the scent of lily of the valley that she wore.

Then he pulled back a few inches so he could talk to her. "My dearest, I think we have brought the thing off. He seemed not so sorry to see you had chosen me as he has been before.''

"He knows he has badly misjudged Sir Ronald. That may have made him think he misjudged you as well."

She tilted her face up to his and Michael, taking the invitation for what it was, kissed her. She sank into his embrace and for long moments she drowned in sensation. Making love had opened her heart to physical love. She found it made every touch deeper and more meaningful. The touch of his fingers on her face as he caressed it while his lips nibbled at hers almost made her swoon. Now she knew what it could lead to, what further delights her body could give her when Michael's was touching it. She snuggled into his arms and held him tight.

"I love you, Michael. I can hardly believe I feel this happy. I never thought I would love anyone. All I dreamed of was nursing and that Papa would not force me to marry someone, for I knew no man would understand my need to care for the sick. And then there you were."

"There I was, falling deeper in love with you with every day. I never dreamed of marriage or love because I was sure a woman would hold me back, demand parties and dresses and attention. And now there is you, a woman who understands my dream, who shares it, and who is beautiful and kind as well. You have to be a dream, Catherine. You are too perfect to be real."

They smiled into each other's eyes, sure their life together would be as wonderful as they believed each other to be.

Epilogue

"Rose! I am so glad you are here!"

It was the day before Catherine's wedding. The spring weather was perfect, all the preparations had been completed, and Catherine was as happy as she could ever remember being. And to complete her happiness, her friend from the Crimea, Rose Cranmer, had unexpectedly arrived.

"If I had known, I would have arranged to stay at a hotel," Rose said when she learned of the occasion to take place the next day. "It cannot be convenient to have a guest at this time."

"Nonsense," Catherine replied briskly. "If you had arrived even one day earlier, I would have insisted you be a bridesmaid with Lucinda. As it is, a number of friends from the Crimea will be there. In fact, there are several friends I want you to meet. Julian's parents. He is not doing well, Rose, and Davy Blankenship suggested you might—"

Rose shook her head vehemently. "No. I could not. Julian's father is an earl or a viscount or something. And his mother is French. I could not think of a single word to say to them."

"But it could mean a job, Rose. A really well-paying job. With no expenses, you could save every penny. In a year or two you could be independent."

Catherine had struck the right note. Rose paused. "Very well, I will meet them. But my plan still is to leave London within a week. I think I will have better luck in Leeds or Manchester."

"We have plenty of hospitals here, Rose. St. Luke's would love to have you. I just thought that working for the Eversleighs would be better for you."

"The best thing for me will be to leave London. I cannot stay here."

It was not the first time Catherine had noticed the sadness in her friend's eyes. She had never asked Rose the cause. She knew Rose had been exceptionally close to her mother and that her mother had died only a few months before Rose joined Miss Nightingale's nurses and left for the Crimea. Catherine did not like to pry, and there was something in Rose that forbade questions.

So now Catherine merely said, "Well, you can't go until after my wedding. Now let's have a cup of cocoa and see if we can get at least a few hours sleep before the big day! Wait until Lucinda sees you tomorrow morning. She will be so excited!"

Catherine enjoyed her wedding.

Michael would be hers forever, and all her friends were gathered around to see that happen. She felt solemn and bubbly at the same time, quite unlike the usual Catherine.

She caught sight of the Blankenships and Mary Ann, seated together. Jeffrey Bancroft was there, looking impossibly handsome and not taking his eyes off Lucinda, who turned her back to him and ostentatiously ignored him. Dr. and Mrs. Dinsmore and all the nurses from St. Luke's were there, as well as a liberal sprinkling of political friends of her father's.

Julian had refused to come, but the earl and countess were in attendance and were looking forward to meeting Rose. They had heard of her almost magical success with the wounded from David Blankenship and were willing to offer her anything to stay with them and try to help their son, who sank deeper into despair with every day.

Her father had insisted on inviting Sir Ronald, despite Catherine's aversion to the man. No matter what he had done, it was important that he keep his mouth shut, and that meant not cutting his acquaintance. Catherine had clenched her teeth and agreed.

Now she was standing in the large ballroom at the back of Stanhope House, greeting her guests and clinging to Michael's arm. The only disappointment was the fact that Michael's family had not been able to come. An outbreak of fever in Edinburgh had kept his father busy, and then his mother had taken sick with it too. She seemed to be recovering, but travel was out of the question.

Catherine had greeted most of the guests, but had yet to catch sight of Rose. They had dressed together, the three friends from Scutari, and Rose had looked lovely in a dress of Catherine's that had been shortened for her. The rose silk had been most becoming to her brown hair and eyes, and she had even managed a smile, though greeting a number of people she did not know had caused her some concern.

"Do not worry. You and I will sneak off to the housekeeper's room and drink champagne by ourselves," Lucinda had promised. Lucinda looked absolutely ravishing in white with a lavish trimming of blue satin the exact sky blue of her eyes. The only trouble, Catherine complained, was that no one but her husband would be looking at her. The eyes of the rest of the world would be on her friends.

Lucinda had laughed at that, and kept all three of them in gales of laughter from that moment on. If her laughter seemed a little brittle to Catherine, she did not want to spoil the moment by mentioning it.

"There she is," Catherine said to Michael, pointing toward Rose. "Over there. I do want her to meet the Eversleighs." She beckoned and Rose smiled and began to make her way toward the bridal couple. "Oh, dear, here comes Sir Ronald. I suppose we will have to be polite for Papa's sake."

Before Sir Ronald could put her manners to their ultimate test, Lucinda said something to him and soon had him deep in conversation with her. Catherine frowned. She would have to speak to Lucinda about Sir Ronald. Admittedly her friend had said not long ago that she planned to marry a rich and prominent man, and on the surface Sir Ronald filled that bill. But she could not seriously consider the pompous Sir Ronald as a husband. Lucinda and Bolton? Impossible. Yes, when they returned from their honeymoon in two weeks' time, she would have a serious talk with Lucinda.

After she had greeted a few other latecomers, Catherine glanced again to Lucinda—still with her back to Jeffrey Bancroft and still talking to Sir Ronald. Catherine looked around for Rose, anxious to introduce her to the Eversleighs, but Rose was not there.

And later, when she went up with the countess to change to her traveling outfit for the honeymoon, Rose's shabby portmanteau was gone.

If you liked MORE THAN A DREAM, be sure to look for Martha Schroeder's next release in the Angels of Mercy series, TRUE TO HER HEART, available wherever books are sold in July 2001.

Practical and intelligent, Lucinda Harrowby is a poor relation who knows she must make some kind of match to secure a place for herself in the world—but she believes she must hide her brains behind her beauty to do so. That changes after she goes to Scutari with Miss Nightingale—and after she loses her heart to Jeffrey Bancroft, a wealthy businessman of mysterious origins.

BOOK YOUR PLACE ON OUR WEBSITE AND MAKE THE READING CONNECTION!

We've created a customized website just for our very special readers, where you can get the inside scoop on everything that's going on with Zebra, Pinnacle and Kensington books.

When you come online, you'll have the exciting opportunity to:

- View covers of upcoming books
- Read sample chapters
- Learn about our future publishing schedule (listed by publication month *and author*)
- Find out when your favorite authors will be visiting a city near you
- Search for and order backlist books from our online catalog
- Check out author bios and background information
- Send e-mail to your favorite authors
- Meet the Kensington staff online
- Join us in weekly chats with authors, readers and other guests
- Get writing guidelines
- AND MUCH MORE!

**Visit our website at
http://www.zebrabooks.com**